THE MISSED CONNECTION

Also by Tia Williams

Fiction

The Accidental Diva

The Perfect Find

Seven Days in June

A Love Song for Ricki Wilde

Young Adult Fiction

It Chicks

Sixteen Candles

Audre & Bash Are Just Friends

THE MISSED CONNECTION

A Novel

TIA WILLIAMS

GRAND CENTRAL
New York Boston

Grand Central Publishing
Hachette Book Group
1290 Avenue of the Americas, New York, NY 10104

Grand Central Publishing is a division of Hachette Book Group, Inc. The Grand Central Publishing name and logo is a registered trademark of Hachette Book Group, Inc.

Print book interior design by Taylor Navis

ISBN: 9781538770269

Printed in the United States of America

To all the "inside girls"—myself, included—who sometimes need a little push outside

Chapter 1

MIGHT AS WELL HAVE A GIGGLE

What nail shape would you like, miss?" asked the manicurist, inspecting Sasha's left hand. "Square? Round? Almond-shaped?"

Distracted, Sasha glanced up from the phone nestled on her lap. "I'm sorry?"

"Almond?"

"Thank you, no, I can't eat almonds," she said, smiling sweetly. "Allergic."

Physically, Sasha Cruz was getting a manicure. Mentally, she was inside her phone, working. She'd just landed the splashiest commercial in her career as a casting director—and so scrolling through audition clips was top priority. She was so distracted, in fact, that she was about to miss a Pivotal Moment.

To be fair, no one expects a Pivotal Moment to happen at an airport mini spa.

It was odd enough that Sasha was getting her nails done professionally. She was damned good at doing her *own* nails. And assessing her own stock portfolio. And rewiring her own kitchen. And silk-pressing her own hair. What couldn't she do? Very few things; namely 1) drive, and 2) confront life without antidepressants. Sasha was raised to be self-sufficient by her single mom, a deadly practical electrician who played no games. "You handle your business! No crying and no suffering!" she'd tell Baby Sasha. Years later, she discovered that her mom hadn't invented this quote. It was paraphrased from an old Juvenile song. But it stuck.

Sasha had arrived at New York City's Fiorello Airport with a flawless, bloodred manicure. But sitting at her gate a full three hours early, she noticed a chip on her thumb. This wouldn't do. She worked hard to cultivate her "minimalist upscale baddie" veneer. Even her casual airport ensemble made a statement. Razor-sharp bob. Winged liner. Impeccable jeans. Tiny tank. Diamond studs (fake). Cashmere throw (real). She looked impenetrable, unruffable, unfuckwithable. A chip in her nail polish was a kink in her armor. After all, as a casting director, she was known for her eye.

It's why Seraphina, the international beauty emporium, had hired her to cast their Autumn Kisses commercial. It was a huge departure for Sasha, whose specialty was popcorn rom-coms and thrillers. But after a yearlong sabbatical—where she did little but hole up in her Prospect Heights, Brooklyn, condo, living off DoorDash and YouTube Pilates—she was a tad rusty. The great news? Seraphina was flying her to their international brand summit in Paris so she could get a "feel" for the Seraphina vibe. Just her and over one hundred execs from all over the world.

To be honest, this was an unnecessary trip. Every girl, gay, and they was familiar with Seraphina's vibe. Where else does one find the world's most covetable perfumes, eye creams, and hydrating-fluffing-smoothing shampoos? But Sasha welcomed the trip. A weekend in Paris was a gift from the heavens, especially after fighting her way back from hell. And her flight phobia was no match for Xanax.

But first, nails. Luckily for Sasha, once she noticed the chip, she also noticed B-Relaxed Spa across from her gate. Its neon cursive sign beckoned to her. The salon was a tiny, hot-pink space with one nail station and two massage chairs—and it was blessedly empty. When Sasha walked in, a freckled, caramel-skinned twentysomething wearing thigh-length braids called out, "Heyyy! I'm Maxi."

Accent via Staten Island, thought Sasha. *Slight lisp via Invisalign. Gorgeous girl. I wonder if she's ever thought about acting?*

Sasha was never not casting.

Maxi led her to the nail station, where they sat across from each other. After deciding that almond was, indeed, the shape in question, the manicurist got to work. And Sasha got back to scrolling. Less than a minute had passed before Maxi said, "Hey, can I ask you a question?"

Sasha glanced up from her phone. Her eyes were blurring from studying the self-tape submissions of dozens of models and actors. It was a lipstick commercial, so she was looking for luscious lips. But "luscious" was so subjective. And the only real direction she had received was via the marketing VP, a fiftysomething dude in leather jeans. "Think cute girls, hot boys who'll agree to wear lipstick, real bodies, all ethnicities. A buffet of diversity. But a *fuckable* buffet." In other words, find models who were "inclusive" enough to score culture points, but sexy enough to please investors.

She stole a glance at Maxi. She had a cute, Kewpie doll–shaped mouth. Her energy was like a bouncing beam of sunlight. Perfect for Seraphina.

Hmm, is she about twenty-three? she wondered. *Maybe younger? Black-girl freckles, caramel skin… Wait. WAIT. Is Paramount still developing that Sade biopic?*

"Sure!" Sasha put on a friendly expression. "You can ask me a question."

"Are you feeling anxious right now?" asked Maxi.

"No, I'm, like, ridiculously relaxed. Why do you ask?"

Sasha couldn't remember the last time she was relaxed. She was high-strung as hell. In general, she felt like the first kernel primed to explode in a microwave popcorn bag. She usually hid it behind self-deprecating banter and a breezy smile. Though right now, after downing a glass of airport bar rosé, her smile was more boozy than breezy.

"Your hand is warm," noted the manicurist. "That's a tension indicator."

Damn. Maxi was right. Nothing got by nail techs and hairstylists.

"Oh, that's just me." She shrugged airily, eyes drifting back down to her phone. "I run hot when I'm in work mode. Like when you have too many apps open and your phone overheats."

"But you're not a phone, you're a person," Maxi pointed out. "You *must* unclench."

Unclench what, exactly? Her brows? Jaw? Butt cheeks? Everything was clenched. Sasha let out a small laugh. "Oh girl, I wouldn't know where to start."

"How about a hand massage?"

"I'm good, really. But thank you."

"I have an idea," persisted Maxi. "Can I do a palm reading?"

Curious, Sasha abandoned her phone for good. She squinted at Maxi, assessing whether she was serious. "I... don't know. *Can* you? Is it on the menu?"

"I've been studying palmistry," she said proudly. "I'm just an apprentice, but I'm good at it. Come on, you got nothing to lose."

Sasha thought about this for five seconds. "You know what? My New Year's resolution was to be more whimsical. Let's do it."

"Yeah?"

"Why not?" She shrugged. "The horrors persist. Might as well have a giggle."

"That's the spirit, diva." The manicurist grabbed her right hand, flipping it over so it faced upward. Lightly, she traced Sasha's palm. "Mmm. Your heart line runs deep. The deeper the line, the richer the love."

"My palm's lying to you, Maxi. I'm poor in love." Not wanting to seem like a sad sack, she flashed a grin. "But rich in vibes."

"Period." Maxi giggled.

Sasha wasn't really joking, though. Dating hadn't been a priority in years. When asked about her nonexistent love life, she always blamed work. She traveled all the time! She was too ambitious! She was the type of woman who intimidated men. "Types" were her specialty. Her career hinged upon finding the perfect person for the perfect role. She was so good at it, she'd typecasted herself.

"Would you consider yourself a hopeful person? Your soul line is showing that you're optimistic."

She couldn't tell the truth, which was that she was chronically depressed, incurably sleepy—and that, on most days, the only thing holding her together was blush. Instead, she said, "I'm optimistic that I can grow to become an optimistic person."

"Love that for you. And I love your bracelet," said Maxi, eyeing the gold cuff on her right wrist. "But I think it's blocking my reading. Here, I'll take it off..."

"No!" In a flash, Sasha clapped her left hand over the bracelet. Her heartbeat quickened and she began to tremble. Abruptly, the oxygen seemed to disappear in the tiny spa.

"My bad! Are you okay?"

"Yes, I'm sorry. I didn't mean to sound so curt." The words tumbled out of her mouth, panicked and apologetic. She took a few deep inhales, trying to regulate her breathing. Oh, this was so embarrassing. "Don't know what happened there."

"You're not fine, you're breathing funny. Here, drink this." Maxi hopped up and grabbed a small paper cone of fountain water, handing it to Sasha. Eagerly, she gulped it down.

"I'm sorry," she repeated. "I just...I never take it off. It's a sentimental thing." Waving her hands in a *don't mind me* gesture, she gave Maxi what she hoped was a disarming smile. Maxi smiled back but couldn't hide her alarm.

The cuff stayed. It was the only thing shielding her scar from the eyes of the world. It was a barely visible, shiny gash—but in Sasha's mind, it was massive, sprawling, all-encompassing. The scar (and its low ache on rainy days) was a constant reminder of that night in October 2022. That night her life turned into a low-budget thriller. A *20/20* episode. An "it happened to me" Reddit post. After that night, she'd learned that the only way to protect herself was to *keep* to herself. Mind her business, not let anyone new into her life, and drown herself in work. Outrun the memories. It worked for a long time—until last year, when her psychiatrist threatened to drop her if she didn't take a work sabbatical.

Your mental health won't improve if you keep running from your past, her doc had said. *Slow down and face it. Feel it.*

So Sasha made some big changes. She stopped working for the first time since high school. She moved from her second-floor brownstone apartment (vulnerable to break-ins) to a high-rise, doorman building (as secure as Fort Knox). Without work to focus on, and nowhere to be, her life became a collection of quiet, unwitnessed moments—played out within the walls of her home. She ordered sushi and binged *Love Is Blind.* She read a captivating book about the history of rats in Manhattan. She installed a claw-foot tub she bought online from Home Depot. And, most significantly, she rarely ventured outside. After a while, friends stopped asking her out. Texts dwindled. But she didn't mind the solitude. It felt healing somehow.

Things didn't get weird till the fourth or fifth month, when Sasha had a terrible realization. She really, *really* didn't mind the solitude. She saw how shockingly easy it'd be to become a recluse (savings pending). Every day, she got cozier with isolation. And it wasn't scary. It was a relief. In fact, she craved it. There was no one to hurt her. No one to judge. No one for her to annoy with her constant, creeping blues. She created her own world. No shower, no problem. Weep through breakfast, nap through lunch.

Sometimes she'd climb in her empty tub with pillows, a water bottle, and a bag of kettle corn. For days, she'd lay there in the dark, bingeing niche history podcasts. Any topic would do, from abandoned malls to bizarre defunct professions ("funeral clown" was her favorite). By the second day in the tub, she'd begin to dissociate. She was no longer Sasha Cruz, deceptively glamorous industry player. She was a bodyless blob, floating away into the pitch-black cocoon of the podcasts—where nothing existed but fun facts, trivia, and lore about long-ago places and people. Dead-and-gone things.

This was worrisome behavior. This was shut-in behavior. But it was hers. She'd built a safe haven. No one talks about how self-satisfying depression can feel.

But then, Sasha caught an endless cold that wasn't a cold, at all. It was aspiration pneumonia, and it landed her in the hospital for five days. Her doc explained that, if left untreated for a few more weeks, it could've killed her. She would've died alone. Possibly in her new bathtub. And that thought, she found, was *not* satisfying. In fact, it terrified her into rejoining the world. Sasha suspected that it wasn't the healthiest choice, allowing fear to motivate another huge life decision. But whatever. There were worse reasons to yank yourself out of a dissociative bed rot.

Step one? Write an elegant, sane-sounding "somebody hire me, please" post on LinkedIn. Before she had time to panic and delete, Seraphina contacted her. And now, the Paris trip would kick off her fresh start. She was thirty-two, back on her feet, and stronger than ever. Was she seeking guidance from a baby nail tech moonlighting as a fortune teller? Sure! But Sasha was a savvy woman.

And savvy women know that wisdom sometimes comes in unconventional packages.

"Got it, your bracelet stays on," said Maxi, as she continued to trace the lines in Sasha's palm. Abruptly, she stopped. Frowned. And then, she pulled a tiny magnifying glass out of her apron pocket. Closing one eye, she held it above Sasha's palm.

Sasha was alarmed. "What happened? What do you see?"

"Nothing, I'm just processing your palm map."

"Is it bad?"

Maxi shook her head, slowly. And then, with a huge smile, she looked up at Sasha. "No, it's great news. You're gonna meet a man."

"A man," repeated Sasha flatly. "That's the great news?"

"I get it, most men are flops. But your palm's saying that the right one awaits you."

"I'm sorry, Maxi, I just don't believe in the soulmate industrial complex."

"Better start believing. You're gonna experience a chance meeting that'll set off a chain of events—events that'll end in happily ever after." Maxi leaned forward, peering into Sasha's eyes. "The right connection can bridge hearts through time and space. The right connection can change the world."

Sasha smiled kindly, but was skeptical of Maxi's overwrought advice. So she changed the subject. "You have an incredible mouth. I'm casting a Seraphina lipstick commercial, any interest?"

"How'd you know I was an actor? I just landed an audition for the new Sade movie."

I still got it, she thought, happily.

"Let's stay in touch." Sasha slid her a business card from her purse. "I'm a casting director."

"God gave with both hands today!" exclaimed Maxi. She pocketed the card, and took Sasha's hand, again. "But back to you. Your palm's telling me you're hiding from your life. Is that true?"

"Welll... not no."

"Life's too short to hide, sis. Aren't you excited to see what happens next?"

Sasha considered this. Maybe "excited" was too dramatic a word. Excitement required a level of trust in the world that she didn't quite feel, yet. But she was curious about the future. And, for the first time in a long time, she was curious about *people*. At the beginning of her sabbatical, she felt relieved not to have to interact with strangers (or anyone, really). People were too unpredictable. But lately, she'd started peering out her bedroom window; spying on the rush hour crowd seventeen floors down on Grand Army Plaza. Behind the safety of her curtains, she'd wonder where everyone was headed, who they were meeting, and what drove them out of bed every morning. Who was out there? Did anyone feel as unmoored as she did? Had anyone else read and loved *Rats: Observations on the History & Habitat of the City's Most Unwanted Inhabitants*?

Sasha did want to know people again, and be known, herself. What was the point of living a life, unwitnessed? And when it came to dating—well, ever since that long-ago October, she'd rejected men as a species and a concept. But she was exhausted from the effort. She was tired of clinging to fear like a security blanket. It was time to open herself up to adventure. Enjoy some light wining-and-dining. Yes, she was a self-sufficient queen, but, for once—why not let a man sweep in and handle the bill, trash day, her orgasms? In her quietest moments, she fantasized about someone telling her, *Don't worry, I've got it.*

Sasha was tired of always gotting it.

"Maybe," she started quietly, "I'm a little excited to see what happens next."

"Of course you are, hon," said Maxi. "And not for nothing? No one wants to die alone."

No one wants to die alone.

In the end, that's what made her believe in Maxi's reading. Somehow, Maxi had read her mind and saw her fears. It was one thing to have the thoughts rattling around in her mind. It was another to hear them spoken aloud by an absolute stranger. Literally, all Maxi knew about Sasha was that she was allergic to almonds.

No one wants to die alone.

That line was still ringing in Sasha's ears, hours later—when she heard it, again. Spoken by a most unexpected gentleman.

Chapter 2

IN BOCCA AL LUPO

Sasha used to love flying. At the height of her career, she practically lived on the red-eye between New York and LA. It felt jet-setty, cosmopolitan. But today? Flights were a high-maintenance nightmare.

Flying required the following: 1) reading the turbulence forecast on Turbli.com; 2) boarding with a buzz; 3) enthusiastically pantomiming the emergency instructions along with the flight attendant; 4) and risking credit card debt to upgrade to first class. That last one was important, because first class offered a private pod with a sliding door. Given her chances of hyperventilating, privacy was key. Especially since the flight was filled with Seraphina execs she hadn't yet met.

But, as Sasha settled into seat 1E, she wasn't thinking about Seraphina or tomorrow's wine hangover. The only thing on her mind was Maxi's palm reading.

I have to admit, she made some brilliant points, thought Sasha, as she attempted to close her privacy door. But it wouldn't budge. Was there a button she wasn't seeing? Sasha tried again. Nothing. Was it stuck? She rang the "help" buzzer, hoping a flight attendant could work some magic. In the meantime, she noticed that the seat next to her, 1F, was vacant. Amazing luck.

Time to settle in. She slipped off her sneaks, cocooned herself in her throw, and geared up for her antianxiety ritual—featuring a satin sleep mask, noise-canceling headphones, and a podcast about the riveting history of American highways.

Within minutes, she was floating in velvety darkness, scored by the soothing, Southern lilt of the host, a female Duke professor.

On the edges of consciousness, she heard the announcement: FLIGHT ATTENDANTS, PREPARE FOR TAKEOFF. The headphones almost canceled out the wooshing sound of the doors closing. She heard the doors reopen. Even with closed eyes, she could sense the presence of a last-minute passenger rushing in. And then, given the sound of a carry-on being loaded onto the overhead bin to her left, that person sat in seat F. Almost immediately, the subtle scent of leather and jasmine wafted over her.

Tom Ford Tuscan Leather. The cologne most favored by the sluttiest NBA and NFL players. Years ago, she'd cast a *Survivor*-type reality show starring rookie athletes camping together during the off-season. She was just a few years older than the twenty-two-, twenty-three-year-old guys, and they were a flirty bunch. But once they realized she was too professional to entertain a toxic-but-sexually-satisfying situationship with any of them, they all became friends. She ended up being godmother to a Detroit Piston's baby! The scent carried sweet memories, transporting her to a younger, freer Sasha. Before she went into hiding.

Hmm. Who was her neighbor? Given how many Seraphina execs were on the flight, he could possibly be one. What if they'd be working together on the commercial? God, traveling with coworkers was so painful. You didn't want Glenn from sales to see you nap-drooling. Now she *urgently* needed to close the pod door.

Blindly, Sasha started groping around her seat again, searching for the button. No luck. With a sigh, she sank back in her plush seat.

But then, out of nowhere, she felt her door slowly begin to close. On its own. Confused, Sasha slid the mask atop her head. Suddenly, the door changed course, sliding back open. She peered over at the seat next to her. And locked eyes with quite a man.

The guy in seat F nodded hello to her. Then, he held up a small, thin remote. "Yours is by your seat. Left side."

Sasha checked. Indeed, there was a remote nestled in her console. "How did I miss this?"

"It's hidden," he said simply. "Apologies for stepping in. I felt bad seeing you struggle."

Seat F had a slight accent. Maybe Portuguese? He had full, dark hair. Five-o'clock shadow. Tailored charcoal suit. His face was chaotic—crooked Roman nose, weathered olive skin, eerily pale green eyes, resting scowl. But the overall effect was arresting. He seemed jagged, rough—a man who needed to rub up against something, to sand down his edges.

Back when Sasha used to date, she'd loved odd-looking guys with presence. And this guy had the presence of a Mafia daddy from a dark romance novel.

Too bad Netflix already cast 365 Days.

"You seem...thrown off. Should I not have intervened?" he asked.

"No, I'm grateful. I'm just not used to anyone helping me."

"A shame." A slight smile broke his scowl. Then, he glanced down, fiddling with the cuff link at his wrist. A lock of hair fell into his face and he raked his fingers through his waves.

It wasn't until he glanced back at her that she realized she was staring. Quickly, she looked away. Sasha often caught herself gazing at people's faces—in a casting way, not a creepy way. But just in case she'd given him the wrong idea, she tucked her hair behind her ear, flashing the fake cubic zirconia wedding ring she wore for protection.

He raised his dark brow. "Allora. Understood. You're a beautiful woman, but I'm gay."

Mortifying. How did she miss this? To be fair, Italian men were confusing.

"I'm so embarrassed." She grimaced slightly. "So presumptuous of me."

"No offense taken," he told her. Then, he busied himself on his phone.

Relieved, Sasha slipped her sleep mask back on. As the plane took off, they fell into silence. The takeoff was a little bumpy—so, Sasha was focusing superhard on the podcast, trying to calm her heart rate. And then, she thought she heard Seat F lightly chuckle.

Sasha slid off her mask again and glanced in his direction. He was suppressing a grin.

"Hello again. I owe you an apology," he confessed. "I lied."

"So soon?" she said wryly.

"I didn't lie about you being gorgeous. You are, and I suspect you know it. But I'm not gay." His pale, almost translucent emerald eyes settled on hers. Despite herself, she sat up a tad straighter. "The truth? For a woman, I know it's uncomfortable being stuck for hours with a man trying to...ehh...hit with you. No, hit *on* you. You should feel comfortable."

She blinked, speechless. How novel, that this strange man cared about her comfort. For a few seconds, she allowed herself to believe it. As a rule, Sasha didn't trust strange men.

Maybe not anymore, she thought. *But once, forever ago, you felt totally safe with a strange man. Instantly and intensely. And it wasn't a lie, or a line. He meant it. And you felt it. But that was an impossible situation and an impossible man. Doesn't count.*

She dropped the thought as quickly as it arose. It was ancient history.

And then, Sasha got suspicious. How did Seat F know that, for her, safety was paramount? Maybe he was a cult leader. She remembered learning from some podcast that cult leaders were adept mind readers. Subtly, Sasha launched into her stranger-danger checklist, studying him for signs of volatility—e.g., clenched jaw, hands in fists, nervous foot taps, dilated pupils, flinty eyes. Nope, he passed the test. She breathed a quiet sigh of relief.

"Well, thank you for the thoughtful lie." The tiniest smile played on Sasha's lips. Then, she remembered she had no real proof he wasn't dangerous, and the smile dropped.

"Prego." A slight smile softened his face. "It means 'you're welcome' in Italian."

She didn't want to encourage conversation, she really didn't. But, for some reason, she couldn't help herself. "Where are you from in Italy? Your accent's charming."

"Southern Italy. A small beach town called Gallipoli. And you?"

Just then, a flight attendant appeared, offering a wineglass on a tray. "Morning, Ms. Cruz. Here's the rosé you requested on the USFlight website three hours ago," she trilled, extremely specifically. "Enjoy!"

Sasha had preordered it, in a move that felt efficient at the time—but was now embarrassing.

"Oh, I will. Thank you." Cheeks aflame, she took a tiny sip. She hoped it looked dainty.

"Lovely surname," he said. "Is it Cruise like Tom? Or Cruz like Penélope?"

"Like Penélope. My father's Dominican. My mom's Black, via Houston."

"Ahh, Texas." He tipped an imaginary hat. "Howdy."

His Italian-flavored cowboy accent was charming. She couldn't help but smile. "Nicely done."

"So, how do you identify? Um, ethnically?"

The question would've been rude if he hadn't sounded so authentically interested. (And if he'd been an American white guy.)

"Well, Black, of course." She paused. "At thirty-two, I'm still working out what it means to be Afro-Latina."

"Thirty-two? I was thinking you have... twenty-five years?"

Flattered, she smiled with actual teeth. "Really? Thank you. It's because Black don't crack. Ever heard that expression?"

He shook his head, eyes dancing with interest.

"We look young forever," she whispered. "Look at Angela Bassett. My future's bright."

"Sì, sì, it's true." He chuckled. "So, you say you're... ehh... *working out* what it means to be Afro-Latina. This means what?"

Wow, Seat F was direct. And a sharp listener. Sharp-listening in a foreign language was no easy feat. Also, this conversation was getting so deep, so fast. It challenged Sasha's stranger-danger rules. But he was pulling her in. She felt as if she was swimming against a current.

"Sometimes I feel like a fraud claiming Afro-Latina identity. My parents were never together, and I don't know my dad." Her voice lowered to a whisper. "I speak Duolingo Spanish. I'm so ashamed. I really regret not experiencing my Dominican side."

"Ahh, but that should be his regret. Not yours."

"Well, it's a long story," she said, knowing she'd said too much.

Seat F cocked his head slightly. He noticed her hesitation and didn't pry. "Santo Domingo is beautiful. Have you visited?"

"A decade ago. Being there was a mind-bender. I saw my cheekbones everywhere."

"Why have you not returned?"

Anxiety, she thought. *Fear born of one specific experience that rippled into every part of my life. Things that used to be easy, like flying, are excruciating now. I hate it. But I can't help it.*

"No time," she told him, and gratefully took a rosé refill from the flight attendant. Without hesitation, she downed half of it. Seat F watched her do this, raised his brows approvingly, and then ordered a martini for himself.

"I'm of mixed ancestry myself," he said. "My father's Italian, but my mother's German."

She laughed. "Biracial king!"

"This... I don't understand?"

"No, it's just interesting, thinking of a German-Italian person as 'mixed.' Americans would say you're white mixed with white."

"Well. Let's not get into the reductive racial politics of your country."

"*Whew.* A six-hour flight isn't enough time."

"Our stories are similar," he continued. "I don't know my mother. I can't speak German. Feels like I have, ehh, a parent-shaped hole in my biography."

"Exactly." Sasha allowed her head to drop back against her seat. She rarely spoke about feeling culturally estranged from her Dominicanness. It was too revealing. What had made her go there with Seat F? And what were the chances that he'd get it? Well, in his own way.

"Esattamente," he said in a low voice. Their eyes found each other. For a moment, Sasha forgot where she was. Talking to him felt familiar. It was like reuniting with someone you'd known so long ago, it predated memory. *Had* she met him before? Or did she inhale the wine too fast?

Her chest flushed hot. She felt a magnetic, elemental pull toward him, as sure as if he were attracting all the molecules in the cabin. She felt summoned by him. Which was so unexpected. For her, even entertaining this guy was nuts. All she'd wanted to do on this flight was learn about the tenacious early twentieth–century Chinese and Black workers who built Route 66.

"Do you know anything about your mom?" she asked, hoping to break the tension.

"I do. She was a young Berlin aristocrat on summer holiday in Gallipoli. She had a romance with a poor fisherman's son—my dad. Then, she got pregnant. Gallipoli is beautiful. It smells like cypress trees and the sea. But, it was a struggling village back then. After my birth, 'poor' stopped being charming, sì? So she returned to Germany. That's how he tells it, anyway." He tilted his head to one side. "What's your parents' story?"

"Well, it's a short one. My dad owned the electrical repair company where my mom worked. He was married, and my mom was his mistress. When she got pregnant with me, he fired her."

"Cristo. I'm sorry." Seat F finished off his martini. "Even if you knew him, how much do you ever *really* know anyone? I've had passionate relationships with people I barely know."

How passionate? she wanted to ask. *And with whom?*

The flight attendant reappeared, handing Seat F another martini and refreshing Sasha's wine. They both took a sip. And then, Seat F slipped off his suit jacket and rolled up his sleeves. Dear God, he'd thrown her off her game. Did she really reveal her tawdry origins? Truthfully, she rarely thought of the beautiful, charming, intensely unfaithful man who sent money sometimes, but never met his daughter. Sasha considered Raul Cruz to be her mom's tragedy, not hers.

"Well. I don't want to bother you. You had on your mask and AirPods before, so..." He trailed off. "Don't let me get in the way."

He even knew when to bow out!

The captain made another announcement about seat belts. Feeling no pain, she slid down her eye mask and reflexively made the sign of the cross.

"Catholic?" she heard him ask.

She slid up her mask. "I was raised Catholic, but no. Religion isn't my thing. On planes, though, all bets are off. I'm interdenominationally open to all symbols of protection. I have worry dolls in my purse. The Egyptian Eye of Ra. A rabbit's foot. A 'Hakuna Matata' magnet."

And a chewed-up pencil from someone I used to know, she thought.

Just then, Seat F pulled out a pen and a cocktail napkin from his jacket pocket. He wrote something on the napkin and, silently, handed it to Sasha from across the aisle. The napkin had FILM FORUM EST. 1970 stamped in gold across the bottom. He'd written on it:

IN BOCCA AL LUPO

"The translation's not perfect, but it means 'good luck and stay safe.'"

Hopelessly intrigued, she whispered the words to herself, and then tucked the napkin into her purse. "A talisman from a mysterious stranger. Thank you."

"Very mysterious, yes. I don't even have, ehh, social media."

"Love that. And I also love the Film Forum. Best indie theater in the city."

"Yes, I live nearby in SoHo about half the year. I go there, alone, every Friday night when I'm in town."

"Nice. I haven't been to the actual theater in so long. I miss it. Especially watching a really dark foreign horror flick in a packed house."

"Horror? I see," he said, tapping a finger on his mouth. "Now's a good time to tell you that 'in bocca al lupo' literally means 'stay safe in the mouth of the wolf.'"

He tipped his chin downward, raising only his eyes to meet hers. Something passed between them, an electric, once-or-twice-in-a-lifetime understanding. For several thundering heartbeats, she lost her breath. God, it had been an eternity since a man had had this effect on her.

"So gothic and dark," she said, once she found her voice. "I love it even more now."

"I thought you might." His eyes crinkled. "I want to take you to the cinema. I mean, I'd *like* to. Apologies, in English I'm too blunt."

"Blunt is good. There's no guessing your intention."

"Guessing games are for children," he said simply.

For Sasha, a woman who'd experienced ten years of New York City dating, a man saying those words was like hearing the herald angels sing.

"Shall we?" he continued. "When we're back in the city?"

She froze. Things just got real. This would be her first date in years. Would she accept? She'd *just* gotten comfortable with grocery shopping herself, instead of Instacarting. Why did she think she'd be okay on a date? Despite her worries, she snapped into project-manager mode.

"Let's do it. There's a great restaurant near the Film Forum. Reservations are tough..."

Then, the scowl came back. "No, don't worry. I'll handle it."

"But I know the publicist. I can get us in, easy."

"I'm sure you can." His potent, pale teal eyes scanned her face. "But I *want* to take care of you. Sì? Allow yourself to be... handled." He paused, running his fingers through his waves. "No, that's not the right word."

Yes, it the fuck is, she thought. *And that might be the sexiest thing I've ever heard.*

"Okay, we have a date." She paused. "I think I'm drunk. I want to sleep, but I shouldn't. What if we crash? What if you snatch my purse?"

"To steal your worry dolls and *Lion King* novelty items?" he said, lightly mocking her.

"Great point."

"Don't worry, I'm too wealthy to steal." His eyes danced. "Though, in America, those are the worst thieves, sì? You're right, maybe you should protect yourself."

She giggled drowsily. "An honest gazillionaire. Refreshing."

"I try to be honest. I have to tell friendly lies so often, in my work."

"What do you do?"

"I'm a luxury hotel inspector. As such, I must be anonymous. Use aliases." He must've noticed that her eyelids looked heavy, because he then said, "Before you go to sleep, may I ask? What's bringing you to Paris?"

"A business trip for Seraphina. The beauty boutique?"

"I know it well. A woman once told me she doesn't trust straight men who know which beauty products to buy girlfriends. She assumes they're, ehh, womanizing."

"Counterpoint? If my guy knew I loved Fenty eye shadow palettes, I'd be impressed. Love a man who pays attention."

Seat F nodded, his finger lightly tapping his bottom lip. Then, he typed something into his iPhone Notes app. Sasha leaned over the aisle and spied on his screen, which said:

NOTE TO SELVES. SHE LIKES FENTY EYESHADOW PALIATTES.

Sasha laughed out loud. He grinned. And then, all at once, she felt the woozy pull of the Xanax and wine, lulling her into sleep. Which could not happen.

Sasha and Seat F had an undeniable connection. But he was, in fact, a stranger. And under no circumstances would she submit to full slumber next to a man she'd just met. Instead, she allowed herself to float into a wine-woozy, waking restfulness. But before she slid her mask down over her eyes, she stole one last glance at him. He was so intriguing. Was it the accent? The asymmetrical features that were so at odds with his solicitous demeanor? The answer didn't matter—because what she saw blew her fucking mind.

Seat F pulled a book from his carry-on. A lock of hair fell into his eyes as he flipped to a bookmarked page. And then, she saw the cover. *How to Not Die Alone* by Logan Ury.

Stunned, Sasha openly gawked at the book. Her mouth dropped open a bit.

Without looking up from the pages, the corner of his mouth curled upward. "No one wants to die alone. Sì?"

No one wants to die alone.

First Maxi, now Seat F. The universe was definitely sending her a message. Thunderstruck, Sasha sat alone with her thoughts for who knows how long, trying to calm her nerves... about everything. Maybe it was time to take a chance. Maybe the great casting director in the sky had decided Seat F was the guy to do it with. Was she ready for this? Probably not, but did it matter? After a while, she stopped asking herself questions. And then, summoning up all the courage lying dormant inside her, she thrust a trembling hand into the aisle. God, she was dying to feel the skin of someone new. Aching for connection. She'd gone so long without it.

Without words, Seat F took her hand in his. His grip felt warm, firm, and correct.

By the time they landed in Paris, they were bonded. They were also bombed. Whether it was the drinks, or the hours of vulnerable, connective conversation—she felt as if she'd slipped into a dream; someone else's dream, someone more lighthearted and hopeful.

But, when they landed, the dream went awry. Sasha couldn't have predicted how overwhelming the Charles de Gaulle Airport would be, especially given her blood alcohol level. To stay attached in the crowd headed to baggage claim, they reached for each other's hands—but how do you hold hands, surrounded by a crush of people, while also rolling luggage? But still, they managed to stay close. Until the taxi stand outside of Departures. They were about to say goodbye (with a hug? a kiss? Sasha would never know), when the dispatcher, overwhelmed with patrons, rushed them into their separate cars. It all happened in a blink of an eye. Sasha and Seat F hadn't exchanged names, numbers, or any info, whatsoever. Well, Seat F knew her last name, but nothing more.

Sasha realized her mistake in the cab, headed for the hotel. Without thinking, she shot off an email to her Seraphina HR contact, April MacGruder (she and April were both Spelman class of '15. They were friendly, but not *friends*). Sasha used her own Seraphina email, Sasha.C@Seraphina.org, which was issued to her for the duration of her casting project. Unfortunately, she was still catastrophically drunk.

In the email, she described Seat F to April—with hectic, misspelled energy—and asked if he worked at Seraphina. Because she absolutely needed to find him. The subject line? "Searching for Seat F."

In her haste, Sasha didn't realize where the email was going. Yes, she'd sent it to April. But she'd also cc'd the entire Seraphina staff. *Global.* Within twenty-four hours, digital chaos ensued.

And Seraphina corporate employees, worldwide, began searching for Seat F.

To: April.M@Seraphina.org; SERAPHINA CORPORATE GLOBAL
From: Sasha.C@Seraphina.org
Subject: Searching for Seat F

APRILL! I met my husband on the plane. Didn't get his info, long stry. Think he told me where he works but I CAN'T REMEMBER? Can u tell me if he's affiliated with Seraphina in any way? Tall brunette, grean eyes, daddy energy? International man of mistry vibes? A manicurist PREDICTED HIM. She said THE RITE CONNECTION BRIDGES HEARTS THRU TIME & SPACE. He's Italian, I'm American, we're from diff parts of the planet but love bridged our hearts! YOU FEAL ME? Anwy, I need him carnally. Please help. xoxo, S

Chapter 3

CAUCASIAN FORNICATION

Sasha was no stranger to humiliation. It followed her around like an illicit rumor or a yippy Pomeranian. This was simply her truth. She was a high-functioning goofball, prone to embarrassing herself. But it wasn't the kind of personality feature you notice at first sight. No, her propensity for weird gaffes lurked just beneath the surface, popping out at the worst moment.

When she was eight, she had a backyard birthday party. After she blew out her candles, her mom tossed a chocolate-covered strawberry in Sasha's mouth (their special custom). Unfortunately, it was intercepted by an oversized butterfly that also landed on her tongue. Her entire third-grade class was there—including bitchy Janae Wells, who took a Polaroid of Sasha, sobbing, a limp wing hanging from her lips. Janae called her "Mothmouth" till graduation.

As a seventeen-year-old majorette, Sasha tried out for the all-state team. Texas is huge, and so were the auditions, held at a Dallas Hilton—in front of hundreds of girls! Sasha nailed her solo (performed to a dizzyingly sped-up remix of Chingy's "Right Thurr"). Until she tripped, tossing her baton toward the celeb judge's table.

To this day, among Texas's most elite millennial former majorettes, Sasha's remembered as the girl who concussed Jessica Simpson.

At twenty-seven, she was chosen to present the Nelson Mandela Award for Diverse Representation at the Screen Actor Guild Awards. At the podium, she peered into the crowd and became tongue-tied with nervousness. All her colleagues remembered where they were sitting when Sasha presented the "Howie Mandela Award."

Terrible. But these humiliations did have a positive-ish side. They taught Sasha not to take herself too seriously; how to laugh at her missteps (or, at least, softly titter). But desperately drunk-emailing an exec at her new job to track down some random guy? And, in the process, mistakenly emailing over one hundred employees all over the world? This was a new low. A professional, personal, and social disaster.

She wanted to teleport to Oz. She wanted to hide under her Paris hotel bed till Christmas. She wanted to crumple up the past twenty-four hours like paper and toss it into an active volcano. Why hadn't someone invented a morning-after pill to consume after committing email fuckery?

The ironic thing was, Sasha didn't even realize her mistake right away. By the time she'd shot off the email in the cab, the driver was pulling up to the hotel. Excited to sleep (and still tipsy), she hurriedly checked in, took a quick shower, and collapsed in bed. Never once did she think to reread her work. Four hours later, she awoke with a groggy yawn. Only then did she open her phone—and she saw, with dismay, that her email had racked up *twenty-five reply-all responses.*

And the number was growing. Before she even had a chance to read them, more responses flooded in. A few minutes later, the number had grown to forty. Shortly after that, she had fifty-nine responses. What was going on? Panicked, she finally reread her email.

She froze solid, her mouth agape in Edvard Munch's *The Scream.*

In utter denial, she read it again. No. No, no, no. Quickly, she scanned through the responses. NO. With growing horror, it dawned on Sasha that hundreds of high-powered Seraphina executives (none of whom she'd ever met!) were invested in her desperate plea to find Seat F. A small selection:

> Greetings, Sasha! I work in public relations at Seraphina Dubai. This man sounds like someone I met at an extremely exclusive and lavish gala last June. Green eyes, you say? Give me till the end of the quarter.
>
> Good day, Sasha and Seraphina family. I run the Seraphina sales team in West Africa. I'm nosy and driven. 350 EURO says I'll find him before next Friday. Who wants to wager?
>
> Don't know your guy, but I have a proposal. I design windows at Seraphina Beverly Hills. One of our VIP customers is an Oscar-nominated screenwriter. A-list. I've contacted her, and she's hot to take your story to the big screen. Could be big. Call me. Let's make magic.
>
> Hi Sasha, I'm VP of Finance at Seraphina Canada. I'm going to Gallipoli on vacation next month. Should I describe your gentleman to someone at the embassy? Please advise.
>
> So cute, omg. Not you treating HR like a dating app! I assist the Makeup Artistry Lead at Seraphina Chicago. I just posted a TikTok asking if anyone knows him. 400 likes, so far!

Slowly, Sasha lowered her phone to the bed and then stared at it, as if she could make it explode through telekinesis. How could she have been so reckless? She wasn't a great drinker. That was the problem. So, when she did indulge, she overdid it and ended up wrecked. But that was no excuse.

How could she show her face at the summit?

Her stomach surged, and her head pounded. After taking a few shallow breaths, the room started swaying. With a dry-mouthed cough, she sprinted to the bathroom—and *just* made it to the toilet before vomiting. Head swimming, she perched on the bathtub rim and folded in on herself, sticking her head between her knees. She focused on breathing in through her nose; out through her mouth. This would pass. She'd survive this.

I'll survive, sure. But at what cost? she wondered, mind racing. *I'm now known worldwide as a thirsty, unprofessional plane-slut with no decorum!*

Once Sasha's breathing regulated, she racked her brain for what to do next—and realized the proper thing would be to call her HR contact, April. She had to face her. Maybe if she played up their Spelman connection, April would cut her some slack? Turns out, there was no need. April was shockingly cool about the whole debacle.

"Sasha, it's fine," said April in her sharp, clipped tones. She'd always had corporate vibes. Even in college, she carried herself as if she might need to fire someone by noon. "You haven't ruined your job. If anything, your email served as an employee bond-building exercise. Everyone's united in finding the whole thing delightful."

"Delightful? I misspelled every fourth word!" squawked Sasha in a scratchy, thin voice. She sounded like she'd swallowed a dry loofah sponge. "I'm so ashamed. And deeply sorry. That behavior doesn't fit the Seraphina brand. By the way, I know he doesn't work for Seraphina! But when I sent the email I was a little foggy. Alcohol-impaired."

"Sasha, relax."

"How can I? Those were private thoughts, not professional ones."

April sighed. "Would it help balance things out if I admitted something private to you?"

Sasha thought about this. "Yes."

"My wife and I met while doing..." She paused and exhaled. "...a Hinge handshake."

"A Hinge handshake?"

"A one-night stand," she whispered. "Colloquially."

"But that's not embarrassing, it's beautiful. Love shows up in all kinds of ways."

"Precisely. This Seat F saga feels unfortunate now, but it'll make a wonderful story at your wedding," she reasoned. "Your email has nothing to do with your body of work. Seraphina wants you because you're *you*. So, let's move on."

"I think I'm going to drown myself in the Seine," Sasha said, thrusting her knuckles into her eye sockets.

"Please don't. The Seine is rancid." She sniffed. "One last thing, I think it's best to disable your Seraphina email address. No one will be able to contact you from the internal mailing list. We'll use your Gmail for the duration of your project."

"Thank you, April."

"Anytime. And Sasha? I do hope you find him."

The Paris summit was Friday through Sunday. But to Sasha, it stretched on for years. As expected, everyone there was whispering about Sasha Cruz and the flight saga. The bright side? No one knew that *she* was Sasha Cruz. The only employees she'd met IRL were her hiring manager and April—and neither was in Paris.

Anonymity was Sasha's only saving grace. So, she bought some enormous, cheap shades off the street, wore them everywhere, and never spoke. When introducing herself during breakout sessions, she called herself Grace (her middle name) Elliot (her mom's last name). And she skipped the networking drinks. As far as she knew, her off-the-radar performance worked. No one connected her to the unhinged email-sender.

But, since it was her first time in Paris, it felt wrong to waste it. So, during her limited free time, she window-shopped along Champs-Élysées, sipped overpriced café crèmes in Montmartre, and snapped an Eiffel Tower selfie. She hoped that immersing herself in tourism would distract her from The Scandal. But, ever so often, the email would flash across her mind and she'd jolt, recoiling in full-body shame.

At the front of her mind, though, was Seat F. Everywhere she went, she hoped she'd run into him. She thought she saw him once in a bakery, but it was a look-alike. She almost called his name, but remembered, with a sinking stomach, that she didn't know it.

But, like April said, she had to move on. What choice did she have? With only one month left to cast the commercial, she had to get to work. Which was exactly what she told Destiny Morgan on the rooftop of Sasha's apartment building back in Brooklyn. Destiny was Sasha's dearest friend. Through all of Sasha's depressive episodes, when she'd successfully managed to alienate (or exhaust) her inner circle—Destiny had stuck by her.

It was a brilliantly sunny morning a few days after Sasha's return. The two friends were on the communal rooftop lounge area of Sasha's building—along with a dozen of her neighbors. As with many of Brooklyn's newer high-rises, the roof was designed to look like an urban oasis, with chaise lounges, wood deck tiles, and green spaces. It was the perfect spot for remote working (i.e., gossiping and tanning).

Sasha and Destiny were kindred spirits who'd met as adults—a rarefied breed of best friends. One of Sasha's first big casting jobs was the film adaptation of a bestselling memoir, *My Life as a Matchmaking*

Maven. The author? Destiny. Her expertise? Creating love matches for Black women seeking to marry wealthy. She was perfect for this career, as she was a Black woman who'd married wealthy three times. From their first brainstorming session at the Hotel Chelsea bar, their bond was immediate. Destiny was ten years older than Sasha, with a voice that purred and a fascinating backstory.

In college, Destiny married her first husband, Jake; a dull, much older real estate honcho. Two years later, he divorced her—after she'd grown two sizes beyond his prenup-mandated weight requirement. When he immediately moved on with a bodacious Ruth's Chris waitress, Destiny sought revenge. First, she befriended the waitress, under the guise of "seeking closure." Secretly, she sussed out her needs (good sex and travel) and then introduced her to a thick-dicked hedge fund zillionaire who, as Destiny knew from experience, could provide both. Within weeks, the waitress dumped Jake to marry the hedge fund guy. As a final nail in her ex-husband's coffin, Destiny officiated the waitress's wedding. Destiny learned quite a lesson from this experience. She had a sixth sense about people's desires. Cleverly, she parlayed this talent into an elite matchmaking service. Her tagline? *Love isn't luck. It's strategy.*

Like an Abyssinian cat, Destiny was languid, fancy, and dedicated to a fluffy life of luxury. Unless the subject was love. In that case, she turned into a steely, ruthless shark. And right now, she was metaphorically circling Sasha in the ocean.

"But baby. All this fuss over one mere man? Have you learned nothing from me?" asked Destiny. The yogafied bombshell was a vision in a cascading, auburn bussdown and a pink bandeau top. She wore pink, exclusively.

"You weren't there on that flight," whispered Sasha, conscious of her neighbors lounging nearby. "Even through all the drama with the email, I can't stop thinking about him."

"Honestly, I'm offended. I've been trying to match you for years!

Every man in my network is top of the line." She chef-kissed her fingertips to her lips. "Vetted and approved by me. And you fall for a random civilian?"

"But that's what makes this so exceptional. The fact that I, a woman who rejects all male attention, spoke to this man for almost six hours straight? It has to mean something."

"Does your picker even work, though? You've been alone for a decade."

"By choice! I was leaning into being single."

"You need to lean into being *plural*," she retorted. "It's important to date widely before you decide Seat F's the one. You need to spread it around. Be a ho, like me." When Destiny said the word "ho," it somehow sounded elevated and elegant, like "courtesan."

"You only date rich old men on their deathbeds."

Destiny stretched languidly. "Mmm, wait till you meet Marlon. He has property in Mustique."

"Yeah? How long ago did Marlon pass?"

Destiny playfully whacked Sasha in the shoulder with her hat. "He's very much alive, thank you. He's sixty-eight and does CrossFit! But back to you embracing your inner ho."

Pouting, Sasha played with the hem of her sundress. "I can't be a ho. I'm too sleepy. Hoes don't nap. Didn't Cardi B say that?"

"No, she said hoes don't get cold. Which is a scientific fact," added Destiny. "Listen, let me build you a roster. I can get you a pair and a spare by close of business Friday."

"You don't get it, Destiny. We talked for hours." Sasha slid off her sunnies, and looked soulfully into her friend's eyes. "The. Whole. Flight."

"So? That's the airplane version of the club boyfriend. Remember those? You'd go out, lock eyes with someone, then date him exclusively for the duration of the function. Never to be seen again." She shrugged. "Some men shouldn't exist beyond the theoretical plane."

"Stop gaslighting me into thinking my experience wasn't real."

Destiny ignored her, pulling up an Excel spreadsheet on her laptop. "Look at all these available men in my contacts. This guy, Eli? He's perfect for you. Full disclosure, he's a little awkward. His personality gives first draft. But he's a HENRY."

"You just said his name's Eli."

"'HENRY' means 'High Earner Not Rich Yet,'" said Destiny, scrolling through her contacts.

Sasha burst out laughing. "I'm through with you."

"Listen, he gives gorgeous head and he'll analyze your retirement fund," she enthused. "But I'm having trouble placing him because he has sleep apnea. Does snoring trigger you?"

Sasha exhaled dramatically, flopping back on the sunbed. "I don't want Eli. I want Seat F. That flight felt cosmic. I've never felt a connection like that, so fast."

That's a lie. Destiny doesn't know about the other time I felt this way. No one does. It's between me and him. Anyway, it was forever ago. It doesn't matter now. And it couldn't matter, then. Different time, different situation.

Destiny turned toward her so fast, her stack of pink bracelets jingle-jangled. She eyed Sasha with suspicion and alarm.

"Am I hearing you say that you're soulmates? What have I told you? It takes four seasons of dating—an entire calendar year—before you can confirm soulmate status."

"You know I don't believe in soulmates. But there was undeniable magic." She nibbled her bottom lip, remembering. "We held hands. Just for a little bit, during turbulence. Like this."

Sasha demonstrated on Destiny, whose eyes slowly widened. "How many seconds?"

"About five."

"Mmm. Anything more would've been creepy. Five is tasteful. Damn, he's good."

"It's funny, though," said Sasha. "I never pictured my soulmate being white."

"Recession indicator," quipped Destiny. Then she began scrolling through her spreadsheet, again. "Wait. You're open to dating white men? Hold, please."

"What are you doing?" asked Sasha.

"Consulting my Caucasian Fornication database. In case you can't find Seat F, I have some backups. What genre of white man are we doing? Fade-and-tatted-calves white? Country-club-chinos white?"

"I'm not looking for a white man!"

Just then, a husky blond guy walked by, and winked. Sasha waved her fingers at him.

"I'm not *looking* for a white man," she repeated, this time in a whisper. "He *happens* to be white. Italian from Italy, to be specific. A coastal beach town."

She gasped. "Imagine us summering in Portofino?"

"First of all, who's 'us'? Secondly, this isn't about Caucasian fornication. I wasn't even thinking about sex on that flight."

"See, but that's a problem," said Destiny. "The longer women go without sex, the less we need it. And we stop even missing it. That's just the law of sexual physics."

"But I get horny sometimes," protested Sasha. "When the laptop heats up on my lap, I get a tingle."

Destiny looked harrowed. "Friend."

"I know, I know. Maybe I'm just not a sexual person. Was I ever? In my twenties, I had three significant boyfriends. I must've enjoyed doing it with them."

Sasha pictured one of those old *Cosmopolitan* magazine coverlines: "Whore to Bore, and Back Again: How to Reignite Your Inner Slut." She wondered if sexuality was like a muscle. If you don't use it, it atrophies.

"I'm sure you were sexual. You know, in your prissy way," Destiny said. "Honestly, I can't see you doing anything to affect the integrity of your silk press."

"Stop it, I'm not precious about my hair. I work out four times a week."

"So you say," joked Destiny. "But yes, you were freer, in general. Before everything happened."

"Yeah, I guess so."

Sasha and Destiny never talked about October 2022. The bracelet, the scar, and the memories hung between them, as subtle as flashing neon lights.

"You can't stay scared forever," said Destiny softly. "I'm not diminishing your experience. But you have a defeated way of living. Don't let that monster... that fucking predator win. Live. Be free. Take chances."

Sasha nodded in agreement. It was easier than explaining the way fear works. After a while, it stops being vivid. It turns into a lifestyle. The fear of the traumatic incident evolves into a fear of everything. Sasha used to be a normal woman, fully experiencing the world. Free. Now, she was in chains—unable to even stay at a hotel without barricading the door at night.

If only the cure was as simple as "Don't let the predator win."

Sasha changed the subject. "Anyway. Maybe Seat F was just a club boyfriend. But I want to see him again. Just to make sure. There was a reason we connected, and I want to know what it is. Does that make sense?"

"Yes. To a woman violently attracted to her MacBook." Destiny reached for her LaCroix on the ground. At which point her spectacular, all-natural double Ds popped out of her bandeau top. "Whoops!"

Sasha reached over, yanking up Destiny's top. "*Please.* I live with these people."

"You know where my titties would be welcome? Italian beaches.

Just saying." She shimmied her shoulders. "Quick question. What if some Seraphina employee actually does find him? What then?"

"I'm choosing to forget that there are strangers all over the world on the case," she said. "Too mortifying. Anyway, HR disabled my account, so I won't receive any more responses. Thank God," she sighed. "I just need to do some detective work, myself."

For the past couple of days, she'd been musing upon fate. Accepting that Seraphina job. Ending up on that particular flight. Sitting in that specific seat, next to that specific man. It felt destined. But she didn't even know his name. He had no social media, and she didn't know where he worked. Was it a lost cause? Or maybe she should do some private investigating herself. Destiny was right. She needed a detective.

Just then, she froze. And gasped so loudly that she startled someone's maltipoo, two chaise lounges away. She swiveled her head toward Destiny. After a few seconds, Destiny's eyes widened and her jaw dropped. And then, they started speaking over each other in rapid-fire best-friendian.

"Wait, you're not thinking—"

"Oh but I am—"

"Have you spoken since—"

"No, not in years—"

Sasha knew a detective. A good one, too. But was she prepared to see him again?

Of course I am, she thought, answering herself. *I don't know what he's up to, or what his life's like now. But we're both adults. And that brief, fleeting moment we had was born out of a heightened situation. We can be professional.*

She whipped out her phone and scrolled through her contact list. There he was, the first name under *D.*

WESLEY DANE, DETECTIVE. DANE & SON AGENCY.

Wes had saved her life once. But reaching out to him might be opening up a world of trouble.

Chapter 4

RIBBED FOR OUR PLEASURE

Thank God I'm not a detective anymore, thought Wes Dane as he lovingly dished a ladleful of brisket into a take-out box. Being an investigator was too high-stakes. And saving people's lives was too draining. It was so much easier to feed them.

And, as the owner of Natural Born Griller, Brooklyn's latest, greatest barbecue food truck, he delighted in doing exactly that.

As Wes handed off the brisket to his customer, an NYU grad student wearing beaded cornrows, he could feel his face light up with unselfconscious happiness. He flashed her a smile—the dangerous one, with the dimple. She blushed. Thanked him with fluttery lashes. And then disappeared in a cloud of citrus fragrance.

Wes couldn't have dreamed up a lovelier Saturday. He felt like breakdancing. Had he ever known such contentment, such unrestrained joy? Doubtful. It was a perfect Saturday afternoon. Today, Natural Born Griller was the featured truck at F.E.A.S.T., the weekend food truck market nestled in Prospect Park (Central Park's chill Brooklyn cousin). Clear skies, eighty degrees. The crowd was a multiethnic combo of food-fluencers, chic couples, and post-gender friend groups in breezy linens. And Wes was parked in a prime location. The top seller spot, at the entrance to the clearing.

Also, he had the longest line (not that he was counting). And the most buzz (according to Eater). And the most faithful regulars (they'd named themselves the "Barbecuties").

Prospect Park was simmering with vivacity. Somebody's speakers were pumping syrupy, smooth Afrobeat. And Wes's world, once so action-packed and unpredictable, had been whittled down to a few small elements: Marinade. Braise. Sear. Grill. And he'd never been happier.

This was the life. The crowd was buzzing, and he adored his customers. They were easy to please! They were *fun* to please. Whether they were starving artists buying their one daily meal, or pregnant folks seized by cravings, or obnoxious foodies looking for the next big thing—everyone wanted a delicious treat to enliven their day. It was just a matter of reading people. Understanding what dish they were in the mood for, and then giving it to them.

Feeding people was compassionate. It was like communion. It was a reciprocal dopamine rush. And these days, most people were teeter-tottering on the verge, trying not to tip over into despair. One good brisket could soothe your psychic wound for five minutes, an hour, an afternoon. And Wes Dane had food for every mood.

That's not a bad tagline, he thought.

"Who's hungry?" he called out.

A tween boy wearing starter dreadlocks and basketball shorts stepped up. Truth Johnson, a repeat customer.

Wes gave him a powerful pound. "What's good witcha, dog?"

"Chilling. You?"

"Grilling."

"That's wassup, that's wassup," said Truth, nodding heavily. "Yo, I came with my girl, this time. She's over by Soup-er Star." He cocked his head to the left. "But don't look!"

"This ain't my first day on Earth, little buddy. Did you offer to buy her lunch, like I told you?"

"Yeah." Truth pulled a crumpled five-dollar bill from his pocket. With confidence, he slammed it on the counter. The cheapest item on Wes's menu was twelve dollars.

"What should I get?" asked Truth. "I heard from two different sources that she borrowed her dress from Neavah Gray. And she's mean as hell. So, she can't spill on it."

"I got you." Wes served up a plate of charred chicken bites. "She can just pop 'em in her mouth, no muss no fuss."

"My man!" exclaimed Truth, and headed to his lucky date.

"Who's hungry?" asked Wes, squinting in the sun. He never wore sunglasses at work. Too impersonal.

A curvy blonde in a purple maxidress stepped up with her friend, a petite, glum-looking woman wearing a band tee and jorts.

"Hi, Wes," said the blonde in a sing-songy tone. "You don't know me, but I follow the Natural Born Griller account on socials. It's *fire*. I'm an associate digital strategist, so I say this from a place of absolute professionalism."

Wes put his hand over his heart, soulfully nodding at her. "I appreciate you. Thank you. I try." Actually, he didn't. His social media intern oversaw all that. For someone who could teach a college course on high-level systems hacking, Wes couldn't get the hang of editing videos. And he hated posting details about his life. The secondhand embarrassment part of his brain was too overdeveloped.

"This is my friend," the blonde said, gesturing to the sad girl. "I dragged her here. She's not having the best mental health day."

"Oh, that's just existential dread," he quipped cheerfully. "Wings for your trouble?"

Flashing his Natural Born Griller grin (again), Wes handed the sad girl a plate of wings. She didn't quite smile back—but her eyes softened, matching his friendly energy. The blonde cheered, paid, and then dragged her away. As they left, Wes overheard their short exchange.

"I told you," whispered the blonde.

"Do you think he knows?" wondered the sad one.

"Oh, he knows," she responded. "Look at his joggers."

Wes glanced down. He was wearing the same gray joggers, crisp tee, and Yankees snapback that virtually every millennial Black Brooklynite had on that summer. He was cooking outside in the heat; he wasn't focused on what he was wearing. But whatever magic the joggers possessed, they just sold almost four hundred dollars in the past hour. He bit down on a proud smirk. Whatever worked.

Wesley Dane was a competitive person. No matter the game, he craved winning. So, when he decided that selling barbecue was his calling, failure wasn't an option. Wes had a few shortcomings: He had no idea how to run a food truck, or even cook professionally. He'd never worked at a restaurant. But starting in his twenties, from early summer to late fall, he'd fire up the grill and his kickback playlist—and everyone he knew would gather at his Fort Greene studio apartment (his space was microscopic, but it had backyard access). Some of his favorite memories happened on those endless Saturdays, with friends from disparate eras of his life munching on his slightly overseasoned, decidedly unaesthetic barbecue, chilling on the couch, the floor, the counters—till all hours. Those parties were a blissful reprieve from detective work.

One night, he thought, *I could live like this forever.* And a light bulb went off. Why not monetize this passion? Sink it into a new business? Find some investors, research grilling on a larger scale, and do this thing?

So, Wes bought a retro, seventies-style truck on a deep discount and fixed it up himself. (He did employ the help of his boy, Spare

Parts Shawn, who supplied him with a brand-spanking-new oven of dubious origin. Wes had a hookup for everything.) When he was finished decorating and renovating, the truck looked like something out of a cool, low-budget action flick. You *had* to notice it.

Then, he brushed up on his grilling chops. The most talented pitmaster he ever met was his great-uncle Rudy, a career cook at several iconic soul food spots. When his wife kicked him out for excessive gambling, Wes allowed Uncle Rudy to sleep on his pull-out couch for a few months—in exchange for teaching Wes all his barbecue knowledge; especially about brisket, which would be his signature dish.

An expert schmoozer, he pulled some strings to garner entry into F.E.A.S.T. Traffic was slow, at first. His truck was untested, and he was parked in the least-desirable position (behind a swing set). Then, it occurred to him—he needed an unforgettable logo. So, he had his cousin, a Spotify graphic designer, whip up a Blacksploitation-style design that matched the truck's throwback vibe. On the logo, Wes was shirtless, wearing roughed-up carpenter pants, Timbs, a scowl, and a spatula jutting out of his apron pocket. His cousin photographed Wes from the ground up, making him (and his spatula, *wink*) look extra-larger than life. It was wild, comic book-y. And plastered on the side of the truck? It was gold.

Everything changed. In the span of one fall weekend, Natural Born Griller became a destination. His lines were long; his customers effusive. But it wasn't until his social media intern pointed him to the comments section of her latest post, that he fully understood his fanbase.

@mollyfranks I'll beat his meat

@carohmel98 Get behind me, sis, I'm about to pull his pork

@brooklynbaddie After I jerk his chicken

@tina1995 I heard he's ribbed for our pleasure

For two seconds, Wes was insulted. *Jerk his chicken?* He'd sunk a good chunk of cash into that truck. He'd sous-chef'ed and lived with his intolerably unkempt Uncle Rudy for months. He expected to be taken seriously. But his indignation was short-lived. Because wasn't this his plan, all along?

Till eleventh grade, he'd been a scrawny late bloomer with braces, massive feet, and insane levels of ADHD. But when his height grew to match his feet (six foot four), his braces came off, and he'd filled out to lean, mean, broad-shouldered proportions, he found himself the object of a weird amount of lusty energy. (Though his personality, which resembled that of a boisterous Labrador puppy no one bothered to crate train, *hadn't* changed.) His transformation did come in handy, though, once he started working as a detective. For whatever reason, his looks made people feel safe—which gained him access to places, informants, and secrets. During a short, post-detective stint as a physical trainer, one of his female clients put it into perspective. "You have pretty privilege, just accept it," the fifty-year-old minx said shortly before blowing him to absolute smithereens. Point, taken.

The vapidity of his new life was healing, after years of taking his sometimes dark, heavy, depressing detective work home. Also, he suspected that it did feed his ego. After all, if he didn't enjoy the attention, would he have agreed to such a slutty logo?

Wes felt lucky that he'd finally stumbled upon professional success, post-detective life. And he was proud of what he'd created. Natural Born Griller had character. More importantly, it had a good-natured owner who made everyone feel special. Because he genuinely, generally, felt like most people were. Most significantly, it was powered by the single-minded focus and uncompromising passion of a thirty-two-year-old man on his third professional pivot after quitting investigative work. Running the food truck was the only thing that stuck. It was a low-stakes, high-reward, nonemotionally taxing job. It was healing.

Detective Wes had a stomach ulcer. Grillmaster Wes slept like a baby. He was never forced to make morally gray decisions. He hadn't had a tortured thought in, damn, who knew how long? These days, his thoughts went no deeper than marinades and rubs. Detective Wes had been a nervous wreck. But Grillmaster Wes was floating on air. He felt in control. Stable. Centered. And he had time to Wordle.

"Who's next?" he said, brandishing a metal spatula.

"Little ol' me," trilled a bright-eyed older lady with a salt-and-pepper pixie cut. Nana was a sixty-year-old, notoriously bawdy Haitian woman who ran a women's health center. She spent her free time doing one of two things: organizing protest marches and stressing out Flatbush's most eligible Boomer men. "How you doing, young man?"

"Just laboring under capitalism, Ms. Nana. They let you out?"

Last weekend, Nana was arrested at a book-banning protest and spent two nights in jail before her Flatbush community banded together to make bail.

"You heard I was arrested?"

"You kidding? I pitched in for bail. Stay on their necks, ma'am. I'd expect nothing less."

"Always." She raised a Black Power fist. "I was arrested in a lace cardigan. So at least I was the most fashionable person in my cell."

"Look at you," he said, his tone admiring and jokey. "Gonna have to call you Mitochondria."

"What?"

"The powerhouse of the cell."

"All right now, AP Biology!" Nana laughed, clapping her hands. "That was a good one."

Wes beamed proudly.

"Baby, I'm starving. You got any smoked wings left?"

"How many you want?"

"Sixty-nine," she said with a wink.

"Ms. Nana, behave yourself," he said, shaking his head. "How 'bout sixty-eight and I'll owe you one?"

She giggled girlishly, bought her wings, and sashayed away.

"Who's next?" he called out.

The next customer was a tall, thirtysomething woman with dark, flowing hair and a pink miniskirt. "Hi! Do you have goat curry?"

"No, actually I only make American barbecue. Soul food by way of Brooklyn," he apologized. "How about ribs?" he offered. "Do you like brisket?"

She lit up at the mention of brisket. "Oooh. Sounds good."

"So," he started, preparing the dish, "when did you move here from Guyana?"

Startled, the woman took her plate. "Wait. Have we met? How'd you know I was Guyanese?"

"Because Caribbeans say 'curried goat.' Guyanese people say 'goat curry.'"

"Stop. You have a crazy attention to detail."

"I know." Wes poured barbecue sauce into a tiny cup for her. "It's a gift and a curse."

It was the only part of detective work that Wes missed. It was fun, using the details he noticed to disarm. Sometimes, like now, he turned it on just to see what happened. He could also tell from the tan line on her finger that she'd removed her wedding ring. And she paid with a man's credit card. Could be nothing. Could be suspicious.

But it was none of his business. Data collecting was just for fun, now. The beautiful Guyanese woman smiled and moved on. Sighing pleasantly, Wes looked out into the crowd. It really was a gorgeous day. God, he felt so centered. He was absolutely at peace. But the sun was at its zenith now, truly blazing. From the glare, he could barely see who was in front of him.

"Who's next?" he called out, twisting the top back on the sauce bottle.

"Me." The voice was hesitant, unsure, and familiar as hell.

"Me who?"

Squinting, Wes cocked his head to the side. Then, the person stepped a bit closer. And he saw who it was. But he already knew. It couldn't have been anyone else, with that signature throaty voice. And he would've recognized the sylphy contours of her silhouette anywhere. Her hair was different, shorter, but undoubtedly—it was her. He hadn't laid eyes on her in five years. Well, that wasn't entirely true. She'd snuck into his dreams. *Often*. Sometimes she blended into the background, sometimes she was the star; but no matter what, she left him utterly dismantled.

It was Sasha Cruz. Again.

"*Jesus fucking Christ,*" he groaned, dropping the bottle in a mighty crash.

And that's how, in the blink of an eye, Wes's past came charging at his present.

Chapter 5

A MISSED CONNECTION THING

And then, things got weird.

While Wes preoccupied himself with swiping up the sauce explosion on his counter, Sasha plummeted into nerve-deep awkwardness, leaning heavily on her nervous tic (i.e., repeatedly and aggressively tucking her hair behind her ears). Behind her, the line rustled with concern, wondering who or what had killed the vibe. Destiny, who'd joined Sasha for moral support—and was spying a few feet away, near the Wok This Way truck—audibly whispered, "Noooo."

What had Sasha expected from Wes when he saw her? Now that she thought about it, she wasn't sure. Pleasant surprise, maybe. A *long time no see* hug, perhaps. She would've taken a fist bump. But nothing could've prepared her for his thunderstruck reaction. The second Wes locked eyes with Sasha, he instinctively drew back, his face an almost slapstick collision of stress, shock, and confusion. The man shattered a glass bottle of barbecue sauce, for God's sake. Was her presence *such* a jump scare?

Besides, *Sasha* should've been the shocked one. Her detective in shining armor had become a natural born griller? Pardon? Not that Wes's truck wasn't cool as hell, all tricked out in retro oranges and browns, like a prop out of *Shaft* or *Boogie Nights*. And his food must've been delicious, given the size of his crowd. But...why, though? He was incredible at detective work. His ingenuity and focus had saved her life. Why give up a career that he excelled in?

Wes Dane never struck her as the kind of guy who'd blow up his life for barbecue.

And she told Destiny as much, twenty minutes before, when they first spotted his truck at F.E.A.S.T. They hid behind a truck, gawking at Wes through the crowd.

"I can't believe what I'm looking at," whispered Sasha to Destiny, who was overdressed for an outdoor food festival, wearing a pink corseted maxidress. And a fascinator. "That's Wes Dane? My absolute God. Is he on OnlyFans?"

"Look at the *women*, though. Matte red lips to eat pulled pork?" Sasha was wearing a short halter top and slouchy jeans. Too casual? "I mean, go off. I love their commitment to the game. But what a scene."

"Did he always look like that?"

"Like a beautiful demon? Yep." She answered without hesitation. "I tried to cast him in a scripted series about a big-city female lawyer who returns to her tiny hometown for Christmas. And she falls for the local sheriff."

"You saw him as the sheriff?"

"No, the sheriff's promiscuous brother. He refused."

"He just allowed a woman to kiss his biceps. I believe this version of Wes would consider it." Destiny squinted her eyes in his direction. "He has no business being that fine."

"Eh. I'm around fineness all the time, at work. Means nothing to me."

Wes wasn't her type, at all. She had no patience for guys that were a bit too pretty and charming for their own good. She'd auditioned a million of them—actors and models who'd had the world handed to them in exchange for the bare minimum, simply because their features sparked joy. She felt thankful that the universe had always protected her from such men.

Well, she thought. *Except for that one time.*

"Wait," said Sasha suddenly. "I do remember him mentioning that he liked to grill on the weekends. But it sounded like a hobby, not a career." She paused again, her mind rewinding, in superspeed, back to their long-ago conversations. What if he didn't remember her? What if he turned her away?

And then, Sasha began to chicken out. "You know what? I'm rethinking everything. I feel weird about this. Maybe I don't need a detective. I can look for Seat F myself."

"Yourself?" Destiny held up an index finger in Sasha's face. "No. I do not believe in breaking a sweat to land a man. This is dating, not an endurance challenge."

"Maybe I should warm up first. You want an empanada?"

Sasha saw that Pastelitos de Titos, a popular Dominican restaurant, had a truck outpost there. Before her life imploded, Sasha always tried to expose herself to Dominican things, to feel like she belonged. But she usually felt like a poser at Dominican hair salons and restaurants, or Spanish-speaking bookstores, stumbling over her public-school-meets-Duolingo Español. Her accent was so poor, she inevitably switched to English. But she was back out in the world. Now was as good a time as any to get back in the game.

"Now's not the time to explore your cultural identity," said Destiny, with no-nonsense finality. She had Sasha's number. "You dragged me out here, *where people are eating outside*, so you can meet Wes. What are you so nervous about?"

"I didn't say I was nervous!"

"It's obvious. Honestly, you're acting like he's an ex. Was there some pumpin' and thumpin' you never told me about?"

"Destiny, please."

"Well, what was your dynamic like, back in the day?"

"Hard to say. It was a dark time," she said haltingly. "I was scared, and he cut through that. He was strong and took charge. We just instantly had this bantery, fun interaction. It was exactly what I needed at the time. I was actually sad when we went our separate ways after the case. I would've liked to stay friends. But it was for the best, I guess." She shrugged vaguely. "That's all I remember."

It wasn't a total lie. Sasha had blocked out a lot of that time. It only resurfaced in vague dreams. The kind where you woke up paranoid and unsettled; but the details were fuzzy.

As soon as Sasha found Wes in her contacts list the day before, she dove into action. She tried calling, but she was sent to voicemail. After leaving a few messages, she texted him; but they all bounced back. So frustrating. Seat F was her future. She refused to let him slip through her fingers.

While she waited for Wes to return her call, she googled his name. And to her surprise, the Dane & Son Detective Agency website didn't show up till the third page. The first two pages were all Natural Born Griller media.

Which led Sasha here. But what had led Wes here?

Kind of ironic, that someone who solves mysteries was now at the center of one.

Wes had hung a sign reading BACK IN TEN from the window and apologized to the Barbecuties for stepping away. Catching Sasha's eye, he cocked his head to the left, gesturing at her to meet him behind the truck.

She nodded, scurrying over to a small, shaded area. And then, Wes slid open the truck door, stepping down and standing in front of her. A hand towel was tossed over his shoulder, a pencil was tucked behind his ear, and he looked outrageously broad-shouldered and startled and concerned. She cupped her hand above her eyes, blocking out the sun as she peered up at him. God, she forgot how tall he was.

"Sasha Cruz. Sasha. Cruz." Wes sounded like he was trying to talk himself into the truth of her presence. "Where did you come from? You scared the hell out of me."

"I'm so, so sorry," she whisper-yelled. "I didn't mean to make a scene or just, like, pop up out of nowhere..."

"Oh, you didn't mean to pop up out of nowhere?" He laughed a little at this, his hand over his heart like he was protecting it from pounding out of his chest. "*Fuck*."

Wes scrubbed a hand over his face, pressing into his eyes. Then, he dropped his hand into his pocket. Shifted his weight from foot to foot. And finally looked into her face. And, oh, she'd forgotten. She'd forgotten the hard line of his jaw. The puffy, sensual contours of his mouth and his long, long lashes—the kind that were truly wasted on a man. The dimple so deep, it flashed and flirted when he spoke.

A long-ago sense memory flooded through her. Quickly, she squeezed her fingernails into her palm, and let it go.

"You're right, this was so unexpected," she conceded. "But in my defense, I tried to call."

"I changed my number."

"That's why my texts bounced."

"But you found me anyway."

"I did. Who's the detective here, me or you?" she joked, trying to lighten the mood.

He smiled hollowly and then glanced at the ground. "Definitely not me."

"You really gave it up, huh?"

"Ages ago."

"Not to pry," she started, tentatively, "but why?"

"I'll tell you over a drink one day." His eyes darted over in the direction of his crowd, and then back at her. It was clear he needed to get back to work. Sasha felt like a fool.

A lengthy silence followed. Two women peeked around the side of the truck, spying on Wes and the random girl monopolizing his time. With studied amiability, he turned on a smile and raised his chin at them. For a moment, he was caught in a beam of sunlight, bathing his face in radiance. Sasha forgot how easily he accepted attention from people. He bloomed under it.

"I'll be right there," he called out, and turned back to Sasha. Almost apologetically, he said, "Folks show up to F.E.A.S.T. starving."

And thirsty, she thought wryly.

"Looks like you only have a few minutes before the riots start," she said.

"Less than that."

Just then, they noticed another customer peeking around the truck. Cheerfully, he held up six fingers. She shot him a thumbs-up and disappeared.

Sasha felt so out of place. "I'm sorry. I shouldn't have shown up like this."

"No, it's just...you caught me by surprise, you know? After three years of no contact."

"Four," she corrected. "And you're the one who disappeared, if I recall."

"I didn't disappear. The case was over," he reasoned. He slid the towel off his shoulder and began wrapping it around a hand, boxer-style. Fidgeting. Was he as nervous as she was?

"I never even got to thank you," she said.

"You didn't need to," he said, glancing again in the direction of his crowd. "I provided a service and fulfilled my contract."

Sasha flinched. "Why are you being so short with me?"

"You do understand I'm at work, right?" He lowered his voice to a movie whisper. "And suddenly I see you in my line—*you*—extremely out of context. You didn't think I'd have a heart attack? What if I showed up at one of your castings?"

She shrugged. "I'd make you audition a piece from *Love Jones* and then cast you in an erotic thriller or small-town rom-com."

Brows furrowed with mock severity; he folded his arms and widened his stance; lowering himself a few inches closer to her height. "You'd make me."

"Easily."

"You think you could *make* me audition for you?"

She arched her brow. "I've broken tougher men."

Wes couldn't help but chuckle at this. And then, with an exasperated groan, he said, "This is not how I thought this day was gonna go."

With a resigned sigh, he massaged a temple. She shot him an almost-guilty grin. And then, the faintest ghost of a smile played on his lips. Was he thawing out a bit?

"Can we start again?" she asked. "Hi, Wes."

"Hi, Sasha."

It felt so unexpectedly dreamy to hear him say her name again. Both warm and titillating, like sinking into a luxurious hot tub. A slightly delirious warmth radiated through her chest. Somehow, her name in his mouth sounded exactly right. She wished he'd say it again—but also hoped he wouldn't.

Did I really forget that my goddamn soul vibrates in this man's presence? she thought, pulse racing.

She had to pull it together. Sasha was strong enough to be around Wes without losing focus. As overwhelming as Wes was, he reminded her of the scariest moment of her life. And she refused to be pulled backward. Wes represented her tortured past. Seat F was her future. She was dying to embrace the excitement of a new person, a new start, a clean slate.

"Respectfully, though," he was asking, "why are you here?"

"I don't know what I was thinking."

"Yes, you do. You always know what you're thinking." His expression went serious. "You okay? Are you in danger?"

"No, no, it's nothing like that, this time. I just..."

She sputtered for what felt like five minutes. Nothing coherent came out. Now that she was here, in front of him, she felt ridiculous. Her Seat F story was going to sound insane. She'd been so focused on finding Wes, that she hadn't given thought to how she'd explain everything. And now, it didn't matter, because he flipped his towel back on his shoulder, and said, "I don't mean to cut you off, but I really need to get back. Cool?"

"Cool," she said, her stomach sinking.

"Cool, cool, cool. We'll get together. Catch up. Anytime you want, off work hours." He smiled. "Good to see you. Glad to see you looking so... umm, good."

And then, Wes offered the slightest half smile. Without looking back, he turned around and headed back up into the truck, shutting the door.

And Sasha stayed rooted to her spot in the shaded knoll behind Natural Born Griller. She felt like a fool. An impulsive jackass. How could she have thought this was a good idea?

While she was standing there, mulling over what to do next, she heard Wes's door reopen. She popped her head up. And there he was, walking toward her, fists thrust in his pockets.

"I'm only gonna ask one more time. Are you in trouble?" He stopped in front of her, looming large. His face was a cloudy mask of concern, with a touch of irritation.

"I swear I'm not," she promised. "Why do you look so annoyed?"

"Because I am annoyed."

"Why?"

"'Cause you know, and I know, that I can't resist helping you," he confessed.

Sasha's stomach dropped. She actually didn't know that. But hearing his confession made her insides flutter in ways she hadn't experienced in years.

"So. Are you gonna tell me why you're here?"

"Because, well... because I need you."

"Again."

"Yes."

Wes tilted his chin up to the sun and exhaled with his entire soul. And then, he looked off to one side, chewing the inside of his mouth. He appeared to be wrestling with the angel and demon on either shoulder. It was unclear who was winning.

"Hold on," he said, and then slow-jogged to the front of the truck. She overheard him make a quick announcement to his customers, and then he strode back over to her. He made a show of setting a timer on his phone.

"Dozens of scantily clad BBQ aficionados are awaiting my riblets. You got ten more minutes."

"Right. Well, I don't want to lead with the ask. It feels impolite. So let me congratulate you on being a... food truckian? What's your title?"

"Small business owner," he articulated impatiently. "Nine minutes."

"You have fans. Of all ages! I saw a FB group dedicated to Boomer Barbecuties."

"Dedicated to *what*? That's, uh, definitely an unauthorized thing. I don't even have Facebook." He cleared his throat, obviously mortified. "Sasha, if you don't spit it out..."

"I need you to find someone for me."

He folded his arms again, his expression unreadable. "I don't do that anymore."

"Are you permanently retired, though? You excel at detective-ing."

"Excelling at something doesn't mean it's your calling. Barbecue is gratifying to me. Food, feeding people, community—it makes me feel useful. You know, as a human."

"You were useful as a detective."

He let out an exasperated noise. "God forbid a Black man pivot!"

"What's *wrong*?"

"This is a lot to process," he said, stepping toward her. "In the past twenty minutes, I've been confronted by a bossy ghost..."

"Me?"

"Yeah, you. I've been pulled away from customers, and now you're questioning my life choices. It's always something with you. You're perpetually running from a burning building."

"I am not, and you're being rude."

"This is just the way I talk."

"No, it isn't. I saw the way you speak to your customers," she said, lightly roasting him. "You're downright flirty."

"I don't flirt with my customers, Sasha."

"Yeah? I've never seen anyone erotically wield a spatula."

"That's not flirting. That's engaging with my environment." Exasperated, Wes shoved his hands back in his pockets. "I'm going to regret asking this. Who are you looking for?"

"A man."

"I've heard great things about Hinge."

"No, I'm looking for a *specific* man. I met him on a plane. We sat next to each other on a flight to Paris. And I can't stop thinking about him."

His mouth dropped open, just a bit. Speechless. "You serious?"

"I'm so serious."

"So, it's a Missed Connections thing? Like those ads that used to run in Craigslist? Like, 'If you're the blonde I gave a seat to on the Q, call this number.'"

"Exactly like that. Look, I know this sounds far-fetched. And it gets weirder. But hear me out. I need to find him because I don't have his contact info."

"Easy. You have his name, right?"

"No."

"But he knows yours."

"Well, no."

"So, neither one of y'all closed?" Wes looked both wildly incredulous and amused. "What's wrong with him? And what's wrong with *you*? Where's your game?"

Sasha tucked her bob behind her ears. "Game? Don't know her."

"Well, what did you do for six hours?"

"We just talked." She paused, realizing she didn't want to share anything else. Especially the hand-holding part. In this day and age, who would hold non-sanitized hands with a stranger?

Wes looked baffled, like he was struggling to understand a conversation in a foreign language. "You were in first class, weren't you?"

"How'd you know?"

"This is sounding like a story about unlimited free booze."

"Welll, that's the thing. These days, I have flight anxiety. So, I was on a cocktail of beta-blockers, Xanax, and wine." She grimaced. "I was wrecked. And by the end of the flight, so was he. Besides, ever since the incident? I don't give my information out."

"Uh-huh. I see."

She could tell he was a little intrigued. He'd even stopped fidgeting and glancing over at his line. While she had him on a hook, she'd keep going.

"Also? Hear me out. A manicurist read my palm and predicted him."

"That's your last 'hear me out,'" said Wes, pinching his brows with his fingers.

"I know how this sounds! I realize I sound delusional. Childish, even. But what happened between me and . . . and . . . I've been calling him Seat F."

"Seat F?" Wes was about to wisecrack but then stopped himself. "Can't lie, Seat F goes kinda hard. Proceed."

"What happened between me and Seat F was special. Different. I'm not lucky with men. You of all people know that. I haven't had the easiest time since I last saw you. I feel like I'm scared of everything. Living. Dying. People. But those six hours with him felt like a gift. It was so special, like I finally got to feel what everyone else feels when they fall for someone, without fear. Maybe being in the air heightened it. Or it could've been the drinks. Or, shit, maybe I hallucinated the whole thing, who knows? But you only get one life, right? One chance to chase down what you want. If he's my guy, I don't want to miss out on knowing him. I'd never forgive myself," she said, taking a breath. "I'm tired of hiding from my life. I do everything from home. And it doesn't help that my industry has gone fully digital. I haven't held an in-person casting in years. It's all self-tapes—you know, auditions that actors record themselves, and send to me. *I have no reason to leave the house.* And I rarely want to," she admitted in a low voice.

Wes's expression had softened. He was taking in her every word, giving her a chance. "I didn't know you were suffering like that."

"No one did," she said, worrying that she had gone too far. "I stayed home for so long, I started to get weird. I'd talk to the TV. Like, if a character said hi to someone, I'd say hi back. Someone cried, I cried. Anyway, the flight taught me that I have a smidgeon of hope left. I discovered that I'm not irreparably broken. That maybe I can feel real things again. Have a real life again. Wes, I have to at least *try* to find him. And you're the only person who can help me."

The park buzzed around them with the sounds of Saturday frivolity. Laughter, music, crying babies, and chatter. But Wes and Sasha were standing alone, hidden behind the truck, the weight of her words binding them like glue. Why did she elaborate like that? She hadn't even given Destiny that many details. It was invigorating, getting it all off her chest. But now that her words were out there, she felt depleted and empty. Was it a mistake to be so honest?

Fuck it. She had nothing to lose.

But just then, Wes's timer went off.

"We made a good team once," she said, eyes pleading.

"I'm sorry, I can't," he said. "I haven't taken a case in years. Even if I wanted to, I'm rusty. And I don't want to. I worked hard to find a stress-free life. I'm done with other people's problems. I hope you can understand."

She nodded silently, fiddling with the gold cuff at her wrist.

"Good luck finding your guy, though. Nice to see you, Sasha."

"You too, Wes."

And then he was gone.

Chapter 6

PROS PLAY HURT

In order to become a functioning human again, Sasha had to *throw* herself outside, as forcefully as a mama bird shoving her chick out of the nest. (Only, she was both the mama and the chick.) On high-anxiety days, this was excruciating. Her apartment was so delightful, so cozy, so hers. At home, she was protected from the world. There was no risk of a shifty-eyed stranger sidling up to her on the train. She didn't need to perform glamour. She could sleep between work Zooms and look fresh as a daisy in seconds because no one knew that, from the waist down, she was wearing panties and slipper-socks.

Nothing Out There felt better than In Here.

But she'd done enough therapy to know that was her anxiety disorder talking. And the longer she wallowed in changelessness, day in and day out, the less hope she had for a functional life. She needed to find her heartbeat, again. Feel the world, again. Anything to liberate her from hibernation malaise. The Paris trip was her big experiment, and she'd passed with flying colors. She boarded a plane. She flew to another continent. She stayed in a hotel without barricading the door with paranoid-survivalist shit from Amazon. She allowed herself to have a "club boyfriend" in the sky. Progress was afoot!

And, at the moment, progress tasted like a strawberry shortcake cupcake at the Little Cupcake Bakeshop. Nestled among Vanderbilt Avenue's pho, furniture, and flower shops, the redbrick café was a delectably wholesome haven for sweet-toothed Brooklynites like Sasha. It was a short walk from her apartment—but still, it would've been so much easier to order on the delivery app. A year ago, she would've. But on this Sunday morning? She tore herself out of bed. Unwrapped her bob. Threw on a tank dress, black-cherry lip gloss, and a straw tote—and dragged her ass out the door. At the end of the eight-minute walk was a single, perfect, pink cupcake.

And more ruminating on what the hell happened with Wes, the day before.

He was so weird with her. Of course it was jarring to be surprised at work. Especially by a person you hadn't seen in forever. But something itched at the corners of her brain—it seemed like more than that. Wes wasn't just surprised to see her.

He seemed in a hurry to get rid of her.

Did I offend him back then? she wondered, racking her brain. *Is it because of what happened between us? Because I crossed the line? Is that why he never spoke to me again?*

There were so many unanswered questions between them. She needed clarity, but she also dreaded revisiting that time. Her head was drowning in confusion. One thing was for sure, though—going to F.E.A.S.T. was a bad idea. And it was a waste, because her detective was no longer a detective. Which looked good on him. Wes seemed lighter, somehow, and she was happy for him. Thrilled. Truly. Finding your calling was a rare gift.

Sasha had thought about him, often, over the years. In her head, she'd built him up to be this savior-hero figure. The Good Guy who'd saved her from the Bad Guy. Sasha only had positive thoughts about Wes. So watching him recoil when he first saw her? It was humbling at best; hurtful at worst. But how obnoxious had she been, expecting Wes to drop everything for her? Even if he'd still been a practicing PI—how dare she assume he'd be available, or that he'd *want* to take on her case? When did she get so self-centered?

Oh wait; she knew when. Self-centeredness was one of the unsavory occupational hazards of becoming a depressive shut-in. When you're the only person you see all day, your only friend in the world, your only *care* in the world—your perspective shrinks to a tiny, you-shaped pinprick. Your brain, your needs, your sadness, your bullshit.

Sucking the frosting off her last strawberry, Sasha decided to stop these thoughts, dead. She got it, loud and clear, that Wes didn't want anything to do with her. And she wasn't owed an explanation.

As she popped the last bite in her mouth, her eyes drifted out the window. Across Vanderbilt, a young Latino couple stumbled out of a well-worn brownstone. Her curls were mussed under a bucket hat; and he had on pajama bottoms and slides. They were clinging to each other, sipping Diet Cokes, and floating on a fuck haze.

This is probably their first time coming up for air since last night, she thought, bitterly. *I hate them. No one should be that happy at twenty-one.*

Her mind immediately drifted to Seat F. What if, at some point in the future, they could be that happy together? Was she delusional for believing there was a chance? Ever since the flight, she'd been replaying their moments together. They seemed to just melt into each other's spaces, until the distance between them shrunk smaller and smaller. Things like that didn't happen to her. Their connection felt so seamless. And then, there was the buzzing thrill of his touch. (Or was it just that she was touch-starved? Either way, it was a thrill.) Sasha didn't believe in coincidences. No, she was supposed to meet Seat F. Their meeting felt seismic. And she needed to know why.

And for a woman with major trust issues? Who, at movie

theaters, looped her purse strap around her leg to discourage pickpockets (because pickpockets are so famous for haunting AMC Theatres)? Opening up to Seat F was massively significant. That's the part she couldn't get over. That she'd shared so much of her personal story, and that it felt so natural.

But now, her one chance to find him had fallen through. Sasha had played the Wes thing all wrong. She shouldn't have barged in on him like that.

Lips pursed in exasperation, she began mindlessly doomscrolling through social media, hoping to stumble upon something, anything to uplift her mood. And just as she clicked on a clip of Botswanan schoolgirls absolutely nailing Beyoncé's "ALIEN SUPERSTAR" choreo, her phone dinged.

Wes. It was a text from Wes.

Wes: Hey

Sasha: Hi!

Wes: You still wanna talk?

Sasha: YES

Wes: IRL, though. I'll meet you where you are, if that's easiest.

Sasha looked up from her phone. She didn't want Wes to come to the Little Cupcake Bakeshop. It was her private place. Whatever Wes wanted to tell her, she'd prefer to hear it somewhere neutral.

Sasha: No, I'll come to you. Where r u?

Wes: On a bike, just passed BK Library

Sasha: Go back, meet me out front in 20

A half hour later, Wes and Sasha were perched, side by side, on a step under the massive shadow of Brooklyn's Central Library. Which wasn't an ordinary library at all. It was a sprawling art deco gem—and the front entrance was iconic, with a fifty-foot facade flanked by limestone columns and bronze sculptures of literary icons and gold accents glinting in the sun. The dramatic steps sweeping up to the entrance were a wedding photographer's dream. Quite the backdrop for Wes and Sasha's conversation.

"Yeah, I'll admit it. I was being curt yesterday." Wes was a long-limbed, athletic vision in warm-up pants, Stan Smiths, and a bike helmet by his side. The iced coffees he brought for himself and Sasha were, untouched, on the limestone step between them. His skin had a slight sheen after riding his bike for miles in eighty-degree weather. But it just gave him a casually sexy, sporty radiance.

Does this man ever have an off day? she thought, trying to mask her obvious staring.

"...and I'm sorry," he was saying. "I hope you accept my apology. I was just surprised, you know? My life has changed so much since 2022. I knew you in a very specific way, during a very specific time, and seeing you out of context was... a lot."

Sasha nodded, so relieved that he wasn't angry with her.

"Seeing you out of context was a lot, too," she agreed. "Like when you're little and you spy your principal at CVS."

"I went to an all-boys Catholic school. My teachers were old Irish winos. Seeing you wasn't that," he said lightly. "I just wasn't expecting to confront my detective life at F.E.A.S.T."

"But are you hiding from your detective life? Half of Brooklyn goes to F.E.A.S.T. You must run into other former clients."

"No, yeah, I've run into clients. And they're supportive, enthusiastic, all good things. It's cool. But your case was different."

"Different?" This was a surprise to Sasha. "I went to you because you'd had so much experience working with cases like mine. I researched. Your specialty was high-stakes, emotional cases. Divorces, missing children. And you were brilliant. So professional, with a healthy remove." She chose her words carefully.

"Thank you," he said. His expression was unreadable.

"So how was my case different from your usual ones?"

Wes frowned a little, thumbing his bottom lip. He seemed to be choosing his words as carefully and thoughtfully as Sasha. They were tiptoeing on the edge of something—being deliberately careful and vague, so as not to plummet into oblivion. If only they could pierce the veil of this halting tension.

"Some jobs were harder than others," he said finally. "Yours was tough. I don't know why."

His nonanswer hung there. Unexplained and unquestioned.

"Why did you give it up?"

"Because I'm not a machine," he answered ruefully. "I couldn't separate myself from the cases. I took everything home with me. And so, my mental health was suffering. I was fucking depressed. Getting too involved has brutal consequences," he said. "I know I seem tough. But I'm mush."

Her eyes scanned the athletic expanse of his frame, his strong hands, his broad back. "You? Come on, now."

"I'm a sensitive soul! If I spend too much brain space dealing with violent boyfriends, evil foster parents, and sadistic stalkers, I get this intense need to burn the world down. I just wanted to embrace a chill, easier life." He offered up a lazy smile. "Barbecue and Prozac help immeasurably."

She gasped a little and matched his expression. "You too? Wes, it takes a hundred and twenty-five milligrams of Zoloft for me to walk out the front door."

Wes lifted his iced coffee. "Here's to Big Pharma."

Sasha lifted hers, too. "And niche history podcasts."

"Yeah? Which ones?"

"I'll text you a list, but my true emotional support pod is *Mobituaries*. Each ep is about an interesting forgotten dead person. *So* mood-stabilizing."

"Here's to podcasts about notable corpses," he declared. "Cheers."

"Cheers."

They picked up their coffees and clinked them together. Then, they sat in silence for a few beats, sinking into the urban chorus of honking cars; middle school boys rough-housing; a smooth-ass older gentleman playing the maracas at the foot of the library steps. It was one of those weirdly cool early summer days, when the sun's beating down, but there's also a crisp breeze. Sasha shivered a bit, covering her arms with her hands. Without hesitation, Wes reached into his knapsack for a hoodie, and handed it to her.

"Really?" she asked.

"Take it. I'm not gonna let you sit here freezing."

With a grateful smile, she slipped on his sweatshirt. It was huge, so she folded up the sleeves.

"Thank you, friend." Her words floated in the air as they sat there, quiet. Just two old acquaintances lost in their thoughts. And protecting their secrets.

"So when was your last case?" asked Sasha, breaking the silence. "What was the final straw?"

He let out a ragged exhale, like a person grown weary of carrying something heavy. And then, he faced her. "You."

Of all the reasons Wes could've given, Sasha could never have predicted that *she* drove him out of the business. "Me? *My* case was your last?"

Wes focused again on the congested sidewalk traffic in front of the library. "The last and final."

"What made you quit, though?"

"Too much to explain."

"But I have all the time in the world. What happened? Was it because of...you know..." She trailed off. They both knew how the sentence would've ended anyway.

"No, no, no. You didn't do anything."

Yes I did, she thought. *You know I did, and we're both thinking about it right now.*

"I just couldn't be in business with my dad anymore," he said. "Long story short, never work with a parent." He looked down at his cup. "How come no one tells you that? That'd be a useful tip to get in your formative years. I feel like I only got bullshit advice from teachers, coaches, et cetera. I once had a professor, this famous Black female activist from the sixties. She told me never to trust a white man with facial hair or a Black man without."

"False. Obama doesn't have facial hair."

"Neither do I! And I'm extraordinarily trustworthy."

Realization hit Sasha, and yesterday's ambush grew even more vivid than before. She groaned, dropping her face in her hands. "Now I get it. Of course you were thrown off, seeing me out of nowhere. Your last case. It must've been triggering."

He shook his iced coffee. "Nah, you're good. Truly. I was just unprepared to be pulled back into my old life."

"You were in Natural Born Griller mode."

Wes tilted his head, his expression slowly brightening. Then he bit down on a chuckle.

"What's funny?" asked Sasha, confused.

"Hard *R*? Really?"

She yelped and burst out laughing.

"Natural Born Grill-*ah*," he pronounced exaggeratedly. "Say it."

"Grillahhh."

"Close enough, Hilary Banks," he said amiably, his shoulder against hers. Beaming, she knocked his back.

"So, Wes Dane," she started, relieved that the tension had dissipated. "Thanks for asking me to meet you. And for meeting me here. I love the library, it's like a set from an old black-and-white movie. So dramatic. I live right over there. See that high-rise?"

"You moved, huh? I remember you were in a brownstone. Second floor."

"I felt safer with a doorman. For obvious reasons," she responded. "So why'd you want to meet with me? If you're no longer a detective and completely uninterested in my case."

"'Cause I'm a nosy fuck."

"Seat F piqued your interest, huh?"

"Definitely piqued yours," he muttered, taking a gulp of iced coffee. "Look, I'm not committing to anything. I just want to ask you some questions."

"Ask away."

"What exactly do you know about him?"

"Welll... not much more than I told you. He's about six feet tall, I think. Rugged features. Scar at his temple, green eyes. Half Italian, half German, but doesn't know his German mother. He grew up in the heel of Italy, in a beach town called Gallipoli. He lives in SoHo about half the year. The rest of the time, he's traveling for work. No social media. And he works as a luxury hotel inspector."

"Luxury hotel inspector. I know a few of those guys. That's an extremely high-paying job. If I'm not mistaken, they're usually anonymous."

"Which further complicates things."

"It's challenging to find a person when you don't know his name *and* he uses an alias," he conceded. "But not impossible. Not for me, at least."

"Cocky," she said, half-jokingly.

"You want an uncocky detective? That's like a surgeon with tremors." He tapped his bottom lip, wheels already turning. "And you feel like he was telling the truth? Being forthcoming? Because I gotta be honest with you. It's sounding like Netflix murder doc behavior."

"Look, I've seen all the *Tinder Swindler*s and *Dirty John*s. And I'm the biggest skeptic. I always assume people are lying to me. But I can't imagine him lying."

"Don't underestimate how banal it is to lie. I could walk with a limp for the rest of the day. Or talk with a Jamaican accent. Introduce myself as Dane Wesley. Lying is so easy." He cocked his chin at her. "You should know."

"Me? What do you mean?"

"You lead with a lie."

"I do not. I always tell the truth."

"You're wearing a fake wedding ring."

With a shocked gasp, she covered her left hand with her right. "How'd you know? No man has ever clocked it."

"No fake is safe around me. It's my job to spot them." He stopped, and corrected himself. "Well, it *was* my job."

"I swear he's not a liar. You're not the only one who knows their way around a fake. I deal with actors for a living, remember?"

"Good point." Wes finished his coffee. "You really feel like he's your guy?"

"Maybe I'm delusional, but I keep imagining him on the other side of the world, looking for me, too."

"What happens when I find him?"

When. Not if.

"Find him first. Please find him. And then I'll figure it out."

Wes's brow was stormy, his expression intense. He seemed torn. "I don't know, Sasha. I just don't know."

"Wes..."

"Fine, I'll do it."

"*What?*" Sasha almost launched herself into his arms. Luckily, she caught herself before logging her fifth humiliation in the past week. "Why? What changed your mind?"

Wes leaned back on his elbows, again, and fixed his eyes on hers. "Because I'm a romantic. And I want you to have a happy ending."

"Seriously?"

"Seriously. There's so much random horror in the world. Some days I feel like we're all living on borrowed time. There's no way to know what's coming. If you have a chance at love, take it. And it sounds like you have a chance."

Sasha's smile started slowly, haltingly. And then it grew to a full beam.

"Thank you. Just... thank you."

"Don't thank me yet," he warned, holding up a hand. "I'm rusty."

"And what about your mental health?"

"Pros play hurt," he said with a shrug.

Sasha chewed on her bottom lip, wondering now if she should back out of this whole thing. "I don't want you to play hurt. I don't want you to hurt at all. If this isn't good for your mental health, I understand. Truly."

"Don't worry about me. Okay? I'm in therapy and I journal! I'm in A-plus emotional health."

"You're sure?"

"Positive."

Sasha exhaled then, her pulse quickening. "This is kind of exciting, isn't it? It's like the part in every thriller when the thief agrees to one last heist. Like Robert De Niro in *Heat*."

"You remember the end of *Heat*?"

"No."

"He got shot to death," he noted dryly. "But here's the thing. Finding Seat F for you feels full circle. Last time I helped you, it was for a dark reason. This is a hopeful reason. A positive reason. If I'm truly dedicated to living a lighter life, this is it."

"So what do you usually do first when you're looking for a missing soulmate?"

"Well, ECID," responded Wes instantly.

"Is ECID some special process thing?"

"No, it means 'Every Case Is Different.'"

"Ha! You'd love my friend Destiny."

"But if we're gonna do this, I have some rules, okay?" He crushed the cup in one hand and leaned forward, elbows resting on his knees. It gave her whiplash, how quickly and seamlessly his energy shifted from sweetie to dominant. "First off, I'm the boss. Understand?"

His tone was so stern, it surprised her. In several titillating ways. She blinked, and then swallowed. For a moment, she felt off-balance. Helplessly attracted. Which was concerning. No. *No.* She realized that, to move forward with Wes on the case, she'd have to ignore the flutter in her stomach. Or at least make peace with it being a purely physical thing—a slight inconvenience that couldn't be helped.

"Yes," she answered, finally. "You're the boss."

At this, the corner of his mouth quirked. "Don't do your own investigating. I need to control every aspect of this process, Sasha. My rules. What I say, goes."

"Got it." She saluted him.

"Secondly, once I find out where Seat F is, I'll meet with him, alone. Under no circumstances can I bring you to him. That's illegal. He has the right to remain private or unfound, if that's what he wants. Instead, you'll write him a letter that I'll deliver to him. In the letter, you'll include your contact information and leave the ball in his court. Understand?"

"Got it. Yes. I knew about the letter from that reality show, *Long Lost Family*," she said enthusiastically. "Ever watched it?"

"No," he said simply. When discussing investigative matters, Wes was no-nonsense. "And there's one more thing. Let's not talk about the past. At all. Life only moves in one direction."

"I agree, fully. I've moved on. And I don't want to reopen everything."

Her words "reopen everything" hung between them. In the silence, Wes's eyes found hers. His gaze was impossibly black, deep, and unmoving, staining her like spilled ink. She tore her eyes away before she drowned. She knew too well how easy it was to get lost in his gaze.

She pressed her fingernails into her palm, bringing herself back to Earth.

"One last thing," he noted. "We need to keep our relationship strictly professional."

She blinked several times. "Well, of course."

"No, not like that. I mean, we really shouldn't even be friends. I crossed too many lines last time. And it had consequences."

She understood where Wes was coming from, hypothetically. But she didn't know how they weren't going to be friends. It was their dynamic. How do you unring a bell? How do you neutralize natural chemistry—even the platonic kind? But, desperate for his help, she agreed.

They shook on it. And, thus, the case began.

Chapter 7

I'M EVERYWHERE

Sasha hated revisiting the past. Like Wes said earlier that day on the library steps; life moved in one direction. But, as she lay in bed, wide awake at 3:00 a.m., her mind went rogue—drifting backward, one year at a time, to her childhood.

Little-girl Sasha had been a different person. Well, not *entirely* different. Same skeleton. Same memories. Same birthmark atop her knee. But she was free from anxiety. She embraced things as they came. Electricians kept late hours, so she had grown up not seeing her mom till bedtime. And by then, Sasha had already finished her homework, made carbonara, read the latest *Hollywood Reporter*, and binged two movies on HBO. She had loved not needing oversight as a kid. And, if she were honest, she knew her mom wasn't capable. For most of Sasha's childhood, Marcia was either rewiring an office building or sleeping.

And though Marcia adored her look-alike baby girl, her primary relationship was with heartbreak.

Self-sufficiency had rescued Sasha. It gave her purpose! What couldn't she do? On her sixteenth birthday, she cooked a three-course meal for her friends. She felt grown. She felt like a character on *Girlfriends*. She felt like nothing bad could ever happen to a person like her, a girl who knew how to caulk a tub and forge a notary stamp.

And, for a long time, this held true. She sailed through Spelman's film and television major. She breezed through a thankless entry-level position at Garfinkle Talent Agency. By twenty-seven, she was a VP. As one of only a handful of top casting agents who lived in Brooklyn instead of LA, she enjoyed a level of freedom unlike most execs her age. The two thousand teens were an electrifying time to be young in New York City. And Sasha was in the eye of the storm, gallivanting through Le Bain, 1 OAK, and the Jane Hotel (actually, she was slightly left of the storm, as she was usually in a corner monitoring box office stats on her phone).

In early 2022, Sasha cast a six-episode army thriller for HBO Max. It was a juicy ensemble cast; she needed eight male actors in major roles. So, she auditioned forty of Hollywood's hottest up-and-coming actors—and, in under a month, she'd cast all eight roles. She had to work quickly because HBO was notoriously fickle. If she didn't come up with talent, fast, they would've lost interest.

The show, *Zone of Action*, was a massive hit. And it landed Sasha an Emmy for Best Casting in a Limited Series, Anthology, or Movie. It was a huge win for anyone, and especially a twenty-eight-year-old Black woman. But she didn't feel it. Sasha never slowed down to feel anything. Instead, she was endlessly compelled to move forward, do more, get greater gains. So that night, she had two glasses of champagne at the ceremony, skipped the after-parties, and went back to her hotel to prep for her next casting.

In the abstract, she knew it was a big deal. But she was too focused on achieving some fuzzy, ephemeral goal that she couldn't quite define. The Emmy was the first stop on the train. But if she got off the ride to celebrate, it might leave without her.

Back in Brooklyn the night after the Emmys, she was having a cozy night in. Around midnight, she was sipping SleepyTime

Tea under a luxurious down comforter—in a shade of saffron she'd landed upon after four months of focused research. Her apartment was her sanctuary. A cozy one-bedroom (that she owned!) on the second floor of a Prospect Heights brownstone. Outside, leaves danced on the early fall wind. Inside, she was warm, toasty, and vibing. Until she heard an outrageous crash in her living room.

Sasha sprinted out of her room and found a brick in the middle of a zillion shards of glass. Someone had thrown it through her window. *What the fuck, what the fuck,* she whispered, gingerly tiptoeing through the glass to pick up the brick. "CUNT" was written on it in white marker. With a yelp, she dropped it immediately.

Heart racing, she scurried back to her room, grabbed her phone, and called the police. A doughy, baby-faced cop arrived an hour later. He looked like a Teddy Graham. Yawning into his fist, he took photos and fielded Sasha's rapid-fire questions. *Surely this was a mistake, right? Any leads? Maybe they were aiming for Gloria Katsune's apartment, right under me? She has enemies because she shoots her water gun out the window at toddlers and dogs. Want her number?*

Sasha was rattled, but not terrified. The whole thing felt like a random act of Brooklyn violence. She threw out the brick. Insurance paid for her window. Life moved on.

The following Tuesday, around midnight, she received thirty phone calls from an unknown number. Still, Sasha wasn't superfazed. It was probably bored teens. There was simply no other explanation. Why would anyone want to harass Sasha?

A week later, same time, Sasha was fresh from the shower, wrapped in a towel and headed to the kitchen. She passed her recently repaired bay window. And then froze. Had she seen something weird outside? An inhuman scowl? Fangs? No, couldn't be. Holding her breath, she retraced her steps back to the window and peered through the blinds.

Someone was standing across the street, under a tree. Staring at her. They were wearing a bright neon-orange warm-up jacket, oversized leather gloves—and a Wolverine mask, the cheap plastic kind you got at Ricky's Halloween superstore. Slowly, Wolverine pointed an index finger and thumb in her direction, and pantomimed shooting her. She screamed. Then, it walked away.

This time, when Sasha called the police, she wasn't calm. She was hysterical. Because now it was official. She was being terrorized. And she had no idea why.

A week later, around midnight, some sixth sense drew her to the front door—where she found a ten-page letter wedged underneath. Ten pages of: "TIME TO PAY THE BILL TIME TO PAY THE BILL TIME TO PAY THE BILL" in all caps. What bill? What had she done? And to whom? Whoever it was, they were hunting her. Watching her. Practically holding her hostage in her own home. When Officer Teddy Graham showed up this time, he told her that "time to pay the bill" wasn't a real threat.

Next Tuesday at midnight, Sasha was ready. She stood in the center of her living room, wielding a butcher knife, her eyes darting between the front door and the street-facing bay window. This time, there wasn't a knock. It was another text assault.

I didn't know you went to Spelman

Nice shirt, whore

I'm everywhere

Dropping the phone, she glanced down at her Spelman sweatshirt. This time, she skipped the police. Trembling uncontrollably, she googled "private investigator or detective brooklyn." After sifting through a few sponsored posts and obvious scammers, she saw:

DANE & SON DETECTIVE AGENCY

> Licensed, experienced full-service private investigators proudly serving New York–area clients, specializing in stalkers, skip-tracing, surveillance, child custody, alimony, missing persons, and high-profile clientele matters.

It wasn't until Sasha saw the word in the profile that it hit her. Stalker. Frantically, she called the agency—though chances were slim that a sane professional would answer a 2 a.m. call.

"Uggblerrggh," a man's voice rasped groggily. "Nadine? I mean, Naomi? Ughhh, I forgot to text you when I got home. I know you hate that. My blood alcohol level's on blackout."

"Who is this?"

A pause. "Who's *this*?"

"I need a detective! I'm in trouble!"

Another pause. More rustling, a pained groan, the sound of a glass clattering to the ground. When he spoke again, his voice sounded much more alert.

"My bad. Wrong phone... Anyway, yeah, you reached a detective. How can I help you?"

"I think someone's trying to kill me. I don't know why... what I did... or wh-who they are. But I'm scared for my life, and the police won't help. I need help. Please."

Sasha never asked for help. But she'd never known fear like this. She felt like this person was behind every corner. Normal, benign activities like grabbing coffee at the bodega were suddenly charged. Was he crouched behind the register? Did he follow her onto the Q train? Was he camped out in a nearby building, watching her through a telescope? Everything was shadowy. And paranoia had set in. And as stated in her favorite novel, *Catch-22*, "Just because you're paranoid doesn't mean they aren't after you."

Hurriedly, Sasha explained this and everything that went down since the Emmys.

"No, yeah, the police won't help," said the voice. "Not at this point."

"Why?"

"Because nothing you've described is illegal. Delivering a letter, standing under a tree, annoying phone calls. No laws were broken," he said.

"He threw a brick through my window!"

"Why didn't you say so? Do you have the brick?"

Her entire body slumped. *God.* "No. No, I don't."

"Do you know this man's identity?"

"Wait, how do you know it's a man?"

"Ever seen *Dateline*? It's always a man."

"Oh my God, oh my God…"

"I know you're scared. I'll find him, don't worry. Come to the office tomorrow…errr, today. Nine a.m. In the meantime, do you have somewhere you can go? A friend's house?"

"My best friend Destiny's out of town for a wedding. There's no one else I can call. What do I do?" Hearing a phantom noise in the kitchen, she spun around, wielding her knife with a shaky hand. "I have a knife!" she screamed, to no one.

"What's your name?"

"Sasha. Sasha Melinda Tameika Ruby Cruz."

"Wow, okay. Hi, Ms. Cruz. I'm Detective Wesley Dane."

"Nice to meet you," she whimpered pitifully.

"I want you to listen." His voice had softened to a soothing, slower cadence. "The perpetrator already did his big one tonight. He won't strike again for another week. He likes being predictable. He gets off on knowing that *you* know when the next attack's coming. But, for extra peace of mind, grab a pillow and a blanket and lock yourself in the bathroom till morning. I'll see you at the office at eight a.m."

"I thought you said nine?"

"Not gonna lie, I feel like you need me sooner."

Sasha hung up, feeling only marginally better. She buried herself under blankets on the couch. Sleep eluded her. Time blurred. October 14, 2022, turned into October 15. And then, around 4:00 a.m., she heard a weird noise just outside the bay window. An eerie, honking, *whoo-OO-oo* sound.

No, no, no, no, no.

She envisioned Wolverine outside under the eerie cloak of night, gearing up to break in and kill her. She needed to get out. Her mind raced. How? Uber. But she couldn't wait there for the car—she had to put distance between herself and the stalker. Fast. With trembling hands, she ordered the car for pickup down the block, at the twenty-four-hour pharmacy. That place would be well-lit and staffed. *Safe.* She grabbed her handbag and her TV remote (she wasn't thinking clearly) and sprinted to her bedroom window. It was at the back of the brownstone. If the stalker was at the front, near the bay window, she could sneak out the back and, taking the next street over, she could escape to the pharmacy without being seen.

Functioning purely on wild self-preservation, she hoisted herself through her bedroom window opening. With an inelegant thump, she rolled onto the fire escape, one floor above the garden. A jagged piece of wire in the ancient window frame ripped through her right wrist. Blood splattered everywhere, but she didn't notice. With a gasping squawk, she hurled herself into Gloria Katsune's overgrown thyme bush. And then she was gone, limp-running into the night.

Once in the Uber, she realized that, in her haste, she'd programmed Destiny's apartment as her destination. But she wasn't home. Numbly, she glanced down at her injured wrist. She knew where to go. Brooklyn Methodist ER. Which is where she stayed, getting stitched up and sleeping off her pain meds—until her 8:00 a.m. appointment with Detective Wesley Dane.

The Dane & Son Detective Agency was nestled above an LGBQT+ bookstore in a charming Fort Greene brownstone. The street was tree-lined and upscale, with santal candle–scented clothing boutiques and lazy cafés. The offices had the same vibe. Cozy couches, framed Kehinde Wiley prints, charcoal area rugs. Minimalist, soothing, tasteful.

Every element in the waiting room was well-appointed. Except for Sasha, who limped in wearing blood-and-dirt-splattered pajamas, a bandage on her wrist, and reeking of thyme. She was a mess, but she was also her mother's daughter. Manners? Impeccable.

"Good morning, ma'am," she said to the silver-haired, older white woman throwing judgmental eyes at her from behind a small desk. The woman wore a pussycat bow blouse and Mrs. Claus glasses. "I have an eight a.m. with Detective Wesley Dane?"

"It's not in my calendar, dear."

"Well, it's a last-minute thing." Sasha smoothed her hair behind her ears, and a tiny leaf fluttered to the floor.

The secretary, Phyllis, frowned disapprovingly, and then led Sasha down a short hallway to two adjoining offices, separated by a glass wall. The nameplates on each door read: WES DANE, SENIOR, and WES DANE, JUNIOR. She deposited Sasha in Junior's office and disappeared.

Standing before her, in front of a modern, bleached-oak desk, was Detective Wes Dane. He was about her age. Late twenties, maybe thirty. And he was absurdly handsome. Egregiously tall. Lashes and dimples rarely found outside of Hollywood. And he was wearing *extremely* good jeans and a blue button-down, sleeves rolled to the elbows. It was hard to reconcile this Tom Ford model with the messy, inebriated voice she'd heard on the phone, just hours before.

For what it's worth, he looked just as shocked by her appearance.

"I was expecting someone older." Sasha was too exhausted to pretend not to stare.

"I get that a lot." He looked her up and down quickly and then averted his eyes. Was he nervous? "I, uh, I have to apologize for how I answered the phone. Rough night. You know how it goes."

"No, you were helpful," she said, swaying a bit on her feet. Her wrist throbbed. They stood there, taking each other in. Something passed between them—a current, an understanding, a statement of unabashed curiosity.

"Where are my manners? Please, have a seat," he said, gesturing at a plush navy couch with matching throw pillows. "Can I get you a coffee? A right slipper?"

"I need a new life," she said.

Wes leaned against his desk, arms folded. With kind, warm eyes, he peered down at her. "I gotta ask, what happened to you?"

Sasha let out a ragged sigh, and melted back into the pillows. God, this was her first time truly relaxing in hours. "I heard a noise outside. Like a 'whoo-OO-oo.' Around four a.m.? He was there. The stalker. So I jumped out the window and ran for my life."

"You jumped out the window?"

"I used to be a gymnast," she explained.

"I'm impressed. But that wasn't the stalker."

"You don't know that. How would you know that?"

"It was a whippoorwill, Ms. Cruz. They're all over Brooklyn this time of year. And they make those noises, early in the morning. I told you, he won't strike again till next Tuesday at midnight."

"Oh. *Ohhhhh.*" She groaned, dropping her face in her hands. "I'm so fucking scared. I feel haunted. And I think I sprained my ankle." She looked up at him. "Not to be ageist, but I didn't expect you to be so young. Will Wesley Dane Sr. be joining us?"

"My father? Nah, I'll be working with you alone. He's on a medical leave of absence."

"Oh. Okay. That's fine, I guess."

"You're in good hands. I promise. I need to ask... Is there anyone who'd want to hurt you? An ex-boyfriend? Ex-girlfriend? Frenemy?"

"No, I have no enemies." She was starting to panic, feeling the rising hysteria. His frustratingly calm demeanor was not helping. "I've only had three serious boyfriends, and we're all on good terms. I had them all over for Friendsgiving last year!"

"I believe you, I believe you," he assured her. "What do you do for a living?"

"Casting agent."

"Hmm. Is it reasonable to say that rejecting actors is a part of your job?"

"Of course. But I'm always kind and sensitive."

Wes nodded, tapping on his bottom lip. "Show me."

"Huh?"

"Show me how you reject someone with kindness."

A tornado of nerves, she pointed to a carafe behind his desk. "Can I have a shot first?"

Wes looked behind him, and then back at Sasha. "A shot of what? It's eight a.m."

She narrowed her eyes.

"Fuck it, I'm still half drunk, myself," he muttered. "Vodka? Whiskey? Gin?"

"Tequila."

Wes poured a shot, handed it to her, and she downed it. She grimaced, the liquid lighting her throat on fire. Then, she snapped into character. Looking Wes directly in the eyes, she took three confident steps forward and clasped her hands together, under her chin.

"Great to see you again. I enjoyed your audition, but unfortunately I've consulted with the director, producer, and writers, and your interpretation of the piece is simply not in line with who they're envisioning. But don't get discouraged, new projects and roles pop up every day. *I believe in you!* That's why I requested you to read for the role. Stay tuned and stay ready, because I'm definitely submitting you for more parts. I'll see you soon, Detective Dane."

Sasha poured on the charm, beaming up at him with a sweet-as-pie smile. He didn't blink the entire time. In fact, he was gazing at her so intensely it'd take a bomb to make him blink.

"Wes," he said, his hands gripping the edge of his desk. "Just call me Wes."

"Wes." And then, she flopped back on the couch, breaking character.

"You're right, that was a compassionate speech."

Overheated and stressed, she stripped off her sweatshirt. Underneath was a flimsy pajama tank. No bra. Her nipples were erect from the satiny fabric. "Thank you."

"You're w-welcome. Jesus, I haven't stuttered since 1999," he muttered. Clearing his throat, he took a seat in the rolling chair behind his desk. "Have you ever come across anyone who's been angry at not getting a role? Crushed? Resentful?"

"No. In show business, you can't take it personally."

"I hear you. But a sociopath, a psychopath, or even just a particularly sensitive person could struggle with rejection. I know I have."

"You don't understand. An actor could bomb one audition but nail the next. He might be the wrong type for one role, but a director's dream on another one. Actors know this."

Wes tapped his palm with a pencil. "And are actors typically known for their emotional stability?"

"God, you're right." Defeated, Sasha held out her shot glass, and he poured a refill. Holding her nose, she downed the shot. The second one really hit, and she started to feel syrupy, heavy-limbed.

If I close my eyes for more than a few seconds, she thought, *I'll fall asleep.*

Sinking back into the couch pillows, she gestured at Wes with her chin. "Can I ask you something?"

"Shoot."

"Do you act? You have a great look for rom-coms. Your face is so unique."

"You think so? I'm flattered." He beamed, a truly dazzling thing. "It's not unique, though. I have a twin sister with the same face."

"Does she act?"

"A fool? Yeah, often."

She giggled. And then she fell silent. Her mood dipped as the realization of her situation came back to her. "How am I going to survive this? The police don't even think it's real!"

"You can file for a stalking protection order. But I have to find him first."

"What happens to me until then? I need twenty-four-hour protection or a bodyguard. Do you offer those services?"

"If you were hiding state secrets, you'd be protected by government resources. But our system is fucked, and it leaves women and children the most vulnerable."

"I can't go back home," she whispered. "My mom's in Texas, but we're not close. I don't have anyone. Can't you bodyguard me? Please."

"What about a hotel? I can help you check in."

"Wes, you don't understand. *He's following me.*"

Just then, she looked up and noticed his secretary leaning in the doorway with two coffees. Her face registered clear disapproval. Silently shaking her head, she handed Wes his coffee and disappeared.

"What was that about?"

"Phyllis has known me my whole life. So she knows I'm about to make a poor decision."

Sasha's face brightened.

"You can stay here. My dad's office is empty. You can sleep on his couch, and there's a bathroom with a shower in the back. I'll bring you towels and a blanket. We've had some long nights here, so we're prepared for sleepovers."

They looked at each other. If instant trust were a thing, it was there in that moment.

"You're saving my life," she whispered, sleep tugging on her voice.

"I haven't yet," he said, chewing on his pencil. "But I promise you, I will."

NON-DELIVERY REPORT

To: Sasha.C@Seraphina.org [disabled account]
From: Patrice.B@Seraphina.org
Subject: Re: Searching for Seat F

Good morning from Algiers! Hope you're excellent! I was incredibly moved by your passion for Seat F. And it occurred to me that I know of a suave Italian man with green eyes. I don't know what this means, daddy energy, so I cannot speak to that. So, this man frequents a café in my neighborhood. He always wears a suit. And he speaks Italian on his mobile phone. So, I went to the café three days ago to find him. He wasn't there, unfortunately. But I stayed, anyway.

After ordering a Café Americain, I waited at the counter with a few other patrons. When the barista called out my name, Patrice, I reached for the coffee—and so did a man. (You see, Patrice is a unisex name in French.) He wasn't your Seat F, but he was quite handsome. Anyway, we're on holiday together as I write. Your love story gave birth to mine.

Merci, and bonne chance on your search!

Patrice Bensoussan
Seraphina Algiers
VP Distribution

Chapter 8

SUPERHERO CINDERELLA

Wes was a hopeless romantic. But not in the traditional, chocolate-and-roses way. Wes had a romantic *worldview*. His way of making this unhinged world tolerable? He elevated banal things so they felt special. He ritualized his life, finding beauty in the everyday.

In the supermarket, he often imagined that he was Jesus's personal chef, shopping for the Last Supper. On Wednesday nights, faithfully, he'd tuck into a corner of Sisters bar to nurse a single, exquisite glass of Malbec and "have a think." He even romanticized his studio apartment—which, when he bought it, was a broke-down, abandoned, seven-hundred-square-foot dump. But he saw the potential, creating a warm space with restored oak furniture, forest-green accents, and artwork by local Black painters. (He'd seen Eddie Murphy's *Boomerang* at a formative age.) The studio was poorly wired and shared a wall with Foam Alone Laundromat. But he'd made the ordinary a sanctuary.

Wes also found a way to make smoking brisket feel special, rarefied. After some trial and error, he had decided that midnight was the optimal time to start smoking his brisket for the next day's offerings. Under the cloak of darkness, alone, cooking outside felt like engaging in some sacred private ritual. It felt reverential, powerful.

Now clad in basketball shorts and a sweatshirt, he trudged out into the darkness of his backyard carrying a tray of beef. Humming an old Jodeci tune, he loaded his meticulously marinated beef into his Traeger grill (which he bought at 80 percent off, thanks to his boy Discount Dario, a crooked stock associate at Home Depot). He needed to focus on his brisket, as the Pig Island NYC barbecue competition was coming up. But he couldn't get Sasha off his mind. What was it about Sasha Cruz? Why did he turn into a simp in her presence? Was it the twinkling angelic chime of her laugh? The simmering-under-the-surface nakedness of her emotions? Her unapologetic directness? Her sinewy, deep caramel legs that seemed to stretch fourteen miles long? Her sultry, feline eyes that twinkled and flashed when she needed him?

I need you, she'd said.

And that's all it took. Wes couldn't say no to her. He couldn't in 2022, and he couldn't now. And even though their relationship was never deeper than client-detective chemistry, he felt helplessly drawn to Sasha. She ignited all his protective instincts in a way that wasn't quite... platonic. Whenever he was in her orbit, he lost his head. Neural pathways, frayed. His palms itched to touch her. It was torture. Sasha was torture. And he craved it.

So much so, that she'd somehow gotten him to agree to track down her man.

I'm being punished, he thought, shutting the grill lid and setting the temp to 250. *I don't know what for, but considering some of the shit I've done, I probably deserve it. Why did she come back now, just when I'm starting over?*

Balancing tongs, marinade, and two trays, Wes opened the

sliding glass door with his elbow, trudging back into his apartment—the thick night air carrying the smoky, spiced scent of slow-cooked brisket. He dumped all his tools in the kitchen, sat down at his rustic coffee table (a gift from his boy Pier 13 Dean, the friendliest furniture cargo thief in Brooklyn). It was almost 1 a.m. His thinking hours. The intimate, secret feeling of being the only person awake on the planet usually brought him clarity. To him, the night wasn't still or quiet. It was alive, pulsing with hidden adventures and night-world magic that didn't count when the sun rose. He grew up in Fort Greene, Brooklyn, when it was *local.* Everyone knew everyone, and a Black family could own a brownstone on the salary of a postal worker and a nurse. Entire lives were lived, lost, and celebrated on these stoops. At night, he felt the pull of a lost time.

Long story short, he had insomnia. Another thing he romanticized.

His studio was cloaked in darkness, save for the lamp at the table, illuminating his journal. While he was waiting for the meat to smoke, he usually jotted down lists, took notes on the day, peeled back his most layered thoughts. The practice gave him clarity. But tonight, his mind kept drifting from his middle-of-the-night musings. His brain had felt scrambled since Sasha stepped out of the sunlight in his Natural Born Griller line, two days before. When her catlike eyes fell on his, he was undone.

I need you, she'd said.

I bet you fucking do, he thought.

Wes rarely thought about old cases. But he'd never stopped thinking about Sasha's. Memories would flood him when the first gust of fall wind kissed the trees—or, to be honest, whenever he smelled thyme. These were amorphous, sense-memory recollections, more ephemeral than specific. Hoping the trauma hadn't colored her life. Hoping that he'd helped her in the long run.

If he'd known she was going to show up at F.E.A.S.T., he

would've had a chance to prepare. But apparently, the Dramatic Appearance was her MO. Sasha had done the same thing in 2022 when she'd shown up to his office hectic and urgent and an absolute mess... and fucking irresistible. Blindingly, unforgettably irresistible. Standing there, with her perfect posture and imperious attitude, totally ignoring the fact that she had leaves in her hair, dirt-encrusted knees, and was down a slipper, like an unhinged superhero Cinderella.

Wes wondered if she depended upon the element of surprise and decided that she wasn't even aware of it. She just had overwhelming energy. He knew it the first night they met, when, somehow, she cajoled him into spending the night in his office. One night that turned into a week. Which was unthinkable. It was so unprofessional. She was a client. His behavior could've been framed as predatory. If she wanted to, she could've sued him to hell and back. Ruined him.

If Wes were a more responsible man, he would've bowed out of Sasha's (first) case the minute she convinced him to let her stay in his offices. And he knew better. That was the thing. He was raised in his father's passenger seat, joining him on investigations. One of the first things Detective Dane Sr. taught him, was that personal feelings should never bleed into a case. They made you messy and clouded your judgment. But Wes didn't know how not to be emotional. He was born with an obsessive attachment to fairness. Bad guys deserved to get hunted down and forced to pay for their crimes. Innocent people were owed safety and peace. It was that simple. He was driven by uncompromising moral certainty, which is part of what made him a great detective.

Whoever had been stalking Sasha deserved to go down. Fine, but when that sentiment was spiked with unexpected attraction and an intense need to protect, lines got blurry.

Ultimately, Wes had to remind himself that he barely even knew

Sasha. And the way her presence unmoored him was his problem, not hers. Wes wasn't the first man to have a crush on an unavailable, beautiful, disaster-prone woman. Before, she was unavailable because she was mid-crisis (understandable). Now, she's off-limits because she's into the airplane dude. A man so unforgettable that she... never bothered to learn his name? It made no sense. And he couldn't fathom a world where Seat F wouldn't leave the flight with all of Sasha's information, *and* plans to see her again. A woman like Sasha Cruz? The hell was he thinking?

The idea was so foreign to Wes, he couldn't help but be fascinated. He had less-than-zero information to go off, but this guy felt unlikely, improbable—like a badly written side character in a student film. He was a question mark and, unfortunately, Wes wasn't wired to ignore those. He had to find him. If for nothing else but to satisfy his curiosity. As an adult male human, he was keenly aware that if a man wanted to be known, he'd be known. A woman wouldn't need a private eye to chase him down. Assuming that Seat F was straight, single, interested, and available—what type of man could experience six concentrated hours of time with a beautiful woman—this particular beautiful woman—and let her slip through his fingers?

Couldn't be me, thought Wes. But it didn't matter what he'd do in Seat F's position. Wes had to take himself out of the case, entirely, or the investigation wasn't going to work. The case was about Sasha, and she deserved a happy ending. Sasha had labeled Seat F a "nice guy." And Wes hoped, for Sasha's sake, that she was right. After everything she'd been through, she deserved happiness. And he'd love to be the one to make it possible for her.

Wes stretched, yawned into his fist, and then flipped a page in his journal. Sasha had hired him to find out Seat F's name and whereabouts. Period, no more, no less. She *didn't* ask him to investigate if Seat F was who he said he was. In lieu of any real facts, he had to start with a few assumptions—that Seat F was interested in Sasha, and that the few details he offered were true. Sasha was no fool; if she said this guy was into her, then he was. Flight anxiety and wine could've fucked with her perception—but the chances were slim.

Wes only saw a few reasons why Seat F would disappear without a trace:

Possibility #1: SECRETIVE. Since he used aliases for his job, maybe he wasn't in the habit of revealing identifying information. Wes imagined that when your profession requires you to go undercover, it can be a hard habit to break. You add liquor to the situation, and it gets murkier. Maybe he was used to living in the shadows, a bit. Flying under the radar.

Possibility #2: MARRIED/TAKEN. Just a Don Draper–style sociopath enjoying a midair flirtation before heading home to his bored wife (or husband) and dysfunctional kids.

Possibility #3: INTROVERT. Shy? Submissive? Maybe he didn't tell her his info because she didn't offer up hers. Maybe he needed to be dommed a bit. Who knows, some women loved bossing around a fumbling, bumbling dum-dum.

Possibility #4: STRAIGHT-PRESENTING GAY DUDE. Could be confusing, especially if he was the kind of man who flirted with all genders and sexual orientations for sport.

If Wes could get in front of him, meet him in person, he'd know in seconds. Okay, so what did he know about Seat F? He jotted down the details in bullets.

- 6 feet tall
- scar at temple
- brown hair
- 45
- luxury hotel inspector
- born in Gallipoli, Italy
- Italian father, German mother
- lives in SoHo, NYC, about half of the year
- no address, phone, DOB, or social media
- no name, no photograph

The last bullet was a problem. A name or a photo could've unlocked everything. Wes could've found him in two hours with a simple skip-trace (a search for a person—aka a skip—who's skipped town, gone incognito, or otherwise disappeared). Usually, the person was right under your nose. They left an ID trail on the online people-finder services: things like mortgages, utilities, landlines, streaming service subscriptions.

But finding a nameless, faceless person was damn near impossible to do. Unless he got his hands on the airline's flight manifest—a passenger list that included every person's name, age, and passport number. The issue? Passenger lists were highly confidential documents, protected by a million privacy laws. They weren't open to the public. Outside of airline employees, there was no way to access the list.

Well, there was no legal way to access the list.

Really, his only recourse was fieldwork. He could visit Fiorello Airport's food courts and lounges. Talk to security guards and gate agents. See if anyone remembered someone who fit Seat F's profile. Of course, the staff was sworn to all sorts of NDAs. And in this economy, no one wanted to put their job on the line. Plus, it'd take a while. As much as he wanted to help Sasha, he didn't have all the time in the world. He had a food truck business to run. And a barbecue competition to prepare for.

Also, fieldwork was boring.

Too bad he couldn't do what he wanted to. In another world, another time, he'd simply bribe an airline worker to release the passenger list. But bribery wasn't an option for Wes, not anymore. No gray areas. Black and white, only. In his new life, clarity was important. And if he started cheating the system there, where would it end?

So the question became—what the hell was he going to do, *legally*?

It remained to be seen. What he did know was that he'd need to create some boundaries for himself, when it came to Sasha. Because hanging with her felt a little too good. And she was in love with someone else. He had to protect himself. He'd take the case, but only because it felt like a full-circle moment. Back then, he found the man who was torturing her. Now, he'd find the man she was in love with. It felt like closure, a balancing of the scales.

But that's not all, was it? He also wanted to prove to himself he could solve one last case. That he was a great detective, after all. That he wasn't the disappointment his father claimed he was.

And then, finally, he could leave the past where it belonged.

He'd just have to be careful, before his secret longing tipped over into something he couldn't come back from.

Chapter 9

PUZZLE PIECES

On October 15, 2022, at 8:00 a.m. ET, Sasha met Wes for the first time. Less than an hour later, they became roommates.

After some pleading, Sasha convinced Wes to let her crash in his dad's office at Dane & Son Detective Agency. But first, she Instacarted some stiff, acrylic sweat suits from Walgreens, and then showered in the private office bathroom. She winced as the scalding water hit her scratches and scrapes and contorted herself to keep her wrist bandage dry—but the shower was necessary. She needed to wash away her harrowing experience. It helped physically. But in her mind, the stalking never stopped. And her tormentor lurked in every shadow.

Wes was sympathetic. But he knew that the longer she stayed, the longer he had to sleep in the offices, too. And the worse it looked to Phyllis, the eagle-eyed secretary. And even though he'd asked her to keep it between them—and sweetened the pot with a 10 percent bonus he'd figure out how to pay later—he didn't entirely trust her.

"Hey," said Wes, sticking his head into Wes Senior's office. He was holding a manila folder.

Sasha looked up at him from her home on the couch. The office was empty, except for a desk, two chairs, and several moving boxes.

"Hey," she said lifelessly.

"It's been seven days," started Wes. "I don't know how to say this nicely. But I'm gonna need to evict you soon."

Sasha heard the words come out of his mouth, but they didn't really compute. She just sat there, feet firmly on the wood floor, knees pressed together, with her hands folded in her lap. It felt comforting to be so rigid, so clenched. Like she was prepared for an attack from all sides. Wes was telling her to go home. And she knew she had to, but she couldn't. What if he was there?

Why was he doing this to her? Who'd go through so much trouble to terrorize her? She'd never hurt anyone. Sasha was bone-tired from going over every exchange she'd had in the past year. She couldn't focus on anything. Every hour bled into the next, as she mostly slept to the soothing sounds of Wes working, next door. The wall between the two offices was thin. She marked the hours by the times Phyllis would check on her, on the way to the kitchen for tea. She'd stick her head in and cough loudly to startle her out of sleep. Then, sucking her teeth disapprovingly, she'd continue down the hall.

Sasha had never felt so isolated. So alone. Every time she considered returning home, she broke out in a paralyzing sweat. All her normal places felt tainted to her. Going home was just another opportunity to be hunted, surveilled, and toyed with. Lying there on that couch, day in and day out, her grip on reality began to loosen. Everything frightened her. Wes's phone ringing next door. A siren, outside. One morning, she dropped a piece of bread in the toaster and shrieked when it popped out. Her nerves were frayed. Thank God Wes was giving her shelter. However illegal or irregular.

"Please don't make me leave." Her voice was gravely and thin. "I'm not ready."

With a heavy exhale, Wes tucked the folder under his arm and rolled an office chair to the couch. Sitting in front of her, wearing a navy Henley, dark jeans, and brown boots, he looked pulled together—if you missed his exhausted, bleary eyes. He and Sasha probably looked like escapees from the same asylum. He, too, had spent the nights in his office, on the couch. They were separated by a wall so thin, Sasha heard the click-clack of his keyboard. She heard him scrawling in his notebook. And the twinkle of ice cubes in his evening whiskey. And neither had slept well. Sasha, due to terror; and Wes, due to worry.

"We need to find you a place to stay that feels safe to you," he explained. "I can't have you here. It's a liability. And Phyllis has a big mouth."

"Please don't kick me out," she whispered. "I can't go home. I'm scared he's there."

Oh, but what if he's here? she thought.

He was everywhere.

The stalker had become almost mythological in her mind. Like he was floating in the sky, or invisible, or able to move through walls. Of course, he couldn't do those things. He wasn't reaching out to her, at all, anymore. Wes had seen to that. He installed programs on her devices, blocking all unknown numbers and email addresses.

The world kept turning, but she was frozen, forever stuck in impotent terror. The fear had nowhere to go. It just festered and grew.

"That's normal, Sasha. You're in a state of hypervigilance. It's a common effect for stalking victims. You've given him superhuman properties."

"Yes, that's exactly it." She leaned forward, elbows on her knees.

"But it's a false feeling. He isn't superhuman. And he's sloppy. He's basically told you when he's going to show up, every week. He's all about a pattern. Not the element of surprise," he said. "People stalk for so many reasons, but the main one? Forcing the victim to engage in a relationship with them. By upsetting you, scaring you, he's lured you into acknowledging him. We've already ruled out a scorned lover. But my hunch is that it's someone with a sense of injustice, who's been wronged. Someone who feels you owe them something. An actor.

"I compiled a list of all the actors you auditioned in the past year. These are printouts of their headshots." He handed her the stack, and a white pencil with DANE & SON DETECTIVE AGENCY stamped on the side, in gold. "Can you go through and mark the ones you rejected?"

Chewing her bottom lip, Sasha flipped through the photographs. Most were men she'd rejected—but there was only one that she'd rejected multiple times. Jones Wright.

"When was the last time you rejected him?"

It came to her immediately. "Oh my God. He didn't get the lead for *Zone of Action*. And it was a huge success. I mean, it won an Emmy."

"Your first incident was the night after the Emmys, correct?"

Sasha gasped—and then her mouth snapped shut like a mousetrap. She looked up from the photos, thunderstruck.

"Those rumors about the male ego? Sad, but true," confirmed Wes.

"How are we going to get him?" In the too-quiet room, her voice sounded shrill, hectic. It was 7:00 p.m., and Phyllis had gone home. Only Sasha and Wes were in the offices.

"As you know, I've had your house surveilled around the clock."

"But you haven't left the office."

"I had a guy do it. One of the most important elements of this line of work? Always have 'a guy.'" He quirked a brow. "Anyway, no leads yet. But today's Tuesday. If history serves, he'll be there around midnight. This time, I'll be there to catch him. Take photos, ID him. So we can nail down his identity and get you that restraining order."

"Good. Good." She handed Wes back the photos and the pencil. "Do you think I should change my number?"

"Better to get a second number," said Wes, "and only give it to people you want to hear from. But check your old mailbox regularly. When someone you want to speak to calls, hit them back with your new number. This way, you're not signaling to him that you're frightened. He wants the rush of knowing he's terrorizing you."

"Oh. Smart."

"And have a friend record a new outgoing message on your old line. In case he's repeat-calling just to hear your voice. A female friend, though. A male voice will piss him off."

Sasha took mental notes, nodding silently. "Thank you."

"Of course."

They settled into an uneasy silence, Sasha's eyes scanning the moving boxes and empty files in the room. "So, this is your dad's office, huh?"

"Yeah. We're partners. We *were* partners."

"Is he retiring?"

"No, he's dying."

The words just hung there. She studied his face. Underneath Wes's neutral expression, Sasha glimpsed a flash of sadness. The dark circles stamped under his eyes were etched with pain.

"Oh, I didn't know. I-I-I shouldn't have…"

"No, you're good," said Wes, waving her off. "He had a massive stroke, and he's in a rehabilitation center now. The strokes keep happening, though. The doctors aren't sure how long he's got."

"I'm sorry to hear that. Are you close?"

"No. But I looked up to him," he answered. "I shouldn't speak in the past tense."

"However you need to speak about him, do that," she said. "I once read something interesting about grief. It pointed out that the ocean appears to be moving, but it isn't. Energy is moving through it. That's what grief is like. It moves through you, and you have to let it."

Wes stuck the pencil in his mouth, chewing distractedly. "That's damned good advice."

"Can I stay longer, then?" She smiled weakly.

Wes shook his head at her ruefully. But it was hard to say no. She looked absolutely lost. And her blanket was slipping off her shoulders.

"May I?" he asked.

"May you what?"

Wes reached over to her, pulling the blanket up around her shoulders. He was effectively tucking her in, even though she was in a seated position. It was such a gentle, tender gesture. A small thing but laced with so much sensitivity. Sasha had a sudden urge to lean her forehead against his chest. God, she was tired. And he was so strong.

"Thank you."

Their eyes met, and a spark flared between them. The air went electric, vivid. But it lasted only a split second, and they looked away, fast. Neither one of them felt strong enough to address what they'd just felt. Sasha was scared for her life. Wes was grieving a dying parent. They were unmoored and not themselves.

"You look like you could use some tea," said Wes. "I think we have chamomile or something in the kitchen."

"Chamomile sounds perfect," she said with a faint smile. "You're so good at your job."

"Nah, this isn't being good at my job," he countered. "A great detective doesn't blur lines with clients. It's about doing the job, coldly and efficiently. Not becoming roommates."

"I'm sorry. I know, I pushed you to do this. Why am I like this?"

"What? Bossy?"

"I'm not bossy."

"Yes, you are."

"Ugh, I know."

He chuckled softly at her abrupt admission. "Bossy is good, though. But my concern is what all of this says about me. I know better than to allow a client to spend the night in my office, on my dying father's couch, while I prepare them warm beverages and stand guard in front of the bathroom while they shower. And yet."

"Here I sit."

"There you sit."

"And you're questioning your fortitude."

He nodded, chewing his pencil. "Weaknesses are dangerous in my profession."

"And rejections are dangerous in mine," she said, shoulders slumping. "I should've been more careful about how I let down actors. Now I'm being tortured for it. How will I ever go back to feeling normal at work? At this point, I should turn myself over to the American Psychiatric Association. Donate my psyche to science."

"The stalker isn't your fault," Wes reminded her. "You have to know that."

"But what if it is? What if I really hurt this man? Said something that stuck with him, or hurt him? I feel like I'm losing my mind." She twisted her hands together in her lap. "I've always been so in control. Since I was a kid. I know how to do everything. By the way, I could repair that drip in your bathroom sink, if you want."

Wes looked surprised. "There's a drip in there?"

"Being efficient made me confident," continued Sasha. "It made me tough. But now I feel broken and exposed. Like, I have no skin." She lowered her voice, shaking. "I'm terrified."

"I know, Sasha. I'll get him. This'll be over soon, I promise."

"I'm only here because I have nowhere else to go. Truly. No siblings, no cousins. My mom's in Houston, but we're not close. She has a sister, but she's MAGA."

"Seriously?" He winced, as if chomping into a raw onion. "Man, Black MAGAs never feel real to me. It's like, are you an actual human, or are you three-D printed?"

"Three-D printed," she repeated with a weak, thin laugh. "Funny." After a lengthy pause, she said, "Wes, I'm sorry about your dad."

"Appreciate it," he said evenly. "It's weird, you know? I'm grieving. But it hasn't happened yet."

He folded his arms across his chest. Something told Sasha not to pry. "I'm still in shock that I'm going to be running this agency alone. No one ever thought I could be a detective. I'm too open with people. I like whimsy and devilry a bit too much." He paused. "One more infraction, then I'm out."

She looked up at him, curious. She couldn't imagine Wes committing any "infractions."

"It's weird that I'm confessing all this to you," he said. "It's usually the opposite. I'm the one people tell everything to."

"In my life, I'm that person, too. The holder of other people's secrets." Her eyes shone in the near darkness. "What makes you trustworthy, do you think?"

"Hmm. I'm legitimately interested. I can ask probing questions without seeming nosy. I don't judge. And I never tell." He chewed on the pencil, again. "I've also been told I look dumb, so that may be it, too. Folks think their deepest, darkest secrets are being tossed into the void."

"You don't look dumb. That's looks-ism. Or some other -ism."

He let out a short, soft chuckle. "What about you? Why do you think people tell you things?"

Sasha settled back into the couch cushions, drawing the blanket up under her chin. "I navigated most of my childhood alone. Part of my survival in school, with friends, or out in the world, was understanding people and what they wanted. Quickly. So, I learned early to ask a lot of questions and listen."

Wes squinted at her, as if trying to see her more clearly. Get to the bottom of her. "What were you like in high school? Student government? No, head cheerleader."

"Majorette captain."

"I was close." He looked fascinated by this information. "Majorettes twirl batons, right? You got good reflexes?"

"Well, I used to."

"Catch," he said, tossing her the Dane & Son pencil. She grabbed it with one hand and twirled it around her finger. All muscle memory. She hadn't tried that in years. She let out a delighted yelp.

"You still got it." He grinned.

"What about you? Newspaper editor? Class president?"

"Vice president. Power without the pressure," he divulged. "I also started a green thumb club, which was a drug front for my fledgling weed business."

"In high school?"

"I thought it was my calling," he said with a chuckle, shaking his head.

"Is this your calling? Rescuing damsels in distress?"

"Nah, I do this 'cause it's the only thing I know how to do." He answered with such ease, she knew it was the truth. "Is casting your calling?"

"It is. I love finding the perfect people to play the perfect part. You don't get that chance in real life. It's like living in a fantasy." She glanced at him. "So, if being a detective isn't your thing, what is?"

"Don't judge me, okay?" He leaned forward, elbows on his knees, eyes shining in the near-dark. "My thing is throwing some shit on the grill. Barbecuing. Hosting. It's so satisfying. I live in this tiny studio on Myrtle. Crazy expensive, considering I grew up in the neighborhood. In 1995, I could've paid rent in loosies and sunflower seeds," he said, disgusted. "Anyway, I love inviting folks over and feeding them. Trite, I know."

"That's not trite. You know your purpose. Would you ever switch professions?"

"Not sure. I'm just waiting for a sign."

"You believe in signs?"

"Maybe." He scratched the tip of his nose, looking contemplative. "I feel like life's fragmented into jigsaw puzzle pieces. Occasionally, a moment, a person, or a place makes perfect sense to you, and the pieces snap together. Like this." He steepled his fingers and then folded them in on each other.

Sasha watched his fingers. "Is this one of those moments?"

Wes held up his hand, arm at a ninety-degree angle, like he was challenging Sasha to arm wrestle. For a moment, they were bathed in silence. All she heard was the soft hum of his computer. And her heartbeat, which was suddenly thundering in her ears.

Sasha slid her hand into his. They twined their fingers together. She inhaled sharply. The warmth of his palm against hers was both calming and stirring. Wes intensified his grip.

"Yeah, it's one of those moments," he said quietly.

And then, they both dropped their hands. Sasha realized she was shivering.

"Let me get you that tea," he said.

While Wes was in the kitchen, Sasha drifted off on the couch. It was a surreal, in-between slumber, where she heard the real-life screech of his kettle, just up the hall—but she was submerged, unconscious. In her mind, she was back in her apartment. Floating from room to room, peering into closets, peeking under rugs, and examining drawers. She was searching for something. From a near distance, she could hear the teakettle screech. Slowly, it grew louder and louder. Until the sound sharpened in her ears. It was right behind her. Panicked, she turned around with excruciating dreamlike slowness—and there he stood. The stalker, in the Wolverine mask. He had no face, but was smiling nonetheless, and she screamed and screamed. Terrified, she clawed at the surface of her consciousness, trying to wake up. Dying to break out of this, thrashing and crying.

She wished she could pull a cord or snap her fingers; anything to stop this noise, this terror. Thrashing and sobbing, she tried to swim out of dreamworld, but it was like being stuck in sludge. Finally, she felt strong hands on her shoulders, pulling her up and out. And then, a voice in her ear, drowning out all other noise—*You're safe, I'm here, I'll save you, wake up, wake up.* The deep rumble of his voice, the warmth of his hands, and his magnetic strength broke through the fear. And he pulled her out of dreamworld. He saved her, just as he said he would.

With a terrific gasp, Sasha's eyes flew open and locked with Wes's. He was kneeling on the floor next to the couch, hands gripping her shoulders. Without thought, just the wild desperation of adrenaline, she flung her arms around his neck, pulling him down to her.

Later, she'd be surprised at her desperation. Sasha wasn't a clingy person. But she didn't feel like herself. All she felt was a tremendous, powerful need. So, she clung to him and buried her face in his neck, eyes squeezed shut. Reflexively, Wes wrapped her in his arms and pulled her even closer.

After who-knows-how-long, he pulled away. "I shouldn't do this."

"Don't leave me!" she demanded with a powerful force that shocked them both.

"I won't. Okay? I won't. Look, I'll sit over on the chair. I'll keep watch while you sleep."

Sasha looked up at him with damp, red-rimmed eyes. "Can you just lay with me?"

"I can't. I really can't."

"Please," and her voice broke. "I'm so scared. I can't calm down. Please. Please. Pl—"

Before she could finish the word, he took a huge breath and made a gravely unprofessional decision.

Wes climbed on the couch with her. Sliding his arm under her shoulders, he pulled her into him so they were flush against each other. Sasha burrowed her face into the hollow under his chin, itching to crawl inside of him; inhale his strength. She couldn't get close enough. A week ago, Wes Dane was a stranger. Tonight, he was her safety.

He rocked her, whispering, "Shhh, it's okay, it's okay." His voice was so low and steady, it became almost meditative, lulling her into a hazy stupor. She didn't realize she was trembling until he told her. She didn't know she was weeping until she felt the dampness on his shirt. But she *was* aware of the heated thrumming at her core. She felt a frantic, desperate urge inside her, building and building. She arched against him, knowing this was wrong but needing it. Needing *him*. Mindlessly, she released a small, impatient whimper.

Wes drew back a little, giving them air. "What do you want?"

Sasha shook her head. She couldn't speak and wasn't even sure how to answer—but it didn't matter. Wes knew. He slipped a strong thigh between her legs, pressing his knee up against her warmth. Pleasure flooded her. She drew in a staggering gasp. She slipped her hands up under his shirt, hungrily, feeling the planes of his back. Tentatively at first, she rolled against his thigh.

"Go ahead," he murmured into her hair. "Take what you need."

So she did, grinding against him, over and over. Wes allowed her to use him, to come apart against him. His hands slid under her sweatshirt, gripping her back tightly. Sasha could feel how unbearably swollen he was in his pants, but his hands never traveled below the small of her back. This was about her comfort, her needs. Her mouth parted against his neck, her choppy moans thrumming against his skin. Her hips stuttered against his thigh, riding him, taking and taking—until she let out a choked sob of unbearable pleasure, sinking her teeth into his skin.

"Let go," he said, his voice a deep gravel. "Let go, you're safe with me."

And so she did. Electricity spiked through her, each wave blurring into the next, until she lay absolutely spent in his arms. Wes rolled onto his back, taking her with him. She'd fall asleep that way, with her head resting on his chest. But as she drifted off—wrapped in this warm cocoon of safety—it occurred to her that she'd practically mauled this man. This man she was paying to help her. What kind of person was she?

"Wes..."

"Just sleep. I got you."

She nodded, fading.

"I got you," he repeated. It was the last thing she heard him say for years.

The next day, she woke up to Phyllis.

"Good morning," she said, with her usual disapproving side eye. "Junior, I mean Detective Dane, is out in the field. But he wanted you to have this note. I assume you'll be leaving today?"

Bleary-eyed, Sasha nodded and took the note. She tore it open, reading hungrily.

"Good morning, Ms. Cruz. Everything's taken care of. I staked out your apartment, photographed the accused, and I've already submitted the proper paperwork for a restraining order. He's exactly who you thought he was. I pulled some strings in the police department, and they were on the scene immediately. He's in police custody, with stalking charges and facing up to three years in prison. Please follow up with Phyllis for any further questions. All the best to you, Ms. Cruz."

And, with distance, her indiscretion with Wes became like a hazily remembered dream. It had all the elements of dream logic—her, in a place beyond thought, just clinging, grasping desperation, and him, her knight in shining armor, swooping in to save her. She assumed Wes would live in the threads of her memory, only.

How wrong she was.

Chapter 10

THERE IS NO TRY

Where were all the luscious lips hiding? wondered Sasha. *Was it really so hard to find a mediagenic, memorable, camera-ready, kissable, friendly-but-fuckable mouth?*

The clock was ticking, and Sasha had only booked three models for the Seraphina commercial. She needed five more. And she feared she'd lost her touch. Sasha was holed up in Elizabeth Street Garden, her workspace for the day. She sat at a wrought-iron bistro table covered with printouts of model and actor headshots—all genders, all body types, all ethnicities. None of them screamed Autumn Kisses campaign. Tapping her foot, she tilted her face up to the sun and shut her eyes.

Focus, focus, focus, she told herself, rubbing her browbone. *You've done this a million times. What's wrong with you?* The Elizabeth Street Garden usually helped her channel her most creative self. Nestled just north of Manhattan's Little Italy, it was a fanciful urban sanctuary with twinkling birdbaths, sculpture gardens, and shadowy trees. It was a charmingly gothic little secret. Like something from an Anne Rice novel.

Today, Sasha couldn't find inspiration. And she knew why. It was so impersonal, trying to create casting gold without actually meeting the talent. Ordinarily, she didn't mind that the industry had gone digital. For someone who could feel anxious around strangers, the less people she was around, the better. But, this was about lips. She needed to see texture, movement, talking—maybe even kissing. An in-person casting was the missing link.

Chewing on her lip, she pulled up Joni Yao from her phone contacts. When Sasha was first hired, the Seraphina Global creative director insisted she was available to chat anytime. Time to take her up on the offer.

"Sasha. Hello." Joni was a friendly, collaborative emo-type with a septum bar and incredible vision—but she was overworked. Thus, her responses were always short. She famously only spoke two words at a time.

"Hi, Joni, how are you?"

"Good. You?"

"Great! But I'm having some thoughts about the Project Pucker casting."

"Mmm. Shoot."

"For the final five, I'd love to hold an in-person audition. Possibly in the next few weeks? Is there a budget?"

"Yes. Yes."

Sasha pantomimed a silent cheer. "Perfect, I'll arrange. Talk soon?"

"Wait." And then, to Sasha's dismay, Joni launched into a multiword monologue. "About your Seat F email—do you ever dabble in the dark arts? I know a kitchen witch who could find Seat F in forty-eight hours. She'll just need a fingernail clipping and four eyelash hairs."

Sasha's entire soul drooped. Dear Lord, she'd never escape that email. She stared down at the phone, scrambling for an adequate response. Until she remembered that April in HR advised her to say the email was an inside joke.

"No need for a kitchen witch, Joni." She hoped she sounded

peppy. "But thank you! That email was an inside joke gone wrong. Crazy, right? Ha ha. More soon."

Sasha shoved the phone in her jeans pocket and sipped her lemonade glumly. This was her life now. She was a joke. The thing is, she'd think the Seat F situation was hilarious, too, if it hadn't happened to her. Why hadn't some programmer or Silicon Valley savant or high school hacker invented a way to permanently erase emails from the interwebs?

The only way to chase that cursed email from her mind was to sink into the memory of Seat F. His voice, his eyes. The feel of him taking her hand in his. Their connection had felt so perfect, like a dream. Over the past few weeks, she kept returning to the feeling he gave her—it was the only way she could exhale, even a little bit. It was uncanny, the way a complete stranger matched her, feeling for feeling, experience for experience. There was a reason they met. She wondered how Wes was doing with the case.

Since they spoke on the library steps, she'd been racking her brain for Seat F details she'd forgotten. Something that'd help Wes's investigation. A missing detail was scratching *just* the edges of her subconscious, but she couldn't access it. Whatever. She had to stop being a busybody. But it was hard to concentrate on anything else.

Work was going nowhere. So, Sasha packed her printouts into her oversized tote and went for a walk. Elizabeth Street Garden was perfectly situated at the crossroads of Nolita, SoHo, and the Lower East Side. Listening to the *Black History Buff* podcast, she walked down Elizabeth Street for a few miles, passing bistros with tables spilling out onto the sidewalk, chic boutiques, and multimillion-dollar townhomes. A warm, flat wind lightly carried the summer-in-the-city scent of heated cement and, well, trash.

Gallipoli is beautiful, Seat F had said. *It smells like cypress trees and the sea.*

As Sasha walked, she tried to imagine cavorting along Southern Italian beaches with him. Was she living in a fantasy? Had she hallucinated him? A few nights ago, she decided she needed something tactile to keep his memory alive. Impulsively, she googled "cypress" and "sea" for a perfume, incense, or anything that carried that scent. When she landed on Molton Brown's Coastal Cypress candle, she actually yelped. And then bought it for next-day delivery.

Delusional? Perhaps. But she kept the candle burning at her bedside every evening, ever since.

Sasha had never allowed herself to be nutty about a guy, rationality be damned. To *fall*. It was all so freeing! Strolling by the Gelateria Gentile gelato shop, she caught her reflection in the window. She looked downright giddy. When was the last time she spontaneously, authentically, smiled all alone? Sasha focused her eyes and zeroed in on a mustached patron demolishing a sundae while reading.

The book he was reading: *How to Not Die Alone*.

She stopped in her tracks, goose bumps trailing up her arms. She openly gawked at the guy—until he glanced up and shot her the finger. Waving apologetic hands, she went along her way. This was a sign too coincidental to ignore.

I feel like a rom-com heroine who falls in love with a ghost only she sees, she thought, allowing her mind to drift. *Like Sally Field in* Kiss Me Goodbye. *Or Demi Moore in* Ghost. *Why aren't there any Black ghost romances? Can we get Zendaya or Keke in a torrid love story costarring a sexily deceased Damson Idris? Why do I have to think of everything?*

Sasha took a left on East Houston Street, heading to the West Village. Before long, she ended up in front of the Film Forum movie theater.

The Film Forum. She paused, a spike of adrenaline surging through her.

I go there, alone, every Friday night when I'm in town, he'd said.

It was Friday. She rushed up to the marquee. The first show of the evening was 6:40. She had three hours. Frantically, she whipped out her phone and called Wes.

* * *

6:30. Houston Hall, a cavernous, crowded beer hall diagonally across the street from Film Forum, on West Houston. We're hiding out in a booth at the window, keeping eyes on the front of the theater. Unobstructed view of neon awning and customers slowly filing in and out of the theater. After 30 minutes, no sign of anyone fitting Seat F's profile.

Sasha was spying on Wes as he jotted down notes in his journal. She tried to be covert about it, but she was sitting directly across from him in a booth—hard to ignore. Every so often, he'd glance up, and she'd quickly look out the window. Their booth was flush against a front window overlooking Houston Street. A prime location to spy on the Film Forum's entrance.

Heart thundering with anticipation, Sasha's gaze traveled back to Wes as he wrote in his small, five-by-seven notebook. Curiously, the corner of each page was stamped with the Wordle logo, and receipts, napkins, and cards were stored between the pages. The random, messy journal was at odds with his crisp streetwear style: short-sleeve maroon tee, slouchy carpenter pants, and impeccable sneakers. Everything he wore hung exactly as it should. He smelled deliciously smoky, like cedar, amber, and crackling fireplace. Odd, in the middle of June. But his scent was heady. Sumptuous.

Wes had shown up twenty-five minutes after Sasha called. She remembered this; his dependability. He was never unreachable. Wes and Sasha had that in common. They both dropped everything for work.

"Out of all the things I could imagine doing at six thirty on a Friday night," she said, sipping her white wine, "spying on the Film Forum wasn't one of them."

"Wild, right?" Wes didn't look up from his notebook. His expression was stern and focused, and his voice sounded a bit… restrained. Like he was actively trying to neutralize his personality, to avoid being overly familiar. She supposed that, per the rules he laid out on the library steps, he was putting a healthy professional distance between them. He was taking this "we're not friends" thing seriously. But it felt so unnatural.

Spontaneously staking out a movie theater was exciting stuff. Sasha was buzzing with anticipation—especially since she was pushing her anxiety boundaries, being away from her apartment basically all day. This was an adventure! But Wes looked like he was balancing his checkbook.

The silence was killing her.

"Big Wordle guy, huh?"

Wes abruptly stopped writing and glanced at her. "Sorry, what was that?"

"The cover of your journal has Wordle on it. Are you a fan? Where does one procure Wordle merch?"

"I have a bunch of these notebooks. I don't remember where I got them." He shrugged. "Everybody likes Wordle. Pandemic hobbies die hard."

Wes spoke like Sasha was dragging every word out of his mouth, against his will. He went back to his notetaking.

"My pandemic activity was Lego," she said, determined to connect with him. "I tried to build a three-foot-tall Yoda. Almost finished, too, but I sneezed and lost balance, knocking his right arm off. The whole thing fell apart. Oh well, I tried."

"Do or do not," he mumbled under his breath. "There is no try."

"What's that mean?"

"It's a Yoda quote." Wes glanced up, again. "Why're you building the Jedi Master when you're a fake fan?"

"Because he was voted 2020's most challenging Lego set. I wanted it to be hard."

"I think you set up your life so that it's harder than it needs to be."

Sasha stared at him, speechless. He ordered another coffee from the waitress and then, calmly, neutrally, clasped his hands together on the table.

She let out a defensive little laugh. "Excuse me?"

"Just an observation."

"I don't complicate things on purpose, Wes." Mirroring him, she clasped her hands together on the table. "Life just gets that way on its own."

"*Your* life gets that way on its own."

Distractedly, he scratched his biceps. Sasha's eyes traveled down to his beautifully cut arm and accidentally lingered there. For one, two, three beats too many.

"Hey." Wes tapped on the table, grabbing her attention.

"Yeah?"

"Eyes up here."

Sasha rolled her eyes. "Don't flatter yourself."

"Don't need to. You flatter me." The left corner of his mouth curved a bit and then went neutral.

Feeling exposed, her stomach fluttered under his gaze. Could he read her mind? She couldn't help but be attracted to him. It was a reflexive, automatic thing, without intent. Like being attracted to a gorgeous doughnut or a Jacob Lawrence portrait. She needed to work on her poker face.

"Are you good with just black coffee? The pinot grigio's decent here."

"I don't drink on the job," responded Wes, with stony restraint.

Sasha's mouth parted, a wisecrack poised on her tongue.

"*Anymore,*" he clarified. "I don't drink on the job anymore. I've changed."

"I see. You're a lot more buttoned up."

"You could say that." Wes took a sip of coffee and peered, brow furrowed, out the window. This seriousness was so unlike him. What was it about him that made Sasha want to push his buttons?

"So, um, I was thinking about our case," started Sasha. "Maybe I could help you? Like, go on your investigative missions. Be the Watson to your Sherlock."

Wes's expression tensed into an exasperated scowl. Sasha discovered that, even while frowning, his dimple popped. It was as if his face was determined to radiate almost-intolerable levels of desirability, even when annoyed.

"It's not appropriate for the client to be present on missions. It could put you in danger."

"Danger?" she scoffed. "We're tracking down my man who doesn't know he's my man. The only thing in danger, here, is my ego."

"It's a conflict of interest. The only reason you're with me right now is because you were already here."

"But I'm an asset. Our skill sets aren't that different. We both notice people for a living."

"I don't need help."

"I know you don't *need* help, but..."

"Look, we said we weren't going to talk about the previous case. But I broke a lot of rules last time, before. I need to put up a firm boundary."

At the mention of their last case, her fingers traveled to her bracelet.

"You didn't do anything wrong," she said, her voice sounding a bit strained.

"I let you live in my office for days. That's a massive breach. You could've sued me for taking advantage of you, a vulnerable client. I could've lost my license."

"But you didn't do anything wrong," she said. "I…we…that was me."

"Let's not talk about it."

"It's just that, it was my fault…"

"You don't have to explain."

"You saved me. The last thing you did was take advantage."

"I could have, though. If I were a different kind of man."

"I knew I was safe with you," confessed Sasha. "I can't explain how I knew. But I did."

"That's naive, Sasha." He frowned. "You know that's naive."

Something passed between them, an energy that left Sasha feeling lightheaded. Had she drunk her wine too fast? Almost automatically, Wes slid her his coffee. Again, he read her mind. Gratefully, she grabbed the mug with both hands, taking a sip. And then, silence bloomed between them. He pulled out his journal to take more notes, and she idly glanced out the window. Memories hung in the air, naked and unaddressed.

"I was being stalked," she said finally. "I was terrified to go home. What you did was heroic, Wes. You did the right thing."

Wes let out a short, resigned breath, as if giving in to the pull of her. "Can I ask you one thing? After the case, did your life go back to normal?"

"Pretty much, yeah," she said breezily. "It's back to normal."

"Good. That's good."

"My 'normal' has changed, though."

"How so?"

Sasha leaned forward on her elbows, her voice dropping. "I was here only twenty minutes before you arrived, and I can tell you that this restaurant has three exits. One behind the bar, one in the back, and the front door. And there's a guy at the bar who's been staring at me this whole time. He's paying in cash and has a wedding ring. Oh, and I can also tell you that there's a window in the bathroom. I don't fuck with public bathrooms that don't have an easy escape." She sat back in her seat. "So, uh, that's my new normal."

Wes's jaw locked, his face etched with concern he couldn't hide. "Understandable. To my knowledge, the stalker experience doesn't leave you. I hate that you need to be on high alert. That's my job. And it's exactly why I need to do this alone. I've dealt with stalking survivors, domestic abuse survivors—it's easy to get pulled into those same fears. I don't want to re-traumatize you."

"You won't, though. I think it'll help to be around you, again. Even just as friends."

"We're not really friends, though," he insisted. "We haven't spoken in years. This is a professional relationship."

"Why can't we be friends?"

"Are you friends with the talent you audition?"

"That's different," she insisted.

He smiled, fiddling with a sugar packet. "Is it? Look, I feel the need to remind you. When I find him, it's against the law for you to be with me. Because you'd be cornering him, unawares, which basically makes *you* a stalker. That way, he'll have the option to reach out to you, and the ball will be in his court. That's how it works."

She was practically vibrating with excitement. "This is thrilling. It's been so long since I've felt hopeful about anything."

"I'm sorry to hear that."

"Come on, we might be sitting here awhile. There are three more showings tonight. Let's get to know each other. How's your day going?"

Sasha was committed to dismantling Wes's walls, whether he liked it or not.

"Before now? I burned two batches of brisket. I'm trying to perfect my recipe for a competition."

"I'm dying to try it. I was too nervous to order something at F.E.A.S.T. the other day."

"You wanna sample my food?" His expression lit up, just a tad. And then, he must've toyed with the sugar packet too aggressively, because it tore. Sugar crystals exploded all over the table. Hurriedly, he swiped the sugar into his palm. "This is your fault, by the way."

"What? How?"

"You make me nervous," he admitted in his real voice. "I'm discombobulated. Stop talking to me, I'm trying to focus. Maybe I do need a drink."

His walls were coming down. She couldn't help but smile a bit. It must've been contagious, because he smiled, too—in an exasperated way. How could she have forgotten his mouth? Was it just that she never really noticed mouths before her Seraphina project? Could be. Perfect Cupid's bow, luscious bottom lip. She wondered... no, it was stupid. But maybe it wasn't. Would he ever think to audition for her commercial?

"Has anyone ever told you that you have a big-screen face?" she started.

"Yeah."

"Who?"

"You, four years ago." He grinned. "You trying to cast me again?"

"It'd be a shame to waste that face. You were made for close-ups."

"Close-ups, as opposed to what?"

"As opposed to background work. Look over there. The bartender has the unremarkable but interesting face of a character actor. Look at our waitress. She feels like a brassy, no-nonsense barkeep at a Western border town in 1850. Juicy role, but it's a side character. You look like a leading man. In a rom-com, specifically."

"Why can't I be in the Western? Would I get to ride a horse?"

"I'm being serious. Listen, there's an audition coming up for my Seraphina commercial. Multi-genders. You have the perfect mouth for it. You'd have to wear lipstick, though."

He shot her a bemused look. "Ain't no way."

"You wouldn't do it?"

"No, and don't give me those judgmental eyebrows. I'm comfortable in my masculinity. My eight-year-old niece made me wear glitter on my face for her Latin ballroom recital," he said proudly.

"That's really sweet. How'd you feel?"

"Like Rick James," he confessed.

She burst out laughing. "Tell me you have a photo, Wes. I'm begging."

He took a swallow of his second cup of coffee and shook his head with a rascally smirk.

"I'll get it out of you," she said.

"You can try," he dared, playfully. "Is this commercial easy for you, after casting big movies and shows?"

"It's harder. I don't know what I'm doing. But it's a fun way to get back to work." She paused. "I need to have fun. I spend so much time focusing on safety. Worrying and obsessing. I feel like I'm choking, sometimes."

"And your guy, Seat F. He made you feel safe?"

"He did," she said softly. "Inexplicably."

"We better find him, then."

"We? You changed your mind about me helping you?"

"I meant *I*. There is no 'we.' I've never had a partner, and I'm not starting today."

"Your dad was your partner, though, right?"

"In name only," he corrected. "Closest thing I had to a real partner was my dog, Easy Rawlins."

"Aww. What kind of dog?"

"Miniature pinscher. They're Chihuahua-sized, but with Doberman aggression. Pure evil. She loved me, but tried to eat everyone she came across, including my sister. Easy died five years ago." He paused. "Not for nothing, I'd rather death had claimed my sister."

"Easy Rawlins? That's the detective in those Walter Mosley mysteries, right? Denzel played him in *Devil in a Blue Dress*. Incredible performance."

Wes nodded, emphatically. "Shit was spectacular."

"Makes no sense, he didn't win an Oscar." She paused, pointedly. "Speaking of makeup *and* Denzel, he wore a full beat in *Gladiator 2*."

He huffed out a short laugh. "Am I getting a Denzel salary for this commercial?"

"If only," she scoffed. "Wait, it just hit me that you gave a female dog a male name."

"I ended up calling her Daughter, anyway. Which became Dottie. Then, Ol' Girl Dot. Sometimes she was Chonk Badonk. LeBronna James. Captain Clapback the Illmatic." He sighed. "I miss that little terrorist."

"Chonk Badonk's looking down on you, I'm sure."

"Believe me, she's looking up."

She burst out laughing. And so did he—his real laugh, the kind where his eyes disappeared. It was so endearing, so contagious. This was Wes Dane's truest form. Light, amiable, and with a throaty-good chuckle that poured over her like sunlight, warming the parts of her that had gone cold.

It might've been one of her most favorite sounds, ever.

"This banter, Wes? This is friendship behavior."

"Okay, we're friends." Wes threw up his hands. "Of course we're friends. Fighting it is exhausting, and life's too short. You still can't come with me on missions, though."

"I know, I know, you work alone."

"Question. This isn't any of my business, but what happens when I find him?"

"Not sure. What do you do when you meet a woman you like?"

"I'm the wrong one to ask," he admitted. "I'm not a relationship guy. At all."

This was interesting information. "No? Lifelong player?"

"No, it's not like that. I've had long-term girlfriends. I even thought I'd get married, once. I mean, I haven't had relationships *lately*. I'm just not interested. Too focused on getting my business off the ground. There's no time."

It occurred to Sasha that this was the excuse she always gave for not dating.

"Makes sense. God, I guess I don't know what I'll do when I'm reunited with Seat F. I haven't thought that far. I'm trying to be chill about all this."

"Yeah, because hiring a PI's a famously chill move," he teased.

"Hopefully, we'll pick up where we left off, and dance into the sunset? I don't think it's unreasonable or embarrassing to want that. I've been alone forever. Why not be strategic about love, the same way I'm strategic about my career, where I live, everything? We've just got one life. I don't want to miss out on love."

"I respect you for being so proactive about it. I hope he turns out to be who you think he is. Truly."

"Thank you, friend."

With soft eyes, he nodded in the direction of her cuff. "I like it."

Sasha looked down. Wes was the one person she didn't have to explain this to. The only other person who knew what happened. "Yeeaaahhhh. Well, the scar was pretty bad. The stitches healed weirdly. This covers it up."

"Do you ever take it off?"

"No." Sasha stared at the bracelet for a long time, her eyes going cloudy. Then she unclasped it, and turned her hand palm up. The jagged, railroad tracks zigzagging across her wrist were on display. She wasn't sure why she did this. But it felt cathartic. He was the one person who knew the scar's backstory. It was part of his story, too.

Wes let out a small exhale. His gaze scanned her scars, free of judgment and with full understanding, and then met her eyes.

"Can I?" he asked.

Sasha nodded. Gingerly, he placed his hand over her scar. "This is a war wound. Your strength is in this scar."

"I'd like to think so," she said with a shy smile. "I'm not quite there yet."

"And the bracelet makes you look like Wonder Woman."

She chuckled, grateful that he inserted some levity into the conversation. "I love your spin. I read somewhere that the key to a fulfilling life is to experience a thrill, even a small one, every day. This conversation has been a thrill."

Wes mulled this over. "I think the key to an exciting life is to share your location with your wildest friend."

"Ha! Why?"

"Because," he started, with a mischievous expression, "it forces you to be interesting."

"Challenge accepted," she told him, pulling out her phone. She shared her location with Destiny, and then texted her, "I'm Watson-ing with my Sherlock. I'll explain later."

Chapter 11

MY CASE, MY RULES

Seat F never showed up at the Film Forum.

Sasha was disappointed, but tried to maintain perspective. Deep down, she knew it was a long shot. After all, she had no idea if he was even in New York. He could still be in Europe. Or anywhere in the world, really. On the flight, he'd told Sasha that he spent half the year in New York. But which half? And what if he split his time unevenly—like, a few weeks in New York, a month in Europe, four days in New York, and so on? And lurking in the back of Sasha's mind, always, was Wes's dose of reality—without a name or a face, this guy's a cipher.

But that was part of the thrill, wasn't it? Right now, he was a fantasy. Seat F was whoever she imagined him to be. Whatever she needed. And, yes, that was mesmerizing to her. Around 4:00 a.m., lying wide awake the night of the Film Forum stakeout, she had a revelation. And she had to tell someone.

Not someone. *Wes.*

She'd always heard about the phenomenon where two long-lost friends reunite, and immediately pick up where they left off, like no time had passed. But she'd never experienced it before. After four years of silence, she and Wes were buddies. That man was a good time. There was a flicker, a spark, when they spoke; and (practically) no topic was off-limits. It'd been ages since she'd felt that lightness. And she had Seat F to thank. Their plane conversation reminded her how it felt to truly connect with another human. While she was on sabbatical, weeks would go by without her speaking to anyone but Destiny. She forgot how to navigate the everyday, normal-ass ritual of two people exchanging intimacies. With Seat F, she'd dipped a toe into feeling seen again—and it rippled throughout her life. Now, she was hungry for more talk. More friends. More Wes.

She and Wes were in cahoots with each other. When they spoke, it was so sparky and exhilarating, like cracking open a window to her mind and giving him a peak. He recognized her—and she, him. And at this moment, she wanted to call him. There's no way he'd be awake at 4:00 a.m., though.

Wes answered on the second ring. His voice was groggy, husky, and surprised. "Why are you awake?"

"Why are *you* awake?" she retorted.

"I was working on my brisket recipe. Something's off, it's driving me crazy."

"You're brisketing at four a.m.?"

"Yeah. Smoking after midnight makes the meat sexier and more dynamic. I have no science to support this, though."

"Ever seen that movie, *Like Water for Chocolate*? Great book-to-film adaptation. The heroine infused her personality into her dishes. When people ate her food, they experienced what she felt when she cooked it."

"Mmm. I like that." He paused. "There's a compliment in there, but I can't find it."

"Natural Born Griller is such a hit, Wes. I know you'll place in the competition."

"I appreciate it, but really, that's not how it works. This is a real food competition, not a popularity contest. But if I place, I get sponsorships, invitations to bigger festivals. Bragging rights. I'm still new on the circuit, so I need to make an impression."

"You're good at those."

Sasha heard him let out a small, sleepy chuckle. "Okay, Sasha. Why're you calling me?"

"I had a revelation about Seat F that I urgently needed to tell you. Related to the case."

"I'm listening."

"I think I *like* not knowing anything about Seat F. Isn't that weird?"

"Yeah, it's weird. Especially since you hired a professional to track him down. Do you want to stop?"

"No, I want to find him. But this part before we do? I kind of like it."

"Why?"

"Right now, it's all possibility. He hasn't let me down yet."

"Why are you assuming he'll disappoint you?"

"If you sleep on the floor, you have nowhere to fall."

"Damn, Sasha, the bar's that low?"

"Talk to any New York woman our age, she'll say the same thing."

At that moment, she saw a bright ribbon of sky peeking out from a crack in her curtains. Was the sun already rising?

"I forgot how easy you were to talk to," she remarked, tucking her hand under the pillow.

"I earned six Communications badges in Cub Scouts," he said, a smile in his voice.

After this, their late-night calls became a thing. Sasha didn't know if it was the relative anonymity of talking without seeing him, or the hazy liminality of the hour, but she found herself becoming more and more candid with every conversation.

* * *

The next night, his call interrupted a dreamless sleep.

"Sasha, wake up."

She sat up in bed with a start. "Are you okay? Am I okay?"

"I'm fine. You're fine, too. I think."

Sasha sank back into the pillows. "Wes, you can't call an anxious person at this hour with urgency in your voice."

"You're right, my bad. I was just wondering...do you remember anything else about your conversation with Seat F," asked Wes. "Any other details?"

"I don't think so. Believe me, I've been racking my brain."

"Sometimes the most innocuous details we tell people can turn into clues. Did you tell him where you like to eat? Your nearest train? Your favorite color? Anything."

Sasha struggled to unlock something. When she first spoke to Wes about the flight conversation, she was positive she'd recalled everything. But the more she pored over those six hours, the more she realized there were pieces missing. Out of focus. It made sense, given she'd drunk so much wine.

And then, she unearthed a buried detail.

"Wes, how could I forget? I told him about my job. Well, in a roundabout way. I said I was doing a 'special project' for Seraphina."

"You weren't specific? You didn't tell him you were casting a commercial?"

"No, it felt too complicated to be like, 'I'm on contract but it's not full-time, it's just for this one project, blah, blah.' It's hard to follow."

"You told him you're New York–based, right?" Wes was listening, but also half talking to himself. "Here's my thought. Most guys, if you tell them you work for a store, they'll assume you work *at* the store. Like, a sales associate, or at the register."

"Mmm. I see where you're going with this. You think he might be looking for me at Seraphina stores around the city?"

"Yup. I'm gonna visit some Seraphina locations tomorrow, see if he's been by," he said. "I'm looking up locations, and I see a handful in the city and three in Brooklyn. And Seraphina's flagship New York store is on Fifth Avenue and Fifty-Seventh."

"I'll meet you there around noon?"

"No, you won't. My case, my rules, remember?"

"I remember, I remember. You're so strict."

"And there's nothing else you remember telling him?"

Sasha took an unblinking pause. There had to be more. Wait, there *was* one more thing. It just popped in her head. Why did it take Wes prompting her for the details to come flooding in? It was like when a skilled yoga teacher gently touches your elbow or hip, and you magically reach pose perfection. All he had to do was give her a nudge, and her thoughts crystallized. She wondered how he did it.

"I just remembered something else," she confessed sheepishly. "I told him I like Fenty palettes."

Wes took a brief pause. "I don't know those words."

"Fenty is Rihanna's makeup line. And she makes eye palettes. An eye palette is several eyeshadows housed in one compact."

"That explanation is less complicated than saying you're a casting director?"

She ignored this. "Wait, I think I remember him writing that down. About the palettes."

"A quick search shows me that Seraphina sells Fenty products."

"Your wheels are turning. I can feel it through the phone. What are you thinking?"

"I'm thinking you should let me do my job." His voice sounded wired, invigorated. "Fuck, I love this part."

"Listen to you." She smiled to herself. "You sure you want to give up detective work?"

He chuckled. "Good night, Sasha."

"'Night, Wes."

The following night, Sasha woke up thirsty around 2:30 a.m. She padded into the kitchen, poured a glass of water—and, naturally, called Wes.

"I've been thinking about what I'll do when I see him again," she said. "And I'm so nervous."

"You? *He* should be nervous. What's tripping you up?"

"Sex," she said without hesitation.

"But that's the easy part."

"Not to me. I haven't done it in years. Studies show that, for women, the longer you go without it, the less you need sex with another person. Especially when we've got vibrators and dildos and smutty audiobooks."

"I better find Seat F before you explode."

"I need to shake the *fear*. I'm just not comfortable around strange men. That's why I was so moved by, uh, Seat F. We were immediately comfortable." She paused, chewing her lip. "Can I tell you a secret?"

This always happened with Wes. Something about his easygoing, nonjudgmental air made her want to spill everything on her mind. No boundaries, no filter. She was about to reveal something she hadn't even told Destiny.

"I can't even…you know. Well, I have trouble…I haven't been able to do…"

"Self-checkout?"

"Wes, that's ridiculous." She couldn't help but laugh at his masturbation euphemism. But it was still depressing. "Ugh. I'm so ashamed."

"There's no shame here, Sasha. Only solutions. Are you saying you can't start? Or you can't finish?"

"I can start! I set the mood. Light a candle. Lower the lights. And then I charge up my Rose—but I feel silly. I have to stop. Somehow, it makes me feel lonelier."

"Maybe your problem is you're engaging in sexual congress with a thorned flower?"

"The Rose is a vibrator, Wes. She's famous." Sasha lowered her voice to a whisper. "When's the last time you masturbated?"

"Alone, or with a consenting party?"

"Alone."

"This morning."

"Was it good?"

There was a pause on the line as Wes considered this question. "I've never kicked myself out of bed."

"God. Life's so simple for men."

"I can't lie, we're all more or less basic."

"Not Seat F," she retorted.

"No?"

"He's not basic. Why would you think he's basic?" She realized she sounded defensive.

"I don't. I have no opinion."

"Yes you do."

"I truly do not."

"Tell me."

"I don't know. He's wealthy, he's ordering martinis, he's got an accent. This is a James Bond bit. Doing a bit, by definition, is basic. Being yourself isn't a viable option?"

"I saw you allow four girls to take a group selfie with you and a chicken wing. Was that not a bit?"

"I was trying to sell chicken. What was Seat F trying to sell you?"

Sasha gasped. "I hired you to find him. Not to insult him."

Sasha didn't want him to poke holes in her fantasy. It had become a ritual for her, waking up and dreaming about where he was in the world, and if he was looking for her. All day long, she'd force herself to remember the details of his face, his voice, the way he helped calm her fears on the flight. She spent so much of the day renewing her faith in this dream. The last thing she wanted was to be made a mockery of. Did Wes think she was a fool?

He'd embarrassed her. But she'd try to defuse it with a little joke.

"Jealousy's an interesting color on you," she teased.

"You think I'm jealous?"

"Most women you speak to are dying of thirst in your presence," she said in a lightly mocking tone. "But I'm a woman, and my attention's elsewhere. I know you're not used to this."

The silence on the other end told her that he wasn't amused.

"That's a wild presumption. Go to sleep, you're delirious."

The next morning, Sasha broke Wes's rules. She showed up at Seraphina, while her detective was working his magic.

She couldn't help but be curious! After an unproductive lunch with an agent at Wilhelmina Models, she set off on an "exposure" walk, roaming aimlessly around Midtown. She wondered how Wes was faring, checking out Seraphina stores. He told her he'd start around 1:00 p.m., and it was 2:00 p.m., now. The flagship Seraphina was only a ten-minute walk across town. What if he was there, right now?

Wes said he worked alone, and she respected that. But she was dying of curiosity. She was desperate to know if Seat F had been looking for her, too! So she dipped into a souvenir store and bought cheap sunglasses, a headscarf, and a fedora. Paired with her trench coat (it had been raining that morning), she looked like the perfect spy.

Ten minutes later, she slunk into the store, with her head tipped slightly downward.

Immediately, she was hit with a gust of fragrance. Where would Wes be? she wondered. He might've already visited and left, but she hoped not. Stealthily, she hung around the blush aisle for a while, pretending to browse, but listening for Wes's voice. A salesgirl asked her fifteen times if she wanted a tester strip, a makeover, anything. To get her off her back, she kept adding products into her basket.

There's no way I could afford all this stuff, she thought. Her basket was so heavy, it was practically cutting into her arm. The longer she browsed, the dumber she felt. Quietly, she tiptoed over to Shampoo, and busied herself reading the back of the bottles.

"Hello, sir, can I help you find something?"

"Hey there! Yes, I'm looking for a gift for my, uh... my girl. My girlfriend."

Sasha's eyes widened behind her glasses. She scanned the store, and her eyes landed on the back of Wes's head. At least she thought it was him. He looked like an anonymous preppy in Dickies, a striped shirt, and Ray-Bans.

"Girlfriend gifts are my specialty," said the salesgirl, a busty, peanut-skinned woman with chestnut ringlets. "You stumbled a bit on 'my girl,' is it a new thing?"

With a nervous laugh, Wes scratched the back of his neck. "It shows, huh? I don't know what I'm doing."

"But you came to the right person! I'm Tilly."

On-assignment-at-Seraphina Wes was a sight to see. Awkward, flustered. He had none of Wes's usual easy confidence. He was a tall, dimpled cutie who wanted to impress his new love.

"I don't know anything about this stuff. She mentioned liking, uh, Fenton eyeshadow pellets? Or is it pendants? I don't..."

Tilly the salesgirl giggled.

"Am I saying it wrong?" How did Wes make himself blush through his rich, walnut-brown skin? Damn, he *was* an actor. He bit his bottom lip, eyes flashing down at Tilly.

"*Fenty* eyeshadow *palettes*. Your girlfriend has good taste." Her eyes quickly scanned Wes, head to toe. "In more ways than one."

Sasha narrowed her eyes behind her shades. Okay, that was out of line. Wes just said he was in a new relationship, and this girl was eye-fucking him? Is girl's-girling a lost art? Granted, this whole act was a lie, but Tilly didn't know that.

He let out an *aw-shucks* chuckle. "Come on, now. You don't have to gas me up. I know you make a commission."

She wriggled her nose cutely. "Can your girlfriend fight?"

Sasha's spine went straight. What kind of saleswoman threw herself mercilessly at her customers? Things had changed a lot in retail since sixteen-year-old Sasha worked at Express.

"My girlfriend doesn't have a reason to fight. I only have eyes for her." He bit his lip sweetly. His dimple flashed. Somehow, he got his eyes to shine with earnest sweetness.

"I'm dying, your love for her is too cute," exclaimed Tilly. "The Fenty palettes are over here. Follow me."

Sasha gulped, realizing they were headed to the aisle diagonal from her. She burrowed deeper into her trench coat.

Tilly handed Wes a few metallic-gold palettes and his face brightened. "These are pretty. Wow, okay. I'll take them."

"Cool, I can ring you up, right here." Tilly pulled a scanner out of her apron pocket.

"I have a dumb question. Is this a unique gift? Like, are other boyfriends coming in here with the same idea?"

"Funny you say that. A couple days ago, a customer bought up all the palettes in our SoHo store. Apparently, he did the same thing at the Tribeca location."

Sasha gasped. Accidentally, she squeezed a body lotion too tight. She felt like she was floating. Her lids shuttered closed, in shock. Seat F was looking for her. He remembered the flight the same way she did. She'd felt so stupid, so gullible, that she was having this one-sided relationship with a drunken memory. But now, there was proof. He felt the same way about her. And he was looking for her, too. Not only that, but he was also risking looking like a creep in the process.

"Wanna hear something funny?" Tilly looked both ways, and then Sasha saw her click off the power on her headset. She lowered her voice, and said, "The SoHo manager is one of my homegirls. She said he was buying palettes for... get this... a girl he vibed with on a plane."

"Like a Missed Connection thing," he said. Which, coincidentally, was the same thing he'd said to Sasha when she first described Seat F.

"Anyway, on the flight, she mentioned loving these palettes. And he remembered."

"Damn, that's romantic. This guy's making me look bad." Wes was wide-eyed.

Sasha hunched down in her trench, trying to mask her smile. She was on Seat F's mind, the way he'd been on hers. He remembered every detail of their conversation. Relief flooded her. And excitement.

Ever since the flight, Sasha had been second-guessing her memory. Had she blown Seat F out of proportion? Was he some sort of waking dream, brought on by altitude, anxiety, and Xanax? Now, she knew that she hadn't dreamed him up. And they were having parallel experiences. Just like her, he'd held on to clues from their conversation and was using them to track her down. It was sweepingly romantic. And affirming.

It was blessed relief, knowing she wasn't delusional. Confused? Yes. Conflicted? Certainly. But she wasn't delusional.

"But there's more. This woman told him she works at Seraphina in New York. So he asked if I knew her. You see the vision, right?" She tapped her temple. "I think he's sending her a message. Think about it—what if she's looking for him, too? If she's really a Seraphina employee, she'll hear about the mysterious guy who's buying her favorite stuff and asking about her."

Sasha's mouth dropped a little. Never in her life had anyone made such a dashing gesture for her. She felt light and swoony, like she was floating away on romance.

"It's like when the romantic poets communicated through erotic sonnets, or whatever."

(Okay, but hearing Wes say the word "erotic" momentarily dysregulated Sasha's brain.)

"Have you tried to find her on an employee database, or something?" he asked.

Tilly shook her head. "How can I, without her name? Anyway, Seraphina can't release employee info to customers."

"Hmm," he said, chewing on the inside of his mouth. "Looking at this dude a different way, this could be considered psycho behavior. Chasing a woman down at her job?"

"You'd think, right? But my girl said he didn't give weirdo. He gave 'wealthy corporate daddy.' I trust her. We're both from the Bronx. We can sense weirdo energy from ten blocks away," she said.

Sasha wanted to yell, *HE'S NOT SHADY, HE'S MY MAN.*

"...but, just to cover her bases," continued Tilly, "when my homegirl found out he was visiting several stores, she put him on our internal watch list."

Wes nodded with interest. "Like a Seraphina Citizens App, with his photo next to 'possible creep'?"

"No, just his name. Beyond that, I'm not sure how it works. Only managers have access, and I'm still in training," she whispered. "You didn't hear me say that."

Omigod. Omigod. Sasha was mere feet away from a person who knew a person who knew Seat F's name. Her heart was thundering wildly in her chest, so powerfully, it felt like they could hear her, two aisles over. Wes was so close to unlocking this whole thing. The mystery of Seat F, the constant wondering, the anguish. Sasha's chaotic pursuit was almost over.

"Wow. You're a great storyteller. And that sounds like a movie."

"Deadass! I should take a screenwriting class."

"Invite me to your first premiere." He offered a shy smile. "Thanks for helping. Sorry I tied you up."

"Listen, you can tie me up anytime," she flirted, and then handed him her Seraphina business card.

With a friendly chortle, he headed toward the door. Damn, Wes was good at his job. But why didn't he push harder to get Seat F's name from the database? Why did he drop the ball?

In a few seconds, Wes would walk past her aisle on the way to the front door. Quickly, Sasha lowered the brim of her fedora and burrowed her face farther down in her trench. She tried to channel invisibility.

He'd just passed her aisle—so close, she could've smelled his warm, woodsy cologne if she wasn't holding her breath in nervousness—when he spoke. This was his real voice, deep and cocksure. Without stopping, or even turning his head to look at her, he called out, "Meet me in the alley on Fifty-Seventh. Now."

"S-sir, are you talking to me?" she whispered in a high-pitched voice.

"Yeah, you, Inspector Gadget. *Now.*"

Outside, it was hot, airless, and out of time, that late-afternoon in June feeling when half the city's summering elsewhere, save for disparate clusters of twentysomethings negotiating their plans for the night. Wes and Sasha weren't twentysomethings, but they were both breathing the same air, lush with possibility.

There were a million stories in the city, theirs was just one. And it was playing out in an alley next to Seraphina.

"What the hell was that, Sasha?" Exasperated to the millionth degree, Wes ripped off his prescription-less glasses and stood in front of her, arms folded.

"Did you know I was there, the whole time?"

"The woman who looks exactly like you, dressed like Carmen Sandiego and standing like a goddamn Easter Island statue in the Shampoo aisle? No, no, you blended right in."

"Must you speak so percussively? You can't fault me for being curious. I had a meeting nearby and I just wanted to..."

"I know what you wanted to do. But I told you. I work alone. You hired me to do this job, right?"

"Of course!"

"Then let me do it!" Angrily, he thrust his hands in his pockets. "Listen, I almost flunked preschool, because I failed the skipping test. Did I know how to skip? Obviously. But when asked to do it in front of an audience, I choked."

Sasha was so charmed by the vision of baby Wes struggling to skip, that she almost short-circuited. "Wes, what are you talking about?"

"Detective work comes naturally to me. Talking to people, gathering information, persuading, all that? It's easy. But I can't work when I have an audience."

"You were doing pretty well to me. That whole bashful act? All the flirting? Wow. Interesting methods."

"Whatever works," responded Wes, just a *tad* defensively. "But listen, if you weren't there, I'd have his name. It was in my hand. Just stay in your lane, okay? Don't you have a commercial to cast?"

"It's not going well. It's going terribly, in fact. And I don't want to face the fact that taking a yearlong sabbatical was a mistake. I've lost my touch." And then, her thoughts took a darker turn. "Or maybe I'm too traumatized to see people the same way. Especially men. Maybe I see a predator behind every face. I'm so tired of being scared, and I just want the thing with Seat F to work. I need something good."

In an instant, Wes's sharp edge softened. "I get it. Because finding him also proves that you can read people correctly. That you're wrong about everyone being a predator."

"Exactly. You understand me."

"Yeah, I understand. Of course I do."

Wes and Sasha stood in silence for a minute. Sasha realized that she was leaning against a city trash bin and she jerked away. The alley was disgusting.

"The good news is, he's looking for you, too."

"That is good news," she said, smiling half-heartedly. "The best news."

"Is it childish that I want to find him before he finds you?"

"Not childish. Competitive," she articulated. "Works for me."

"I *do* work for you. So, let me continue to do my job."

"I will. And I apologize for the spy costume. I love to theme dress," she said with a small wince of shame.

Wes eyed her for a moment, contemplating something. And then reached out with one hand, gently removing her sunglasses. He stuck them atop her head. "I need to see your eyes to say this."

"To say what?" She peered up at him, trying not to be moved by the tenderness in his gesture.

"I'm not jealous of Seat F."

She blinked. His words were so blunt, they knocked the wind out of her. "Of course you're not. I don't believe that; it was a dumb joke."

"Jealousy is wanting what someone else has. And he doesn't have you yet." His eyes blazed, pinning her to the spot. "Does he?"

It wasn't really a question, because Wes knew the answer. And so did Sasha—a fact that knocked her on her ass and yanked her clean out of her Seat F fantasy. Wes was right. Seat F was a vague outline of a person. He was more of a concept than an actual guy. How could she be devoted to an invisible man?

Wes's words were bold, direct. A challenge. Sasha swallowed, shaking her head. She couldn't think of a goddamned thing to say.

The air between them swelled with a question, unanswered. And the memory of a long-ago indiscretion neither wanted to face.

NON-DELIVERY REPORT

To: Sasha.C@Seraphina.org [disabled account]
From: Mingzhu.L@Seraphina.org
Subject: Re: Searching for Seat F

Greetings, Sasha!

I've waited a few weeks to respond, because I felt so silly. But I love mystery novels and your Seat F email intrigued me. So, I did some sleuthing of my own.

Seat F is an international man. Why wouldn't he spend some time in Hong Kong? And if he did, he'd surely visit Ozone at the Ritz Carlton. European businessmen love this bar. My cousin met her Italian ex-boyfriend there! So, my girlfriend and I went there for a drink, and to ask around and see if anyone knew him.

No luck. But, at one point, my friend went to the loo, and I fell asleep on a couch. When I opened my eyes, I realized I was leaning on the shoulder of a dashing man! And we discovered we attended primary school together! We've been inseparable ever since.

I wish I'd found your love, but I'm happy I found mine. Good luck on your search. If you're ever in Hong Kong, you've got a friend in me.

Mingzhu Lim
Seraphina Hong Kong
Director Marketing

Chapter 12
HEAD CASE

And then, Wes's phone went off, ringing into the quiet. He checked the number and groaned. "Jesus. My sister."

Sasha was grateful for the interruption. The phone pierced through the almost unbearable tension between her and Wes. Her head was spinning. With just a few words, Wes had left Sasha an emotionally conflicted wreck. But now, it was like it hadn't even happened. Wes was totally preoccupied with his phone.

"Your sister? It c-could be..." Sasha stopped herself and cleared her throat, trying to quell the breathy hitch in her voice. "It could be good news."

He snorted at this. "You don't know my sister." Putting the phone to his ear, he mouthed *Sorry* and stepped away.

Sasha tried to pretend she wasn't watching him. His face registered fifteen different shades of displeasure. She had to pull it together. What was she going through? After years of not feeling a single flutter for anyone, she was suddenly attracted to a man? *To two men?* She wondered if this was a normal phenomenon. If, when women emerged from celibacy, they became indiscriminately horny. But Wes wasn't exactly an indiscriminate attraction.

As much as she tried to run from it, it was there. A flutter, a surge, a flash of electricity, whenever she was near him. Actually, she didn't even need to be physically near him. Just on the phone with him. Reading his texts. Imagining him saying the words out loud. The thing that sent her running from him—the fact he'd witnessed the scariest time of her life, the reminder, the living time stamp of him—it was also the pull. Wes understood her on a level that no one else could access. Even Destiny got annoyed with her bizarre quirks and seemingly random phobias since the 2022 incident. Wes had been there, though. Wes had saved the day.

But he wasn't a relationship guy. For good reason, he wanted to keep things professional. Wes was even resistant to being friends, until she cajoled him into it. He was unavailable, and so was she. She'd just have to remind herself of this. And ignore the fact that, with one utterance—*He doesn't have you yet, does he*—he'd so easily, confidently, crushed the idea of anyone else from her mind.

Stop it, put it away, remember what you're here for, she told herself, covertly training her eyes on Wes as he paced, talking to his sister. What was happening on the other side of the call? Judging from his infrequent, interrupted responses, Wes was being strong-armed.

"Brooke, I told you I'm not going..."

"You know I have to work..."

"Grilling *is* my work..."

"Oh word? Brooke, you design splash parks! I *feed* people, while you expose them to waterborne syphilis. How *dare*..."

"Fine. Fine. Fine."

Wes made an exasperated sound, and shoved his phone in his pocket.

With a defeated slump to his shoulders, he walked back over to Sasha, who was trying to fake a nonchalant air. She raised her phone, saying, "Just got a notice that my Uber's ten minutes behind."

He nodded. "Yeah, no, all good. I'll wait with you."

"So, uh, what was that about?"

"Just my sister, Brooke. Being my sister, Brooke."

"Your twin sister." She was dying of curiosity. The mother of the glitter princess! "I couldn't help but overhear that she's a water park designer? So fascinating."

"Yeah, well, if you ever wondered where an engineering doctorate gets you these days, look no further."

"What happened on the call?"

"I just agreed to something I'm going to regret. But there's no arguing with my sister."

"What did you agree to?"

He sighed. "You remember that I was a partner in my dad's firm, Dane & Son Detective Agency? A bench in Fort Greene Park is being dedicated to him this weekend. He passed not long after I wrapped our case, back in 2022."

"I'm so sorry, Wes. I didn't know he passed."

It was an empty, trite thing to say. How would she have known? But the look on his face was so conflicted, so stormy—she was grasping at how to respond.

Sasha remembered his office, empty next to Wes's. He didn't say much about him during her first case. But she'd picked up that he was somewhat of a hero—a complicated hero—to Wes. His father was clearly a tricky subject. She hoped Wes felt comfortable enough one day to tell her more.

"No, you're fine," Wes assured her. "The bench has been in the works for a while. And it's an honor. It's just that my sister is…" He stopped himself. "I'm trying to think of a diplomatic way to say this. Her energy's just dark. She's like one of those Spirit Halloween animatronics."

"So specific," she said, raising her brows. "Is there a way to compartmentalize? Block out your sister, but go to honor your dad?"

"Nah, it leaves a bad taste in my mouth," he admitted. "The whole thing is so performative, putting on a show for folks who knew me as a kid that I have no relationship with now. I can visit the bench whenever I want. I don't need to prove anything."

"You don't. And everyone grieves in their own way."

Wes scratched the back of his neck, drawing his mouth to one side. "Maybe I'm just being an asshole. What do you think I should do?"

Sasha wanted to be sensitive. But she had to tell the truth. "I don't know enough about your relationship with your father to make an informed—"

"Just tell me."

"You should go."

"*Damn.* I knew you'd say that."

"I just don't want you to regret not being there for such an important day. You're his namesake. And you followed in his footsteps? I'm sure he was so proud of you. And it sounds like you feel the same about him. What's a few hours to support your family? Some light punch, a few speeches, shake a few hands. In and out."

"Family isn't intrinsically a good thing," Wes pointed out. "It just means they're *familiar.* If familiarity mattered, water wouldn't boil fish."

"You're really such a philosopher," she said, authentically impressed. "You're right. If your family's that toxic, don't go. Your mental health is the most important thing. That said, there might be cake."

He chewed on his bottom lip, peering down at the floor. Sasha could tell there was so much more to the story than he was saying. And every part of her wanted to know it. Curiosity flooded her. Wes was a mystery. She wanted to figure out her new (old) friend. She wanted to know more.

"They're toxic," he said, finally, "but I have my moments, too. I've done things I'm not proud of."

"Everyone has," said Sasha.

Wes looked pensive. Unreachable. "Not like me."

She didn't know what he meant, but she didn't want to push. Instead, she said, "If you need some emotional support, I could join you."

"I don't need emotional support," he said quietly.

"What do you need?"

"New relatives," he said with a small laugh, trying to lighten the mood.

"Wes."

"Seriously. After my dad died, my mom's brain powered down. One minute she's normal, the next minute she's mean as hell. Especially to me. And she got remarried to a former Harlem Globetrotter who keeps running for mayor as an Independent."

"Your stepdad is Sweet Willy Watson?"

"And Brooke's just pathologically rude. No social graces, whatsoever."

Sasha winced. "It's really that bad?"

"I can't, in good conscience, expose you to these ding-dongs."

"Well, after everything you've done for me, I owe you."

Wes stared down the alley at the street, wrestling with something. "Nah, I'm good. Thanks for offering, though."

When Destiny invited Sasha to a "couples" scalp massage at Head Case Spa, Brooklyn's destination for soothing scalp treatments, she eagerly accepted. She'd read that their cranio-massages left even the most high-strung New Yorkers floating on air. And floating was what Sasha needed. For the past few nights, she'd had deep anxiety nightmares that bled into the following day—just a jumble of barely logical snapshots from October 2022. But, hopefully, the treatment would give her relaxation.

The spa was a Mediterranean-inspired oasis, with elegant arches, mosaic tiles, and the delicate sound of water flowing over stones.

Washcloths were draped over their eyes, but reed diffusers awakened their other senses, wafting a geranium-lavender scent through the air. As Sasha and Destiny sank into weightlessness on their plush cots, masseuses rubbed detoxifying salt scrubs into their scalps.

And while this was all happening, Seat F was somewhere out there looking for her, too.

"Soooo... how do you see things playing out, when you finally meet Seat F?" asked Destiny, practically echoing Wes's question, a few days before. "Honestly."

"Honestly? In my fantasies, our worlds would collide," said Sasha, who was lying on a luxe cot a few feet from Destiny. "Climate change would reverse. Flowers would bloom. Pangea would reassemble."

And, please God, my inconvenient attraction to Wes Dane would fade.

"I love the new you. Look at how unreasonably romantic you've become." Destiny stretched languidly, wiggling her ballet slipper–pink toes. "Imagine telling people the story of how you met?"

"Oh, our meet-cute would be highly abnormal. And you know I like neat, clean-cut things."

"You eat corn on the cob with a fork and a knife."

"I've been putting off telling Wes how I eat barbecue ribs," she said with a little chuckle.

If she and Destiny weren't wearing washcloths over their eyes, Sasha would've seen her *Oh really?* expression.

"Odd meet-cutes are my new micro-obsession," continued Sasha. "I'm obsessed with this IG account where the host interviews random couples about how they met. And I've fallen into a YouTube rabbit hole researching celeb relationships. It makes this thing with Seat F feel more real."

"You should talk to my parents. They met at a support group for people chronically unable to pass driving tests. Imagine?"

"See? I love that," enthused Sasha. "Did you know that Stevie Nicks married her best friend's widowed husband? And Serena

Williams met her husband at a restaurant, which seems normal. But no. He was sitting at a table she wanted, so she told him a rat was under a chair so he'd switch tables. Queen shit."

"Advantage, Serena!"

"Colman Domingo met his husband in a Walgreens parking lot and found him when he posted a Craigslist Missed Connections story."

"So, you and Colman are practically on parallel timelines."

"Girl. And he's been married to his guy for over a decade."

"I love this for you, that you're feeling all hopeful about men. You're healing!"

If only it were that easy, she thought. The whole reason she was here, blowing up her silk press to steam her scalp, was to heal. To relax. To calm her nervous system. Healing was always on her mind. And always a bit elusive.

"I doubt if I'll ever be all-the-way healed. But I'm feeling hopeful. And guess what? Wes and I found out that Seat F's looking for me, too."

"You and Wes? I thought he told you not to get involved with the case?"

Sasha grimaced. "He did. But I might've snuck into one of his missions. I didn't think he'd catch me. I was just so curious."

"You're such a control freak. Girl, let that man do his job."

"I know, I know. But I felt spiritually called to spy on him. I can't explain it."

"Interesting. Maybe you just want to be around Wes."

"I'm sorry?"

"You heard me."

Sasha wasn't ready to admit this to Destiny. She was barely able to admit it to herself. To come clean with her, Sasha would need to confront the fact that she was trapped in the twistiest, most nonsensical hell of her own making.

"You know Wes Dane isn't my type."

"Do you know how often people misdiagnose their so-called types? It's why no one does BuzzFeed quizzes anymore."

"I know that I'm not into playfully flirtatious men. Impossible to tell their intentions, don't you think?"

"Don't ask me. I don't know how to flirt playfully. I go in for the kill."

"Our relationship is hard to explain." She waved a hand, attempting to dismiss the topic.

"Try me, babe."

Sasha steeled herself for this explanation. She'd never told anyone about the night they'd shared years ago, and she wasn't ready to do so now.

"Wes and I had an intense night, back in 2022. I was scared and he was...perfect. Perfect. But he knew me at a scary time. One I'm always trying to forget. Sometimes when we're talking, I dissociate a bit, because everything about Wes reminds me of me, a stalking victim, being terrorized, and having nowhere to turn. He pulls me into the past. Through no fault of Wes's, of course," she explained. "Anyway, Seat F feels like a new page. I can control how much he knows. What he sees. We haven't escaped the fires of utter chaos together. It doesn't feel so heavy."

"Makes sense," Destiny allowed. "It's worth noting, though, that you said Wes's name several times in the last five minutes."

Sasha had no response to this. Pouting, she asked, "Can we get Popeyes after?"

"You forget, baby, I'm a love professional. I just want to help. I can't imagine a more complicated scenario than developing a crush on the guy I hired to find my crush."

It was a terrible thought. Messy. Confusing. And, as she'd discovered today while taking a break from researching meet-cutes, Reddit had no convincing advice for "how to tell if you're inconveniently attracted to the wrong guy." Sasha decided that, if she felt a tiny spark for Wes, it was surely misplaced gratitude for saving her ass—in 2022 and today. Every time her thoughts drifted to him, she steered them in the other direction. Toward Seat F. The one predicted by the manicurist. The one who held her hand through turbulence. The one who was looking for her, as she looked for him.

Remember the whole point, thought Sasha. *Remember what you're doing.*

"But, if you're truly not into Wes," started Destiny, "do you mind if I add him to my database? He's such an eligible bachelor. Truly one to watch."

"Excuse me?" Sasha flinched, totally caught off guard. The idea was preposterous. She couldn't figure out a proper response, so she burst into nervous laughter.

"What's so funny?"

Sasha wound down her giggles, letting out a drawn-out sigh. "Oh, Destiny. He's not a matchmaking kind of guy."

"You think I couldn't find him a partner? *Me?* In 2017, I successfully matched a Delta with an AKA. Don't play with me."

"I just mean, he doesn't need one. He gets enough women, believe me. He even has groupies. They're called the Barbecuties. Can you imagine?"

"What that tells me is there's a market for him. And I could possibly be sitting on the love of his life. If you don't etroduce us, I'm sliding into that young man's DMs."

"Umm . . . maybe. I'll let you know." Sasha adjusted her eye mask. "But I'm warning you. He's kind of a player. By his own admission, he's not a relationship guy."

"Ahhh, I see. He's not available, so you're talking yourself out of being attracted to him."

"Destiny, I'm not attracted to him! He's an attractive man, but he's not *my* man."

"Fine, but I must reemphasize the fact that you should be diversifying your portfolio, man-wise. I worry about all this energy for Seat F. I meant it when I said I like seeing you romantically hopeful. I just don't want the hopefulness to become delusion. You met Seat F once. In the sky. Off the Henny."

"Listen, there's a greater force at play. The manicurist said that the right connection can bridge hearts through time and space. She was on point! By the way, soothsayers are very trendy. There's a new palmistry café opening in Crown Heights."

"And? Brooklyn loves a fuckass coffee shop. Ever been to Cockatoo Café? It's a coffee shop featuring live, uncaged exotic birds. Imagine a myna bird flying away with your croissant in its claws?" She yawned indulgently. "Not all trends make sense."

"Palmistry does, though. That woman was onto something. I see signs everywhere. As a love specialist, I'd think you'd be more open to the whimsy of this."

"I'm a realist. It's the only way you get numbers like I do. My job is to make the connection happen, fast. The possibility of you actually finding Seat F is slim. And the biggest love red flag? Insurmountable obstacles. You're mistaking the thrill of a crush with the thrill of the unknown."

"Maybe," muttered Sasha, unconvinced.

"Promise me, if you ever meet him, that you'll bring a chaperone. I'll go with you. Or, better yet, Wes. I don't like that we don't know anything about him. Promise?"

With a resigned exhale, Sasha responded, "Promise."

Chapter 13

COMING UP ROSES

Sasha was trying like hell to sleep, but it wouldn't come. She chewed a melatonin gummy, ate an edible, and took a Tylenol PM. Still nothing. For hours, she lay awake, feeling restless and ungrounded. Eventually, her mind drifted to Deep Thoughts. She began asking herself the big questions. Where was she going in life? How would she get there? Who even was she?

Who I am, she thought, *is a woman who is suddenly, desperately horny.*

She rolled onto her back in the cool cocoon of her sheets, determined to solve her problem. Her fingers dipped under the waistband of her cotton boy shorts, sliding down, down, down. Slowly, she stroked herself, sending pleasant—but relatively placid—ripples through her body. Jesus, she was wound tight. She was unsettled about the case and feeling unproductive at work. If she didn't take the edge off her personality, she'd never find sleep. And definitely not an orgasm.

It had been so long since she'd had an actual orgasm, that she didn't aim too high. But she never stopped trying.

Restlessly, in the dark, she pulled up Seat F sense memories. The feel of his rough hand in hers. His bold, expensive scent. The surreal, almost translucent wintergreen tint of his eyes. The florid accent. Her eyes fluttered closed, and she let out a long, uneven sigh. Instead of calming her, thinking of him made her feel hectic. Confused. Desperate. Where the fuck was he? Why did she meet The One, only for him to slip out of her grasp? Evade her? It was maddening. With a frustrated sound, she reached for her bedside lamp, flicking it on. And then, she lit her cypress-and-the-sea candle. She tried to send her thoughts to Gallipoli, a place she'd never been, with a man she barely knew. Her lids fluttered closed.

Let go of the tension, bitch, she told herself. *Just let go. Relax.*

But never in the history of *over*focusing on *un*focusing did anyone actually relax.

Time for the Rose. Her palm resting in her panties, Al Bundy–style, was no longer good enough. She needed more than relaxation. She needed an orgasm. Fucking terribly. And just because she'd been blocked for years, didn't mean it'd be that way forever. With an almost-pissed-off scowl, she pressed the vibrator button to level three (there were five), and slid it over her clit. Her cotton panties were the only barrier.

Sasha drew in a deep breath, held it, and let go. And then, she tried to think of sexy things.

A$AP Rocky's cheekbones, she thought desperately. *Gucci's Jackie 1961 handbag.* Their Eyes Were Watching God. *The chocolate treatment at Body By Brooklyn spa. Old black-and-white photos of Black cowboys. SZA's rasp. Curiosity. Anaïs Nin's diaries. The caramelized edges of a peach cobbler. The entire cast of* Sinners. *Humor. Dimples.*

Her eyes flew open. Dimples? Hold on. What?

Yep, dimples, she thought. *A thigh-melting smile. A raspy, late-night voice. Strong hands. Sinfully suckable lips you can't help imagining skimming the length of your throat. Soulful, intense eyes framed by mesmerizingly long lashes that have absolutely no Black-ass business adorning a man. Grill game. Loyalty. A name that begins with* W.

Wes. Wes. Wes.

Oh. Ohhh. Okay, now she was starting to feel something. Searing warmth radiated from the Rose. Her lids shuttered closed. No. Wes wasn't supposed to be the thought that made her pussy throb. His face wasn't supposed to make her thighs tremble. But it was probably a normal association, seeing as how they'd just discussed the Rose a few nights ago.

She turned the vibrator up to four, sending a jolt of electricity through her. With a small moan, she arched her back, riding the waves of pleasure. Heat was building, her pulse was racing, but she couldn't quite get there. In fact, the more she imagined Wes doing Wes things—cracking wise, writing in his notebook, chuckling in that adorable, eye-disappearing way—the more frustrated she became. Simply imagining him wasn't enough. It wasn't good enough. She needed more.

Sasha Cruz, thirty-two, made an executive decision. And it was crazy. It was something she would've never done a year before, but it was happening. She was going to call Wes. She fucking ached to hear him. His voice in her ear might send her over the edge. And he didn't have to suspect anything. They talked every night, so it wouldn't be cause for alarm. Plus, it was 2:30 a.m. She decided anything that happened at this hour, could be stricken from the record.

Her left hand held the Rose in place. With her right hand, she grabbed her phone off the nightstand and thumb-dialed his number. Then, she put the phone on speaker and propped it next to her ear, on the pillow.

She was sweaty, hot, and unbearably flushed. But she channeled all her experience coaching actors through auditions, and told herself to act normal.

"Hey," answered Wes, sounding drowsy-cozy. "Wassup."

His voice was low, deep, and raspy with sleep. Wes's languid rasp, so intimate in her ear, sent her spinning. She imagined him next to her, close enough to touch, to bite, to kiss.

"Hi," she breathed into the phone, trying to steady the tremor in her voice. She pressed the vibrator deeper into her, and the electric surge was almost too good. She squeezed her eyes shut, swallowed a whimper. "Wh-what are you doing this weekend?"

"You good? You sound different. Are you high?"

"No." The vibration of his voice thrummed through her, arching her back, pebbling her nipples under the thin cotton of her nightshirt. The rush was excruciating, obliterating. She worked her hips, sinuously, against the Rose. Against his voice.

Wait, she thought, *what are we talking about? Hurry, think of something.*

"Sasha?"

When Wes said her name in that breathy, sleepy, slightly confused way, she almost came from that alone. Just from the way her name sounded in his mouth, in the dark. Her toes curled. She bit down on her bottom lip hard enough to draw blood. Oh God, was she doing this? She was really doing this.

"You told me you used to teach boxing, right?" she managed.

"Years ago, but yeah. You want me to train you?"

"Yes. Yes!" She turned the Rose up to five, and her eyes rolled back in her head. "I—I want to learn self-defense. I need... I need..."

"What do you need?"

Oh God. Now, everything he said had a double meaning. She would not survive this conversation.

"If I could fight," she huffed, "I'd feel safer."

"I hear you. But you should know, I was teaching off the books. I don't have a certificate to train or anything. You sure you don't want to take a real class?"

"No, I want you." She choked back a moan on "you," and pushed the vibrator deeper into her clit. Pleasure seared through her, and she arched again, riding the wave in agonized silence.

Why did I say I wanted him? she thought. *He's gonna know, he's gonna know…*

"You want me." He paused for a moment, and then let out a low, soft chuckle. "Good to know. Your place or mine?"

"Yours," she breathed. "Yours."

"Mine. Cool." Pause. "Do you have asthma? You're breathing a lot."

"Everyone br-breathes a lot. If we didn't, we'd be dead."

"Wait, you're serious about training at my house? You really wanna come?"

Jesus, the word "come." The way Wes said it, it was just…it was too…

"Do I wanna…what?" Sasha was close. She rubbed the Rose against her panties, the delicious friction almost too much to take, now. Her face rolled against the pillows and she swallowed a moan, trembling uncontrollably.

"Come."

A spike of electricity tore through her. Wes's voice licked into her every opening, tasting every thirsty, needy, desperate part of her, driving her utterly insane. She needed it again.

"You're breaking up," she lied, trying to keep her voice steady. "Can you repeat that?"

"I was just rhetorically asking if you really wanted to come."

"Wh-what?"

"You still can't hear me? You must have T-Mobile. Verizon ain't cheap, but it's worth it." Then, he raised his voice, intentionally articulating every word. "Do. You. Wanna. Come."

"Yesss," she groaned, turning her face to one side, burying her moans in the pillow. She was losing it, fast. She was so close, she was *soaring*. A few beats passed; or maybe it was several beats, she couldn't tell. Time was liquid, and so was she—her panties were drenched.

Bucking helplessly against the Rose, her thighs began to quiver and her breath hitched.

When Wes spoke again, it was different. Something changed in the brief, loaded pause since he last spoke. Sasha thought she heard him suck in a sharp breath. His gasp felt close, excruciatingly close. She was losing her mind.

"Oh." His voice was a low rumble, deep in his throat.

She held her breath, waves threatening to explode. Did he know? She couldn't speak, or she'd cry out. She'd give herself away.

"Sasha."

He spoke her name like a command. It was too delicious to process. It was coming from a place she'd never heard—and it was guttural, dominating, and dirty as fuck. Wave upon wave of arousal crashed through her.

Jesus, did Wes know what she was doing? He couldn't possibly. No one in their right mind would rope an innocent bystander into a solo wank. Maybe she was imagining that his voice changed. More than likely, she heard the voice she wanted to hear—because, on some secret level, she craved it. But the chance that he *was* aware? It made the whole thing riskier, more dangerous. God, she was going to regret this in the morning. She was going to regret this forever. On her deathbed, she'd remember this moment with bone-deep mortification. But right now? Oh, right now she was in shambles. Wes Dane owned her. She was hanging on his every syllable.

"Sasha."

His voice was hot wax dripping down a candle. *Fuck.* Fuck, fuck, fuck. She was teetering on the edge, her orgasm building to perilous heights. The whole world was narrowed down to this. His voice in her ear.

"Y-yes?" she panted.

"Come."

It sent her to the fucking moon. She sucked in a loud breath, clenched, and finally, fucking *finally*, after who-knows-how-many-years, she came. And it was so overwhelming, so piercing, that she squeezed out a small tear.

Some dizzy-floaty moments later, she came to. She felt a light sheen of misty sweat on her skin. Her breathing was starting to slow, but her heart continued to pound. And then, she noticed that her phone had slid to the ground. With a yelp, she yanked herself out of her postorgasmic haze, and picked it up.

"Are you there?" she asked. But the call must've disconnected when it landed on the ground. Wes was gone. Had she made noise? God, did he know? What was so hot five minutes before was now depraved beyond all human comprehension. What had gotten into her?

She drifted to sleep before she could answer.

It was impossible to tell when the nightmares would come. Sasha could be having a perfectly status quo day. Smooth sailing. But then, as she drifted into sleep, the terrors would come. A disjointed, unsettling collage of feelings—nothing tangible—just remembrances of feeling hunted, chased, and gripped in paranoia. No people were in these dreams; just shadows darting in and out of sight. Sasha was lost at sea. And then a hand would come out of nowhere, grasping at her clothes, her hair, an arm—anything to pull her to safety.

It always ended the same way. In Sasha's dream, the hand was disembodied, but she knew who it belonged to. This time—the night after her Rose encounter—she rushed into consciousness with a breathless gasp, and her phone was ringing. Startled and disoriented, she reached for her phone on the nightstand. She had no idea what time it was.

"Hello?" She was groggy, and still halfway stuck in nightmare-world.

"You up?"

It was Wes, with uncanny timing. His strong hand just pulled her out of a nightmare. And now he was speaking in her ear. She was suddenly, blisteringly wide awake. Omigod. Omigod. It all came rushing back to her. Was Wes calling to talk about her insane Rose call? Of course he was. What could she possibly say? She was too mortified and ashamed to speak.

Her insides were screaming. Did he know? It was the morning after her risky call. After she hung up the night before, Sasha had been on pins and needles for ages before falling asleep—replaying the conversation, again and again. The way he'd sounded. The way she'd sounded. The shocking impulsivity that was so unlike her. What had possessed her? It's like she'd had a personality transplant.

One thing was true—Wes opened something up in her. It couldn't be denied. But she didn't know what it meant. Wes was everything she didn't want. Too handsome, a bit of a lothario, definitely aware of his charm. Sasha's dad was like that. And he'd given her mom a lifetime of heartache. Wes Dane wasn't an option.

Second, it felt like cheating on Seat F. She realized this sounded insane, given that their relationship began (and ended?) over the length of a transatlantic flight.

Third, was it a breach of moral code to nonconsensually ride the waves of someone's voice to completion?

But the worst part was what it revealed about herself. The orgasm that had so frustratingly eluded her, for years, just roared back into town. And not because she had a gorgeously spiritual, man-decentering, *fall in love with your yoni* style erotic breakthrough. Or because she was fantasizing about her fated soulmate, Seat F. No, it was because she was imagining Wes Dane simply existing on the other side of the line. Wes Dane, who was minding his own business, trying to process why she'd chosen T-Mobile over Verizon.

Wes Dane, her recently reclaimed friend, with whom she was supposed to respect professional boundaries.

She tried to convince herself it was cool. It was a small moment of sexual weakness. Men were always getting caught doing some weird sexual shit. Look at politicians and university presidents. Far be it from a woman to let her hormones take over, for once.

She'd been holding her breath since she woke up that morning, hoping against hope that Wes hadn't picked up on what was happening on her end of the call. In between meetings, she turned off all the lights and hid under the covers, feverishly scrolling through social media. She had to distract herself or her mind would snap.

But it was time to face this.

"Did I wake you?" Wes was asking.

"Yes, I... no. Sorry, I'm a little off."

Should she bring it up? If she did, and he wasn't aware, she would die a thousand deaths. If she did, and he *was* aware, then she'd also die. If she didn't bring it up, and he was aware, the awkwardness might also kill her. So, no matter what, death was imminent.

"You sound weird," said Wes. "I know why."

Dear God.

"You had another nightmare." He'd fielded a similar call before, the previous week. "Here's what you do. Go get some ice. Hold it in your hand, and let it melt. Physiologically speaking, it'll calm your nervous system."

"How do you know?"

"I'll tell you some other time."

Her fears were, haltingly, beginning to subside. Wes didn't sound like someone who telephonically overheard her enjoy the most exquisite orgasm of her life. He was being his usual self—candid, sweet, thoughtful. The ice thing was a sweet suggestion. If Wes had any awareness of what she'd done, Sasha would've picked up on some awkwardness. He probably wouldn't have called her at all. Actually, no; Wes was so direct that he would've immediately called her back after the phone cut off last night, demanding an explanation. In any event, the fact that he hadn't mentioned anything was a good sign.

Hesitantly, she allowed herself to believe that things were status quo.

"When's the last time you left the house?" he asked.

This question left her stomach in knots. Wes could tell she'd been a shut-in for days? She was so embarrassed. There was no rhyme or reason to her anxiety episodes. She could be relatively fine out in the world for two days, but then retreat into hiding for a week.

"When we were at Seraphina."

Her words were met with a weighted silence.

"That long, huh?" His voice was measured and nonjudgmental. But it was clear he was worried. "I'm going to regret this. But will you come with me to the bench dedication tomorrow? It'll be good for you to get out. And you'll feel safe with me, right? I apologize in advance for my feral family."

"I thought you weren't going."

"I wasn't. But I thought about your offer to be my emotional support person." He took a breath. "I'll allow it, if I can be yours."

"That's a great idea."

"Or a terrible one."

"I'll be on my best behavior."

She heard him let out a terse chuckle. "You'll be the only one."

Chapter 14

FAKE DATING

"What can I say about Detective Wesley Dane Sr. that we don't already know? He was a pillar of the community. A father, brother, and son to all. Detective Dane was a child of Fort Greene, Brooklyn, before it became... well, you know..."

"Mighty white!" someone yelled out from the crowd, to knowing laughter.

"Before the transformation, let's say," city council member Marilyn Juarez said with a wink.

Sasha, Wes, the Dane family, and about sixty members of the community were gathered in Fort Greene Park's central lawn, under the spotty shade of a group of 180-year-old silver linden trees. Councilwoman Juarez was standing at the bench, which was draped in tarp. She didn't need a microphone; her voice boomed.

"As someone who grew up attending art, fitness, and college prep classes at the rec center he funded and built on Myrtle Avenue—the one that gave little-girl me a safe place to land—I can tell you that I wouldn't be standing here today without his love. As a detective, he was devoted to lifting his community. He reunited missing children with their parents. He helped DV victims build a case to convict their abusers. He broke the case of mistreatment at the Mount Saint Mary's Nursing Home, right here on Vanderbilt. And I've never met a man with more integrity. I'll never forget his words at the 1998 Boys & Girls Club Christmas benefit: 'Whatever you choose to do, choose the honest way over the easy way. It'll come back to you with dividends.'"

Sasha glanced at Wes. He was standing next to her, wearing a deep khaki suit and a synthetic smile. She nudged him a bit with her elbow, getting his attention. *You got this,* she mouthed. He blinked a few times, bringing himself back from wherever he was. *Thanks,* he mouthed back, looking down at her. The tightness in his expression softened.

Sasha had been so nervous about going to the ceremony with Wes. Whether it was a platonic or romantic situation, meeting someone's family always deepened the relationship. All morning, she obsessed about what to wear. And how would she introduce herself? As a client? A friend? She supposed it didn't really matter. No one would be paying attention to her—it was a big moment for the Danes. Not their plus-ones.

Sasha wondered how Wes Dane Sr.'s legendary status affected Wes. And why hadn't he ever moved away? There was no outrunning your past when you stayed in the same place your whole life. Sasha couldn't fathom it—she left Houston for college, and after graduation, she moved to Brooklyn. No looking back. So, Sasha had no reference for what it was like to live, as an adult, among people, places, and memories from her childhood. How "stuck" she would've felt. If she'd stayed in Houston, she'd still be the girl with the popstar-concussing baton. Thank God she broke free.

For whatever reason, Wes never took that chance. She wondered why.

"...and Wesley Senior instilled the same values in his beloved twins, Brooke and Wesley Junior," continued Councilwoman Juarez. "Now, I know y'all are grown and in your thirties, but to me, you're still the kids going door-to-door, gathering baby essentials for new moms in need."

Several "awws" came from the crowd. An older gentleman in a fedora and suspenders said, "Hmm-hmm. I remember Junior with his Superman cape and his stutter. Thought he could save the world!" Laughter and more "awws" erupted.

The old man looked delighted. Wes looked like he wanted to astral-project.

"Detective Wesley Dane Sr. taught his children to be productive, forthright citizens, and his influence is seen in them today. Brooke, as a commercial engineer with a doctorate and real estate here and in Martha's Vineyard, and Wesley Junior, proudly following in Wes Senior's footsteps as a"—checks notes—" uh, oh I'm sorry, he *was* a detective. Now he owns a chain of barbecue restaurants!"

Sasha angled her head toward Wes's and whispered, "A chain of restaurants?"

"Fucking Brooke," he hissed. "She wrote this speech."

"Did she exaggerate your dad, too?"

"No, he was a pillar of the community," whispered Wes. "Everyone's hero. But I never saw that, though. He was so hard on me. I think I was grounded for a decade straight."

Sasha looked at him, trying to process this outpouring of vulnerability. She had a million questions, but now wasn't the time to ask them. Wes was so kind, so bighearted. She couldn't imagine a parent being harsh with a kid like that.

"Please join me," Councilwoman Juarez was saying, "in dedicating this park bench to Detective Wesley Dane Sr. One of the true heroes of old Fort Greene." With a flourish, she lifted the tarp off the bench. It was shiny walnut with an engraved plaque affixed to the back. The crowd clapped and cheered. "Deejay, spin us a tune!"

The deejay, who was a deacon at Emmanuel Baptist and not qualified to spin anything, turned on a Spotify playlist. As Frankie

Beverly and Maze sang through the speakers, people began mingling, dancing, and heartily congratulating the Danes.

Though she obviously never knew Wes's dad, Sasha was in awe. He sounded like a saint. It was almost too good to be true. She tried to imagine little-boy Wes collecting formula and diapers from neighbors, lugging a big bag from door to door like a mini Santa. Trying to live up to the legacy of his beloved dad. It must've felt constricting, following in the footsteps of such a heralded figure—and saddled with his name, no less. There was no escaping being held to his example—and it was probably a lot of pressure on a kid or teen or young man trying to make his own mark in the world. Honestly? With all this talk about Wes Senior's honesty and integrity, even Sasha wanted to rebel.

A flurry of people walked by, slapping Wes on the back, congratulating him. Sasha stood by his side, smiling brightly. She would've felt out of place, had Wes not introduced "his friend Sasha" to everyone who spoke to him.

"We miss your dad every day, Junior."

"The kindest man I ever met."

"When'd you get so tall, son?"

"Retired NYPD, here. Went to PS 20 with your dad. Never could convince ol' boy to join the force. Why? He was too principled to be a cop. *Ha ha!* No, all jokes aside, he never once compromised his beliefs to solve a case. That man was a saint."

It was one compliment after another. Wes was all pasted-on smiles and blank-eyed hugs—until he was intercepted by a tall, lanky beauty wearing a micro pixie haircut and a sleeveless jumpsuit. Her face was a feminized version of Wes's, and it looked pissed off.

"So. You decided to join us," she said, planting her fists on her hips.

"A chain of restaurants, Brooke?"

"Oh, grow up. Dare to imagine a brighter future for yourself." She dismissed him with an impatient wave. And then, she noticed Sasha. With raised eyebrows, she quickly scanned her outfit—a chic, teal sundress with a sweetheart neckline. Under Brooke's pointed gaze, Sasha felt like she was giving a bit too much boob.

"Brooke, this is my friend Sasha Cruz. Sasha, meet the Omen."

"Pleasure to meet you," Sasha said with a smile. "Your pixie cut is so pretty."

"I hate it." She spoke with startling bluntness. "I bleached my hair and it broke off, so I had to go short."

Wes shook his head in deep sibling disgust. "I know you don't get them often, but it's customary to say 'thank you' upon receiving a compliment. We've talked about this."

"Well, I love short hair." Sasha tried to smooth things over. "You can lean into bold earrings. That's always fun."

Brooke stared at Sasha for a beat too long and then let out a short laugh. "You're cute. I like you." She cut her eyes at Wes, muttering, "She's not your friend. Be so for real."

Wes opened his mouth to respond, but Brooke cut him off. "Were you seriously gonna miss this? What would Daddy think?"

"The good news is, we'll never know." Wes looked exhausted by the conversation, and it hadn't even lasted two minutes. "Well, it's been riveting, but..."

"I can't be the only one to uphold his legacy, Junior. I have four Corgis, an *actual* career, a daughter, and Timothy-Joshua to oversee." When she said "Timothy-Joshua," she pointed in the direction of a paunchy white man with a blandly sleazy vibe (flashy watch, attention-seeking mustache). He looked like the kind of person you meet just as you're hitting rock bottom in Vegas. At his side was a pointy-featured, terrifyingly poised tween in starter heels. "If I can make the time, you can make the time."

"Really? Why don't you write a speech about it? In this one, make me an aerospace engineer so I can rocket right the fuck out of here."

"I cannot run Dad's affairs on my own. I planned this entire event by myself! The decor, the guest list, the catering..."

"I'm surprised. The pigs in a blanket have Timothy-Joshua written all over them."

Brooke gasped and then narrowed her eyes. "At least I'm married."

"At what cost, though?" They all turned to look at Timothy-Joshua, who was doing the Nae Nae while holding a mini fan in front of his face.

Sasha was fascinated seeing this side of Wes. Together, he and Brooke seemed like overgrown thirteen-year-olds locked in an ancient sibling battle. She almost felt like she was eavesdropping.

"What ever happened to that writer-girl you were dating?" Brooke asked him with a pointed smirk. "The journalist? Sasha, do you know her?"

Writer-girl?

"Um, I don't think so?" she said vaguely. A waiter with a tray swept past her, and she took the opportunity to change the subject. "Oooh look, mini crabcakes!"

"First of all," said Wes, "stop trying to be controversial, Brooke. You're overheating your last remaining brain cell. Secondly, don't act like you handle everything yourself. Mom oversees Dad's estate, not you."

"Mom? *Our* mom? This morning, she got confused by the map on the bottom of a Whitman's Sampler box."

Wes and Brooke peered over their shoulders, and Sasha followed their gaze. A petite silver-haired woman in a floral sheath dress was dancing with a seven-foot-tall giraffe. He'd paired his wide-shouldered, burgundy suit with a matching fedora. Sweet

Willy Watson. Sasha recognized him from several mayoral elections. The speakers played "Best of My Love," and they both body-rolled toward each other.

"They're adorable!" raved Sasha.

"They're kissing," gasped Brooke. "Ugh, let me go pull Mom away from that pinkie-ringed pimp. Wes, circulate. Act like you've been somewhere before. Sasha, it's lovely to meet you. Hope I see you again." With that, she swanned away.

"Wow," said Sasha. "She's . . . a firecracker."

"She's an emotionally lawless villain," he retorted. "Crazy to think she was the golden child, while I was the problem child."

"I honestly can't imagine you being anyone's problem, Wes."

"I mean, I wasn't *easy*. I was mischievous, but I got pretty good grades, and I was everyone's friend. I got in trouble for fighting at school sometimes. He hated me for that. Told me I embarrassed him. Said I was 'physically undisciplined.' That was probably true, but I was bullying the bullies. My dad was all about rescuing underdogs. You'd think he'd appreciate that." He looked around at the crowd. "All these people loved him. No one ever considers what heroic people are like at home."

His tone was casual, direct, conversational. But the message was heartbreaking. She couldn't imagine feeling like an embarrassment to a parent. Her mom bragged about her every chance she got. Sasha's childhood wasn't perfect—and, much of the time, she felt like she raised herself—but she grew up feeling valued. For all her mom's faults, this was a priceless gift.

Sasha felt righteously fired up, like she wanted to rescue his inner child, somehow.

"I'm sorry your relationship was hard. Honestly, it breaks my heart to hear."

"I'm good. Really. You can't change the past, right?" With that, he dropped the subject. He grabbed two cups of champagne from a passing tray and handed one to Sasha. They clicked their cups together. The mood was lifted a bit. "I'm sorry about Brooke."

"Oh, I can take it," she said lightly. "Funny that she doesn't think we're friends."

"You caught that, huh?" He let out a short chuckle. "Yeah, that's her antisocial way of saying you're pretty. While also insulting me. She knows I don't have a girlfriend. What, does she think we woke up from a one-night stand and I dragged you here?"

This was an offhanded comment, but it sent Sasha's mind into a small erotic spiral. Helplessly, a delicious vision flashed in her mind—the two of them, tangled in rumpled, morning-after sheets, a beam of sunlight streaming down on their intertwined bodies, as they luxuriated in their blissed-out little world.

Sasha nervously smoothed her hair behind her ears. *I'm never using the Rose again. She's a cruel mistress.*

But, as she recovered from Feeling Things, Sasha had a bright thought. This was more proof that Wes hadn't clocked the Rose incident. Or else he would never have made such a suggestive comment.

"How are you doing in this crowd?" Wes asked. "Let me know if it's too much, okay?"

"I'm good. But thanks for checking in." She couldn't say what she wanted to say, which was that she'd never had anyone check in like that. She'd never opened up about her anxiety in a way that would *invite* anyone to check in. This was a friendship milestone. And she felt like she was blooming under his attention.

"What's making you smile like that?" he asked, taking a sip of his champagne.

"If I told you, you wouldn't believe it."

Just then, Sasha felt a tap on the back of her right shoulder. As Wes's expression darkened into preemptive annoyance, she spun around. It was his mom. Up close, she seemed more delicate than the fully embodied woman gleefully dancing with her man. She had a fragility that felt immediate, as if the ghostly specter of a nervous breakdown wasn't far off.

"Hello, young lady. Aren't you fresh as a daisy?" she exclaimed. "Wes, what's her name?"

"Sasha," sighed Wes. "Hi, Mom."

"*Tasha.* Lovely name." His mom had the hopeful, wide-open expression of a Facebook Boomer on the verge of succumbing to an internet scam. She batted her lashes at Sasha. "How long have you been dating my sweet boy?"

"We're not dating, Mrs. Dane. We're just friends."

"Well, I hope you stick around."

Sasha was taken aback. "What do you mean?"

"She's calling him a slut," said Brooke, who showed up again out of nowhere.

Mrs. Dane wrinkled her nose. "I hate it when you use that fast language. Your daddy would've hated that."

Just then, Councilwoman Juarez pulled Brooke and Mrs. Dane away to meet her new assistant. It was the perfect time for Sasha to address his mom's allegations.

"Are you a slut, Wes?" she asked teasingly.

"Me? No, not currently."

"Your mom thinks you are."

"I think labeling me a 'slut' is disrespectful to the smart, beautiful, interesting women I had the privilege of consorting with for brief yet meaningful amounts of time."

She let out a short laugh. "Diplomatic. Nicely done. So, you had a wild past?"

"I was just easily seduced," he admitted, plainly. "In my post-college years, I lost my footing a little bit. Years of unserious, unhealthy behavior. And, yeah, too many women. Unfortunately, I wasn't really boyfriend material. Whatever that means."

Before Sasha could think of a response, Brooke and Mrs. Dane returned.

"So," started Mrs. Dane, "how long have you lovebirds been dating?"

"Sasha just told you; we're friends."

"Well, you certainly look like a couple. Is this fake dating?" asked Mrs. Dane. "Like in romance books?"

"I love fake-dating tropes," said Sasha. "Have you read *The Wedding Date*?"

"Jasmine Guillory? Of course. What an author," she gushed enthusiastically. She nudged her son. "I really like your quote-unquote friend."

"You really think I'd bring someone here to trick people? What for?"

"Me thinketh that Wes doth protesth too much," trilled Mrs. Dane.

"You doing Shakespeare, or did your dentures slip?" muttered Brooke.

Mrs. Dane ignored her. "And what do you do for a living, dear?"

"I'm a casting agent," said Sasha. "Mostly film, but I've done a lot of TV. I'm working on a Seraphina commercial right now."

"Seraphina? My favorite store. You must be very skilled at what you do."

"She's being humble," interrupted Wes. "She cast a fourth of the rom-coms and thrillers on Netflix. Remember *Let's Knot and Say We Did*? You quoted that movie for a month, Mom."

Sasha looked up at him, with heated cheeks and a surprised smile. She was so touched that he knew that. "Did you read my IMDb?"

"Maybe." His eyes crinkled. "I've been researching you."

"I'm flattered. Did you watch *Let's Knot and Say We Did*?"

"Yeah, over the weekend. That guy who played the brother of the sheriff? Perfect casting."

Her mouth dropped. "Stop it. You really did watch? I'm impressed. You're not the demo."

"If you worked on it, I'm the demo," he stated simply. Wes's and Sasha's eyes met. He eyed her like he had an endless urge to drink her in, to memorize her. It was absolutely destabilizing.

So destabilizing that they forgot they were in front of an audience.

"Friends, my entire ass," mumbled Brooke.

Sasha quickly changed the subject, snapping them out of their trance. "Detective Dane Senior sounds like an exceptional man."

"Oh, he was divine," sighed Mrs. Dane. "His peers would tell him that to be a great detective, you need to cheat. Operate in gray areas. But not my Wesley. He was so principled. No hacking, no illegal snooping, no bugging phones, or all that stuff *you* do, Wes." Mrs. Dane placed her fists on her hips. If Sasha wasn't mistaken, a flash of anger erupted on her face. Something in her demeanor changed. And just like that, she went dark. "Wes, I'm relieved you stopped trying to follow in his footsteps. Because your father was special. A saint. And Lord knows, you're no saint."

It was a terrible thing to say. And it was so shocking coming from a person who, seconds before, seemed like a harmless, slightly wacky woman. Wes had warned Sasha that his mom was toxic—but Sasha hadn't been able to see it. Mrs. Dane didn't seem plugged enough into reality to inflict real damage. But in one breath, she flipped a switch, and her effervescent personality curdled into something sinister. Brooke was just a bitchy, bratty sister. But Mrs. Dane was operating from a place of grief and resentment. Now, Sasha understood why Wes didn't want to come.

Wes, Sasha, Mrs. Dane, and Brooke all stood in a force field of awkwardness. In the background, the upbeat pep of Will Smith's

"Summertime" provided a tone-deaf backdrop to this uncomfortable moment.

"Mom, stop." Clearly, Brooke didn't tolerate anyone but herself messing with Wes.

"Wes, I know it caused you so much pain," she continued, "trying to keep time with an icon."

"I think he's got it," warned Brooke. "Enough."

"Now you can forge your own path. With Tasha. Now go and be the best truck driver you can be. Your father wore himself out, rescuing you so often. Lord, all those charges. Trespassing without consent."

Wes didn't blink. He didn't become visibly angry or even defensive. Instead, his defense mechanism was to go calm, absorbing her insults without reacting. To Sasha, it was clear this wasn't his first time fielding outbursts like this. "It was a child abuse case. I had to get that kid out of there."

"Then there was the illegal GPS tracker he put on a guy's car."

"He was terrorizing his ex-wife," explained Wes. "I was building a case."

"It was illegal. All those citations risked your father's pristine name and reputation." Then, Mrs. Dane raised her voice. "You risked his reputation! *Do you understand that?*"

Brooke stepped in. "Mom, enough. You're embarrassing us."

"No, she's being truthful." Wes appeared disturbingly calm. The only thing throwing off his act was the clench of his jaw. "Mom's entitled to her opinion."

Wes might've been cool and calm, but Sasha was incensed. She was so offended by his mother's treatment of him that it surprised her. This wasn't her family. Their dynamics were none of her business. But nevertheless, she felt strongly that she needed to defend him.

"Mrs. Dane, with all due respect, Wes isn't a truck driver. He owns a food truck. He's been written up in *Eater*, *Infatuation*, and *Grub Street*. He has the featured spot at F.E.A.S.T. every weekend. That's a huge deal."

Wes stilled, gazing at her with absolute wonder. Mrs. Dane looked at her like she was an absolute fool.

"Oh, Marsha," said Wes's mom. "You don't understand. I'm glad he has a new job. He was too emotional to be a detective. So many mental health issues. He used to have night terrors and wet the bed. You need a level head as a detective. All those citations!" Mrs. Dane grabbed his arm. "Thank God you found a new start. With your temperament, detective work is too risky. It's like your dad used to say, in searching for monsters, be careful not to turn into one yourself."

What the hell did that mean? wondered Sasha.

"I'd just like to see you settle down," she said, still hanging on to Wes's arm. "You had so much promise. I hate to see you flail. Your father died so disappointed in you. All that drinking! The women!" Mrs. Dane turned her attention to Sasha. "And then, after my husband died, you know what his only son did? He played Wordle. All the time. He went all the way to Palo Alto for the national Wordle competition and lost. It was sad. *I don't even know what Wordle is!*"

Sasha blinked. Wordle. He actually competed in a Wordle championship? Is that where he got his journals? This man contained multitudes.

"I didn't lose," he mumbled. "I came in second."

"Everything that isn't first is losing," snapped Mrs. Dane angrily. "Ask Hillary Chicken!"

Brooke looked at Sweet Willy, who'd appeared by Mrs. Dane's side. "Hillary Chicken? Has she been drinking on her meds?"

Sweet Willy Watson smiled apologetically. "I'm gonna tell you what my Pop-Pop once told me. He said, 'Son, this, too, will pass.

Sometimes you have to cut off your balls to save your ass.'" He tipped his fedora and two-stepped back onto the dance floor.

Sasha was furious on Wes's behalf. His mom was mean. His sister was bitchy. How dare they cast him as some deadbeat loser. He was a canny, savvy entrepreneur. It struck her how destructive a death can be, for a family. She wondered what they were like when Wes Senior was alive.

"Well. That's just about all the dysfunction I'm willing to experience today," announced Wes. "Sasha, how about brunch at Walter's?"

"Have fun!" exclaimed Mrs. Dane, as if she hadn't scorched the earth. "Sasha, next time I see you two, maybe you'll be an actual couple."

Sasha forced a tight smile. "Between you and me, Mrs. Dane, I'm hopeful. If he'll have me."

Wes blinked rapidly. His mouth parted, but nothing came out. He looked flabbergasted.

"You'd date my son? But you're such a catch."

Sasha moved closer to Wes, hooking her arm in his. "No, Wes is the catch."

"Oh, don't be silly." She laughed.

That was the last straw. Sasha turned to face Wes. With a soft smile, she raised up on her tiptoes. Closing her eyes, she kissed him on the cheek. When she came back down, she locked eyes with him. And what she saw made her stomach flip. Wes looked like he'd been sprayed by a flurry of automatic bullets.

And then, he grabbed her by the hand, and they got the entire fuck out of there.

At the outskirts of the park, Wes and Sasha were embroiled in tension.

"You didn't have to do that," he said. "I was fine."

"No you weren't. I couldn't let her talk about you like that."

"I was fine, Sasha." With a terse expression, he unbuttoned his suit jacket. "Don't feel sorry for me. Besides, they're right to be ambivalent about me. I've done some terrible things. Things I regret every day."

Confused, Sasha stepped closer to him. "What terrible things?"

But Wes's expression was far away; he was somewhere else, entirely. Somewhere unreachable. Abruptly, he shook his head, as if deleting the past twenty minutes from his memory.

"Wes," she repeated, "what terrible things?"

Lost in thought, he ignored her. "I'll have Seat F's name by tomorrow. I know what to do."

Chapter 15

BARTER ECONOMY

Wes was going to solve Sasha's case. That was no question. But, after the dedication ceremony, his strategy changed.

No more doing things by the book. No more attempting to emulate his sainted father's integrity. Integrity took too long. And who was he trying to prove himself to, anyway? His dad? Way too late to change his mind; to convince him that he was a worthy business partner and son. Wes Senior had fired him while he was in hospice. And a few months later, he'd suffered a fatal stroke. And, just like his mom had articulated so clearly (despite slurring every word prior), he'd died disappointed in his only son. So, it no longer mattered how he conducted this case.

He was a joke to his family. His sainted father was gone. And Sasha Cruz had pity-kissed him at 1:43 p.m. in the middle of Fort Greene Park.

His head was still spinning. That moment managed to obliterate his ego while also being the absolute highlight of his year. It was like she'd uppercut him in the balls while slipping him a winning lottery ticket. And she'd only kissed him because she pitied him, not because she wanted him. To her, Wes was just a savior figure. A good friend. An emotional support person.

Her emotional support person whose voice, *simply his voice*, made her come.

That call. Did she think he didn't know what she was doing? Did she think he couldn't hear her? The hitching of her breath, the soft, airy moans, the barely suppressed whimpers—he was on the other side of the call, coming apart. And harder than he'd ever been in his life.

Was she trying to torture him? If so, it was working. It was so illicit, so dirty and intimate. After hanging up, he stared at the wall, buzzing with a furious, unmet ache. Sasha left him with his dick in his hand, jacking off like a teenager, desperately imagining it was her. *Her* hand, *her* outrageously sensual mouth, *her* tongue, *her* everything. That call was erotic torment. And he was the idiot who, for the first ten minutes, actually thought she was calling in search of his boxing services. Once he realized what she was doing, it was like the bottom dropped out of his world.

They weren't dating. He wasn't even in the running. They were professional associates with a friendship that was getting deeper and richer with every nighttime call. The problem was, he'd started looking forward to those groggy, sleepy talks. The rest of his day was stressful—he was hustling, romancing investors, perfecting recipes, or obsessively researching competitions around the country. Exciting stuff, to be sure. But five minutes of Sasha, on the phone, in the dark, was his new reason for living.

And acting normal around her was becoming excruciating.

The way she looked at the bench ceremony almost ended him. The contours of her waist, her sleeper-build breasts spilling out of that low-cut dress. The soft protectiveness in her face when she leaned up to kiss him. Wes was so tired of pretending that her every move didn't knock him sideways. At the ceremony, it was especially tough to hide his feelings, because he was also trying to hide that his family was laced with dysfunction. He wanted to protect Sasha from their bullshit. She'd been through enough.

And so had he, honestly. Wes had an intense need to finish this case and get back to who he was before Sasha Cruz got under his skin. He'd been close to getting it out of the Seraphina sales associate, by way of her manager's consumer "threat" database—until he was distracted by Sasha. He'd considered circling back with the associate, but it was quicker and cleaner to start fresh. And he knew where to start. The top-secret USFlight Airlines manifest.

The manifest would list all of Seat F's information. But it was a sealed document. The only way to gain access was to bribe an airline employee. Lucky for him, bribing was his specialty. Well, quickly assessing who was bribable was his specialty.

After making a few calls, he discovered that USFlight employees hung out at Upstairs Cocktail Bar in Jackson Heights, Queens. Nestled above a restaurant called Unidentified Flying Chickens (the most confoundingly baller name for a Korean spot, ever), the low-key speakeasy was about five minutes from Fiorello Airport. Perfect. He formulated a plan while speeding down the Brooklyn-Queens Expressway. Admittedly, it wasn't that involved. The plan was as follows: chill at the bar for a while, eavesdrop on some conversations, find a USFlight Airlines worker, and play it as it lays.

Despite feeling certain about leaving the detective world, there was no denying it—the high of undercover work was unmatched. His new career was fun, honest work; but it was safe. Straightforward. You buy materials, cook, and hope you can sell enough to profit. It was gratifying, but it wasn't *thrilling*. Not like this. Not like dropping into a situation, cold, all synapses firing—with no way to prepare—and surviving on wits and wiles, alone. Each moment could mean everything or nothing. Only the most plugged-in, alive professionals knew the difference. Was he still mentally nimble enough to think on his feet?

God, I missed this, he thought, pulling into a parking space just off Roosevelt Boulevard, a consistently crowded main thoroughfare. After walking a few blocks, he spotted Unidentified Flying Chickens, slid on a pair of horn-rimmed glasses (no prescription), and ducked into the hidden door by the restaurant. With his NYU trucker cap, NYU tee, and Carhartt trousers, he was going for a "cool grad student vibe." Approachable, open, and unthreatening. Heading up the narrow, green-lit stairwell, he caught his reflection in a mirror and decided he looked the part.

The speakeasy was dimly lit with a tucked-away bar. It was a cash-only, pop-radio, cigarette-smoke, no-food type of scene. There were a few stools at the bar, some two-person tables against a back wall, and a few sunken sofas. Through the smoke, Wes checked out the crowd. It was 6:00 p.m., happy hour. And, true to his research, about half the people still had on their USFlight uniforms. He spotted an empty barstool, next to two uniformed USFlight employees.

Quietly, Wes made his way through the tight crowd. He straddled the seat, asked for a drinks menu, and opened his ears.

There was a woman next to him, chatting it up with a balding Asian guy in glasses. Judging from the cadence of their conversation, they were tipsy, but in a fun, loose-lipped way—neither had entered messy territory. The woman was coffee-skinned, tall, maybe six foot one, with dramatic makeup and a high ponytail. Her USFlight hat was crumpled in her lap. And she was mid-cheers.

"Here's to my last day," she exclaimed, holding up a shot glass.

"Onward and upward, queen." Her friend clinked his glass to hers. "I still can't believe this is happening. That Mark actually fired you. Man, *fuck* Mark."

"Me too, but that's corporate America," she said.

"That's America, period," he pointed out. "Discrimination and hate and judgment."

"And small-dicked bosses named Mark with cigar breath and failed hair plugs from Turkey," she added.

"I'm gonna miss you, Roslyn," he wailed. "Let's Zoom every day."

"No, FaceTime," said Roslyn. "Mark already canceled my USFlight Zoom account. And confiscated my ten-year anniversary pin in front of the whole team." She quickly looked both ways and then lowered her voice. "The motherfucker ripped it off my vest and threw it away himself."

"*Not in front of the whole team,*" gasped her friend.

"Had the nerve to say *I* was the one throwing away ten years. Not him."

"Wait, is he allowed to do that?"

Time to jump in, thought Wes.

"Actually, that's assault," he mumbled under his breath.

Roslyn and her friend turned in his direction, two sets of eyebrows raised to the heavens.

"Oh. Oh, sorry. I didn't mean to butt in," he apologized with a sheepish grimace. "I couldn't help but overhear."

"No, it's my fault, my voice carries," said Roslyn, with a delicate flutter of her fingers.

"Mark sounds like a real asshole," said Wes. "And it sounds like you escaped a toxic situation. I had a bad day at work myself, so I can relate."

Wes didn't have a bad day at work, nor did he have a story prepared.

"I promise you," said the friend, "whatever happened to you today, it couldn't be worse than what Mark did."

"Well, I can't resist competition." Flashing his dimpled smile, Wes lowered the brim of his cap and folded his arms. "Let's go. What's the backstory, Roslyn?"

"Oh, I'll tell you. But let's do shots first."

Wes declined (he needed his wits), but Roslyn and her friend downed another round.

"You sitting down?" asked Roslyn figuratively. "Long story short, I'm a flight attendant, okay? Ten years with the same airline."

"Incredible run," said Wes. "You're obviously a dedicated worker."

"Extremely, okay? So, I was floored when, two weeks ago, Mark dismissed me from a Tallahassee flight for quote-unquote wearing club makeup. Club makeup? He's a sixty-two-year-old geezer from Anne Arundel County, Maryland. What's he know about the club?"

Wes's jaw dropped. "Damn. I'm halfway through law school, so I can tell you that's definitely not legal."

Subtly, Wes checked Roslyn's body language. She was sitting with her feet propped on the ledge under the bar. Subtly, he propped his feet up, too, mirroring her—to signal to her subconscious that he was safe, and on her side.

"There's more," said Roslyn. "Last week, he took me off first class. I've served first class for seven years."

"Seven's a holy number. It represents spiritual perfection," declared her friend. That last shot was a doozy.

"Nah, I'm so fucked up about this. Why'd he take you off first class, Ros?" asked Wes, eyes meeting hers with a wide-open, vulnerable earnestness. He was outraged—so his expression was real.

This situation is none of my business, thought Wes, *but I'd love to have a few words with Mark.*

"He said my presence is too distracting for first class." Her voice rose with indignation. "Too distracting? I can't help it that my face is tea, my body's tea, the hair's tea, it's giving Bob Mackie, and he can't even spell 'glamour.'"

"And yesterday, Mark pulled her from flights, altogether," said her friend. "He told her that she was upsetting passengers. And it made more sense for her to work in the back office. At a desk. So, she quit."

Wes felt like he was missing a key piece of this story. What was she doing on these flights that was so distracting? Did she sit on somebody's lap? Steal a puppy from its carrier? What was she guilty of? "I'm sorry, I have to ask why..."

"It's 'cause I'm a trans woman," said Roslyn. "That's it. That's the whole reason."

"But he can't do that." As soon as he said it, he knew how bumblefuck naive he sounded. Obviously, he knew that trans people experienced discriminatory workplace practices every day. But he'd never been face-to-face with someone who'd been through it. His pulse began to race. Involuntarily, his vigilante spirit began to kick in. Maybe he needed a drink, after all.

"If you felt like pursuing it," he said, "this could be a massive lawsuit. The state has laws that protect your rights at work. He's counting on you not to pursue legal action. You could sue the whole airline."

Just then, someone waved at the friend from across the room. He waved back, promised Roslyn and Wes that he'd be right back, and then excused himself. Roslyn was left sitting next to Wes, looking utterly dejected.

Roslyn's reddened eyes narrowed in anger. "Fuck USFlight Airlines."

"And fuck Mark," added Wes.

"Fuck intolerant, small-minded, tacky, right-wing bigots."

"Yo, fuck the entire system, for real."

They clinked glasses again. "You said you had a bad day, too?"

"I did, yeah." And then, he did something he'd never done before. Blinded by his outrage about Mark, Roslyn, and the whole USFlight debacle, he let his guard slip for a moment. And he spoke without thinking. "I think I torched my entire career. But, unlike you, it was all my fault."

"Couldn't have been. You're so sweet! What's your name?"

"Timothy-Joshua." He replied with his cursed brother-in-law's name without blinking.

"What happened to you today, Timothy-Joshua?"

"So, like I said, I'm in law school. But I make extra cash assisting at my old man's law firm. I liked it, you know. I have a solid legal mind. And working for my dad was cool. He's well respected, smart. I was learning a lot." He paused, and then called the bartender. He ordered a vodka double. "Anyway. Long story short, we were hired by a woman who was being stalked. But my dad was busy, so he had me handle the case. And I crossed the line."

"How?"

"He never bothered her again; it doesn't matter."

"How did you cross the line?"

"I surveilled him. I waited for him, outside of her building. I sat in my car, all night, every night, till I caught him. I saw him stand outside of her window, then try to break in through the back. She wasn't there, thank God. And I don't know what he intended to do. I'll never know. None of my business.

"From the car, I took photographs with a long lens. So I'd have clear shots of his face, and of him attempting to break and enter. And then I walked over to him. Calmly. Rationally. I confronted him, you know, told him if he had a problem with her, he needed to solve it. Get out of town, change his name, never come back. But then he started talking crazy, you know. Called her names. Dehumanizing, obscene names. Fucking degrading. And he didn't know her at all. But she'd rejected him. And he couldn't live with it. It was a professional rejection, not even a personal one. Didn't matter. He took it personally."

"Tell me you knocked him out."

"I did knock him out. In one punch. I broke his jaw." The mask had completely fallen. Now, Wes was himself. He wasn't a naive law student. He wasn't on a case. He was finally wrestling with something that had weighed on him, forever. "Then, from the scene, I called the police with an anonymous tip. And I submitted the photographs from an untraceable email. Went back to the car, watched him get arrested. No one knew I called. But my father found out." He took a drink. "You always take an ego hit, getting fired. But when your parent does it, it hits different."

It wasn't just that, though, was it? thought Wes. *Before I even touched him, I made him throw a brick into her window. A brick that I brought. I framed him. Yeah, he'd done it before, but this was tampering with a case. It was false evidence. That's what put my father over the edge. That I cheated. The small fact that I'd let a client move into our office just added fuel to the fire. Phyllis couldn't resist telling him that while he was at the rehabilitation center. Of course he died disappointed in me. I'm sure she made it seem like I'd turned the family business into a brothel.*

"I'm so sorry. Let me guess. Were you in love with her?"

He shook his head. "Nah. Just a close friend. You ever have one of those nights that feel out of time? Like, they don't match with the rest of your life, but it's so good? We had one of those. So, when this guy was saying such vile shit about her, I turned into an aggro, obvious, cliché douche. I just saw red."

"Would you do it again? Even though it hurt your relationship with your dad?"

Wes never thought about this. He didn't allow himself to think this.

"Yes. For her, I'd do it again."

"You're her hero."

"Nah, I don't think so," he said, slowly, working it out in real time. "If what I did was heroic, I'd be proud of it. And I wouldn't have done it in the dark."

Roslyn nodded at this, understanding. "Where is she now, this woman?"

He downed his shot and then looked at her. "Somewhere I can't reach."

"For her sake, I hope she comes out of hiding. Hot and sad is a wicked combination."

"I'm not sad, Ros. I'm contemplative," he corrected with a half smile. "Besides, she's not thinking about me. Believe me." He realized he'd gone too dark, slipped into being too real. Back to Roslyn. Eye on the prize. "If Mark hadn't fired you, would you have quit?"

"King, I'd set fire to the airline, if I could."

"What if I told you that you could."

Suspicion danced on her brow. "You serious right now?"

"I'm serious. You can take them down. And I'll help you."

She sat back in her chair. Elegantly, she folded one leg over the other. "I'm listening."

"I can't promise anything," he started, lowering his voice. "But I know a journalist. The *Times*, *The New Yorker*, *The Atlantic*."

"How?"

"A woman I used to date," he said, which was true.

"I've dated a few writers, too. They're so complicated and take forever to figure out, like sexy little Rubik's Cubes."

"Understatement," quipped Wes. "Anyway, she's always hungry for long-form investigative pieces. Everything you told me tonight is damning. You wanna fuck the system, for real? Let's go."

"You'd introduce me?"

"Consider it done," he promised. "I just need a favor. It's so stupid, though. You probably can't even help."

"Try me, handsome."

"It feels serendipitous that I'm sitting next to you. I'm in the neighborhood 'cause I was just at Fiorello Airport, trying to find information on a USFlight passenger. No luck."

"Yeah, passenger info's classified."

"Right. So I was coming here to blow off some steam, or whatever. But I feel like the universe wanted me to meet you. Nah, but I need this guy's name. Long story, but I need to get in touch with him. He's a partner in a firm, and I'd do anything to work there. I've had a tough year, Ros. I'm ashamed to resort to this. But, between us, I just really need a win." His voice cracked, just enough, on "win."

"Oh, Timothy-Joshua, don't be ashamed," whispered Roslyn. "And you wanna know if I have access to the flight manifest?"

"Do you?" Wes shot her a soft, almost timid look. As if it truly pained him, just to ask.

"Till end-of-day tomorrow, when all my passwords die. And you're lucky, I don't give a good goddamn about giving it to you. Mark messed with the wrong woman. 'Cause I'm not the one. *Or* the two."

Wes's eyes lit up. He'd had to think on his feet, how would he bribe her? Cash would've been the easiest, most obvious route. In fact, he never left the house without two hundred dollars on him, in cash. For bribery emergencies. But he prided himself on never relying on it. He used his wits instead. Besides, cash briberies were tacky. And he was, legitimately, invested about Roslyn's firing. He didn't want to use her. He wanted to help her.

America had basically turned into a barter economy, anyway.

"Here, I can pull it up now, on my work phone." Ros pulled her phone out of her handbag, thumbs flying. Wes told her the flight number, seat number, and time of departure. It took her about five minutes to pull up the flight manifest. She showed him her screen.

"Is this the guy?"

It was a photograph of a man in his midforties, with features identical to the ones Sasha described. And below it, was the following information:

Name: Teo D. Scera
Citizenship: USA, Italia
Sex: Male

A triumphant smile slowly spread across his face.

"That's him," said Wes, shaking Ros's hand. "Thank you."

At home, that night, it took him under an hour to find his address with the info provided. When he did, he stared at it for a while.

565 Broome Street, Apt. 14D
New York, NY 10012

Why did it feel so familiar? He knew that building, somehow. A quick Google Maps search showed him the front of the building. Yes, he knew that massive high-rise—but why? Had he seen it in a movie? Had he been inside? Broome was a major thoroughfare in SoHo, he must've passed it a million times biking through the city or something. Stuck, he decided to take a shower and clear his mind. In the middle of the shower, though, it hit him.

Imani McIntyre. His ex. She lived right next to that building, on the same block. She also happened to be an award-winning journalist. Jesus, did all roads lead back to her?

Wes dashed out of the shower, soaking wet, and called her immediately.

"Imani, what you doing?"

"Shit. Just working on an exposé about a ring of clergy people who embezzle money from churches to fund whorish, decadent lifestyles under different identities. You?"

"Same," he said, not listening. "I need your help."

"What now?"

"You know that high-rise on your block? Didn't you tell me you use the gym in that building?"

"Yeah, the doorman secretly cut me a key if I promised to slide him some homemade edibles every Saturday."

See? he thought. *Barter economy.*

"Can you keep a lookout for me? For a guy named Teo D. Scera. He lives in that building. Find out if he's in town?"

"What's in it for me?"

"I just landed you a huge story for the *Times*. A USFlight Airlines takedown. You in?"

Her laugh carried through the phone. "You know me too well, Detective."

NON-DELIVERY REPORT

To: Sasha.C@Seraphina.org [disabled account]
From: Deirdre.F@Seraphina.org
Subject: Re: Searching for Seat F

Haigh, Sasha! Firstly, I want to thank you for sharing this email with all of us. Even if it was mistakenly sent, it's brought so much joy to our offices here in Dublin. We have a bet going to see who'll find Seat F, first! I was sure it would be me. I'm such a matchmaker. I've married off one brother, and two female friends. So, I got to work on your behalf!

I visited the Italian consulate, hoping that someone there could point me in the right direction. But I was told they didn't have enough information to go on. It was a pretty day, so afterward I went for a walk in a nearby park. I'm strolling along, not paying attention, and BAM. A jogger ran smack into me. The collision was so great, she stumbled backward into a puddle. When I helped her up, I almost lost my breath. She was (and is) a knockout. Being a gentlewoman, I loaned her my jacket. And she promised to return it to me—but only if I'd meet her for matcha. (!!!)

She's the one. When you know, you know. Here's hoping you'll find this much happiness with Seat F.

Deirdre Fitzpatrick
Seraphina Dublin
Supply Chain Lead

Chapter 16

NOSTRADAMUS WAS A PHARMACIST

An entire day had passed since the bench ceremony. But Sasha was still shocked by her behavior. How could she kiss Wes like that, in front of his mother, sister, and Sweet Willy Watson? She'd written and deleted about fifteen texts to Wes. She called him once but chickened out before he answered.

The kiss was supposed to be for show. A sign of solidarity. A message to his family that Wes, and his choices, were valid. But it didn't feel like a fake kiss. It felt natural. The second her lips touched his cheek, she wanted to fast-forward to 1:00 or 2:00 a.m.—*their* time, when they could talk shit about everyone at that party, laugh about it, and sink into their quiet, off-hours world, where there were no mean grieving mothers, emotionally undisciplined sisters, lofty expectations from beyond the grave, or a case to solve. Just the two of them in the dark.

It killed her that Wes thought she was pitying him. She wasn't. She didn't kiss him because she felt sorry for him. She did it because she felt an allegiance with him. And, in that moment, when he was being so maligned, she wanted him to feel it.

It was deeper than that, though. Sasha was just drawn to him. But she had no idea how to explain a feeling she couldn't name.

It was late, but she didn't want another day to pass before she explained all this to him. And she wanted to do it in person. This was a bold proposition—but no bolder than kissing him in the middle of his dead dad's celebration.

But before she could call him, he called her.

"Wes! Hi!"

"Hey. I have something important to tell you. But I can't do it over the phone. Can we meet for coffee in the morning?"

"Why wait? Want to come over?"

"To your place?" Silence. "You mean, right now?"

Maybe it wasn't a great idea. Had she overstepped? After the call and that kiss, she couldn't trust her instincts when it came to Wes.

"Well...I mean, I'm wired, I'm not going to sleep anytime soon. Might as well."

The answer was a fervent *yes*. Sasha told him her address. And then, slowly, she lowered the phone to her side. Stunned. Because that's when it hit her. She'd never had a man, alone, in this apartment.

Shortly after her stalker incident, Sasha moved apartments and never looked back. The only other person who'd visited her new apartment was Destiny. No men. And this was intentional. Home is the place you should feel the safest. Protected from the world, shielded. When your safe place has been invaded—and with such ease—the natural response was to barricade yourself. Make your home truly impenetrable. It started by moving to the seventeenth floor of a doorman building. It ended in not inviting anyone into your home.

Sasha forgot what it was like to have anyone else in her home. She stood in place, staring at the mirror above her couch. She was wearing baggy sweat shorts, a men's tank top, and her hair swept back in a white bandana. She looked like a backup dancer for Aaliyah. Her first impulse was to rip off the bandana, flat-iron the creases in her bob, and change into something less Y2K.

But why? This was *her* home. This was what Sasha was wearing in her home.

By the same token, there was sawdust, loose wires, and power tools strewn about her kitchen—but that's because she'd been rewiring her lights for the past three weeks. Was she supposed to hurriedly tidy that up, too? She was tired of putting on a front to please everyone. It was exhausting, trying to control the way people saw her. *I'm glamorous, I'm smart, I'm pulled together.* To what end? Her whole life, she'd been polished like a gem—as if a flawless image translated into a well-edited, well-lived, precious existence protected from the evils of the world. It didn't guarantee anything but great selfies.

Sasha didn't feel like putting on a presentable outfit or sprucing up her kitchen. So she didn't. And the relief was exhilarating. It was a breakthrough moment in a season full of them. Slowly, Sasha's chains were loosening.

A year ago, she only left her home for a few work lunches a month. This week, she'd left the confines of her apartment almost every day. Even if for a moment—even if just to grab a cupcake. And tonight, an actual flesh-and-blood man was coming over, but it was okay. He wasn't the stalker. He was Wes, who saved her. Wes, who she trusted. It was fine. She was fine.

Sasha opened her eyes. She breathed in, held it for thirty seconds, and breathed out. Gingerly, she walked over to her couch and sat down. She placed her hands on her lap and waited.

About thirty minutes later, the buzzer jolted her out of her seat. She hopped up and pressed the buzzer by her door. Before she knew it, she heard the knock. Quickly, she checked her reflection in the mirror again. She stood up a little taller, patted her bandana, and stepped back, opening her door.

And there he stood. Wes... the thirty-two-year-old college student? Why was he wearing so much NYU merch? Didn't he go to Hampton?

"I would've met you on campus, you know," she joked.

"It's a disguise. Long story." He leaned against her doorframe and swiveled his cap to the back. NYU LAW was embroidered above the snap. "I can pull off sleep-deprived postgraduate student, though, right?"

"You do. It's kind of disturbing."

Wes cocked his chin in her direction, a teasing glint in his eye. "How was your visit to *106 & Park*?"

She huffed out a laugh. "This is my home repairs look!"

"No one should look this cute doing home repairs," he mumbled, almost to himself.

"What'd you say?"

"Not important."

They stood in the doorway for a moment, stuck in a liminal, not-here, not-there space. *The kiss, the kiss, bring it up, hurry up,* was practically running through Sasha's mind on a ticker tape. But now that Wes was standing in front of her, everything she'd planned to say—every excuse, every apology—dissolved into thin air. And he was completely unreadable.

In lieu of panicking, she simply pretended it hadn't happened. Flashing a slightly forced smile, she welcomed him in. "Come on in, NYU."

Wes was in her home. For real. Even as they sat in her colorful, eclectic living room—Wes manspreading on her couch; Sasha perched, somewhat stiffly, on a side chair—she struggled to wrap her brain around this fact. It *felt* like he'd been all over her home. While on the phone, Sasha had spoken to him from her bed, the bathtub, the kitchen island. But now, he was here in the flesh, peering around her space with barely masked wonder—like he was peeking into one of those dioramas from fifth-grade science class.

Seat F was the reason Wes was back in her life. Seat F should've been top of mind when she saw Wes. But, oh, he wasn't. Not when Wes showed up at 11:00 p.m., looking like someone's too-fine boyfriend they should never allow out of the house.

Right now, he was studying a few books he'd brought over from her bookcase. *Caribemotion: Living the Dominican Republic*, *Being La Dominicana: Race and Identity in the Visual Culture of Santo Domingo.*

"This cover is beautiful," he said, lightly running his fingers along the vibrant typography of *The Classics Collection: Santo Domingo.*

"I love that coffee-table book. It's one of my favorites."

"Why not display it?"

"I don't know, it feels performative. I'm not from DR. And my Spanish is so embarrassing. I don't want anyone to think I'm claiming a culture I haven't experienced." She laughed a little. "Not that anyone ever comes here."

"I get it. Though, as someone who is here," he said, raising his brows pointedly, "I don't think you look performative. You're proud of your heritage. It adds another layer to you."

"Thank you," she said shyly. Which was odd. She never felt shy in Wes's presence.

"Sounds like you need to book a trip, soon."

"Maybe," she said, taking the book back from him.

"Your apartment is so perfect." His eyes scanned her living room, in obvious awe. "It looks like a movie set."

"I'm a bit of a perfectionist. In my first rental, I bought coasters to be fancy. I was eating dinner on a cardboard box, but my glass had a coaster."

Subtly, Sasha inhaled the scent of the Coastal Cypress candle burning on the coffee table. She couldn't allow herself to forget why she reconnected with Wes in the first place. He was here to find her fated flight boyfriend. The man who was also, simultaneously, searching for her, too. But her exchange with Seat F was starting to feel like a dream. Hazy and sweet, but slipping away, just out of reach. Sasha needed to see him. She needed to touch him, to ensure that he was real.

If Wes didn't find Seat F soon, she couldn't be held responsible for her actions.

"Your friend messaged me," he was telling her, while munching on a pretzel stick. Neither of them had a real appetite that late, so Sasha had grabbed a bag of pretzels and two cans of Pellegrino from the pantry.

"What friend?" It popped out of her mouth before she remembered that she only had one. "Destiny?"

"Destiny, yeah. She wants to add me to her dating database." He chuckled a little at this, shaking his head. "I never considered a matchmaker, but maybe I need one."

"I'm so mad at that girl. I'm sorry, I told her not to do that."

"Why? Don't gatekeep her services."

"I just don't think you need a matchmaker. You don't strike me as someone struggling to find a woman."

"Well..." He paused, thinking it over. "No, I can't say that I've struggled. But I've never met the right woman. The one."

"But you're also not looking. Didn't you tell me you're not into relationships right now?" Sasha asked this in the most nonchalant way possible, as if she hadn't committed his statement to memory.

"I'm not aggressively looking. But the door is cracked." Wes chose his words carefully. "I mean, isn't everyone? I don't want to spend Sunday nights alone. I want to have a best friend who I'm desperate to fuck and feed and take care of and travel with and spend the rest of my life learning. I'd be lucky to find it."

He glanced at her, almost shyly. Sasha offered a tight smile, and then quickly reached for the pretzel bag. She hadn't blinked the entire time he spoke. His words reverberated through her, landing in some faraway place, untouched and hidden. An inconvenient ache throbbed between her thighs. Were his words sexy, or was it the way he said them? Or was her stomach fluttering because she pictured herself as the object of the fucking, feeding, and best-friending?

Everything he named was what she wanted, too.

With Seat F, she reminded herself. *It's what you want with Seat F. This man is not available. Don't go backward. Life only moves in one direction, remember?*

"You seem surprised," he said quietly. "You're not the only one tired of doing life alone."

"No, no of course not." She grabbed a handful of pretzels and settled back in her chair. "And I'm not just tired of being alone. I'm tired of being scared. I just want to trust again. I want to be normal."

"It takes time. It's a trite thing to say, but it's true."

"I just feel stupid. I wasn't beaten or abused." She held out her wrist, uncharacteristically uncovered. "The only injury I sustained, I did to myself! So many stalking survivors have had it worse. Why am I so traumatized?"

He relaxed back against her pillows. "What would make you feel safe?"

"Outside of screening everyone I interact with? Being intimidating, maybe. Knowing how to fight. Men don't have to worry about things like this. What a luxury it must be, having physicality and strength on your side."

Wes popped another pretzel in his mouth. "Right, you told me on the phone the other night. When you asked me to train you."

Sasha's stomach seized. A blazing flush spread over her cheeks and chest. God, the call. She prayed that her face didn't give anything away.

"I took you seriously, you know. I even bought a set of new punch mitts." He cleared his throat. "Okay, don't take this the wrong way…"

"Oh no."

"…but boxing might help in other ways, too. You know. Orgasmically."

"Oh God." She dropped her face in her hands. "Why is it so easy to talk about this shit on the phone, but not in person?"

"Don't be embarrassed for saying what's on your mind. Look, there's real scientific data suggesting that regular cardio enhances your sex life."

She grabbed the pretzel bag from him. "I don't want to talk about this. I didn't invite you here to discuss my orgasm challenges."

He bit down on a smile.

"You're loving this, aren't you?" she said. "You think this is funny."

"I don't! I'm just trying to help. I was also thinking, maybe you're focusing too much on *sex* sex. Maybe think about what turns you on outside of actual sex."

"If you say 'sex' again, I'll kill you."

"I'm serious, Sasha. Think about it. What turns you on. Just tell me."

"I don't know!" She threw up her hands. "Ugh. Okay, let me think. The back of a man's neck, between his shoulder blades? Listening to someone nerd out on something. I'm not just saying this, but I think barbecue ribs are sexy. I'm dying to try yours. But don't make fun of me, I eat ribs with a fork."

He stared at her, horrified. "That's bone-chilling. Take it back."

Giggling, she kept racking her brain. Sasha had to admit; this was sort of fun. "Oh, and I love when a man cracks open a soda can, or a beer can . . . anything like that."

"A soda can? Oh, you're a freak for real."

"You know what else is sexy?" Grabbing the pretzels and Pellegrinos, she stood up and gestured for Wes to follow her. "Come with me, you have to see this."

Sasha padded through the dining room to the brand-new island, in the middle of her open concept kitchen. Lightly, she ran her fingertips over the smooth oak surface. "I think this kitchen island is sexy. Is that weird?"

"No, it's niche." Wes smoothed his palm along the surface. "You don't want anybody who doesn't think this kitchen island is sexy. This wood is perfect. And the varnish looks like salted caramel, or something. Did . . . did you make this?"

She beamed, proudly. "You can tell?"

"I can. It's very you." He nodded appreciatively. "I'm no expert, but I did a ton of research on wood pieces when I decorated my apartment. This work is incredible, Sasha. I'll teach you how to box, if you teach me how to build furniture."

"Depends on how soon you solve my case," she joked. "And speaking of . . ."

"Sorry, hold on." Performatively locking eyes with Sasha, he slowly cracked open his can of Pellegrino. It made a loud, satisfying hissing sound. She burst out laughing.

"You couldn't resist, huh?"

"Resist what?" He took a big, lusty gulp, a mischievous smile playing on his lips.

"I should never have told you."

"You should *always* tell me."

They were laughing, joking, but so much was hanging between

them. The kiss. The call. The electric charge in the air that they were both trying desperately to ignore. They danced on the edge of it, where it was safe and uncomplicated. Until, as history showed, she slipped up and took things too far. As evidenced by that nonconsensual orgasmic call, and that (also nonconsensual) ill-timed kiss, something about Wes Dane made her engage in risky behavior.

"Hey." She walked to his side of the island, so they were face-to-face, standing in front of each other. "I'm sorry about your dad's ceremony. The kiss. I never should've done that."

Wes let out a slight, barely audible exhale. Clearly, he'd been waiting for her to address it. "No need. Apology accepted. But can I ask why you did it?"

"I didn't like the way your mom was talking about you. I felt protective of you, defensive. Wes, you're one of the best people I know. Granted, I don't know you *that* well. But ever since we met at your office, you've been nothing but a kind, empathetic, understanding friend. And you *are* a catch. But I shouldn't have interfered."

Wes's brows furrowed inward. "You see how it made me look, though, right?"

"How did you look?"

"Everyone at that party asked me who you were. I insist we're just friends. And then you kiss me out of nowhere? I looked like a liar, an unserious person. It was embarrassing." He paused. "Generally, I don't care what anyone thinks of me. But there, it mattered."

A wave of nauseating regret pooled in her stomach. "No, I get it. I don't know what came over me."

"It was definitely a bold swing."

"It was, and I wasn't thinking."

"When you don't think," he said pointedly, "all hell breaks loose."

And then, there was a palpable energy switch in the air. It was as if a veil dropped, and everything they'd been holding back came flooding to the surface.

Sasha winced. "Listen, I feel terrible. I made a mistake, but my intentions were pure."

"Pure. Interesting." Buying time, he took another drink of Pellegrino, then set the can down. "Can I ask you something? How are you going to feel when I track him down?"

"Happy. Thrilled. Ecstatic. Why?"

He cocked his head slightly, studying her. "Yeah, you look ecstatic."

"What's that supposed to mean?"

"Nothing. I just urge you to be realistic about this case. Because you will meet him."

Sasha let out a nervous chuckle. "Um… I know? It's why I hired you. I want to meet him. What are you implying?"

"Are you serious about finding this guy? Or is this about escaping into a fun little adventure? Is the chase the thing?"

It wasn't just the condescending words that took Sasha by surprise. It was Wes's tone. He sounded fed up, almost angry. Why did he think she wasn't taking the case seriously? And he had no right to question her motivations.

"Excuse me?" She took a step closer to him. "Are you insinuating that my decision to track down a nameless Italian who's possibly my soulmate was a flippant decision?"

He let out a short chuckle. "Repeat that sentence, and you tell me."

"Don't laugh at me. I didn't come to this decision lightly. I'm an adult, okay? I'm a serious person. I have a matching luggage set and life insurance!"

"You're a serious person? Since when is a manicurist qualified to predict the future?"

Indignant, she grasped at straws trying to find a comeback. "Why would being a manicurist preclude her from being a mystic? *Nostradamus was a pharmacist!*"

Wes looked at her with utter bafflement. "How can you be such a realist and so whimsical at the same time? You're the most confusing person, Sasha. It's like splitting an atom, trying to reason with you."

"I'm being whimsical on purpose, Wes. Because I'm *not* whimsical. I'm a thinker, a planner, a worrier. I'm forcing this, because, yes, I do want an adventure. Is that so wrong? Who knows if we'll be here tomorrow. I wanted to take a chance. Is that so wrong?"

"I just want to make sure this is what you want."

"I swear to God, if you condescend to me one more time in my own kitchen..." She paused, calmed her breathing. "Whether I'm sure or not is none of your business."

"What if you're putting yourself in danger again?"

Incensed now, she took another step toward him. He remained unmoving, his energy tight as a drum. "How *dare* you. You, of all people, know what I've been through. You're gonna weaponize my trauma against me? Try to talk me out of it for fake concern about my safety?"

Wes flinched, his cool beginning to evaporate. "Fake concern? Fake? What would I get out of pretending to care?"

"But why *do* you care so much?" she yelled, losing it. "My reasons are none of your business. Your job is to find him. Period."

"I'm speaking to you as a professional," he seethed, each word taut with tension. "There are too many unknowns. You meeting him doesn't feel safe, Sasha."

Sasha paused, her eyes narrowing. "You know what? I was joking before. But I do think you're jealous."

Wes stilled. The clench of his jaw was the only sign that her words affected him. "Why do you need me to be jealous so badly? Are you trying to get a rise out of me?"

"No! I don't need..."

"Fuck this," he muttered. In two breaths, he was standing just inches in front of her. He planted both hands on the kitchen island, on either side of her hips. With a small gasp, she craned her head up to meet his gaze. His expression was pure heat, burning her alive.

"I'm only gonna say this once." His voice was tense, strained. Like he was trying to cage something wild in him. "You understand? And then we bury it forever."

She nodded, her head swimming.

"I'm not jealous. I'm perplexed. I'm fucking *baffled*. Because if I were him on that flight, and you were looking up at me with that face and those eyes and that smart little mouth and that stitched-together toughness barely masking vulnerability? You'd have left knowing a lot more than my name."

His confession knocked Sasha silly. It wasn't just the words, it was how he said them—gruff, vulnerable, angry. The words poured out of Wes in a molten rush, like they'd been pent up forever, too powerful to deny one second longer. She drank in his face—heavy-lidded bedroom eyes and a mouth she ached to taste.

"I... I didn't know..."

"Yeah, you did. Shut up."

Forcefully, Wes slid his hand up into her hair, grabbing a fistful and tilting her head back. Without giving her a moment to collect herself, he crashed his lips against Sasha's, drawing her into the hottest, rawest, most erotic kiss she'd ever had in her life. It was obliterating. Stunned, she whimpered into his mouth—*his sinful fucking mouth*—lost in the dizzying power of this kiss. And it was so delicious, she could barely kiss him back. He ravished her.

And the voltage stunned them both. Together, they toppled clumsily back against the table, Wes on top of her, his erection thumping against her cunt, only separated by a few layers of fabric—and they kissed through it all. With a ragged groan, he gripped her hair tighter, pulling her even closer in a way that felt territorial. *Final.* And she responded with a trembly swoon, going limp in his arms.

He'd kissed the truth out of her.

Roughly, he pushed up her shirt, unclipped her bra, and stared at her. "Jesus, Sasha," he groaned, drawing a nipple into his mouth, kneading the other with greedy fervor. She rubbed against him, squeezing his dick through his pants. God, he was big. He was *huge*. She couldn't get to it fast enough. Had she ever wanted anyone this nakedly, this shamelessly?

The next few seconds were a frenzy. Wes tore down her shorts; she yanked up his shirt. Somehow, her panties went flying and landed atop her Keurig. As he kicked off his pants, Sasha reached down into a side drawer on the island and pulled out a condom. Too far gone to interrogate why this woman kept condoms in her kitchen, he held both of her wrists over her head, in one hand. She was pinned beneath him. Helpless. This was exactly where he wanted her. They were forehead to forehead, now. Chests heaving. Breathing in sync. With the smallest smile of satisfaction, he captured her mouth with a possessive growl. He kissed her slower, this time. Dirtier. She moaned into his mouth as he teased her with his dick—running the tip up and down her folds, rubbing it against her clit, teasing them both until it was too much. Till she gasped out, "*please*," and he had no choice.

Wes thrust into her. Deeply. And he stayed there, slowly grinding against her. She cried out in pleasure so intense, so shocking, her brain went hazy. She tried to meet his thrust, but he held her firm.

"Sasha," he said, calling her to attention. Grounding her.

"Yes?" she breathed out.

"That call. Did you need to hear my voice? To get off? Or did you need me to tell you to do it?"

Her eyes flew open. And then, still impossibly deep inside her, Wes slid his free hand down between them, lazily stroking her clit with his thumb. Pleasure surged so fast, it was scary.

"I don't kn-know what you're talking about."

"You want me to spell it out?" Wes's mouth was at her ear, his voice sounding as tortured as she felt. "'Cause I could talk about how I heard your breathing change. How you moaned. I could hear you, Sasha. Did you think I couldn't?"

So he knew. He really did know.

"Answer me," he ordered, stroking her clit faster. She moaned, trembling uncontrollably now, and he held her wrists tighter. Teasingly, he ran his tongue along her bottom lip, then nipped it. His mouth was so delicious. His thumb was torturing her. She was desperate for friction, dying for him to fuck her.

"I don't know why I called," she cried out. "I just needed you."

"Say it again."

"I needed you."

"To do what?"

He pulled out then, leaving her desperate, gasping, wanting. *Jesus.*

"I needed you to make me come. Wes, *please*..."

"Fucking say it again."

"I needed you to make me come."

"Good. Remember it."

And then, he slammed into her. Over and over, he fucked her like this, deep and steady and hard, through an orgasm that left her in pieces. And when he followed, seconds later, he buried his face in her hair, groaning out a curse, reveling in this feeling, this woman. On stolen time.

When it was over, he carefully unwrapped her legs from his hips and pulled up his trousers, backing away from the island. The room, suddenly, went cold. Struggling to catch her breath, she propped herself on her elbows.

"I need to tell you why I'm here." His voice was unsteady, gruff.

"What?" she panted, confused.

"I know his name."

She was too fucked-out to think. "Whose name?"

He handed her a piece of paper, on official Dane & Son Detective Agency letterhead. On it, he'd scrawled a name in black ink:

Teo D. Scera

She lay there, sprawled on her kitchen island, puffy-lipped and trembling. Her mouth felt bruised, her pussy was throbbing—her whole body was on fire from his hands, his mouth, his dick. But another man's name was clenched in her fist. Seat F. Stunned, she looked up at Wes.

"Happy to be of service," he said in an emotionless tone.

And then he left.

Chapter 17

CLEVER, KIND, AND BEAUTIFUL

Sasha was elated, conflicted, sore, stunned, and exceedingly well fucked. She had it *bad*. She dragged her ass to bed without changing into pajamas, because her clothes smelled like Wes. She curled up with the sweatshirt he'd loaned her on the library steps, teddy-bear style.

Did she light the Coastal Cypress candle?

No. Notably, she did not.

She was in a blissed-out haze. As she drifted into sleep, the only thing on her mind was Wes. His hands, his words. His easy dominance. His searingly erotic mouth; his touch that was both worshipful and punishing. The stealth way that he was always one step ahead of her. Sasha actually thought she'd gotten away with that Rose call. But he was a detective, after all. How could she think he wouldn't know? Wes had her number. He knew where her deepest vulnerabilities lay. Of course he'd known, all this time, that she was desperate for him. Because the phone thing? That was shamelessly desperate behavior. And so was gasping his name as she came, twice, on her beloved kitchen island. Where she'd minced vegetables for gumbo prep just six hours prior.

The only other thing on her mind? Seat F's name. Teo. *Teo.* It didn't seem real. And it hadn't escaped her that Wes had punctuated their client-detective situationship consummation with that reveal. Pretty dramatic, even for him. Did he do it on purpose, just to torture her?

Of course he didn't. They got carried away before he had a chance to tell her why he'd come over, in the first place.

But just as sleep overtook her, she remembered the expression on his face when he left—an uneasy mix of triumph and defeat. What was he thinking?

She awoke with a start the next morning, the question still fresh in her thoughts. Had he called? Jolting upright, she reached for her phone on the nightstand and saw that, yes, he'd texted.

Wes: GM. I overstepped last night. I'm
sorry. Can I take you to coffee today?
We have some case details to discuss.
Brown Butter at 11?

Slowly, she sank back down into her pillows, but it felt like plummeting from a great height. She wasn't sure what she'd wanted to hear from Wes, but it wasn't an apology. His words felt so removed, so short. Clearly, he wanted to put last night in the past. Maybe he was right. Their situation was a mess, from top to bottom. And they'd just made it messier.

Swallowing down the lump in her throat, she nodded at the phone, as if it was Wes. And then texted back.

Sasha: Yes. See you then.
And no need for apologies.
We both overstepped! xoxo

* * *

At 10:50 a.m., Sasha hopped out of an Uber on Tompkins Avenue, across the street from the rustic-casual Brown Butter café. Ever since her anxiety diagnosis, she liked to arrive early to events and meetings, to give herself extra time to prepare—regulate her breathing, hydrate, psych herself up for being social. She figured she'd just order a coffee and wait for Wes at the bar. Turns out, there'd be no prep time. Because Wes was already seated out front in one of the café's turquoise cocktail tables. With a woman. A stunning woman.

Sasha went rigid; utterly unable to move. Who was he with? Certainly, Wes could hang out with whomever he wanted. They weren't dating; they weren't even supposed to be sleeping together. But she still felt an instant punch of hurt and jealousy—neither of which needed to make sense. Wes was the first man who'd been inside her home, *inside her*, in too long to count. She felt safe enough with him to lose herself. To her, last night didn't feel casual. It felt meaningful.

And another thing—Wes knew she was showing up in ten minutes. Did he time this encounter on purpose? Did he *want* Sasha to see him with that hot tamale?

Luckily for her, Wes's back was facing away from the street. So, he didn't see Sasha or her facial journey, which ranged from shock to horror, and back again. She tried to shake it off and think of this from a progressive perspective. They were adults. They had no ownership over each other, and Wes was free to engage in a coffee tête-à-tête with anyone he damned well pleased.

All salient points, she thought. *Now I just have to believe them.*

Sasha straightened her spine and strode toward them. The good (terrible?) news was, Wes and the woman were so lost in conversation, neither noticed her approaching.

Wes leaned over the table, looking effortlessly cool in a breezy, short-sleeve button-down and linen trousers. His body language projected "eager listener," while the mystery woman's gave off "power position." She leaned back in her chair, sultrily, with her legs crossed and her bejeweled fingers fluffing her coily hair.

But as Sasha got closer, she realized she wasn't just any woman. She was Imani McIntyre. Notable journalist and seductress-about-town, Imani McIntyre. What the hell was Wes doing with her?

Sasha hadn't ever met her, personally, but she'd mingled in her vicinity at various Black women in media conferences—and a few nightspots in the late twenty teens. Everyone knew who she was, anyway. A legendary journalist. It girl. Rare nepo kid who surpassed the success of her famous parents (sports journalist "Big Mac" McIntyre, and abstract artist Virginia Tse). Imani wrote long-form exposés about corporate raiders, crooked politicians, murderous millionaires, and such. Thanks to her juicy tell-all writing style, Imani's pieces usually went viral.

Also, she was just cool. She oozed it, without seeming to try. Today, she wore a bra top and a low-slung kilt with work boots. Fern tattoos snaked down her abs. And whatever she just said had Wes laughing his ass off.

"Hey, hey, hey," trilled Sasha with fake breeziness, slipping off her white sunglasses. She'd felt so cute in her red shorts set, but next to Imani's abbed-up energy, she felt like a discarded Shirley Temple at last call.

Wes and Imani looked up from their conversation. For a split second, he looked rattled. But he recovered quickly, flashing a smile and standing up to give Sasha a (demonstratively) friendly hug.

"Here, you can have my seat," he said, pulling out the chair for her. He grabbed another one from an empty table and pulled in between the two women. "Sasha, meet my friend Imani. Imani, this is Sasha."

Calling on all her Hollywood schmoozing experience, Sasha

buried her raging discomfort and beamed at Imani. "Great to meet you! Wes, did I get the time wrong? We were meeting at eleven, right?"

Imani sipped from her straw, studying both with a removed, eagle-eyed calm. She also seemed to be floating on a substance not available on the menu.

"No, yeah, we said eleven," answered Wes. "But Imani surprised me. Out of nowhere."

Sasha picked up an amiable-but-strained tone from "out of nowhere." Wes seemed to be signaling to her that Imani's appearance wasn't planned. At least that's what she hoped. Sometimes delusion looked like no other good ideas.

"Oh nooo, sis," wailed Imani, clutching her chest. "I should've asked Wes if it was cool before I just showed up here."

"Trust, it's cool, cool, cool," said Sasha, pretending not to care. "The more the merrier."

"You know, we *do* know each other," said Imani in a conspiratorial tone. "Remember the kickback at that rapper's house after Le Bain? Like ten years ago?"

"Yeah? Which rapper?" asked Wes, also pretending not to care.

"Oh, it's all a haze," answered Imani. "I was on deadline and fried, and I was trying to find a bedroom to crash in. And I pass the kitchen, right? And I see this girl, legs sticking out from under the sink. I was like, sis, you good under there?"

"Wait, I remember this," said Sasha. "I think I said something like, 'This faucet's on sicko mode. I'm fixing the pipes.' In 2018, I described everything as 'sicko mode.' That was you? I couldn't see who I was talking to."

"Well, I thought I'd hallucinated you, until someone told me your name. It was my ketamine era. You understand."

Sasha, who'd never tried a single recreational drug, nodded in solidarity.

"Okay, but who was the rapper?" Wes was ignored, yet again.

"I'm a huge fan," Imani told Sasha. "You cast that HBO movie about the Bahamian anesthesiologist who moonlights as a sex worker and falls for her client, the recently widowed secretary of state? I saw your interview on the aftershow."

Sasha couldn't help but be flattered. And for a moment, she backburned her flaming ball of confusion over Wes. "No, I'm a fan of *yours*. One of my favorite reads of the past three years was your exposé on the Black shaman who married that Norwegian princess."

Imani chuckled and tossed back her coils. "Ahhh yes. One of my favorite pieces. Would you believe I got tipped off from a leak on Reddit?"

"Well, where there's Reddit, there's fire."

Sasha was turning on the charm. Putting on a bit of a show for Wes, showing him that this bizarre situation didn't faze her, whatsoever. Nor did last night. Nor did any of the unease between them. She was cool as a cucumber.

Imani laughed. "Aren't you an adorable little bean sprout?"

"I'm... five seven. But I'll take it."

Wes cleared his throat. "I love this reunion so much. So, so much. But Sasha, I owe you an explanation. I was here for our date—"

"Not a date. A meeting," corrected Sasha.

"Right. And Imani was in the vicinity and surprised me. Spontaneously."

"Spontaneity is so important." Imani flipped her hair again, sending the scent of French cigarettes and tuberose across the table. "The downfall of social culture is planned meetups."

Sasha started to laugh, but then she saw Imani was serious. "Well, that's certainly one of them."

"Wes was already on my mind, because he called me yesterday. So, this morning I'm visiting my eco-friendly psychopharmacologist up the street, when I see his location. He was only three minutes away! I had to pull up."

As Imani talked, Sasha could practically see Wes's soul leave his body.

"I'm glad you brought up that call," he jumped in. "Sasha, the reason I called Imani concerns you, too..."

"You have his location?" Sasha asked Imani with a tight smile.

"Oh, I never check it. It's leftover from when we were lovers."

It was like the whole world blinked at once. Sasha cut her eyes at Wes. Wes shifted in his seat, looking puckish. He let out an awkward, forced chuckle. "It was years ago."

"Wes was at a low point. Depressed, sleeping for days. I was worried, so I made him share it."

"I wasn't depressed, I had Covid. Let's not make a bad thing worse." Wes flagged down their waitress and preemptively ordered Sasha a white wine.

"It wasn't Covid, it was melancholia. You'd just gotten fired from the agency. You were a shut-in. Every time I saw you, you had melting ice in your palms. So odd. Anyway, I forgot I had your location." She wagged her finger at him like a schoolmarm. "You think I want to know where *you* are at all times? You're so bad."

Wes rolled his eyes at Imani—then, she dissolved into husky laughter, resting her hand on his arm. A nauseating wave of jealousy rolled through Sasha's stomach.

She tried to look unbothered. "Were you two boyfriend and girlfriend?"

"She's so cute," said Imani, looking at Wes with amusement. "Imagine me believing in girlfriends and boyfriends?"

"We dated briefly," explained Wes. "Extremely briefly. An extremely long time ago."

"I don't believe in labels," said Imani. "I'm solo-polyamorous."

"Isn't that a label?" asked Sasha lightly.

Imani floated past this question. "In poly relationships, you're in one primary couple, and all other sexual partners are secondary. Same with solo-poly, except that the primary couple is you with *yourself.* I have lovers, but they're all secondary. You see?" She winked. "I'm all about freedom and hedonism and safe words."

"In summation, solo-polyamory is a pseudo-intellectual label for fuckboy," explained Wes, eager to wrap up this portion of the program. "Anyway, the reason I called Imani..."

"Chill, Wes." Imani shot Sasha a mischievous look. "Speaking of safe words, what's yours? You can't truly know someone until you've learned their safe word."

"Will I need one for this conversation?" Sasha laughed nervously.

"She doesn't have a safe word," interrupted Wes. "Imani, enough with your little tests. You always do this."

Always? How many times had they been in a similar situation—sharing coffee in their cozy, intimate bubble, when a random girl shows up, blowing the equation? Sasha felt like an interloper. She felt like walls were closing in on her, even though she was outside. She and Wes were so intimate just ten hours before, and now she was seated across a bohemian bombshell who seemed to know Wes in a way that she never would.

And then, Competitive Sasha arose from the depths of her personality. She wasn't going to let this textbook cool girl throw her off her game.

"Wes, why do you think I don't have a safe word?" asked Sasha coolly.

"No reason," started Wes. "You just don't strike me as a safe-word girl."

"Oh really? And what kind of girl is that?"

"One with risky kinks," he answered.

Offended, she huffed out a short laugh. "I think you know I'm not a prude."

"Then, tell us your word!" prodded Imani. "Come onnn, it's a safe space."

Sasha swallowed, racking her brain for a word.

"Filibuster."

Imani clapped her hands together with delight.

"Filibuster is bananas," grumbled Wes, trying to hide the amusement tugging at his lips.

"She's so clever, Wes!"

"I know," he said shortly. "She's clever, kind, and beautiful. But can I *please* get to why we're all here. Sasha, I didn't, uh, get a chance to tell you last night. But I have an update. I know where Teo lives."

Sasha was stuck on "clever, kind, and beautiful." Did he really just describe her that way, so casually? Her stomach fluttered, and she prayed she didn't look as giddy as she felt.

Imani tapped on the table in front of Sasha. "Wes found your dude's address."

"Wait, what?" Sasha sucked in a sharp gulp of air. She missed this piece of information, entirely. Whether it was losing her attention span, her decorum, or her panties, she always got lost in his presence. "You found him? When? How?"

It felt so anticlimactic, Wes dropping such important information at Brown Butter. In front of an audience. Why wouldn't Imani go away?

"Hold on, I need to prepare for this." She whipped a lip gloss out of her purse, applying it with no mirror. "Now I'm ready."

"You sure? Should we ask them to dim the lights?" Wes was going for light sarcasm but landed closer to "pouty."

"Tell me."

"He lives at 565 Broome. In SoHo."

Sasha felt a jolt. Teo had a name and an address. He was an actual person. She'd been waiting for signs from the universe that he wasn't a figment of her imagination—and these things made him real. Identifiable. And after waiting for weeks, hearing these details was surreal.

And, after last night, hearing *Wes* deliver them was downright disorienting.

"Teo D. Scera." Sasha said it again, stretching out the vowels. Then, she repeated it, this time with an Italian accent. "Teo D. Scera, who lives on Broome. Wow. This is real. He's real. I'm so relieved."

"I've already tracked him down," said Wes. "It's why I called Imani. She lives on the same block and knows the doorman."

Sasha let out an "ohhh," finally understanding why Imani was there.

"It's risky to discuss these things on the phone," explained Wes. "So, I wanted to meet her in person. But later today, obviously. After you and I talked."

"Wait. Wait, wait, wait," said Sasha, trying to wrap her brain around this new revelation. Teo. Teo. She had to practice saying it. She drew her wrist up to her nose—the scent of cypress lingered. She was brought back to the flight. Their connection.

One step closer, she thought. *I'm probably just stunned. Processing so much information.*

"Have you ever seen him, Imani?" She turned to face her. "Probably just under six feet tall? Piercing, irresistible green eyes?"

Wes grabbed a piece of French bread from the basket, and bit into it like he wanted to fight someone.

"Oh him? I know who he is. He stays in the gym. He's strict with it. I know jujitsu, so I can tell when people have impeccable movement patterns." She smiled mysteriously. "Jujitsu practice taught me to access my divine feminine in a unique way. Authentic womanhood is falling in love with the way you move, don't you think?"

"Sure," said Sasha, downing her white wine.

"I met Wes in jujitsu class. He thought he was a skirmishing expert because he used to box." She tsk'ed at him. "It was cute beating you that one time."

"Beat me? You tricked me."

"My bra was loose. Who knew a rogue nipple could topple a man's equilibrium?"

Can I use my safe word now? wondered Sasha. She felt small and inconsequential in the face of their spicy shared history.

"Anyway, Sasha, your plane guy's extremely into core work and squat thrusts." Imani winked. "Bodes well for you."

"Let's stick to details that pertain to the case," interrupted Wes.

"But you allowed the rogue nipple anecdote?" Sasha scoffed.

"He carries himself like a worldly, wealthy man. I've only seen him in gym clothes, but it looks like nothing wrinkled or synthetic has ever touched his skin. And he's got a fascinating face. He's like if Adam Driver, Rami Malek, John Turturro, and young Al Pacino had a baby."

"That's a whole lotta nose," muttered Wes. "Long shot, but any idea when he's in town?"

"No, but the last time I saw him was two weeks ago. We even chopped it up a bit."

Sasha sat up straight, as if yanked upward by a celestial string. "*You spoke to him!*"

"I did. I'd just returned from a work trip to Accra. We were talking about how low-budget American flights are. He mentioned taking a flight with terrible service, but the upside was he met a woman. Was that you?"

Sasha gasped. This was real. *He* was real. "He was talking about me!"

Wes, all business, focused his attention on Imani. "Do me a favor, hang out in the gym more often. And call me immediately the next time you see him."

"Say less," Imani responded. "I owe you, after you leaked the USFlight Airlines story."

Sasha wondered what they were talking about. It was like a secret tie that bound them, a connection she couldn't reach. And then, she felt her chest start to tighten with anxiety. She felt territorial. And she knew it was a childish, unearned emotion. But just the night before, they were ravenous for each other. Emotionally, she was still there.

"Oh shit, gotta run," said Imani, checking her phone. "Wes, you know that piece I told you about on the phone?"

He glanced, quickly, at Sasha. "No, what piece?"

"It was late, you were probably half-asleep. Anyway, I need to go to Luxembourg—just got a tip that one of the church robbers was last seen there. Ugh, Europe in June is *the ghetto*. But I can visit my mom's artist flat in London, after."

Wes sipped his water. "She's still doing Muppets portraiture using her fingerprints?"

"Toe prints." Imani stared at her phone, lost in thought. "Hmm. The target churches are always in small European villages, with no resources to launch an investigation. Where in Luxembourg would he be?"

Sasha was reeling. Imani and Wes had late-night conversations, too? Wes knew Imani's mom? Worried that her distress would show on her face, she blurted out the first thing that sprang to mind.

"Umm... d-did you know that our noses are always visible to us? I learned this on a podcast about the history of perception. Our brain filters it out, or else we'd never notice the rest of the world." Sasha paused for emphasis. "Imani, the robber's probably right in front of you—just think of him as your nose."

"Brilliant." Imani pointed at her, almost accusatorily. "Bitch, I fuck with you, *hard*."

With that proclamation, Imani McIntyre was out. She twirled

away, a cloud of curls and cleavage—but not before air-kissing Sasha and wrapping Wes in a breast-centric embrace.

Then, it was just Wes and Sasha, sitting alone at the tiny, turquoise table. Sasha was caught in the crossfire of a million conflicting emotions. She didn't know how to feel, or what to think. But she did know one thing. Wes sparked with Imani. He sparked with his Barbecuties. He damn near sparked with his coffee cup.

Whatever unnamable thing he had with Sasha wasn't special. It was just his way.

Twenty minutes later, they were still there. Wes ordered appetizers for her, but she had no appetite. And the two of them were talking circles around the elephant in the room. They were so affected by each other's presence: Sasha's hands were trembling, and Wes couldn't stop folding his napkin into origami. The air between them seethed with everything they hadn't said.

"Imani's sweet!" Sasha said enthusiastically.

"If by 'sweet' you mean imperious, then sure. But she has a good heart. Unless it's a Blood Moon, when evil Imani reigns." He took a sip of water. "Her words, not mine."

"I do love a witchy girly."

Sasha searched Wes's face for some sign that last night even happened. Did it matter at all? She couldn't tell. His eyes were infinite pools of inky darkness, revealing nothing. So intense, so mesmerizing. She saw him above her, his exquisite face, his expression as he fucked her so well, so thoroughly, that her thighs were still liquid. There was no way to hide her inconvenient, ravenous lust for him, anymore. He knew all about it. He'd tasted it. There was nowhere to hide.

She'd never felt more naked in front of a man. More confused. More jealous.

"So, when did you date?"

"Why?"

"Just wondering. You have chemistry."

"No, we have history," he corrected. "We've been friends a long time. Why?"

"I'm just curious. I'm sorry, it's none of my business."

He chuckled humorlessly and took a drink. "It really isn't. You know. Considering."

"So you had a shut-in experience, too? Why didn't you tell me?"

"Never came up." It was clear he didn't want to elaborate, and Sasha didn't push. Instead, she fiddled with her gold cuff for ages, fighting off tears that made no sense. Why was she feeling emotional? Wes wasn't acting like himself. And she didn't feel like herself, either. He sounded bitter, and she sounded jealous.

She cleared her throat. "I brought the letter. Um, the one you'll give to... Teo, when you see him. I did what you said. I put in my phone number, my email, everything. So he can contact me, if he wants to."

With trembling hands, she pulled an envelope out of her purse and slid it across the table. Wes nodded, pocketing it. "Thanks, I was going to ask about that."

They sat in excruciating silence for what felt like hours. Finally, he spoke.

"Are we gonna talk about last night?"

Her eyes found his. They stayed tangled in each other's gaze for a few heartbeats; until his eyes flicked down to her mouth, lingering there, before traveling down to the mark he'd left under her jaw. She saw his jaw clench. And then, he tore his eyes away.

"I'm sorry. For everything," he said.

With that, he broke the tension. But it also broke Sasha. This wasn't how she hoped this conversation would go. On some level, she wanted him to tell her it wasn't a mistake. Tell her to forget

Seat F, to listen to what her brain, heart, and pussy were telling her, and stop running from him. She hoped he'd legitimize her feelings. But it was unfair to expect Wes to do all the heavy lifting. And, besides, Wes didn't feel the same. He wasn't shy about the things he wanted. If he was serious about her, he would've told her. And she wouldn't have felt like a third wheel with Imani.

And then, a terrible thought crossed her mind—if Imani had been in her place last night, would he have fucked her the same way? Was Sasha just an available body? She stopped these thoughts before spiraling further.

Instead of pouring out her soul, she simply said, "I'm sorry, too. It was both of us. Something happens to us when we're in each other's space." Her words tumbled out. "The call, the kiss at the ceremony. Last night. It's like the walls come down, and we lose ourselves to this unavoidable attraction, and I think maybe..."

Suddenly, Wes reached around the small table and grabbed her chair leg, easily dragging her closer to him. She gasped, startled. And then, he tucked his index finger under her chin, tipping her face up. She was close enough to feel his minty, warm breath on her skin. God, she wanted to taste his mouth again. She ached for it. Lightly, he ran his thumb over the bruise on her neck. A temporary reminder of a heated moment neither one of them could help. Her nipples peaked. Her heart pounded in her throat.

This man was irresistible.

"You make me feel fucking crazy." Wes's voice was even, controlled—but Sasha felt a subtle tremble in the hand under her chin. "Please stop making me feel crazy."

"I'll stop if you will," she breathed, fighting off a swoon. "We have to. It complicates things. Blurs lines."

"Let's just be normal. We can be normal, right?" It sounded like he was trying to convince himself, more than her. And then, he dropped his hand. The absence of it left her dizzy.

"Yes. Normal." She nodded, gulping down a glass of water.

"That's my water," noted Wes.

"Sorry," she said, grabbing hers. "Honestly, it's just hormones. We're not teenagers, we can control our lustful urges. And I have too much lapsed Catholic guilt to keep doing this."

"Let's just focus on the case. We're starting over from here, blank slate."

"Right. Let's do a reset."

"Just not a manual reset." He smirked, crookedly.

She let out a grateful little laugh at his corny joke. "Thank you, friend."

"For what?"

"Your maturity. For not letting this get weird. It's generous of you."

Wes toyed with his knife, his expression opaque. "Don't thank me yet."

Chapter 18

FANTASY ALWAYS WINS

Blank slate, he thought, playing back his words to Sasha. *Idiotic. And impossible.*

It was around 6:00 p.m. the next day, and the weather had taken a dismal turn. It was rainy, gloomy, and gray—which reflected Wes's general mood, as anyone walking by his Natural Born Griller truck could plainly see. He was parked at Pig Island, one of New York's most elite barbecue festivals, out in Staten Island. After applying twice before, he was finally accepted, thanks to his popularity at F.E.A.S.T. But at F.E.A.S.T., he was a big fish in a small pond. There was only one other barbecue truck (and it was vegan). Plus, the fragrant scent of smoked meats was louder than, say, a dessert or sandwich truck, so he had a leg up on the competition. But at Pig Island, among thirty of the buzziest, most seasoned barbecue chefs, trucks, and restaurants in the New York area? He was an unproven newbie with a vibey truck.

He couldn't focus, anyway. The only thing on his mind was Sasha, stripped bare, unfolding under him like a flower. God, he'd lost his head in her kitchen. Wes had no intention of taking things that far. But he was sick over Sasha. Heartsick, soulsick. Sick of pretending not to care, and even sicker of *yearning*. She'd infiltrated his heart, his thoughts, his filthiest fantasies, his whole world—and going crazy for a woman who was crazy for someone else wasn't his style. It was unbecoming, thankless work. Why waste his time playing a game he could never win?

No one liked to lose. But for Wes, defeat was repellent. And so, he'd never longed for things that were out of reach. He didn't chase windmills. He only attempted shots he could take. Not necessarily easy shots, but ones that weren't futile. Natural Born Griller was a perfect example. Years ago, when he, a detective-cum-trainer-cum-boxer who'd never professionally cooked anything but taxes (a brief side hustle, whatever), decided to launch a food truck business—he never doubted himself, because he knew he had the discipline and hustle to make it work. In his bones, Wes knew he'd win, or else he wouldn't have tried. Because trying and losing—especially losing publicly? No. Too harrowing to contemplate. It was hard enough carrying around the private suspicion that he wasn't quite good enough to deserve good things. Subliminally, he'd learned this from his parents. *In our day, there was no ADD, there was just lazy. No McDonald's 'cause Wes can't stop kicking the pew at church. We'll have Brooke present the Good Citizen award because Wes forgot his tie (again). We're not testing him for dyslexia, he just needs to apply himself.* The subtext was that he was a loser. He couldn't bear the thought of proving it.

Sasha was a gamble he couldn't win.

Wes had been with all kinds of women—bougie, boho, hood, fat, skinny, married, weird, tall, petite, sanctified, menopausal, hyperflexible—because he was a lot of women's type. And the attention was gratifying to him in a way that demanded in-depth therapy work. But he had to wonder if a few of those women would take him seriously in a nonsexual context. Yes, he owned his apartment and his business. But his apartment was matchbook-sized, and his start-up hadn't yet turned a profit. He drove a 2016 struggle-Nissan. The only way he could fall asleep was if he was buzzed, high, or both. His savings were dwindling. He had good taste, but all his furniture was sourced from his contact, Pier 13 Dean, who stole pieces from freight boats. Most Sunday mornings were spent trying to remember the name of the woman he'd just put in an Uber. He had seasonal allergies and expired contacts, and too many flaws to name. A certain kind of woman would need to squint to see Wes Dane as a serious person.

Sasha Cruz was that kind of woman. She had an Emmy. She owned an apartment in a luxury building in a fancy zip code. She carried a barrel-shaped Louis Vuitton purse. But it was more than looking expensive. She seemed otherworldly—a luminous, bronze-skinned glamour girl who consistently showed just enough cleavage or side-boob or leg to fuck him up for days. Again, *she had an Emmy.* She fearlessly jumped out of a window when she thought she was in danger. She was a force. She needed a man that matched her energy. Sasha deserved a debonair guy, a dollar sign in a custom suit. Some captain-of-industry type who knew about St. Barths and caviar families. Wes was a lot of things, but he wasn't that.

That was Seat F. Teo. He was a fantasy, but Wes was a flesh-and-blood human. And the fantasy always wins.

He scrubbed his face with his hands, drowning in self-loathing. To her, he was only good for his PI services and an orgasm. He was tired of being used. He was tired of letting her do it. Never again.

Of course it was easy for Wes to say this, now, from the safety of his truck, all the way out in Staten Island, with miles separating them. But would he remember it in her presence? Doubtful. Whenever he found himself in her orbit, he lost all faculties. He became willing to do anything for her. Even find her lost love.

In the history of stupid things done for a woman, he thought, *this is the stupidest. I'm basically cucking myself.*

But when he kissed her, his blood quickened in his veins. And it was worth it. Knowing that, with one look, one touch, or the sound of his voice, he owned her for that moment at least—well, that was worth it, too. There was power in it. Because, as she continued this ridiculous search for this hypothetical soulmate with a digital footprint so nonexistent he was either Jason Bourne or AI—Wes knew, and Sasha knew, who she truly belonged to. And Teo might get her in the end, but he'd taste Wes's name on her tongue. He'd sense her desperation for someone else. And that, too, was worth it.

But was Sasha's sexual desperation truly about Wes? Or was it just that he was *there*? If so, it wouldn't be the first time he was treated like a himbo escort. Wes was used to that. But this was the first time it hurt. He didn't know this much hurt existed.

What also hurt? Realizing that he was in way over his head at this competition. He'd had four customers in the past two hours. His fellow grillmasters were leagues beyond him, experience-wise. His competition was a lumberjack wearing a lab coat full of festival medals, spit-roasting a whole hog. Next to him, a team of women wearing traditional Lenape clothing were serving chili-and-maple-sugar–glazed wings that *leapt* off the bone. A guy in a BLUE LIVES MATTER cap was causing a commotion with something called Freedom Pork Belly (this played in Staten Island). In this crowd, Wes was invisible. Actually, that wasn't entirely true. A few folks had taken selfies with the truck. Optimistically speaking, if they tagged Wes in the photos, that was a win.

Not a financial win, though. He'd spent four grand on meat, spices, and marinades, and was getting a bit itchy. And he was convinced this brisket was his most delicious batch. One of his few customers, Chase Trellino, a massive barbecue-head who'd followed him from Brooklyn, even said so. Wes didn't have to win the competition, though. He didn't even need to place in the top three. As long as the esteemed judges (two Michelin-star chefs, a

New York Times food critic, and...Method Man?) voted him into the top five, he'd be qualified to enter his truck at EAT ME, the biggest BBQ festival on the East Coast.

But Wes's head wasn't in the game today. All he could think about was Sasha. He was so tired of being *aware* of her. He wondered how to become un-obsessed with someone.

Wes looked out into the rain, as smoke from the grills and spit roasts wafted through the crowds. Umbrellas brushed against each other, as hungry barbecue-heads mingled and ate, nodding their heads to the deejay's yacht rock tunes. The summer storm had cast a humid pall on the event, which nicely complemented his psyche. He hadn't had a customer in ten minutes, though. Might as well work on the case. He was under the gun now. Sasha's letter to Teo was practically burning a hole in his desk at home.

Pulling out his notebook, he went over his notes. Before he'd left for Staten Island that morning, he'd also called every hotel inspector agency in every cosmopolitan capital—New York City, London, Milan, Paris—and no one had heard of Teo D. Scera. Except for the receptionist at the Cayne Agency NYC. She recognized Teo's name, not because he worked there, but because, a few years ago, a woman named Kim, claiming to be his ex-fiancée, had called looking for him.

So, Sasha wasn't the first woman Teo had pulled despite revealing practically nothing about his personal life. And he'd proposed to this Kim. Wes couldn't say he was surprised. But the proof affirmed his creeping suspicions.

Wes discovered that Kim lived on the Upper West Side. He easily found her contact info and, after a short call (in which he impersonated an NYPD officer working on a missing persons case), she invited him to tea at Gotham Lounge. Kim Gold was a striking, Natalie Portman–esque brunette in finance, maybe forty, who dated Teo ten years ago. She'd been looking for him because she was engaged to a new man, and wanted to return the jewelry Teo had gifted her.

On their initial call, Wes had asked her to bring to tea anything that might help the case. And so, with a solemn expression, Kim slid a small stack of postcards across the table. As Wes flipped them over, scanning them, she explained that postcards were their "thing." Wherever he traveled, he'd write her love notes on postcards and bring them home as souvenirs. Wes was surprised that she was willing to part with them and told her as much. "I'm too busy to be sentimental," she responded. Plus, she said she didn't speak Italian and never understood the notes, anyway—she'd just been swept away by the romance of it. (Sounded familiar.) Wes pocketed the cards in his messenger bag, to revisit later.

Curiously, Kim only had glowing reviews about Teo. "Yes, he was gone quite a bit. But I travel for work, too. It never bothered me. When we were together, he was so solicitous, so generous. Gifts and experiences and beautiful sex and kindness. Teo never gave me a reason to think he was anything but in love with me. Honestly, I miss him."

It struck Wes how sharp, intelligent, and professionally accomplished Kim was. Her profile was uncomfortably similar to Sasha's. Would such whip-smart women fall for a scam? Love grifters were usually attracted to down-on-their luck, vulnerable women who centered men in all things—and whose hunger for love blinded them. Kim didn't seem like the type. And Sasha definitely wasn't. In her own words, she was *forcing* herself to be romantic, to take a chance on a wild card. If Teo was a grifter, it seemed that Sasha and Kim would've sniffed him out.

Except that love blindness was a real thing. And it infected people, indiscriminately. It didn't matter how successful or accomplished you were. Anyone could be starved for affection, or willing to believe anything to find it. You could be brilliant at work, at life, in friendships—but not have the defenses necessary to avoid being preyed upon by a manipulator. In many cases, the heart overrides the brain. Was that what was happening with Sasha?

And to that end, something about the postcards bothered him. He couldn't figure out what.

God, Wes hated Teo. He'd never hated anyone so intensely. He loathed that he knew he was a bad guy, but didn't have enough information to prove it. He hated that this snake oil salesman had Sasha's attention. But, worse than anything, he hated the chance that Teo was dangerous. Sasha had hired him to find Seat F, but for him, the goalposts had changed. Now, he was trying to build a case for Teo being a fraud.

With a groan, he reached into his fridge and pulled out a beer. Vendors were forbidden to drink alcohol at Pig Island, but Wes wasn't going to make it through this gray, slow day without a beer. Really, he just needed one sip. He took a healthy chug. Glumly, he sat with his head in his hands, elbows on his counter. He tapped his fingertips over his cheekbones, peering with envy at the lines at the more established trucks.

I hate everything, he thought, and downed the whole beer.

Wes couldn't get a handle on Teo. Earlier that morning, he'd put in a call to a connection at United States Bank, Luchini Lou. He'd gone to high school with this guy, a bored teller trying to save for a summer house. It cost a pretty penny to get info out of Lou, which was a cost he'd ordinarily bake into his detective fee. But Wes couldn't bring himself to charge Sasha anything but the bare minimum. So he reached into his savings for this one. Hopefully, it'd be worth it.

Just then, a customer appeared at his window. Lost in thought, it took him a second for his vision to adjust to her presence. Then, his spine straightened and he offered an affable smile.

"Rainy enough for you? What are you in the mood for?"

"I'm not here to eat." A thin-lipped, older woman wearing salt-and-pepper dreadlocks, jeans, and a blazer squinted at him and gestured with a clipboard. "I'm an inspector from the New York City Department of Health."

Shit. Now he recognized her—it was Marianne Ralph, the legend. Every four months, the Department of Health checked in on all trucks with no warning, just ambushing them at festivals and competitions or curbside. The element of surprise struck the fear of God in all the pros that Wes met in the business. And Marianne Ralph was one of the toughest inspectors. She'd brought the hot dog guy outside of the Metropolitan Museum of Art to tears, and he'd been in the game since the Reagan administration. Luckily, Wes had never been dressed down by Marianne, but he supposed he was due. Good thing he'd followed the vendor and DOH rules to the tee.

"I'm Marianne Ralph," she said unnecessarily.

He turned on some dimply charm. "Can I see your badge?"

She didn't laugh. "What are you selling here today, uh, Mr..." She turned a sheet on her clipboard and then nodded. "Mr. Dane."

"Not much, really just brisket. It's my signature dish."

"Do I have your consent to enter the truck? I need to inspect the food."

Before he could properly respond, Marianne Ralph was inside his truck, peering into a pot of brisket simmering on the stove. "How was this prepared?"

"I smoke the brisket and pork prior, of course. It takes about ten to twelve hours to smoke. Then I just transport them here in these containers." He showed her his glass containers. "And I let them simmer on the stove."

"Mr. Dane, are you aware that brisket needs to be vacuum sealed and in a specific environment?"

"It's sealed, see?"

"Not vacuum-sealed. And did you write down the temperature you smoked it in?"

"Well, no...but the last inspector didn't mention writing down the number."

As his heart thudded, she handed him his container. Scowling, she scribbled a few notes on her clipboard and then dropped it in her oversized bag.

"Mr. Dane, this is an extremely FDA-regulated space. It brings me no pleasure to tell you this. But your brisket and pork need to be stored in a very specific environment. Your last inspectors were cutting corners."

"But I didn't know, Ms. Ralph. I'm relatively new to the business. Can I get a break? Pay a fine?"

She held up her hand, cutting him off. She dumped the contents of all the containers and pots into the garbage. With a dour expression, she pulled a half-gallon bottle of bleach out of her tote bag.

"Wait." Immediately panicked, he held up his hands in a *don't shoot* gesture. "W-wait, what are you doing? No, no, no, no..."

Slowly, she poured the bleach in the trash.

"You killed my brisket." In shock, Wes's words ran together. *Youkilledmybrisket.*

After Marianne left, Wes sat down, hard, on his wooden bench by the grill. The loss was staggering. With entry fees, and the price of ingredients, he'd just wasted almost five thousand dollars. Without even any hope of placing, because now he was disqualified. This competition would've brought him sponsorships, cash prizes, and further acceptance into this competitive world. And his food was delicious. This was a waste.

Wes wanted to give up. Set his truck on fire. But unfortunately, he loved this fucking business. He'd get it right, he'd just have to come back stronger and sharper at the next competition. One day, he'd tell the story of this wildly aggressive, punitive bleaching on the *Afros + Knives* podcast, and it'd be a colorful anecdote on the way to success. Besides, no one said it'd be easy. Nothing was easy. He cracked open another beer.

Mother*fuck*.

He needed a win.

While Wes was packing up, mentally counting the thousands he'd lost today, his phone buzzed in his pocket. It was an unknown number.

"Wes Dane, here."

"What's good witcha, playboy?"

It was Luchini Lou, his contact at United States Bank. Because of the precarious content of their call, he couldn't identify himself to Wes, or call from a traceable number. And they needed to talk fast.

"What you got?" asked Wes, sitting up straight and grabbing one of his Wordle journals.

"Sent you the report via locked email. You know the password."

Wes checked Gmail on his phone. "Got it. More later."

Wes clicked off and pulled up the email. Attached was a PDF of Teo D. Scera's latest bank statement. It wasn't anything too out-of-pocket. There were charges from Milan, Côte d'Azur, Johannesburg, Paris. He was obviously a world traveler. He didn't own his condo, he paid monthly rental fees. There were a few odd things, though. He had several charges at hotels. If he was a luxury hotel inspector, wouldn't the charges be on a corporate card? Or comped? He shouldn't be paying for rooms, meals, Wi-Fi—or anything.

And then, there was the fact that there were five people listed on his business savings account. All men, or people with traditionally male names. Were they all him? That was a possibility. Wes searched all five names and came up empty. There was no information on any of them—except for Sam Canter. His profession was unknown, but he was apparently the head of a charity called Two Tunics.

A quick search showed that it was a charity to raise funds for the unhoused. Taken from the Bible quote: *Whoever has two tunics is to share with him who has none, and whoever has food is to do likewise.* He also saw that the charity was sponsoring a gala at the Pierre Hotel that Friday.

In a flash, he slid the truck window closed and called Two Tunics.

"Good afternoon. Yes, maybe you can help me. I'm researching my dissertation about corruption in American charities. Two Tunics's reputation is crystal clear, though. Is there anyone I can talk to about the day-to-day operations? Pick their brain?"

"Of course, who are you looking for?"

"Sam Canter. If he's available."

"Oh, Mr. Canter is rarely available. He's an extremely busy man. This charity's just one of his many projects. He's hosting a huge event on Friday, so he's meeting with event planners all day. Call in a few weeks."

"Well, thanks for your help! Maybe I can catch him at the gala."

"It's not open to the public. Besides, Mr. Canter never attends, himself. He's the brains behind the operation. But he's always well represented by the entire Canter family."

"Hmm. What's the price of admission?"

"You said you're doing your dissertation?"

"Yeah."

"No offense, but you can't afford a ticket on a student's salary. The gala's for top donors and media. And family members of the board."

Long after Wes hung up, he stared at the bleached-out meat in his garbage, thinking. He'd bet a year's salary that Teo would be at this gala. He *hoped* Teo would be at this gala. Because then, Wes could wrap this case up. His job was to find him and deliver Sasha's letter inviting him to meet her—and he could do it, there. But first he needed a ticket. Easy, all he had to do was impersonate a hedge fund douche calling to RSVP. And he knew a guy.

Adrenaline racing, he called Digital Dayquan Dotcom. D3 could build a website in a pinch. If he'd taken his mood stabilizers that day, he could do it in under an hour.

"D3. It's Wes. How you feeling?"

"Emotionally regulated. What's good?"

"I need to impersonate a hedge fund guy to get into an event on Friday. What's a good asshole name?"

"Roland Weiss," he said with no hesitation or explanation.

"Bet," said Wes. "I'm Roland Weiss. Now, I need a personal brand website. Add some fake client testimonials and, listen up, 'cause this is important, I need a quote from a financier called Sam Canter. Link some fake financial articles to the site, too. Also, I need a fake Roland Weiss LinkedIn profile. Have your usual bots follow it."

D3 yawned. "I gotchu. It'll be four hundred dollars."

Wes paused before answering. He was sitting in front of a garbage can full of dead brisket. Thousands down the drain. Four hundred dollars? He wasn't even willing to part with forty.

He thought fast.

"Your mom still pushes Mary Kay?"

"Mm-hmm."

"I'll cater her next party, free. All-you-can-eat barbecue. And I usually charge five hundred dollars."

"How that benefits me, though?"

"D, you live in her basement and don't pay rent or cook. You'll benefit by eating."

He paused for five seconds. "You got a deal, dog."

Two hours later, Wes redialed Sam Canter's office—posing as Roland Weiss's assistant.

"Good afternoon, I'm calling to RSVP to the Two Tunics gala," he said, his voice sounding tinny and uncanny through the voice changer he held to his mouth. (In his truck, Wes kept a small briefcase full of detective-y gizmos and disguises.)

"Roland Weiss? W-E-I-S-S? I'm afraid I don't see him on the invite list."

"It's understandable. Mr. Weiss was due in Qatar with... with Sir Luther VanDrossian on the evening of the gala, but he had a scheduling hiccup, so he's now available. I understand Mr. Canter invited Mr. Weiss to sit at one of his family tables." He paused. "Comped tickets, of course."

"I think you're mistaken, sir."

"Mr. Canter and Mr. Weiss are old associates. We're a hedge fund based in Denver. Check our site."

Through the phone, Wes heard the receptionist tapping on a keyboard. "Ahhh. LeBron James and Steph Curry are clients? Dope."

Fucking Dayquan, he thought. *Always taking it too far.*

"I see. My intern must've made a mistake. Mr. Weiss and a plus-one are good to go."

Thank God. He was in, and hopefully he could convince Sasha to come. She could watch Teo from afar, from a safe distance, and get a sense of who he was—without wearing wine-and-Xanax goggles. And with Wes there to monitor all of this, ensuring her safety.

He'd refrain from giving Teo her letter until she okayed it. Either Sasha would want to move forward with Teo, or she wouldn't. But Wes would be done with it.

Suddenly, he was compelled to pull one of Teo's postcards out of his messenger bag. Why did these bother him? He read over the love note:

Io non ho paura. Di quello che non so spiegare.

According to Google translate, this meant:

I'm not afraid. Of what I can't explain.

They were the lyrics to a 2011 Italian pop song, "lo Non Ho Paura." Wes wondered if Kim knew these were song lyrics and not original thoughts. Corny motherfucker couldn't even write his own love notes.

That's when it hit him. Teo hadn't *mailed* any of these postcards to Kim. He physically handed them to Kim. They weren't postmarked. Which led to only one explanation. He didn't want them postmarked—because then, his true whereabouts would be exposed.

Chapter 19

WE TALKED ABOUT THIS

Sasha had Wes's Wordle journal. Well, at least one of them. She knew he had several.

Sasha had coffee with a talent agent, went to a dentist appointment, and was back home in her own kitchen, searching through her tote for some gum—when she found it. How had his journal ended up in her purse? Short of sprouting wings and flying, she couldn't imagine what it was doing there. All she knew was that she couldn't escape Wes. She couldn't get him out of her mind. And, in all honesty, she wasn't really trying.

Since the case started, she'd been trying to convince herself that her crush on Wes was a harmless, reflexive thing. Of course, she'd developed a softness for him—this man had rescued her from a stalker. She'd sought him out at her lowest, weakest point, and he saved her. And now, he was saving her again, by finding her missed connection. Her fascination with him was just misplaced gratitude, right? *Teo* was her fated guy. *Teo* was the one who dropped out of the sky, drawing her in on one single flight. *Teo* was the reason Wes was back, in the first place.

But the electricity between Sasha and Wes was too seismic to ignore. Plus, she'd realized something. Before Wes, she'd never had truly obliterating, mind-melting sex. She'd had okay sex. Like, good enough—but paint-by-numbers. Unremarkable. Unfurnished. Wes lit her ablaze.

When they were kissing in her kitchen, there was one utterly destabilizing moment when they pulled away—for air, but also to openly gaze at each other in damn near worship—and she knew that she never wanted him to leave. Teo was a question mark, but Wes was *here*, flesh and blood, touchable, fuckable, lovable, and she wanted him. It was that simple.

And she'd intended to tell him as much. So, when he texted that sleeping together was a mistake, it devastated her. When she saw his easy, lived-in chemistry with Imani, she was jealous. And when he reconfirmed, after Imani left, that they needed to ignore their attraction and focus on the job at hand—she was shattered. Because what she wanted, deep down, was for him to drop the case. And after that? She wanted him to take her and run off with her into the sunset.

But Sasha couldn't ignore the truth. Wes just didn't feel the same way. And why would he? Beyond him saying he didn't want a relationship with anyone right now—Sasha hired him to find another guy! Only a masochist would take on this situation. But when she hired him, how was she to know that all these feelings would bloom? In the furthest recesses of her mind, she suspected it'd always been there; she was just too traumatized in 2022 to see it. How stupid she'd been, to seek him out. How ill-advised. Only a woman woefully out of practice with men and relationships would make such an immature, short-sighted decision.

She was a woman askew.

And, God, a big part of her wanted to end the case. Because the possibility of Teo was no match for the reality of Wes. But there was no reality of Wes, was there? He'd told her, in several ways, that they had no future. What other choice did she have, but to hear him?

Sasha was spinning. She wanted Wes, but that was a mistake. She also wanted to stop the case—but, given her instincts of late, this was probably the wrong call, too. No, she'd stay the course. She didn't want to call it off and then, for the rest of her life, wonder if she'd been too hasty. She didn't want to make yet another short-sighted decision.

Chewing on her bottom lip, she brought the journal into her bedroom, and set it on the bed. She was dying to look through it. But that was a bridge too far. Like peeking into someone's diary. Plus, he'd expect her to do it. She didn't want to be predictable. With elite-level self-control, she left the journal on her bed, and took a long, hot shower. Afterward, she slipped into a satin robe and then walked by the bed, allowing her fingertips to graze her duvet. They trailed over the journal nonchalantly.

Nothing to see here, she told herself. *Just some field notes containing information about Teo, things Wes hasn't told me. I know there's more. I can feel that he's holding back. It wouldn't hurt just to take a peek.*

Looking quickly to her left and right, she picked up the book. She thumbed through the pages. Endless notes, handwritten, flew by in a blur. It wasn't exactly reading it, if she was just flipping through! Hungrily, she tried to catch a word, a phrase, anything. Curiosity flooded her.

Am I hoping to find more details about the case, she wondered, *or details about me?*

Leaving the question unanswered, she lit her Coastal Cypress candle and tried to remember how good her conversation with Teo felt. Slowly, she lowered herself back on her pillows, the journal resting on her stomach, under her hands. Her eyes shuttered closed. And, almost immediately, Wes eclipsed Teo in her mind. All she could think of was his journal, and that he wrote all his most important, intimate thoughts in there. His insides spilled out over the pages. Looking in his private notebook felt too voyeuristic, like spying on his brain. She couldn't do that. She trusted Wes, implicitly, and it was important to Sasha that he trust her, too.

Sasha had to return it to him. Sooner rather than later.

Opening one eye, she checked the time on her phone. It was 8:30 p.m. She texted him and waited twenty minutes for a response. Nothing. She texted again. More crickets. This was not ideal. Sasha absolutely couldn't keep this notebook overnight. Sasha didn't trust herself not to have every word committed to memory before midnight. Plus, once Wes realized it was gone, she didn't want him to think she was holding on to it, on purpose—out of nosiness.

The thought crossed her mind that she could just drop it off at his house. She knew he lived next to the Foam Alone Laundromat in Fort Greene. If he wasn't home, at least she tried. It was a risky move, showing up to his apartment, out of the clear blue. But "risky" hadn't been stopping her lately.

In fact, nothing had been stopping her lately. She'd left the house more times than she had in the past year. It was empowering. Earlier this morning, she took the train for the first time in a small lifetime. It wasn't that she was feeling less anxious. It's that she wasn't *caring* as much about it. Which was the trick. Feelings of paranoia, agoraphobia-lite, and fear were no surprise, given her past trauma. And everyone felt panicky and weird sometimes. The difference between someone with an anxiety disorder, and a quote-unquote normal person was that the normal person didn't let the fears take over. They felt them, noted them, and moved on with their lives. They didn't allow the demons to haunt them continuously, day in and day out. There was a liberating lack of obsession.

Lately, Sasha'd had more "normal" encounters with anxiety than usual. This was one of them. She was being so spontaneous. The fact that she was actually leaving her house this late—and didn't even know what to expect when she got to Wes's place—was uncharted territory. But something in her felt exhilarated from not knowing. It was like watching a thriller on the edge of her seat, wondering what was going to happen next. Trying to guess, weighing the outcomes. Except this was real life. Her life had become an adventure.

Before she could change her mind, she lunged out of bed. She threw on some black leggings and a cropped sweatshirt, messily twisted her hair into a clip, and blended a rose tint onto her cheekbones and lips. Her heart was thundering in her chest. She wasn't sure how Wes would perceive this burst of spontaneity, but the notebook felt like it was on fire in her hands. She had to deliver it to him.

A short time later, she found herself standing outside of Foam Alone Laundromat. On the doorbell plate by the front door, she saw DANE next to apartment four. With a trembling finger, she pushed his buzzer. And then she waited. And waited. Sasha stood outside of the building for ten minutes. Each second that passed, she wondered if he was ignoring her, asleep, or just not home. Most normal people were out, weren't they?

She felt a small pang. Even though she and Wes had put it to bed, the smoldering encounter at her apartment lingered in her mind. *He'd* lingered. She could still feel him all over her. If only she had the kind of personality that could fuck and forget. No doubt, Imani could do that. Imani seemed to be a sexual gladiator, the kind of love-'em-and-leave-'em woman Sasha had always yearned to be. But as pro-sex as Sasha was for everyone else, she was hesitant when it came to herself. She suspected this came from living with a mom who seemed ruined by sex (Freudian, but true). The way young Sasha saw it, Marcia had valued hormones over logic, and the cost was high. She was left with a fatherless child who, though loved, had complicated her life immeasurably—and had transformed her from Hot Side Chick to Scorned Woman in under nine months. Heavy shit to ponder in middle school.

Okay, but back to Imani, she thought. *Is Wes upstairs with her right now? Or someone else? Wait, is Wes solo-polyamorous?*

As she wrestled with such questions, she decided to buzz one last time. And, shockingly, Wes buzzed back. Without hesitation, she raced in and hurried to Wes's first-floor apartment door. Before she could connect fist with wood, it flew open. And there was Wes, standing before her. Half naked. Wearing nothing but a towel slung around his hips, a toothbrush lodged in his mouth. He also had a towel wrapped around his head, which was bizarre since—what hair did he have to dry? He wore a close fade.

Sasha stared. No, she *gawked.* For some reason, being half naked made him look even taller than six foot four. Droplets of water pooled in the valley of his collarbones, spilling down the wide, sculpted expanse of his chest. Her eyes traveled down the sinewy muscles of his arms, down his abs, and, Jesus Christ, his thighs. She wanted to bite each one. She traveled back up to where she was avoiding. The barely disguised bulge behind the towel. Thick and long, and it wasn't even hard. Fuck. Fuck. Fuck.

Wes popped the toothbrush out of his mouth. Absentmindedly, he wiped his mouth with the back of his hand. His tongue darted out to the corner of his mouth, licking up some errant toothpaste. His half smile was dangerous, knowing.

It was the single sexiest gesture Sasha had ever seen.

"Hi." Wes sounded as if he'd been expecting Sasha. As if, despite everything he'd said, her showing up on his doorstep was inevitable.

"Hi." It came out in a whisper, her voice momentarily giving out. She cleared her throat. "You always answer the door like that?"

"You always show up unannounced?"

"Well, no, not usually. But I have something of yours."

"Of mine? What do you have?"

She took the journal out of her bag and handed it to him. "It was in my bag, I have no idea how it got there. Must've been a mix-up at Brown Butter the other day."

"I didn't know I'd misplaced it," he said, brows creasing. "Did you... uh, did you read anything?"

"No, of course not."

"I mean, you could've. It's not like there's anything in there that..." He trailed off, with a shrug. "You know."

Sasha didn't know, but she nodded. "As soon as I realized I had it, I brought it over. I didn't want you to think I was holding it hostage. I've been trying to contact you for hours."

"Ohhh. Yeah, I was busy performing poorly at a barbecue competition. Anyway, thank you," he said casually. "Where are my manners? Come in."

"No, I really shouldn't. I see you're settling in for bed. I should go."

"Don't go. Come *on*, you're already here." He moved back a few steps, widening the door with him.

Goddamn it, he was such a ham. And the king of mixed messages. Standing there, wet, in only a towel? Was he teasing her, after putting up such a firm boundary yesterday? Testing her, seeing if she was strong enough to resist him? Sasha never met a competition she didn't want to win.

"It's tempting," she said with a smirk, "but no. You, yourself, put a ban on all flirtatious behavior. Let's not get ourselves into another situation."

"No, no, you're right." He paused, his voice taking a serious tone. "And thank you for coming. I'm not going to pretend I don't know what a brave move that was for you to leave your house, at this hour. Alone. I'm proud of you for doing that."

"Thank you," she said softly. "I'm proud of myself, too."

Her heart leapt. A beam of warmth spread from the center of her chest, radiating all over. Without having to explain, Wes knew this was a leap for her. It felt so magical to be seen. To be understood. With Wes, she felt like she was no longer living an unwitnessed life. She couldn't have stopped the wide smile spreading across her face, if she tried.

"Will you come in now?"

"Oh fine," she said with mock exasperation.

He took a few steps back, opening the door wider and allowing her to step in. As she walked past him into the hallway, she took in his scent—warm, vanilla, cedar, smoky. It stirred all her nerve endings.

Inside, she looked around. His studio was cozy, well-designed and warm. She'd expected more of a bachelor pad, with single-straight-guy artlessness. But the decor was tasteful and masculine, awash in camel and charcoal tones. He had an incredible, oversized black-and-white print hanging over the couch—a shot of kids playing in a New York City street. The mat was a deep, forest green—an inspired touch.

"What's this print?" she asked, pointing to it. "It's stunning."

"You like it?" He walked over to the couch. She couldn't help but focus on his back, strong with sculpted shoulders. She wished she didn't know how good his skin felt on hers. How strong he felt above her. How easily she came undone under him.

Shut your whore mouth, she told herself.

"Yeah, that was a fun day. I was nine, it was the hottest summer on record in Brooklyn. The hydrant was blowing water everywhere."

Sasha's jaw dropped. She walked over to the wall and stood next to him, taking it in. "You're the little boy caught in midair, flying through the water spray?"

"Always so chaotic. I couldn't sit still. It's a great shot, though. I don't remember who took it. But it was taken on this exact block, so I thought it'd be cool to blow up."

"A true child of Fort Greene. You're adorable." She winced slightly. "You *were* adorable."

"Thanks. Yeah, that photo's special." He turned to face her, and she faced him, too. "I was going to call you tomorrow, but since you're here…I have an update for you. Do you have an evening gown?"

"An evening gown? Why?"

And then Wes explained the gala on Friday, that there was a good chance Teo could be there. And that, hopefully, they could wrap up the case for good. Of course, Sasha was in. And she pretended to be excited. But the idea of seeing Teo and Wes in the same place at the same time was too mind-bending to process. Especially right now. She couldn't focus on anything but dripping, bare-chested Wes in a towel.

"I was just about to get some water," Wes was saying. "You thirsty? Hungry? Can I interest you in a rib with a fork?"

"No, I really can't stay. I just wanted to drop off the journal."

"This is an anticlimactic first visit to my apartment. But I'm glad you're here."

"Same. I love seeing where you live." Feeling awkward, she fiddled with her gold cuff, looking down at her hands.

The apartment was silent. Everything was still. And then, the thing that happens with them, happened. The same way it always did. Standing in front of him, breathing the same air—all her nerve endings came alive. Whatever chemistry they summoned together, it made her feel deliriously off-kilter and yet perfectly balanced.

And just like that, their carefully negotiated boundaries went *pttht.* It was like the power suddenly went out, worldwide. Lights out. Bets off. No rules.

"Sasha," he said, waiting for her to look at him. When she did, everything else receded. She saw the rise and fall of his chest, his gaze flick down to the sliver of stomach showing between her sweatshirt and leggings. His jaw tightened, and he clenched and released his hands at his sides, as if trying to find the strength to hold it together. She certainly couldn't. He was irresistible, with his wicked eyes, and overwhelming strength, and lusty mouth, and open heart—and she wanted to devour him. She felt out of control.

There was no point in pretending it wasn't going to happen. Again. Neither one of them was strong enough to fight it. And, come on. Wasn't that really what she was there for?

"We talked about this," he said as a warning.

Sasha nodded, biting her lip. Her mouth watered. She glanced down at the towel wrapped low on his hips. There was no way to miss how fucking hard he was, tenting the towel. All of that "no more crossing the line" talk was bullshit. No matter what, they'd find a way to end up here. They always did.

"Remind me what we said," she whispered.

His gaze was molten. "Get on your knees, first."

Beyond thought, she dropped down where she stood. He moved two steps closer. She pressed her mouth hotly against his bulge, tracing the outline of his dick over the towel. He fisted his hand in her hair. Her claw clip went flying. A low groan rumbled in his throat.

"This just confuses things," he managed, his voice a low growl. "Blurs lines. We need to focus."

She grabbed the sides of the towel and yanked it down. There was something so tawdry about him being naked, while she was fully clothed. She handled the heavy length of him in her hand and dragged her tongue from the base to the tip. He let out a choppy groan. God, she loved that sound. She just wanted to drive him as crazy as he drove her. With showy, excruciating slowness, she spit in both hands and swirled them up and down his length. He hissed, biting down on his bottom lip till it whitened.

"If I remember," he rasped, through gritted teeth, "you said we needed to control ourselves. Isn't that right?"

She nodded, and then fastened her mouth on the tip, sucking wetly as her hands kept working him up and down, over and over.

And then she stopped. Peering up at him under her eyelashes, she dropped her hands, clasping them primly at the small of her back. His eyes flashed with immediate understanding.

"Can I?" he asked huskily.

"Do it," she breathed.

Wes tightened his grip on her hair and sank deep into her mouth. Slowly, he pulled out, and then sank back in, expertly fucking her mouth—and the delicious submissiveness of it all made her lose it. Her eyes teared, her cunt ached... and God, was it possible to come like this, untouched? Abruptly, Wes pulled her off him, making a little pop sound with her mouth.

"More?" he asked.

As an answer, she stuck out her tongue. He tapped it with his heavy, straining shaft.

"What happened to that Catholic guilt?" he teased, his voice going straight to her cunt. "Look at you now."

And then he sank in as far as he could go. She trembled, taking it, her thighs going liquid. If she could've screamed, she would've. If she could've begged harder, faster, more, she would've—but somehow, he knew. He gave it to her, over and over. And when he warned her he was coming, he tried to pull out—but she shook her head, *no*, sucking him down. Draining him.

When his world stopped spinning, Wes hooked his hands under her arms and lifted her onto the couch. She felt his hands sliding under her ass, pulling her toward him. In a frenzy, her leggings and cotton bikini briefs disappeared, and his mouth was on her. Wes ate her like he kissed her, with all-consuming ravenousness—expertly teasing, sucking, and licking, drawing one orgasm out of her, and then another. Or maybe it was the same one, surging again. All she knew was that his mouth was *pornographic*. He unraveled her.

And afterward, they lay there together, a sweaty, messy tangling of limbs. Gingerly, he slid his right arm under her shoulder blades and drew her to his chest. She went willingly, as limp as a ragdoll. It was the only place she wanted to be. She pressed her nose against the base of his throat, inhaling his scent. He awakened every sense in her.

I don't believe in anything, she thought, *but this. Him and me in the dark, trembling and overstimulated and certain. Wasn't this always the answer?*

She pulled back from him a little, looking up at him. His eyes drank in her face, feature for feature. Reverently, his palm traveled to her cheek, his thumb tracing her bottom lip. Her tongue met the tip of his thumb. With an anguished groan, he lowered his face to hers, drawing her into a slow, searing kiss. They were already buzzing, half weak from orgasms, so the kiss was a hazy, languid pleasure. As she quivered under him, it occurred to her that she could've stayed that way for the next five days. Or forever.

Wes broke the kiss. Forehead to forehead, they breathed each other's air for a few blissed-out moments. Nothing else mattered. No boundaries, no professionalism, no rules. She was gathering the courage to tell him this; to explain how badly she wanted him. How stupid she'd been. But then, his voice broke through the silence.

"This isn't good for me," he said.

Her thoughts cracked down the center, crumbling to the earth.

And then, in a moment of explosive vulnerability, he added, "It's killing me."

"It's killing me, too, Wes," she whispered.

"No, it's not, Sasha. Not in the same way. Every day, I rack my brain for how I could win. How I could make you forget him. But I have nothing to offer you. I have a past. I've spent two separate nights in jail for aggravated assault. I owe thousands in unpaid parking tickets. You're lying on a Mafia rug. Today, a gargoyle bleached my brisket."

Sasha thought she misheard him. "A Mafia rug?"

"I'm not wealthy. I'm not international. And I'm not a fantasy. I'm just some guy; not exceptional enough for a woman like you to bother getting to know. But you make me feel special. You make me feel necessary. I'd do anything for you, Sasha. Unfortunately for me, that means I'll complete your case." He pressed his lips against the top of her head. "But the prize is that somebody else gets you."

"Wes, please listen. I have to be honest. Please trust me when I tell you..."

"How can I trust you? I can taste you in my mouth—me, the guy looking for your guy. I can't be alone with you for more than five minutes without needing to feel you, kiss you, touch you. Make you mine. It's torture. And you know it. How do you think that makes me feel? Have you *ever* considered how this makes me feel? And I fucking hate him. He's a fraud, Sasha. I'm almost able to prove it. But ultimately, you didn't ask me to judge him. You asked me to find him. Tomorrow, I'm delivering him to you in a tux. After that, I'm not letting you use me anymore."

Nodding, eyes tearing, she gently untangled herself from him and stood up, unsteadily.

"I'm sorry," she whispered, pulling on her clothes as she headed to the door. "I'm sorry."

She was sorry as she ran down the stairs and out onto the street, and sorry in the Uber home. In the backseat, she crushed her purse to her chest, as if her heart would seep out of her chest otherwise. As if it were the only thing keeping her intact.

NON-DELIVERY REPORT

To: Sasha.C@Seraphina.org [disabled account]
From: maxi.morgan2006@gmail.com
Subject: Re: Searching for Seat F

Hi Ms. Cruz. You might not remember me, but I read your palm at Fiorello Airport earlier this month? You gave me your business card with your email. Hope it's okay that I reach out!

I was a palmistry novice when I did your reading. After doing many readings since then, I realized that I made a small mistake. I remember telling you that you'll experience a chance meeting that'll set off a chain of events that'll end in happily ever after. And that the right connection bridges hearts through time and space, etc.

Well, that's true. But I'm now realizing that the "chain of events that'll end in happily ever after" is referring to *other* people. You're going to meet a man, and somehow, that meeting will bring love to strangers. Many, many strangers. I don't know how I messed that up! But I apologize.

Let me know if you've had this chance meeting yet. And if you were satisfied with your reading, please leave me a positive review on Yelp. Link below.

Maxi Morgan
Nail Tech & Palmistry Expert & Actor
Flushing, Queens

Chapter 20

LIKE YOU'RE MINE

Sasha was balancing on her tiptoes atop a four-foot ladder. She was also wearing a full face of makeup and a sweeping, full-length evening gown. With her left hand, she steadied herself against the wall. With her right hand, she stretched up to tinker with Destiny's smoke detector. Why had she never noticed how intolerably high her best friend's ceilings were?

"What *can't* she do?" murmured Destiny, as she watched Sasha from the plush safety of her rose-sprigged, antique four-poster bed. Currently, they were in her bedroom, but her whole apartment was decorated in high boudoir style—lace-trimmed displays, gilded mirrors, antique furniture, and pink accents.

It was the night of the Two Tunics charity gala. Destiny offered to style Sasha's bob in sexy, tousled waves, so she came over to get ready. But as she sat at Destiny's vanity, the smoke detector beeps drove her crazy. So, efficient to the bone, Sasha hoisted the ladder out of a closet, and changed the batteries herself. She needed to keep herself occupied. Because she felt like she was suffering a breakup—a breakup with a man who was never hers, in the first place.

Once she got home last night, she crawled into bed, fully clothed, his scent still covering her. His touch still burning into her skin. And she didn't sleep. Instead, she wept bitter, broken tears. She cried over the revelation she'd reached way too late. She cried for hurting Wes, and for not having the courage to tell him how she really felt. Sasha was in pieces.

But she had to put herself back together. Because no matter how she felt, Sasha was going to see Wes again, tonight. And possibly Teo. And she had to take it like a woman. After all, this situation wasn't happening *to* her. She'd unknowingly *orchestrated* it. It was all her fault.

She was too embarrassed to tell Destiny the truth. So, instead, she busied herself with home repairs.

"Please don't fall. My insurance has lapsed," said Destiny, sipping Fleur de Geisha tea.

"I've never fallen off a ladder in my life," said Sasha. "And why don't you know how to reinstate your insurance? And fix your smoke detector? You'd die first in *The Hunger Games*."

"I told you, my Taskrabbit's coming over tomorrow to do repairs. He could've done it."

"*You* could've done it."

"I'm too delicate for such matters."

Folding her gown's hem over her arm, Sasha carefully climbed down the ladder. "Fire safety isn't a joke. Promise me you'll learn how to change your battery, friend."

"This isn't about fire safety. You're trying to channel your nervous energy."

"Why would I be nervous?"

Sasha sat down at Destiny's flashy mirrored vanity and eyed herself in the reflection. Admittedly, she felt fantastic in the gown—a bias-cut peach satin slip dress that clung to her figure, leaving nothing to the imagination. Her eyes were melodramatic and smoky; her hair fell in glamorous waves. Tasteful Swarovski crystal jewelry twinkled at her ears and cleavage. On the outside, it was all working—but inside, she was a boiling cauldron of turmoil. Her stomach was flip-flopping, and her palms were permanently damp. With a small grimace, she grabbed a *New Yorker* magazine and fanned her face.

"It's clear you're nervous, baby. You just climbed up a ladder in formal wear."

"Formals always throw me. You're all glam, you have to performatively be on your best behavior. It makes me goofy. At the junior prom, I bit down on a cherry tomato and it exploded all over my dress." She sighed glumly. "I looked like *Carrie*."

"What's freaking you out the most about tonight?"

With a stressed-out sigh, she caught Destiny's eyes in the mirror. She still wasn't comfortable sharing the full truth about her and Wes. "Going to a fancy gala with Wes, maybe? Experiencing him in formal wear? Even though the date is just for show, it's still nerve-racking."

"Huh. Interesting. I had assumed the possibility of seeing Teo again was making you nervous."

"Oh. Oh, of course. That goes without saying," she said quickly, brushing a touch of powder onto her nose. "But I don't want to get my hopes up. It's almost too good to be true. So I'm managing my expectations. If he's there, it'll be a happy surprise. If he isn't? Well, maybe we'll gather some clues."

Destiny clapped her hands on her thighs. Then, her drooly Saint Bernard, Miss Piggy, came bounding into the room, wearing a pink statement necklace. She leapt onto Destiny's lap.

"Sasha, are you sure about Teo? I'm worried that you're so caught up in the fantasy, you're forgetting he's just some guy. Hopefully, he's exactly who he presented to be on the flight. But there's a chance he won't be. Honey, he could be the kind of boyfriend you need to crate at night. He could be *poor*. It's a crapshoot."

Sasha turned around on the stool, facing Destiny. "I'm not caught in a fantasy."

Sighing heavily, Miss Piggy flipped on her back and zonked out.

"You are. And is it just a way to avoid what's really in front of you?"

"What are you talking about?"

"Wes."

Sasha folded one leg over the other and arranged her gown over her knee. "Whatever do you mean?" she asked in a posh British accent.

"Don't be cute. How many times have you hung out with him in the past week?"

"But we're not just 'hanging out.' We're basically coworkers."

"There's something you're not telling me, Sasha Cruz," announced Destiny, fussing with Miss Piggy's necklace. "I know you. Look at how you're wiggling your foot. You always contract restless leg syndrome when you get stressed out."

Sasha let out a massive exhale, her shoulders slumping. She hoped her makeup masked her blotchy eyes from crying all night long. "Okay. Okay, I'm tired of running. I'm going to tell you something, but you can't judge me."

"No promises, babe. Shoot."

"I'm...I like him. I'm crazy about him, a little bit. I don't know how this happened. We keep slipping up with each other." She dropped her face in her hands, and then, "You know, orgasmically."

"Ahhh!" screamed Destiny, startling Miss Piggy out of sleep. "You did it. I knew it. Besides, you're always with him. If you hang out at a barbershop long enough, you're gonna get a haircut." She beamed. "You really like him, huh?"

"Too much." Sasha chewed her lip. "I've never felt like this. But what if it's just the trauma talking? He was there at the scariest point of my life. What if I'm just projecting all these savior feelings onto him? But I ruined everything, anyway. I was too scared to get hurt, so I never told him how I felt. And last night, he told me he couldn't see me... that way... anymore. That it was killing him."

"Killing him? He's down that bad? What are we gonna do?"

"Nothing. We do nothing. It's for the best, anyway. I'm scared he would've hurt me. He's not a relationships guy, and he's a tad ran-through, and he's extremely close to his ex..."

"What does the ex look like?"

"She's Imani McIntyre."

Destiny's jaw dropped. "Don't piss me off. That strumpet?"

"Swear to God. I saw her the other day. Apparently, she's tapped into her 'divine feminine.'"

Destiny winced. "Yeah, let's keep him away from her."

Sasha stared off into nothing, trying to mentally prepare herself for letting Wes go. "This is for the best. I just have to keep reminding myself. Wes is..."

...wonderful, beautiful, caring, romantic, delicious...

"...sort of my favorite person. But our connection goes back to a time when I felt scared and vulnerable. I want to start over, feel strong. I mean, look at my progress! I'm headed to a gala full of strangers. And I'm surprisingly okay with this. This is a massive step forward, and I don't want any ties to the past."

"Self-preservation, I get it. But you can't help how you feel."

Destiny was right. She couldn't help her feelings. But she did have control over whether she acted on them or not. Earrings jingling, she stood up, grabbed her evening bag, and kissed Destiny on the cheek. It was time to go.

Later, as her Uber driver drove across the Brooklyn Bridge, as a syrupy amber sun set over Lower Manhattan's chrome skyline, she dug into her bag. She was looking for her good-luck charm. The thing that she carried with her for the past four years whenever she needed a surge of positivity. Protection.

Her fingers found it in the dark. An old pencil, with Dane & Son Detective Agency stamped on the side in gold. Grooves from the previous owner's teeth marks were embedded on it, as he liked to chew it when he was thinking. At least he did the night he tossed it to her in his office—and she caught it, in prime majorette style. She fondled it lovingly, then tucked it back in her bag.

An ironic talisman for a woman who didn't like to look back.

Wes couldn't find Sasha. Granted, they'd agreed to meet out front at nine, and he was fifteen minutes early. But he was nervous. He was downright losing it. First of all, the last time he wore a tux was at Brooke and Timothy-Joshua's wedding. But his sister made him tailor it to hell and back, so at least it fit well. But he felt weird walking in it. He also felt weird pacing back and forth along Sixty-First Street between Madison and Fifth, keeping an eye on the Pierre's grand entrance. Waiting, waiting. Waiting for his date who wasn't a date; his lover who wasn't his lover. Even though he was the one who stopped them from going further, it was still a near-impossible thought. He needed Sasha Cruz in his life—in an urgent, undeniable way. And Wes didn't know how to deprive himself from what he wanted. But this time, he had to. He'd suffered enough humiliation. Every time he touched her, he lost.

No more. Wes was no more than a hired hand in her love story with someone else. And he'd be stupid to keep forgetting it.

Wes stopped across the street from the Pierre. Throngs of well-heeled guests mingled at the entrance. A few publicists were standing in the grand doorway, checking in couples and ushering them inside. Wes fiddled with his cuff links, squinting at the guests from across the street. Was Teo already in there? Was he waiting in the line? Nah, he didn't strike Wes as someone who'd wait in line. He just wanted to meet this motherfucker, face-to-face. He knew, deep in his bones, that he was a bad guy. A possibly dangerous one. Too many red flags, too many unanswered questions, too many inconsistencies. And when it came to Sasha, all his protective instincts kicked in. He wouldn't let anyone hurt her. He had to protect her.

Where was she? Taking a deep breath, he looked to his right at the massive Central Park vista, glowing a dusky, russet gold as the sun disappeared in the sky. To the left was Madison Avenue, she'd probably be coming from there.

Just then, his phone rang. He pulled it from his jacket pocket—it was Imani.

"Hey, I. What's going on?"

"I saw him. I just saw him, Wes." She sounded out of breath. The words tumbled out of her. "I just left the gym in his building, and I saw him walk out the front door and get into a limo. He was wearing a tux. What does the tux mean?"

Wes sucked in a sharp breath, and then let it go. He was coming. He was near.

"It means he's on his way to the Two Tunics gala. And Sasha's finally gonna meet him."

"Lucky girl." She giggled. "He looks like a spanker."

"If he ever laid a hand on her, I'd fucking kill him."

"Listen to you. You'd *kill* him? Over a healthy, mutually negotiated spank?"

"I'd kill him over nothing, Imani. He's not a good guy. And I don't want him anywhere near Sasha."

"Mmm, the plot thickens. Oh, I forgot to tell you. I saw him yesterday, too. Walking down our block with an older gentleman. My third eye homed in on him."

"Why didn't you tell me this?"

"I have my own life! Anyway, the man with Teo was wearing priest garb." She paused. "Or maybe he was a neo-goth."

"That's a staggering difference."

"I think I'm just seeing priests everywhere, because of my article. Did I tell you they launder the stolen church money by funneling it into fake businesses? If you were a shady priest, where would you put your cash?"

"I'll get back to you on that. Gotta run. I owe you and your third eye."

Wes's pulse was racing. A vein in his temple throbbed. It was all but confirmed. Teo D. Scera would be here tonight. Where the hell was Sasha?

Fucking calm down, he thought. *Just go in, you can wait for her in the lobby. You look like an asshole.*

Quickly, he looked both ways and walked across Sixty-First, toward the hotel entrance. Used to making himself as inconspicuous as possible during investigations, he kept his head facing down, so as not to look anyone in the eye. But then, out of the corner of his eye, he caught a glimpse that took his breath away. He stopped dead just outside the entrance. It was Sasha, stepping out of an Uber several feet away from him. A Pierre doorman reaching his hand in and helping her out.

Seeing her was a punch in the stomach. She was more beautiful, more utterly, intolerably, irresistibly *scrumptious*, than he'd ever seen her. She was poured into a slinky dress the exact color of the sunset over the park. Had he ever seen a cleavage so creamy, so golden-bronze and succulent? With her tousled hair and puffy, red lips, she looked like she'd been making out for six hours. That's how she looked after he kissed her, devoured her, made her come. It's how he dreamed of her.

"*Fuuuuck,*" he groaned under his breath. Frozen in place, he watched her walk—no, saunter—to a publicist at the door. In a daze, he watched her mouth form the words, *hihowareyou*. Wes realized he was entering creep territory, so he forced himself to make a move. Clearing his throat, he walked up behind her.

Wes wanted to get her attention, but was careful not to scare her. He knew how jittery she was in crowds. So, in lieu of tapping her on the shoulder, or calling her name, he simply cleared his throat. She whipped around, a blur of waves, creamy shoulders, and rose-crushed lips.

Her chest rose sharply as she sucked in the smallest gasp. Her eyes scanned him, from his face, down to his shoes, and back to his eyes. Wes didn't know if it was the lights from the Pierre—or something else—but her chestnut eyes were sparkling.

"Hi," she breathed.

"Hello," he managed stiffly. "Hey."

"H-how long have you been standing there?"

"Me? I just got here."

"You look..." Trailing off, she tried again. "You look *cinematic* in this tux."

"I feel like a limo driver." Wes couldn't take his eyes off her. "But you? You're so beautiful. You look..."

...like you're mine, he thought.

And for a moment, just one, dizzying, perfect moment, he allowed himself to pretend it was true. That she'd shown up for him. Not Teo, just him.

He'd never wanted anything or anyone this badly, in his life. It was a helpless, crazy feeling. But Sasha wasn't his, and never was. Unless he was on the other side of the phone at a vulnerable, horny moment at 2:00 a.m. on a Tuesday.

Or if she's scared for her life in a detective's office.

Brain scrambled, he repeated himself. "You look beautiful."

She smiled shyly. "Thank you."

A light in her eyes flared and then faded. Just then, Wes noticed the redness in her eyes. Had she been crying? He couldn't bear the thought.

The air was thick with emotions—regret, want, exhilaration—and everything that they weren't saying.

"So," he started, "should we go in?"

"Let's do it," she said, and her bright tone sounded forced. "Quick question. Can we wear surveillance earpieces?"

A smile tugged at the corner of his mouth. "You think you're in *Mr. and Mrs. Smith*, don't you?"

"I told you, I love to theme dress," she said, and then pulled two pods out of her clutch. "I bought these earpieces at the spy shop on Seventh Ave. Here's yours."

Wes bit back a chuckle. "I figured you'd do that. So I brought real ones. Here's yours."

He pulled an actual, legit set out of his jacket pocket, and handed her a pair. She grinned conspiratorially.

"One step ahead, huh?" she teased him.

"Always. Let's go."

With his palm on the small of her back, he led her inside. As flares went off inside him, he kept telling himself, *Remember it's a job, it's a job, it's a job, you fucking idiot...*

...you fucking idiot, Sasha thought. How could she let herself be so nakedly obvious? When she first saw Wes, she couldn't pretend not to care. She wasn't prepared for Tux Wes. Crisp and impeccably tailored, it was cut to flatter the hard lines of his long legs, the breadth of his chest. She swore she could see the bulge in his groin. He looked like a Pinterest-board boyfriend, or a vintage Old Spice ad, or a dating app billboard blatantly misrepresenting the caliber of idiots *truly* on the app (ugh, why was she always casting).

When she met his eyes and he smiled at her, she was gone.

Fucking gone. For a moment, she didn't have the strength to pretend that Wes Dane hadn't turned her inside out. For God's sake, he knew not to creep up behind her, because it would scare the shit out of her. When it came to her, Wes grew a Superman cape out of thin air. That's how it felt. He was her hero.

Why did she hire him in the first place? Did she forget how it felt, that one night, to be close to him? To feel grounded in the fortress of a stranger's arms? Did she forget how good he felt? It was pure insanity, calling him back into her life, without expecting complications and confusion.

But the timing just wasn't in their favor. She had to face it. People were wildly attracted all the time, it didn't mean they were supposed to be together. The examples were endless. Issa and Lawrence. Carrie and Big. Joker and Harley Quinn. Olivia Pope and President Fitz. Miss Piggy and Kermit.

Look at J. Lo and Ben Affleck, she thought. *They can't stay away from each other, but the marriage never sticks. There must be a reason for that. Beyond them both being problematic Leos.*

She just had to move past it. He could have a place in her life. But it couldn't be romantic.

This is what she told herself as he placed his wide, strong hand on the small of her back, leading her through the grand doors. The heat from his palm radiated through her, tingling her skin. They got on a mirrored, art deco elevator with an older woman, draped in a red duchesse satin gown. They all nodded hello to each other. And then, Sasha and Wes stood behind her, a respectful distance from each other. The ride seemed to take forever. Her eyes darted toward his, and then away. He stole a glance, too, and then focused on the floor numbers. A slow smile played on Wes's lips. Then, he chuckled a bit, quietly.

What? she mouthed.

Your earpiece is on backwards, he answered.

Oh, she said, fumbling.

"I got you," he said out loud. The woman glanced up at them in the mirror.

Wes stepped toward Sasha, gently backing her against the wall. With furrowed concentration, he readjusted the piece in her left ear. His scent was intoxicating. For a moment, she allowed herself to drink in his beautiful face—blatantly and indulgently.

Kiss me, she thought, *kiss me, please, I know we're not supposed to, but I can't go one more second without it.*

"Is that better?" he asked.

"Sorry?" Her brain had short-circuited. She had no idea what he was referring to.

"Your earpiece."

"Oh! Yes."

"Good." With a satisfied, rascally twinkle in his eye, he dropped his hand. "And Sasha? Stop staring at my mouth. I'm not doing your commercial."

The door opened, and the woman stole one more look at them, eyes wide, before walking off.

With inside-joke chuckles and intoxicating closeness, the two stepped out of the elevator together, glamorous beyond measure, momentarily forgetting the real reason they were there.

Chapter 21

TOXIC MÉNAGE À TROIS

Sasha and Wes stood on the outskirts of the ballroom. The almost century-old space was a splashy eruption of lavish Jazz Age decor. At the head of the dance floor, a deadly serious-looking band was playing a jaunty version of "24K Magic." Just beyond the wiggling crowd of revelers, twenty circular tables were dressed in cream-and-gold tablescapes, each with its own, unique orchid bouquet. The crowd was a lively bunch of middle-aged moneyed folk—Upper East Side types for whom the ticket, limo, Oscar de la Renta gown, and auction bids were a mere drop in their financial bucket. Tonight, the 1 percent was feeling themselves as they gathered to support the noble mission of...

"What was the name of the charity, again?" asked Sasha, crushing her table assignment in her palm.

"Two Tunics," responded Wes.

They were slightly uncomfortable. After recovering from the sensory shock of seeing each other looking Oscar-night elegant, they fell into silence. The echo of last night reverberated between them. Sasha felt something final in the air. Teo was in this room. When Wes found him, it was the end of the case—and them. If the stakeout at Film Forum was the beginning, tonight was the ending.

"Two Tunics," she repeated, trying to ground herself in the conversation. "What does that mean, I wonder?"

"It's a biblical reference. Something about if you have two tunics, you should give one away," explained Wes, somewhat clunkily. "To a person who, you know, doesn't have one."

"Got it. This reminds me, I got the chicest embroidered tunic in Seville with Destiny." She fidgeted with her bracelet. "I wonder where that is."

"You think these people know they're here for a charity?" wondered Wes. "Or this just a rich person version of meeting at the spot."

A man walked by, then, accidentally stepping on the back of his date's heels. She playfully slapped his arm, saying, "These heels were six hundred dollars, Craig!"

Eyes wide, Wes whispered to Sasha, "For a pair of *shoes*, though?"

"I've spent close to that on a gorgeous heel," admitted Sasha. "But those aren't even good. Polka-dot suede?"

"No amount of money can unlame you," he surmised.

"What should we do, now?" Sasha fluffed her hair, eyes darting around the room. "Hit the dance floor?"

"Nah, it's a little early to put my pinkie ring up to the moon."

"Fair. So, what's the plan?"

"Separate. Circulate. Interrogate. Meaning, we're going to go our separate ways, and strike up conversations with partygoers. See if you can ask leading questions that would bring us to Teo's whereabouts. Nothing too obvious."

"No, I'll be so subtle," she assured him.

"Just remember, we can hear each other in our buds," said Wes, "so if you get into trouble, just holler. I'll give you some direction. Tell you what to do."

He's good at that, she thought, her cheeks blazing. Goddamn it, she had to rid such thoughts from her mind. But how? Wes was too beautiful. And the night was too gorgeous. Every sensation felt heightened. Even now, she and Wes were standing so close together, their pinkies unbearably close—the memory of his touch thrummed under her skin. She stepped away.

This is killing me, he'd told her. Their toxic ménage à trois might've been killing him, but it was slowly torturing her. She couldn't see a way out. Wes Dane consumed her thoughts! But he very clearly said he wasn't an option. So, there was nothing left to discuss. If she'd learned anything from her mother, it was that chasing a man is an invitation for them to run in the opposite direction. You could blink and miss twenty years of your life, saving yourself for a man.

But Sasha couldn't shake off how she felt in his orbit. Right now, she was pretending to care about what a stranger spent on her shitty shoes, while her heart beat outside of her chest.

The world tilted on its axis when they were together.

"Should we separate?" he asked, turning to face her.

"Yes, I'm ready. Let's do it."

"How's your anxiety right now? Are you okay? With all the people?"

She wanted to say, *With you here? Of course I'm okay. You make me feel invincible, like nothing scary is allowed to happen to me. You're my layer of protection. My grounding force. My good guy in a room of wolves.*

In bocca al lupo. Stay safe in the mouth of wolves. Sasha sucked in air, sharply. Teo had said that on the flight, hadn't he? It was an odd line to remember now, of all times.

The truth was too complicated, so she pretended to be fine. "You know what? I feel pretty un-anxious right now."

Sasha glanced up at Wes. He was already looking at her. Quickly, he began concerning himself with his cuff links.

"Just tell me if you need me," he said, "and I'll come find you."

"Got it." Sasha nodded. "See you on the other side."

With that, she turned on her heel and headed into the crowd. Somehow, she could feel his gaze warming the bare skin of her back. Was Wes watching her? She was dying to look back.

Hell yes, Wes watched her walk away. He drank her in—the slinky grace of her body, the liquid sheen of her gown, the luminous bronze of her bare shoulders. *Fuck.* A vein in his temple throbbed. Basically, he was watching her glide off like a goddamn swan into someone else's arms. And it left him in near-physical pain. Good thing she hadn't looked back. Because he would've called this all off.

Which would've been a mistake. He needed to find Teo tonight. His only goal was to make it to the other side of this fun-house mirror investigation. And move on.

Once Sasha was out of sight, he wandered over to a floral bouquet display. Just to stand and collect himself. A wild spray of flowers fell out of the floor vase, spilling over. Forever the kid who, even after being told not to touch anything at the department store, knocked over mannequins and clothing racks—he gingerly ran his fingers along a petal. He wondered what kind of flower it was.

"An impressive arrangement, isn't it?"

The voice was coming from the other side of the flowers. Wes leaned forward a bit and saw a guy who looked a lot like him. They exchanged an African American Nod of Solidarity.

"You the florist?" asked Wes.

The guy chuckled a little. "No, my wife is. Ricki Wilde, of Wilde Things Harlem? She's a genius with perennials."

The guy looked so proud, he was practically levitating. Wes smiled at this. "I don't know anything about flowers, but your wife's talented, man. I'm Roland Weiss."

"The name's Ezra Walker," he said in a deep, rolling Southern drawl. "You involved with the charity?"

"No, I'm just a donor." He stood up straighter. "I run a hedge fund."

"Reckon I enjoy seeing a Black man run a hedge fund."

"Appreciate you. Yeah, it's a lot of pressure. Nice to get out for a night like this. Even though I'm, uh, not here solely for pleasure. I'm meeting a business associate, Teo D. Scera. We have some... we have a few... *hedge topics* to... iron out."

Wes was glitching. If he hadn't spent the last twenty-four hours trying to figure out how to get unobsessed with a woman, he would've invested more time researching finance buzzwords. He was walking into this disguise cold.

"You know him?" asked Wes, innocently.

"Never heard of the fella, no." Ezra sipped a whiskey sour. "Hold on, you said his name's Teo? Come to think of it, I did overhear someone introducing himself with that name. Over by the bar." He gestured with his glass. "Eye-talian accent, sounded like?"

"That's him." Wes neutralized his expression. "Well, I should make my way over there. Good to meet you, man—"

"If you don't mind me saying," interrupted Ezra, "you look familiar. Does someone in your family run a food truck?"

"My cousin! That's hilarious. Yeah, he's trying to perfect a brisket."

"I was visiting a friend in Prospect Park and saw him. Brisket, huh? I'm an expert in South Carolina barbecue. You tell him the secret is orange juice in the marinade." Then, Ezra's phone buzzed. "My wife's calling me over to the table. Pleasure to meet you, young man." Ezra slapped Wes on the back and disappeared into the crowd.

Young man? They were about the same age. Orange juice, though. That was smart.

Wes pressed a button on his earpiece. "You hear that?"

No response from Sasha. He tried again.

"Teo's here," he whispered. "Can you hear me?"

No answer from Sasha. But he was picking up environmental noise from her end. Was her input mic on? He could hear her, but she couldn't hear him. He peered over the crowd but didn't see her. So, he texted her a message, instead.

Inspector Gadget. Where u at? He's here. If u get this, turn on your earpiece with the small orange button.

Sasha didn't answer. Wes didn't want to think the worst.

That she'd gotten to Teo before he did.

Sasha wasn't having any luck. She'd sidled up to a couple at the bar, dropping Teo's name. Nothing. Then, she'd gone back to the check-in desk, to ask if he'd checked in, but the woman said she couldn't give out that information. How did Wes make investigating look so easy? She wondered how Wes was faring. She adjusted her earpiece but couldn't hear him. Feeling restless, she made the executive decision to head to the ladies' lounge. Refresh her lipstick. Give herself a pep talk. Reset.

Sasha strode across the room, weaving in between the tables, till she reached the lavish lounge. It was almost the size of her apartment. The art deco sitting room featured a circular velvet settee in the center of the room, surrounded by several vanity stations for touch-ups. Automatically, Sasha scanned the room for windows. There were two on the back wall. And this was the first floor, an easy escape, if needed.

Exit strategy planned, Sasha strode over to one of the vanities. In the midsummer humidity, her waves had frizzed a little. With an impatient sigh, she tried to smooth the fuzz with her fingers, to no avail.

"I have anti-frizz spray if you want it?" said a woman in the mirror, next to her. Draped in red satin, she was an elegant beauty, with glowing, golden-brown skin. Her hair fell in rippling, jet-black ringlets to her clavicle. Yes, she'd borrow serum from this woman.

"You just saved my life," said Sasha, running a small dollop through her hair.

"Please, I feel your pain. My Dominican stylist gave me this stuff, and I swear by it."

"They truly are all-knowing," said Sasha.

"Heavy-handed with the heat, though," the woman pointed out.

"Girl! I still have heat damage from a 2025 blowout," said Sasha. "But I regret nothing. My hair was laid."

"You live on the edge." The woman laughed. "I'm Patricia Moreno."

"Hi, I'm Sasha Cruz."

With the unique fervor that happens between women in public ladies' rooms, they were instantly bonded. "Can I ask, are you Dominican?" asked Patricia. "I always know my people."

Surprised, Sasha gasped a little. And then smiled at Patricia, in the mirror. She'd never been identified this way, before.

"I-I am," she said. "Half. But I don't—" She cut herself off.

"What's wrong?" Patricia looked concerned.

"I don't speak Spanish well. And I didn't grow up in a Dominican community. So, it means a lot that you could tell."

Why was she apologizing for her father's mistakes, to a stranger?

"Sasha, no one can take your heritage from you. You are what you are."

Feeling slightly buoyed by her vote of confidence, Sasha said, "I can read Spanish a lot better than I speak it. I've read a few novels in Spanish, actually."

Patricia shut her clutch with a satisfying click. "Yeah? ¿Cuál es tu libro favorito?"

Too insecure to use her Spanish, Sasha responded, "I'm making my way through the Reina Roja series. I love a thriller."

"Listen, I have a book club. All Dominican girls. I started it with my sister-in-law and my homegirl, and we're at thirty-five now. Wanna join? It's my month to bring someone new."

"Seriously? But you don't even know me."

"I'll get to know you." She shrugged, patting her T-zone with translucent powder. "It's fun. We make dishes inspired by the book, we drink, we theme dress..."

"Theme dress?" Sasha gasped. "Done. I'll bring the moro de guandules."

Patricia handed Sasha her phone. "Put in your info, I'll text you mine."

Sasha did. Patricia couldn't imagine the significance of their exchange. The fact that, instead of rushing in and out (which was her usual routine in public bathrooms), she spoke to a stranger. She had a full-on conversation, bonded, gave out her *real* phone number, and revealed a piece of herself. This was a staggering amount of growth to experience in a ballroom bathroom.

Patricia took the phone back and smiled at her new friend. "I should get back. I left my fiancé at our table with my colleagues, and he hates Wall Street banter." She smiled. "Why are you here, new friend?"

Sasha didn't feel like lying. She knew what her story was supposed to be. She was Wes's—no, Roland's—business partner, here as his plus-one. But she was tired of lying. And she wanted to say the words out loud.

"I'm here with an associate." She swallowed. "But it's tricky. We're supposed to be professional partners. But we're more than that."

"How much more?" asked Patricia.

Sasha grimaced a little. And then, she blurted it out. "I'm crazy about him. I'm overwhelmed by it. When he's near me, my brain shuts off and my heart explodes, and I can't resist anything about him," she said. "It hurts, because the odds are against us. But I'm in love with him. Every moment we're not together feels wasted."

Spontaneously, Patricia gave Sasha a hug. Sasha hugged her back, this kind, openhearted stranger with exquisite hair.

"Don't waste any more time," said Patricia. "Tell him."

Afterward, they said their goodbyes. Patricia slipped into a stall and Sasha headed back out into the ballroom.

At the border of the dance floor, she collided with Wes.

Wes walked right into Sasha.

He'd been pacing the length of the ballroom, searching for her. Since Sasha's earpiece wasn't working and she wasn't answering texts, his protective instinct surged. Had her anxiety ratcheted up? Did she leave in a panic? Was she with Teo? If so, was she safe?

But, about five minutes ago, her earpiece kicked in. And Wes could finally hear her end of the connection. But what he heard, he wished he hadn't.

It hurts, because the odds are against us. I'm in love with him. Every moment we're not together feels wasted.

Wes didn't know who Sasha was talking to. But it was obvious who she was talking *about*. All signs pointed to Teo. The odds were, indeed, great. And she was obviously in love with him. Look at the lengths she'd gone to find him. This wasn't news to Wes. But it was a wake-up call, hearing Sasha say those words—directly into his ears, no less, the raw emotion in her voice on full blast. *I'm in love with him.* The truth was inescapable.

This was on his mind as they stood facing each other, while partygoers around them slow-danced to a terrible, big-band version of "This Is How We Do It."

"Oh, hey. Where were you?" His voice sounded off-kilter. He'd just been assaulted by so many emotions, he didn't know how to be normal. And her beauty wasn't helping. There was a feverish flush to her cheeks. She was wringing her hands together, her eyes bright. She looked impassioned, like she was on the precipice of a revelation. What was going on with her? And was she not wearing a bra? He hadn't noticed before. But the silk of her low-cut gown clung to her erect nipples.

My God, he thought, *the things I'd do to her right now if I could.*

"I was in the ladies' lounge," she said. "Where were you?"

"Your earpiece must not be working. You couldn't hear me?"

"No! And I forgot I even had them on. Um... could you hear me?" Nervously, she smoothed down her hair—rustling up her fragrance, some darkly sexy combination of vanilla and rose. It was stultifying.

His heart was breaking.

"No, I couldn't hear anything," lied Wes. "Maybe mine's faulty, too."

"What should we do now?" she asked.

"You should dance," suggested a string bean of a man wearing all black. He held up a full-frame Canon camera with an external flash. The event photographer. "But first, look at me."

Wes said, "Nah, we're good. But thank you."

"Come on, you're a beautiful couple. And the night is young."

"We're not a couple," corrected Sasha. The photographer huffed off, shaking his head.

She looked at Wes. He looked back. And he decided that, if this was going to be their last night together, he wanted one more chance to breathe her air.

He tilted his head, lightly scratching his jaw. "Should we?"

"Dance together? Here? Now?"

Wes drank her in, this extraordinary woman gazing up at him with wide, feline eyes, and he had no choice but to touch her. Stepping forward, he closed the space between them. Boldly, he slipped his hand between her arm and waist, stopping at the small of her back. He pulled her against him. In the gesture, her spaghetti strap slid down her shoulder. It took every ounce of willpower he had to not run his tongue along the luminous skin there. Instead, he gently slid the strap back up on her shoulder.

Sasha took in a soft, shuddering breath. Her hand found his, and he placed it over his heart. His brain went fuzzy.

They swayed slowly, barely moving, with no regard for the song playing. Their breathing was in sync. With merely an inch between them, from head to toe, they were close enough to smell, taste, feel—but they didn't. They couldn't, not anymore, and certainly not there. Wes understood this, but it was excruciating. Feeling the warmth of her skin through her dress was insane. Intolerably erotic.

Tell her, he thought. *Tell her before you lose all decorum and fuck her right here.*

"He's here," Wes blurted out. "Teo's here."

He felt her stiffen. Something flared in her eyes and went out. "How do you know?"

"I asked around. I haven't seen him. But listen. I want to meet him before you do. To make sure you're safe. Understand?"

"Of course," she said. "Good. This is great. Exciting."

Wes said nothing, just continued to hold her close.

"What's going to happen to us?" she asked, a tremor in her voice. "We'll still talk, right?"

"Honestly?"

"Please tell me the truth."

"I can't be your friend. I'm sorry. I want you to be happy. But I can't see you and pretend not to feel anything." He cleared his throat. "It's too easy to forget that I'm just a guy you hired."

She nodded, in a daze. "I still have your pencil."

"My what?"

"Your pencil. From that night. You tossed it to me, and I caught it, majorette-style. It has Dane & Son Detective Agency printed on it. And your bite marks," she said with a weak smile. "It's silly."

Unconsciously, Wes tightened his hold on her. "Why did you keep it?"

"I wanted a Wes souvenir, I guess. To remember how you cared for me. That it's possible to find a kindred spirit, even in the dark."

Wes didn't think the hurt could slice deeper. All he could manage was a crooked half smile. "I was doing my job. But it's good to know that I meant something. That I left an impression." He paused, trying to streamline his thoughts. "Why are you telling me this?"

"Because I want you to know," she said, "that you're not just some guy I hired."

The inky depths of Sasha's eyes fixed him to his spot. They stopped moving, still locked in their extremely close but not touching embrace. Well-heeled couples swirled and swayed around them, to a song Wes couldn't even identify, because it didn't matter. He dipped his face into her hair, breathing her in. At that, she made a sweet, breathy noise—and it hit him so hard, he shut his eyes. Like when you squeeze them shut on a roller coaster, to ground yourself.

"Who am I to you?" she asked, eyes pleading. "You told me all the reasons it wouldn't work. But how do you feel?"

And then, only then, did he let her go. And turned back into Detective Wes. "It doesn't matter. Because the truth is, I *am* a guy you hired," he said lightly, still with a half smile. "And I still have work to do. Right? Here's what's gonna happen. I'm doing one last sweep of the place. You wait for me at that cocktail table, over there. I don't want you speaking to him before I do, so call me if you spot him first. And I'll come over."

Jarred by his sudden energy switch, she said, "Perfect. Yes. Great plan."

"When I find him, I'll text you. While we're talking, you come over and lurk nearby. Size him up. Decide if you want me to move forward with the letter. If it's still a yes, I'll make sure he has it before the night's over."

Just like that, the spell was broken. Sasha headed for the cocktail table. And Wes? Well, Wes went straight for the bar. And he downed three shots of whiskey, one after another.

He was furious with himself that it had come to this. That he needed to get drunk to face this fool. With a ragged groan, he scrubbed his face with his hands. This was his fatal flaw. When life got too intense, his compass vanished. Confidence plummeted. He got drunk. He fought. He bent rules. He hadn't changed at all, had he?

Caught between self-hatred, jealousy, and thunderous heartbreak, he ordered another shot.

By the time Wes looked up from his mini-bender—his vision blurred and out of sync—he realized the world had continued to turn without him.

His gaze fell on Sasha, standing at a high cocktail table to the far right of the bar. There was a man standing with her. Both were wearing stunned, giddy expressions.

And he knew, without a shadow of a doubt, this was Teo.

Chapter 22

THE PETTIEST BITCH YOU KNOW IS A STRAIGHT MAN

The funny thing was, Sasha didn't see Teo at first. She stood there at the high-top table, lost in thought. Suddenly, her dress felt too naked. The silk too thin, the spaghetti straps too bare. Earlier in the night, the gown felt chic. Now it felt thirsty—and she was cold. Her head ached. When was the last time she'd eaten something?

Overwhelmed, her eyes welled up. She opened them, wide, trying to keep the tears from falling. She wasn't a crier. (Much to her chagrin, at times. Sometimes she wished she could just push out some tears. It'd be cathartic.) But Wes's tone on the dance floor rattled her. He was so far away. It was like he'd rewound time, back to the morning they met, years ago, before they magnetized each other, when he was just a detective and she was a distressed client and the lines were clear-cut.

If Wes had asked her, Sasha would've run off with him. And stayed forever.

But he didn't. And Teo was here. Maybe it wouldn't matter when she saw him again. Maybe the world would melt away, and she'd be reminded of why she started this search in the first place.

And then, a tear fell. Sasha grabbed a napkin and folded it into a tiny triangle, dabbing at the corners of her eyes, gingerly. *Fuck, fuck, fuck.* Public weeping was so passive-aggressive. *Oh look at me, I'm emotionally undisciplined in front of an audience, someone feel sorry for me.* She didn't need help. Maybe she never did. She'd made her whole life happen for herself. Why couldn't she have found Teo on her own?

Which begged the question. Why did she need to call on Wes?

Ignoring her internal voice, Sasha continued patting at her eyes. At one point, she dabbed so furiously, the sharp point of her napkin triangle poked into her eye. She yelped and flicked her hand, sending the napkin flying. Sasha heard a gruff sound of surprise. Then she spun around. Her napkin had hit an innocent bystander in the face as he moved through the crowd. (This was not unlike her move during the all-state Texas majorette tryouts. Adult Sasha was just teen Sasha with premium bedding.)

The man had stopped in his tracks and was rubbing his eye. Was that...Teo?

Before Sasha had a chance to speak, he beat her to it.

"Seraphina," he said, dropping his hand to his side. A smile softening the rugged edge of his features. Like an ice cap melting. "Is that you?"

"Did...Did you call me Seraphina?" she whispered.

"It's how I've referred to you, in my head." His eyes crinkled. "And to anyone who'll listen."

He's been talking about me, too, she thought. *I'm not crazy. I'm not alone.*

"I've been calling you Seat F."

"Seat F?" His brows met, quizzical for a few seconds, then he chuckled. "Oh. Sì, of course. My seat. I can't believe I'm looking at you. How... What are you doing here?"

"I was invited," she said, her voice sounding high and unfamiliar. He looked exactly as she remembered. About five foot eleven, mint-green eyes. Dark, salt-and-pepper hair. His smile was crooked and imperfect, which added to his charm. She remembered why she'd been so intrigued. He was tough yet gentle; mysterious but direct. Everything about him was a thrilling contradiction. "Why are you here?"

"I know the owner of the charity quite well."

They stood there, smiling, not quite knowing what to do.

"It's you," he said under his breath.

"You're how I remembered."

"You are, too. And much more. We were stupid not to exchange information."

"What were we thinking?" asked Sasha with a little laugh.

"We weren't. We were... well, I was intoxicated. In more ways than one. And I've never regretted something more."

"I've been waiting for this moment. Wondering what I'd say, how I'd act."

"As have I. I almost hired an investigator to find you, but I didn't want to be like a... how you say... stalker. It's distasteful."

Sasha nodded in vigorous agreement. "Isn't it just?"

"I looked for you, however. On my own. I wondered where a woman like you would go. I even visited a few Seraphinas." He shook his head, brows knitted. "Was I wrong in thinking you worked there?"

"You were right. But I'm casting a commercial for the brand. I don't work in the stores. I should've been clearer!"

"Ah. Ahh. I see. No, you did the right thing, withholding that. You shouldn't divulge such things to a stranger." His eyes crinkled.

"In any case, I told myself that if we're supposed to meet again, the universe will make it so."

"And it did."

"Shall we introduce ourselves?"

"Yes," she said enthusiastically, "but let's make it count this time."

"Allora. Yes. This is a moment of significance."

And then they both made a show of readying themselves for the Introduction That Was Weeks in the Making. He set his martini down on the table and then took a performative breath. He straightened his already flawlessly tied bow tie and checked his cuff links. She tossed her hair, mussing her soft waves, and smoothed her gown over her hips. Shyly, she took him in, once again. Thick, heavy waves of hair practically begging to be pulled, yanked, mussed. Peridot eyes shining like stained glass. Tux so well-cut, Tom Ford likely paid him to wear it. He cut an alluring, powerful figure.

Most crucially, though? He had *certainty* in his gaze. Intention. He knew what he wanted and wasn't afraid to claim it.

Fuck Wes, she thought resolutely.

"What's your name?" he asked.

"Sasha Cruz. And you are?"

"Besotted."

Sasha let out a small, short laugh. "Nice."

"But I'm also Teo D. Scera."

Even though she knew his name, it sounded glorious coming from him. In his native tongue, his voice was florid, husky. It sounded like cathedrals and siesta-sex and good pasta and decadence. "Pleasure to meet you. Again."

"No, no, no. Pleasure's mine," he said. "Again."

They shook hands, and she remembered his touch. Firm, confident, bold. He didn't let go. Neither did she. They stood there, joined at their hands, like they had all the time in the world. And then, because she was feeling spontaneous, and because she wanted to put as much distance between herself and this gala and run headfirst into her future, before Wes saw her and the glass shattered, before she remembered that she'd practically begged him to stop her, Sasha said, "Do you want to get out of here?"

Keeping his eyes on her, Teo set his martini glass down on the table. "Let's go. Le Veau d'Or?"

She blinked. The chic bistro was a ninety-year-old Upper East Side institution. Romantic, ritzy, and impossible to get a table. "I'd love to. But we'll never get in."

He smiled. "Remember what I said on the flight? I'll handle it. Let me do that. Please."

This was the lure of Teo. She thought back to when she struggled to close the remote door on the flight. The way he stepped in and did it for her. He lightened her load. Would she have figured it out? Of course. But she was tired of figuring everything out, on her own. And somehow, he knew that.

Teo was exactly how she remembered. In him, she saw possibility. An unknown future. Slate wiped clean. Just then, he offered Sasha his arm. She slipped her hand in the crook of his elbow.

"Take me to dinner," she said boldly.

Together, they headed toward the exit, passing the bar along the way. Sasha's feet barely touched the ground. This was what she wanted. Until she looked up and locked eyes with Wes.

Wes was leaning against the bar, propped on an elbow. And there was a look on his face she'd never seen before. His eyes were reddened, devoid of light. Distractedly, his fingertips were tapping on his shot glass. His brow was furiously knitted, like he was trying to solve a calculus problem—or strenuously focused on appearing sober.

"Sasha Cruz! Funny seeing you here."

He was speaking just a shade too fast. Yep. He'd had one drink too many.

"Hello!" She dropped her hand from Teo's arm.

"I was looking for you. You were supposed to text me, remember?" He eyed Teo.

"Right, right. I forgot. Well, great seeing you—"

"Apologies, where are my manners?" Wes thrust his hand in Teo's direction, without moving from the bar. Teo had to step closer to Wes to shake it.

"Teo D. Scera."

"Roland Weiss. I'm an old friend of Sasha's."

"Ahh. Do you work in casting together?"

"No," said Sasha. "No, he runs a hedge fund. He's a VC."

"Ahh. A venture capitalist." Teo gave him a nod of approval. "What sector do you invest in?"

Panic flashed in Wes's face. He was in no state to convincingly answer this question

"No, I'm a VC as in vice... chancellor," he sputtered. "At a university. A small university. A college, actually. Online."

A vice chancellor? Oh, Wes was bombed.

"He was a personality hire," said Sasha quickly. "Teo, we should go before the restaurant closes."

"An online college," said Teo, with a pleasant smile. "Noble work. How did you meet Sasha?"

"She's on the advisory board. For the college. That reminds me, Sasha, we have that board meeting tomorrow morning at nine." He raised his brows pointedly. "I'll have my secretary send you a car. Would hate for you to miss it and let down the fifteen other board members. All of whom are former MMA fighters."

Wes was being absurd, but she knew what he was doing. Letting Teo know that if he had any designs on robbing her blind or bludgeoning her to death tonight, there would be people expecting her at a certain time. He'd be held accountable should anything happen to her.

Wes was eyeing Teo. Behind his casual, relaxed body language, she spotted the tension in his jaw. He held the glass in a white-knuckled fist. When did he get hammered?

"So," started Teo, "what brings you to this fundraiser?"

"I've donated to this charity for years," he said. "Thousands. Of dollars, not years."

"Impressive, on an academic's salary."

"Well, I'm also financially involved in several start-ups. I've gotten lucky."

Teo's brows rose with interest. "Is that so? Which start-ups?"

"I don't like to brag," said Wes. "Have you heard of the Rose?"

"I'm not familiar."

"Look it up," responded Wes, while Sasha stared daggers at him. "What brings you here?"

"My business associate runs the charity. I'm not affiliated, but it's a noble cause. The last person I'd expect to see here was Sasha. We met on a flight to Paris recently. A missed connection, you might say. I was a fool not to get Sasha's information. I've never regretted anything more."

Sasha and Teo glanced at each other. Warmth spread to her cheeks.

"Romantic," said Wes flatly. "Anyway, if you're not in the car in the morning, I'll assume this guy's the culprit."

"Are you worried about me kidnapping her?" He laughed good-naturedly.

Wes looked at him. "What's funny?"

"It's humorous, the idea of me committing such a crime."

Wes chuckled, hollowly. "I guess that is funny, considering that kidnapping takes strategic thinking."

Teo frowned in light, amiable confusion. "You, eh, don't take me for a strategic thinker?"

"You had six isolated hours to zero in on Sasha's name, and that tripped you up. No, I don't take you for a strategic thinker."

Sasha read a social satire piece once, theorizing that "the pettiest bitch you know is a straight man." The proof was right in front of her. Currently, her Spanx thong was cutting her in half—she longed to rip it off and choke Wes with it.

But Teo seemed amused. "Are you baiting me?"

"Why, you feeling baited?" asked Wes.

"Roland, that's enough," hissed Sasha.

"I won't be insulted by an online vice chancellor."

Wes turned to Sasha, gesturing at Teo with his glass. A bit sloshed onto the floor. "You hear this elitist fuck? *This* is your guy?"

"You know, you're quite rude," said Teo, with an almost surprised tone. "But you're also entertaining. I can't decide if I like you or not. Ehh, I'm of two minds."

"Well, I'm of two tunics," Sasha blurted out nonsensically. The tension was making her anxiety flare. "Teo, this man is my friend. He's not usually like this. Unfortunately, he's inebriated beyond belief."

"It's true. I'm an inebriated man saying inebriated shit," admitted Wes. Then, he looked at Teo with stony resolve, his entire demeanor switching up. "But on this, I'm clear. You hurt her, and I'll fuck your entire life. You feel me? I played Little League with half the bookings officers in this city."

"So, if I hurt Sasha," said Teo, "you'll have me jailed?"

"No. I'm saying that *I* won't be. Understand? No matter what I do. And before you ask, yeah, it's a threat. Welcome to America, dawg. Cops are corrupt." Wes finished his drink, and then added, "It's a fucking travesty in every instance but this one."

Teo didn't address this veiled threat. He just nodded mildly. And then, he asked Sasha, "Is this friend important to you?"

"He is," she confessed. "Very."

"Then, excuse me. I'll get him a glass of water." Teo flagged a bartender, following him to the other end of the bar.

Sasha whipped around to face Wes.

"What the fuck are you doing?" she spat. "What happened to you?"

"What, am I the only one drinking at the function? Look at the dance floor. Sixty-year-old white people out there throwing ass to a Carlos Santana featuring Rob Thomas cover. They're the problem."

"Wes, please. Don't ruin this. Pull yourself together or I'll kill you." She spoke so fast, her words bled together.

"You can't be serious with this guy. That mama-mia-ass accent? Come *on*, Sasha."

"Oh really? How many languages do you speak?" She ripped the glass out of his hand. "And did you really just threaten him?"

"It wasn't a threat. He hurts you, I'm ending him. I've done it before."

"Done what before? Listen to you! When did you even have time to get this drunk?"

"I'm not drunk. I'm six foot four, do you know how much I'd have to drink to feel it?" He exhaled a bit too hard, and his balance went wonky. Groaning, he grabbed the edge of the bar for balance. "Yeah, I'm drunk."

"This is your *job*. I can't believe you did this. You don't get to do this!" She moved closer to him, whisper-yelling so no one could hear. All around them, revelers were reveling, but her life had split down the center. "Every time we got close, you pushed me away. So you don't get to have a temper tantrum."

He blinked, slowly, and then eyed her through his absurdly long lashes. "Don't I?"

Even in this state, petulant and angry, his face got to her. At once, he was goofy, vulnerable, menacing, ridiculous, and utterly, thoroughly, in the wrong. But in his mess was the truth. And it was clearer than if he'd said it out loud.

"Let me be happy, okay? You found Teo for me. Your work here is done. Put the last month behind us and move on. I'll never forgive you if you ruin this for me."

"He's a fraud."

"And I'm a fool," she said bitterly. "Go home."

Just then, Teo returned with the water. He handed it to Wes. "Drink this. I haven't known Sasha for long, but I doubt she'd have a friend who was an, eh, actual threat to me. Sì? And a friend of hers is a friend of mine."

"Say 'friend' one more time, Super Mario."

"And I decided I can't leave you in this condition. My driver's circling the block. Where do you live? Nearby? Can I drop you off somewhere?"

Something sparked in Wes's eye—undetectable to anyone but Sasha. But it disappeared in a millisecond. And then he sighed as if giving up the fight. "Brooklyn. But I don't need a ride."

"He can take an Uber, it's fine," said Sasha frantically. "Honestly, he's not even that drunk, he's just dramatic."

"I insist. Sasha, you also live in Brooklyn, yes? I'll drop you both off. Roland will take the passenger seat. Let's call it a night."

This was an obvious power move. Teo was domming Wes. On top of that, he was showing Sasha that he cared about what she cared about.

Sasha chewed her lip, the situation giving her heart palpitations. "Are you sure, Teo?"

"Any friend of yours is a friend of mine. Sì? I've been in his position. Tomorrow night, he'll be home, alone, regretting his actions. But we'll be dining at Le Veau d'Or. It's the least I can do."

Even though Sasha knew it was a power play, she was taken by Teo's chivalry. She was also taken by the micro-expression on

Wes's face. Something was brewing behind his eyes, she just didn't know what. An idea. A spark of a plan.

What was coming next?

Wes found himself sitting in the front seat of Teo's Escalade. A uniformed driver was speeding down the West Side Highway, as Lower Manhattan's jagged skyline flew by. His drunkenness was clinging to him, stubbornly—and the sharp, nauseating scent of leather and shoe polish wasn't helping.

Sasha and Teo were seated in the back, but there was a partition separating them from the front. In the ten minutes since they'd piled in the car, Wes had been straining his ears to listen to their conversation. Even in his state, he was dedicated to catching Teo in a lie. His Wordle journal was on his lap. His pen was poised. And his instincts told him that this bozo was going to give himself away. Right now, Teo was in "impressing the girl" mode. Playing at chivalry by rescuing Wes. Rising above his antics. Sweeping Sasha away in a chauffeured car.

Teo was feeling smug. That's when men get messy.

Lightly, Wes tapped on the glass. The partition was opaque, dark, but it was basic glass—not the heavy, laminated kind. The issue was that it was sealed along the edges, which solidly kept out sound. Wes cupped his hand at his ear and pressed it against the glass. Still nothing. He leaned his head back against the seat, annoyed as fuck. He knew what he had to do. But he'd been hoping to avoid it.

Fishing around in the inner pocket of his jacket, Wes pulled out a tiny black gizmo. An HY929 listening device—a bug attached to earphones that, when attached to the partition, would enable him to hear their conversation clearly. He never left home without it. Spy shit 101.

The driver, a Slavic-looking young man with a retro mustache, shot him a quizzical glance. He was probably twenty-one or so, but his livery uniform and 'stache added an air of gravitas.

Wes put his index finger to his lips. *Shhh.* Quickly, he inserted the earphones into his ears and showed the driver the gadget. Then, he pointed to the partition.

The driver pointed to a camera affixed just above the rearview mirror.

Without skipping a beat, Wes dug back into his suit jacket pocket of tricks. He pulled out two twenties and handed it to the driver. The driver snorted, shaking his head. Fine. It wasn't enough. Everyone had a price. He returned to the well, and handed the driver two hundred, cash. The driver's eyes widened to comical proportions. Instantly, he flipped down the visor and slipped the cash behind a pocket-sized photo of Pope John Paul II.

He'd been carrying that bill stash around for years—insurance in case he encountered a situation where he couldn't use his wits to bribe someone. Tonight was the night.

"Our secret," said the driver in a rolling Czech accent, hitting the camera's off button. Grinning, he held up a fist. Wes bumped it with his.

Then, he pressed the bug to the glass. And listened.

Chapter 23

CYPRESS AND THE SEA

In the backseat, Sasha's head was spinning. Nothing could've prepared her for this bizarro-world car ride. Her intoxicated former—*something*—was sobering up in the front seat. Her dashing current—*something*—was cracking open a Malbec for them. Making matters worse, traffic was horrible, so they were inching along at a snail's pace. It was the longest, most emotionally complex ride from the Upper East Side to Brooklyn ever attempted.

There was no precedent for how to behave in such a situation. But her past month had been so topsy-turvy, so unbelievably surreal, she just went with it.

In fact, she channeled her spirit from the flight. The idea that the world held great mystery and promise; that it was time for her to embrace adventure. Sasha couldn't control the slings and arrows of outrageous fortune. Best to let go and jump, once in a while. Or she'd end up a prisoner again. Holed up in her apartment, slowly disappearing among the battered remnants of her personality.

This was one of those let-everything-go moments. Thanks to the partition, she was physically cordoned off from Wes—so it wasn't *that* difficult to pretend he wasn't there. Especially since she was furious with him. She couldn't believe he'd imploded so ridiculously. After everything, that was how he behaved when it mattered most? Hurling insane threats at Teo? He'd been all bruised ego and misplaced aggression, and she never saw Wes as the kind of man who'd fall prey to either.

Just another thing to accept at face value. She couldn't change him. Couldn't make him speak up when it mattered. What she could do was sink into her conversation with Teo—a man who happened to be one of the kindest, most intriguing people she'd ever met. And so much more than he seemed.

"... and I'm ready to leave the hotel inspector world," he was saying as he poured Sasha a glass of wine. "It's just too nefarious."

"What do you mean?"

"In the luxury hospitality industry, I do business with men of extreme wealth. Unchecked men can be dangerous. Just like your friend said about American police. I'm not immune. I've taken liberties."

"That's quite an admission." She took the glass from Teo. "Liberties like cold-blooded murder? Or getting funny with your money?"

"The latter," he admitted. "There's no way to get to my income bracket without blurring lines."

"At least you're honest."

"Here's to honesty," he said, lifting his glass to Sasha. They toasted and each took a drink. "I've grown tired of traveling all the time. And living anonymously. All the aliases! I want to be who I really am."

"Well, what drew you to being a hotel inspector?"

"It sounded exciting. In Gallipoli, there were only a few career possibilities. Tourism, fisherman, or priest. I grew up in the Church."

"Same," she said. "But I realized early that Catholicism isn't for me. I wish I'd found a spirituality to replace it. But it's hard for me to believe what I don't see."

"Pessimist?"

"Realist."

"You must have faith in something, no?"

She smiled. "Myself."

"Lonely, no?"

"Maybe. But every time I've bet on me, I've won."

Teo met her eyes. "Do you think I can convince you to bet on someone else, for a change?"

"You can try." She took a sip, not breaking eye contact. "But I'm a tough convert."

"A challenge," he pronounced. "As a boy, I thought I might be a priest one day. But no. I'm a bit too much of a . . . what's the word? Hedonist. At one point, I was hoping there was a way to do both, but no."

"I see you're not familiar with American megachurches. It's certainly possible to be godly and thotty. Ever been to Atlanta?"

He laughed. "I never wanted to have an ordinary life. I wanted to experience everything. Fully. Wealth, experience, and yes, women."

"La dolce vita."

"Sì, signora." He swirled his wine. "My career helped me create an extraordinary life. You must feel the same with your work, no?"

"I do. That's one of the reasons I love casting. I can create extraordinary moments. Read a director's mind by finding the perfect people to act out the perfect situations. It's a rush."

"Like slotting puzzle pieces together."

Just then, she was hit with a flashback of Wes in 2022 saying that some moments snap together like two puzzle pieces. He'd clapped his hands together, punctuating the thought.

But Sasha shook her head, sending the thought skittering back into her memory bank. Or up to the passenger seat, where it belonged.

"How did you get into casting?" asked Teo, watching her intensely as she spoke.

"When I was eleven or so, I got an infection after a root canal. I was bedridden for an entire summer, and I watched every age-inappropriate movie on cable. And I just became obsessed with all the actors. I remember seeing Leo in *Titanic* and *The Basketball Diaries*, and I was like who knew he could do such drastically opposing roles. Who saw those ripples in his talent? The infinite variations in his personality? That's how I learned what a casting agent was." She shrugged. "That was it for me. I started reading *Hollywood Reporter* and arguing with adults about Oscar nominees in AOL chat rooms."

Teo looked delighted at this revelation. "Did that get you into trouble?"

"My mom never found out." She grinned. "But going toe-to-toe with film bros made me a shark."

"Don't strike me as a killer."

"In business only."

"You must meet so many characters."

"I do. And you're one of them."

They locked eyes. A spark of possibility crackled between them. Moonlight poured over half of Teo's face, while the other side was bathed in shadow.

"Hearing you say you need a change? So do I. The past five years haven't been easy. I've been living with anxiety disorder," she confessed quietly. Was it too soon to admit? Possibly, but she didn't care. She had nothing to hide. "I've been spending a lot of time alone. Which is where I've been happiest. I have a dream of just escaping everything. Moving far away, where no one knows me. Never to be seen again."

"If that's what you really want," started Teo, "I could make that happen. Easily."

"What do you mean?"

"I bought a ruined villa in Gallipoli. Years ago. I've been fixing it up, slowly but surely. It's built on a cliff over the sea, isolated from everything. Surrounded by cypress trees."

Cypress and the sea, thought Sasha, inhaling the scent in her mind.

"You'd never want for anything. And you'd never have to see anyone you didn't want to. Sì? It's hidden from the world."

Who was this man? Teo was like a magician granting her the wish. Sealing her away from everything that scared her. She'd been waiting for this. She'd been aching for this. And in that moment, as the Lower Manhattan night skyline rushed past them, it was all she wanted to do. Go. Go. Go. Escape. Leave it all behind. Everything, including all the work she'd done on her anxiety. Yes, she'd made huge strides. The fact that she'd felt sort of comfortable at a massive gala would've been unthinkable a month ago. But life was short, and the world wasn't getting any safer.

Go. Go. Go.

Wes and the driver, Jakub, had become fast friends—with their phone translation apps as their lifeline. Jakub let him play Spotify deejay. He also slipped him a few caffeine pills, which had helped him sober up. Jakub used the app to ask Wes the best shopping neighborhoods to take his girlfriend, Irina, when she arrived next month. Wes was more than happy to forge a relationship with him. Because he couldn't focus too much on the fact that Sasha, *his Sasha*, was in the backseat with another man. Settling her feline gaze on him. Flirting with him. Touching him, possibly. Ruminating on it would drive him insane. He didn't even want Teo to *look* at her. It was unthinkable.

Also unthinkable? His suggestion that whisking Sasha off to some castle was a good idea. Didn't Teo just hear her say she suffered from anxiety? Why would he feed into it? If he cared about

Sasha, wouldn't he want to help her overcome it, or work through the trauma that brought her there? No, he offered her a Band-Aid just to impress her.

Wes cared about what scared Sasha, because he cared about her. That villa-on-the-sea bullshit was about Teo only. A soulless flex.

He didn't even ask why she wanted to hide away.

Perspiration dotted his upper lip. Involuntarily, his hands curled into fists. Seeing him crashing out, Wes's good buddy Jakub offered him a mini bottle of Aquafina. He downed it, gratefully.

Calm down, he told himself. *Relax. Breathe. Listen.*

The conversation between Sasha and Teo hadn't yet revealed much, but Wes could feel a revelation brewing. It was tingling at his fingertips. He could almost touch it. He listened, again.

"...so, in Paris, you were staying in the 6th arrondissement?" asked Teo. "So was I. A shame we didn't meet."

"Such a missed opportunity," she said, sipping her wine. "But there's no playbook for how you act in those situations."

"Certainly not."

"Where were you headed?"

"I stayed in Paris a few days, visiting a few friends," he explained. "Then I traveled about four hours to Luxembourg. A small village called Larochette? It's a lovely medieval town, built around the ruins of an ancient castle."

"Sounds glorious. Had you been there before?"

"Sì, sì, I did some business there. So, I was tying up loose ends."

"I've been dying to ask. What were some of your aliases? Did you ever use funny ones? I read somewhere that Elton John makes reservations under the name Binky Poodle Clip."

"I know Sir Elton! Perfect alias for him," he divulged. "Hmm. Some of my names. Mo Hanly. A. J. Lhuellah. Ted Nanoi."

Wes scribbled the names down. And then he stopped, his pen freezing on the page. Where had he heard those names before?

They were odd. A tad...off. Just weird enough to be memorable. Quickly, he riffled through his notebook, stopping on the page where he'd jotted down Teo's banking information:

Seat F shares a checking account with four other people. Genders and whereabouts undisclosed. But are they real people? Or pseudonyms for Seat F? Investigate—

Mo Hanly

AJ Lhuellah

Ted Nanoi

Sam Canter

Well, well, well. Proof from Teo's own mouth. So they weren't other people. They were all aliases. But he'd only named the first three. Why not the fourth?

And then Wes remembered the name of the person, Teo's associate, who ran Two Tunics. Sam Canter. He was Teo as well. That's *his* charity. His gala. Why all the secrecy? What were the reasons someone would start a charity under a pseudonym? An urge to remain anonymous due to grace and humility? Eavesdropping on this braggy jackass for fifteen minutes negated that possibility.

Wes paused a moment, peering out the window at the Hudson River, as slow-moving barges floated to New Jersey docks. With what budget could Teo operate a charity that large, roping in important leaders of industry, entertainment, and business? How did he pull off such a feat? Unless it was a scam. (If Anna Delvey could do it, anyone could.) Maybe he was laundering cash. Wes combed through his conversations over the last few weeks. Recently, he'd had a conversation with *someone* about laundering money. When was it? Who was the person?

He racked his brain to remember.

Imani. It was Imani, telling him about the exposé she was writing. Something about nuns and priests stealing from churches.

"Did I tell you they launder the stolen church money by funneling it into fake businesses?" she'd asked. "If you were a shady priest, where would you put your cash?"

Wes continued staring at the highway, mind racing. The subjects in Imani's piece were clergy, who went through the trouble of getting hired at churches, only to rob them blind, disappear, change their identities, and live extravagant secular lives full of fucking, eating, drinking, carousing, and spending—and then, months later, they start over. New church, new name, new European location. He remembered Imani saying that the villages were always conspicuously small, with few resources to launch a criminal investigation.

Wes's wheels were turning. The name of Teo's charity was from a Bible verse. True, but a charity steeped in biblical lore wasn't unique. Was it?

Wes took another look at the names, wondering where they'd come from. There had to be a pattern.

Unconsciously, he let his eyes unfocus a bit. In his mind, the letters floated around and reassembled into different configurations. New words. This was his Wordle strategy. (This skill also made him dangerous at Scrabble and *Jeopardy!*) He simply softened his gaze a bit, until the right word rose to the surface. For several minutes, he scrambled, unscrambled, and then tried again. The answers evaded him—until, suddenly, they didn't.

The words came together, one by one.

Mo Hanly = Holy Man

AJ Lhuellah = Hallelujah

Ted Nanoi = Anointed

Sam Canter = Sacrament

His jaw dropped. Jakub looked at him. Concerned, the driver gave him a hopeful thumbs-up. Wes returned the gesture and then went back to his notebook. Was the Catholic slant of these names a coincidence? Clearly not. These aliases were dreamed up by someone tickled by word puzzles—and who knew their way around a church.

Just then, he remembered another detail from his conversation with Imani. One of the church grifters' last sightings was in Luxembourg. And then a flurry of rapid-fire thoughts flew through his mind.

Teo just visited Luxembourg.

He said his "associate" ran Two Tunics, but it's actually him.

He's lying to Sasha.

He's definitely not a hotel inspector.

What the hell is he, then?

His name, Wes told himself. *Look at his name.*

Teo D. Scera

Wes scrambled the letters in every way possible. Sarecdeto, Tedosacer, Dostaceer. Sacerdote. Nonsense words. They didn't make sense. Well, they didn't make sense—in English.

Lightning-fast, he clicked on his translator app and chose "Italian->English." He entered the first three words. None had an English translation.

Finally, he typed in "sacerdote."

When he saw the translation, he almost laughed.

Priest. It meant priest.

Chapter 24

A THRONE OF LIES

MESSAGES

WESLEY DANE TO SASHA CRUZ, 9:54 p.m.

Wes: We're getting out now. Tell him to drop you off now.

Sasha: Shutup

Wes: Tell him to drop you off NOW

Sasha: STOP EMBARRASSING ME

Wes: Jakub is my boy he'll pull over if I tell him to and please believe me when I say I'll make this a thousand times more embarrassing for you TELL HIM TO DROP YOU OFF NOWNOWNOW

Sasha: Who tf is Jakub?

Wes: I DON'T WANT HIM TO SEE WHERE YOU LIVE DO IT NOW

You know what? You can drop me off here. I mean us. Me and... Roland. Right here on Flatbush. It's between both of our houses."

"Allora. Are you sure? It's almost ten o'clock. It's Brooklyn. Is it safe?"

"We're right at Grand Army Plaza, it's bougie. See? People are outside, leaving restaurants, the museum. Summer hours in the city, you know. I'm just gonna get Roland some bodega coffee, perk him up a bit. Make sure he's okay."

"Well, if you're sure."

"I am," she said quickly. "Thank you for making sure my friend's okay. I owe you."

"You owe me nothing..."

Sasha's phone started blowing up again, and she turned off the ringer.

"Spam," she said nonchalantly. "But I really do need to get out here." Sasha tapped on the partition, and it rolled down. "Here's fine, sir! Right in front of the library."

Before Teo had a chance to get out and open her door, she gathered the bottom of her gown in a fist and hopped down from the Escalade. At the same time, Wes's door flew open. He whispered something to the driver, gave him a pound, and then joined her on the sidewalk. The Escalade went speeding down the street with a dramatic, smoky screech. Sasha and Wes were left in its wake, standing before the majestic tower of the library, the front lights glowing in the night sky.

From an outsider's perspective, Sasha and Wes looked like a fashion editorial. Glamorous and elegant as hell, moodily illuminated by the glow from entryway lights. But, oh, the reality was different. They stood there, facing each other, a tornado of hectic, frenetic drama.

"You scared the shit out of me, Wes! I have anxiety, you can't send me texts like that! I almost had a stroke!" Her hand was over her heart. "Jesus, I'm having palpitations."

"I know! I'm sorry, I didn't have a choice. I had to get you out of there. Fast."

"I didn't even get to say goodbye!" she yelled. "And when did you sober up? Do you know that driver? What the entire fuck is going on?"

"I had to get you out of there," he yelled back, pointing uselessly down Flatbush Avenue, in the direction of the long-gone Escalade.

"Why?"

"He's a fraud. He's running a grift, Sasha. He's been lying to you this whole time."

Sasha stared at him for a split second. Then, she peered up at the moon as if to say, *Sis, are you seeing this shit?* The night was humid, hot, and still. Perspiration misted her chest and the nape of her neck. Her heart was racing. Wes stood in a wide-legged stance, facing her, his arms crossed across his chest. He looked eight feet tall, dead serious, and extremely sober. And annoyingly handsome. They glared at each other for a few seconds, breathing hard and collecting themselves.

"What 'whole time'? I've spoken to him a total of, maybe, eight hours and thirty minutes. What grift?"

Wes stepped toward her. "I don't know how to say this. It sounds unbelievable. But trust me, it's true."

"Jesus Christ, spit it out! I just jumped out of an Escalade in four-inch heels, Wes. Tell me *something*."

"Fine," he said with a defeated exhale. "He's a priest."

"I'm sorry, I didn't catch that. A what?"

"A priest."

Sasha stared at him. "Are you well?"

He scrubbed his face with his hands and began stress-pacing. "I told you it sounded crazy. I couldn't believe it, either. But I called Imani from the car..."

She flinched. "You called Imani?"

"Yeah, it was quick. Like two minutes. She's working on an exposé about this clergy ring that embezzles money from European churches. It's a whole thing, I can't go into it right now. But he's one of them. I called her to ask if this ring is dangerous. They're not. No reports of assaults; no one hurt, trafficked, or killed. Nothing like that. They're fucking just... robbers. They steal from their churches, run off with the cash, travel and party, and then start over at a new church. They're hard to trace, because they change their identities each time. Seat F's one of them."

Sasha poked out her lips, nodding. "I see. How'd you come to this conclusion?"

"I figured it out in the car."

She realized she'd been clutching the hem of her gown so tightly, her knuckles were aching. She dropped it. "How?"

"I wiretapped the partition."

"You wiretapped us? That's a real thing? Like in John le Carré novels?"

"Are you being serious right now?"

"Wait," she said, the weight of this sinking in, "you really spied on me? That's such a violation!"

"You know a better way to listen through sealed glass?" he shouted. Then, he stopped pacing and stood in front of her, looking tortured and impassioned. "He gave himself away. Those names he told you? The aliases? They're all Catholic anagrams. Two Tunics is his charity, under the name Sam Canter. Which is an anagram for Sacrament."

Sasha stared at him, incredulously. "Putting those Wordle skills to use, I see."

"You're not taking me seriously."

"How can I? You're saying Teo is a part-time holy man? Please be for real."

"He is! Sasha, he's sitting on a throne of lies!"

"A throne of lies, huh? And you expect me to take you seriously?"

"This isn't a joke," he said. "Teo D. Scera is an alias, too. He didn't tell you his name on purpose. Because you'd search it, and you'd see he had zero digital footprint. And it'd look suspicious. It's all a twisted game."

"If it's a twisted game, then why was he looking for me, too? Why would he do that, if he didn't want to be found?"

Wes emitted a frustrated sigh. "That I don't know. Maybe that part was real, I don't know. He's had relationships before. I spoke to an ex of his. Said he was cool, but always traveling for work. He'd always bring her postcards when he returned."

"I don't want to know this. Why are you telling me this?"

"He didn't mail them, Sasha. He physically handed them to her, to avoid a return address. To keep his whereabouts unknown." He paused, for emphasis. "A lot's unclear, but I'm sure of one thing. He's a liar. And I don't want him near you."

"As if you have a say." A hot breeze blew through them, rustling her hair, sending it frizzing into oblivion. And then, something snapped inside her. She was immediately, unassailably, irreversibly enraged. Taking two steps toward him, she slammed her palms into his shoulders and shoved him, hard. Caught off guard, he stumbled back a step.

"How dare you," she seethed. "How could you do this to me. A priest? That's the best you could do? This is demented."

"That guy being a priest is demented. As if God would fuck with him in the slightest."

"You've gone to great lengths to get me away from him. Point taken."

"This isn't about us. It's about keeping you safe. You wanted me to investigate. I did that. You don't like what I found? That's on you." Wes's face was a furious storm.

"You don't want to be with me. But you don't want me to be with anyone else." Her voice wavered with emotional exhaustion. "This isn't about my safety; it's about your ego. You hate not getting the girl."

Wes made a gruff noise that sounded like an audible eye roll.

"What ego? After dealing with you, I don't have one."

"Neither do I!" she exploded. "You fuck me senseless, in the most passionate and soul-shattering way, and before I can catch my breath, you're all, 'we can't be together, I'm not good for you, don't forget our boundaries.' I've been in a permanent state of confusion since you came back into my life. It's hell."

At that, Wes moved closer, into her space. She backed against the stairs' railing. With the crook of his index finger, he tilted her chin upward to face him. The abrupt motion—and his closeness—sent a wave of heat surging through her, leaving her throbbing.

"Confusion?" he raged. "You fucking *melt* when I touch you, like you're doing right now, and I never felt anything like it. It rips me to pieces, Sasha. Because it's too close to the real thing. The way you look at me? It's like you want me to devour you, like you crave it, like it's a need that never even *existed* before me. And I lose myself, every time. Because I can't resist you. I never could. But when it comes down to it, you'd choose this fake elite Euro fuck who's running the world's most unnecessarily sacrilegious grift." He let his hand drop. "You don't know confusion."

"You never told me you felt like this," she breathed, her voice cracking.

"What would be the point? You chose someone else."

"I didn't know I had a choice, Wes."

He stepped away from her. Thrusting his hands in his pants pockets, he looked down the street at nothing. When he spoke again, his voice was careful. Like he was trying to keep steady on a rocking boat.

"I have something to tell you."

Sasha was still trying to catch her breath. Calm her pulse. "What is it?"

"My father fired me because I crossed the line with you. But it wasn't just about me letting you stay in the office." He cleared his throat. "The night when we…when I caught your stalker? I didn't just catch him. I set him up, so it would be an easy arrest. Made him fingerprint a brick and throw it through your window. It didn't feel out-of-pocket. He'd done it before. But I broke code." He brought his hands together, cracking a knuckle. "And that's not all. I hurt him. I knocked the shit out of him. And I regret it. I do. But he was terrorizing you. I've seen that stalking pattern before. It could've ended badly," he said, shaking his head. "I couldn't let him hurt you. I'd do anything to protect you."

The hot breeze hit them again. And Sasha finally understood. This was why he reacted the way he did when she showed up at F.E.A.S.T. for the first time. This is why he needed to put up boundaries with her. His blurring of lines in 2022 had cost him his career—and most importantly, his relationship with his dad before his death. She'd upended his entire life.

"Wes," she started, "why did you agree to take this case?"

"It felt like closing the loop, helping you find happiness. You deserve it."

"You did that for me?"

"There are no bounds to what I'd do for you."

They stood there, on the precipice of something. But then Wes broke the spell. He pulled out his phone and typed something in.

"Your Uber's coming in five," he said, sounding utterly depleted. "I'm walking home. Good night, Sasha."

And he left. Sasha didn't wait for the car. She walked the several blocks home in her heels, the straps scraping off her skin. She was bleeding, but she didn't feel it. At home, she climbed onto her kitchen island, curled into a ball, and stayed there, awake, for hours.

The next morning, when Sasha was waking up on a slab of wood, Wes was lying on Imani's zebra-print couch. Feet up on the arm, hands behind his head. She was perched on an overstuffed Restoration wing chair, smoking her a.m. joint through a vintage 1930s cigarette holder. If you didn't know they were good friends, you'd think Imani was a therapist, and Wes was her patient.

In all fairness, that's practically what was happening.

"I can't thank you enough," she was saying. "You saved my piece. I thought I'd have to kill it."

"I wish I could tell you I'm happy about it."

"And to think he's right next door? Are my investigative skills rusty? Maybe I need to go on sabbatical. My girlfriend owns a cottage on a glacier in Gstaad, maybe I'll pull up."

"Only you would 'pull up' to a glacier."

"You can only get there by dogsled." She took an extravagant pull from the joint, and exhaled through her glossy lips. "But I hear you can't be on your period, or the dogs lose their sense of direction."

This didn't sound true, but he was too hungover to investigate further. She handed him her cigarette holder, but Wes shook his head. His head hurt too badly to function. Even smelling the weed was making him nauseous. Groaning, he flung an arm over his aching face.

"What did you drink last night?"

"Everything," he mumbled.

"Hold on, let me get you a Hangheal Liver Detox supplement."

"No, I'm good," he said, holding up his hand. "I know you told me this already, but I need you to swear to me that this ring isn't dangerous."

"I told you, it's just a bunch of partyers. They get off on the thrill of getting away with something. Carousing on someone else's dime. Convincing the world that they're something they're not, whether it's a nun or a slutty, multimillionaire heiress."

"Or a hotel inspector."

"It's getting away with it." She shifted in her chair, tucking her feet under her butt. "That's the high. For the piece, I've spoken to a few psychiatrists and professors specializing in people with double lives. They feel that rules don't apply to them, because they're exceptional and deserve more than normal people. The scam feels like manifest destiny. What they're owed. And what's crazy? They can feel love. Authentically. It just has limits. No one person ever outranks their needs. And their number one need is lie, cheat, and steal. That's what this Teo D. Scera, or whatever his name is, is doing with Sasha. It was fun to romance her on the plane. It might've been real, for the moment. But the grift will always be more real."

"I want him dead," he grumbled. "If I didn't get out of the car when I did, things would've gotten untenable."

"Too bad you didn't," she said. "Imagine the publicity I'd get! My piece will get him and the whole ring arrested, for sure. But imagine how viral it'd be if he turned up dead?"

"That's dark, even for you."

Imani slid her cigarette holder onto an improvised ashtray—which was actually a jade bowl decorated with a mosaic Medusa. With a knowing smirk, she peered down at her old friend.

Feeling the weight of Imani's gaze, he opened his eyes and

looked her way. She looked like the Cheshire cat, all slinky and smirky, her leopard-print muumuu hanging off her shoulder.

"What are you looking at?"

"You like her," she trilled. "I have a Pulitzer, I know what I'm talking about."

"You don't have a Pulitzer."

"I will once I publish this 'Holy Ring' piece," she said with a wink. "Don't change the subject. You're obsessed with her."

Somewhat clunkily, he changed the subject. "What I'm obsessed with is my new orange juice brisket recipe. I just got accepted into the Mad Dog & Merrill Midwest Grill'n competition out in Green Bay. This is big shit. It's *televised*," he said. "With this OJ thing, I could possibly place. Or at least recoup my losses from the last one."

"That's dope, friend. No doubt you'll place. But stop trying to run from this conversation. You're down astronomically bad, friend. And so's she. I don't think she looked at me once during that lunch. I know this is the real thing. My third eye is *pulsating*."

"You're a writer. You're prone to exaggeration."

"Maybe. Maybe not. But I know what I saw. That's why I put your journal in her bag."

He sat up. "I know you fucking lying."

She giggled. "It was clear you weren't going to do anything about it. So, I gave her a reason to go to you. Did it work?"

Wes dropped his face into his hands. "Yes," he said, his voice muffled. "Yes, it fucking worked."

Laughing, she smoothly dodged the throw pillow Wes chucked at her. It collided with a nude self-portrait she'd sketched while at a Nigerian prince's seaside villa. The materials: canvas and cobalt eye pencil.

"What's the plan, Wesley Junior? You gonna let Cardinal Coitus win?"

"It's not a competition. Stop stirring up drama, this is my actual life."

"I've never seen you like this. About anyone."

"That's because I've never felt like this. Not even close." He stared at the ceiling. "I never knew that the precise temperature of someone's skin could have such an effect on me. Is that even a thing? Her skin's so... I don't know. It's toasty. It's perfect."

"Oh, you're *gone*."

"I can't think, I can't sleep. I think I'm coming down with something." Glumly, he coughed twice into his fist.

"You're not sick, you're in love. This is new for you. The few relationships you've had crashed and burned. Because you only considered toxic women you couldn't have a future with. You don't think you deserve nice things."

"I don't deserve her. She spent six hundred dollars on a pair of shoes."

"So have I! She had the money, so she treated herself. Good for her. Don't get insecure because she's a bad bitch. Are you not a bad bitch? What happened to your confidence? Stand up!"

"Imani, please."

"She's under your skin. It's already done. You'd be a fool not to fight for it."

"She doesn't really want me. She thinks she does, but it's not real. It's some savior thing. I'm the person she runs to when she needs help. When a stalker's after her. When she's horny. When she has insomnia. When she's launching a missing person's case. When she's horny."

"You already said that."

He opened one eye. "Bears repeating."

"Nigga, that's... several instances. Sounds like she needs you all the time."

"She chose somebody else. What am I supposed to do?"

"Fight for her."

With an impatient huff, she stomped to the couch and nudged him in the leg. Begrudgingly—and gingerly—he scooted over, making room for her to sit down.

"It's complicated, Imani," he groaned, squeezing his eyes shut. "You don't get it."

"Look at me."

With a begrudging sigh, he lifted his eyelids. It felt like benching four hundred pounds.

"There is a reason she dug you up out of her past." She scooched her butt down, to reach his level of slump. "I'm not a mind reader, baby. But she told me herself she hadn't dated in a while. Here's what I think. That flirtation on the plane might've awoken a sense memory. A dormant desire, if you will. Something subconscious, but strong enough for her to reach back in the past for you." She shrugged. "I've circled the block for less."

Nodding slowly, Wes looked off into the distance. "Damn. That was half third-eye logic, and half sensible."

"My sense isn't common, but it's always correct," she said. "When are you gonna see her again? You solved her case, so you'll meet for payment, right? Or do you have a QR code or something?"

Wes made an offended snort. "No! I didn't charge her. This was a favor. And an experiment for me. I wanted to see if I still had it. If I could solve a case, on my own, my way. To prove to myself that I was actually good."

"To prove to yourself? Or your dad's memory?"

Silently, Wes rubbed his temples and let out a low, rumbling groan. He didn't answer, but he didn't have to. Imani knew him well.

Just then, he heard a rustling. The beaded, fringed curtain that was her bedroom door blew open—and out swanned a curvy, dark-skinned goddess wearing auburn braids and a kimono. She blew Imani a kiss, waved at Wes, and floated into the kitchen.

"You let me in when you had someone over?"

"She's my friend. We had a platonic sleepover." Imani shot him a sphinxian grin.

"You wanna be bisexual so bad. I hope you told her you're straight."

"She knows! Don't worry about my business, worry about yours." She grabbed her joint and stood up. Heading toward the kitchen, she called out, "Love like this won't strike again. Go get your woman, Wes."

Chapter 25

SALVATION IN A STRANGER

Later that afternoon, Sasha was sitting in her safe place, the Little Cupcake Bakeshop. She was on her third strawberry shortcake cupcake. Her second latte. Her sixth text, and fourth missed call from Teo. If that was even his name.

Sasha was operating on only two hours of kitchen island sleep. The rest of the night she'd spent thinking. How the hell did she get here? Obsessively, she kept replaying the flight conversation in her mind. Was there anything that felt weird? Con artist-y? Deceptive? And she just couldn't come up with anything. If he hadn't been that forthcoming with personal information, so what? Neither had she. Sasha had never been in the practice of showing all her cards to a stranger—not even before the 2022 incident. The fact is, it just hadn't seemed weird to walk away knowing practically nothing about each other.

But now, she was second-guessing everything. Was he even from Gallipoli? Was he even Italian, or just an excellent mimic? She knew a few actors who could instantly copy any accent, speech pattern, or dialect. It was a skill akin to a musician playing a song by ear after hearing it once. He'd told her he was a hotel inspector, which required aliases. Was that his way of telling her that he lived a double (or triple, or quadruple) life? And his *in bocca al lupo*—"in the mouth of the wolf." Was he referring to himself?

Everything he said now seemed to be code for an alternate truth. But she was no dummy. And she was savvy about people; her profession demanded it. If he was an international, world-class grifter, how could she—of all people—miss it? Or was he just that good?

A priest. A priest? Really? It was too far-fetched to believe. It sounded like a Shonda Rhimes fever-dream plot from an old episode of *Scandal*. A White House aide getting mixed up with a holy man posing as a senator, or some such.

Honestly? Would watch, thought Sasha ruefully.

It couldn't be true. Two insane incidents didn't happen to the same woman. Was she born under a faulty star? Was her karma fucked? Was this because she was an ex-Catholic agnostic heathen who hadn't been to church since 2008, when she attended an ice cream social celebrating Obama's inauguration at St. Mary of Sorrows? Sasha just couldn't wrap her brain around the fact that she was possibly hoodwinked by an actual, ordained priest who robbed churches in order to fuck, party, and spend. There were so many easier ways to have a good time. But it was the thrill of getting away with it, Wes had said. The rush of fooling otherwise smart, capable, clever people.

It was chilling, finding out you were possibly a mark. That you were targeted by a world-class liar and duped with shocking ease. Sasha wasn't just second-guessing her initial exchange with Teo, she was second-guessing all her adult life choices. Which decision had brought her here? Bingeing cupcakes and feeling like the dumbest woman in Brooklyn.

On the one hand, she wanted to give Teo a chance to clear his name. And she hoped that it wasn't true, of course. But, at the beginning and end of everything, she trusted Wes. Even as she lashed out at him last night, refusing to take his revelation seriously, she had a creeping suspicion that he was right. She knew he'd always tell her the truth. Wes was her lighthouse. Her safety. Her fearless protector. And the truth was, he was so much more than that. She'd only had the nerve to admit it to her new friend and book club president Patricia in the ladies' restroom. It was a spontaneous exchange with a stranger, the kind that happens several times a night in women's bathrooms all over the world. It didn't feel quite real.

Because she hadn't yet faced it herself. Last night, hearing him say those words, shook her. He'd kept her at arm's length for so long, she thought she was alone at sea with her feelings. She'd been terrified to mention their connection, because he'd been so clear with her about boundaries. Maintaining the client-detective line. But he didn't look at her like a friend. He didn't kiss her, or talk to her, or fuck her like a friend. After being with him—even in the most uncharged, platonic situations—she stumbled away blinking into the sun, so lost in him she practically forgot her name.

But if she faced that Wes was crazy about her (perhaps as crazy as she was about him), then she'd also need to accept that searching for Teo was a mistake. Mortifying, after moving mountains to find him. Not to mention after humiliating herself in front of Seraphina's global team. She'd so badly wanted to be right about Teo. To orchestrate her own happiness. To deliver herself out of a terrifying, yearslong funk, into something life-affirming, something sweet. She wanted magical, luscious, light, dark, soft, urgent, transformative, soul-rearranging, fucking seismic, forever connection.

She got it. But with the wrong (right?) person. And now, she might've lost it before it was ever truly hers.

For as long as I live, she thought, *I'll never forget the way he looked at me at the library steps. Like I've always been his. Like I'm insane for not realizing. Like saying it out loud would break his heart.*

Before he walked away, Wes looked as defeated as she felt. Like timing wasn't in their favor. They kept missing each other, misreading each other, and telling lies to protect their fragile hearts. And now, it was too late. Eyes misty, she took a final bite of the cupcake and washed it down with Evian. It didn't taste like anything. Everything sweet was drained from the world. So much so, that she had to push herself out the door, because the lure of agoraphobia-lite tugged at her again.

But back to the priest thing. She googled the ring of clergymen and found some articles in local newspapers in France, Austria, and Spain. Tales of churches going broke and shutting down. There were leads each time, former employees, but they seemed to vanish into thin air. Untraceable. Who would be sinister enough to burgle a holy house? Who, indeed.

Even armed with this information, though, even knowing that Imani (fucking Imani, all roads did lead to her) was writing a splashy article about the ring, she still couldn't reconcile Teo with the crime. She didn't listen to any of his voice notes, or even read his texts. But the next time her phone rang, she answered.

"Sasha, you're there," said Teo, his voice tinged with relief.

She tossed her cupcake wrappers in the garbage, mouthed *Thank you* to the waitress, and headed outside into the glaring afternoon sun. The glare hit her like walking into a wall. Sliding on her sunglasses, she sat down on a bench outside the bakery. Here, she could focus.

"I'm here." For privacy, she pulled her Yankees snapback down low.

"What happened last night? I've been calling you, messaging you. I was worried."

"Why were you worried? What do you think happened?"

"I don't know, you and your friend practically leapt from a moving car. It seemed like an emergency."

"Because it was." And then, she told the truth because she didn't have the energy to pretend anymore. In any area of her life. "My friend's name isn't Roland, it's Wes. And he isn't just my friend. He's a detective. I hired him to find you."

"Ahh. You did. I suspected."

Why did he suspect this? He didn't sound surprised at all. His calmness was unsettling. If he'd had a detective investigate her whereabouts, Sasha would've felt threatened, terrified, and utterly confused.

"You suspected he was a detective? How?"

"No, I didn't take him for a detective. I assumed he was a scorned lover. But I knew you'd hired one. I felt like someone or something, a shadow figure, was gaining on me. Trying to, eh, trace my steps. It wouldn't have been the first time." His accent was becoming less Hollywood Italian with every word. It was a subtle shift, but there.

Sasha hadn't moved a muscle since he started talking. Inexplicably, she put the phone facedown on her lap for a moment, and whipped her head to the left, right, and even flipped forward, checking under the bench. Her feet locked in a wide, defensive stance, she stood up and peered behind her. He wasn't in the bakery. No one was watching her. No one was hunting her. And then she had a small, out-of-body moment. It was almost as if she'd drifted outside of herself and saw herself from the outside, in.

She was capable of saving herself. Wes assured her, via Imani, that Teo wasn't dangerous. But if he was there, and if he had posed a threat, she would've handled it. She would've fought, clawed, kicked, screamed. Sasha knew this about herself. And if she couldn't win, she'd have gone down swinging. She knew this about herself, because that's what she did in 2022. When threatened, she got scrappy. She grabbed a knife. She parkoured herself out the window. She slept in a hospital and found the perfect detective to handle it.

She orchestrated her rescue. She didn't take any of it lying down. She didn't realize it then, but it gave her a surge of power today.

She wasn't a victim. A crisis magnet, maybe. But not a victim.

"So you knew I was investigating you," she said carefully, settling back down on the bench. "What do you mean, it's happened before?"

"When you've amassed a fortune, strange things begin happening. People assume you're cheating. Like you couldn't possibly have come by it honestly. As if there's an honest way to amass a fortune."

"Cynical."

"No, no. It's simply the truth."

"Are you calling from a burner phone?"

He chuckled again, as if this answer was obvious. "Always."

"I see. Anything else you want to tell me?"

"I'd like to see you again. I'm sorry that last night went so wrong. I hope we can try again? Start over? I'm quite fond of you, sì?"

"What does 'sacerdote' mean in English?"

"Priest."

"You realize it's an anagram of your name, right?"

"Of course I know. I'm surprised you know. For English speakers, it's not something you discover unless you're looking for it." His tone revealed his amusement. "You were looking for it, weren't you?"

She sucked in air. "It's true, isn't it?"

Silence. More silence. Swallowing. "You've got a good detective."

"Jesus Christ."

"Please don't take His name in vain."

"Oh, do fuck yourself." She spat. "Are the names part of the fun? Leaving little clues, hiding in plain sight?"

"It's one of my favorite parts. I studied linguistics in divinity school. Words, they're sexy."

His voice was iceberg cool. Almost pleasant. He was so remorseless, it was jarring. How do you engage with a person who'd flagrantly lied, but didn't regret it in the slightest? There was no room for discussion. It was maddening. Not only had he hoodwinked her, but he also refused to receive her anger about it. Sasha was raging at a wall.

"There must be a special conference room in hell for monsters who take advantage of churches, where people go to celebrate community and faith. What's wrong with you?"

"But Sasha, I have faith, too," he retorted. "I love God. And He loves me and all my faults."

"Convenient," she remarked. "Why'd you even look for me in Seraphina? What was the point?"

"I wished to see you again. That was real."

"I can't believe this is happening," she muttered to herself under her breath. "Am I hallucinating? Did I fight my way back from oblivion to end up in a Netflix love-con doc? This is insane. This is a farce."

"Sasha, please listen. I told you I'd grown tired of aliases. And of so much traveling. I meant this—just not as a hotel inspector. I told more truth than I ever do. I never speak about where I'm from, or my parents, my childhood. I even told you that, as a boy, I thought I'd be a priest."

Sasha's shoulders slumped. She'd forgotten that anecdote. If only she'd realized his throwaway comment was a peek into his present.

"I felt," he was saying, "that with you, I could be myself."

"Which is who, exactly?"

"I can't tell you that. Not right now. But I'd like to see you."

"You can't be serious. See me? Forget you know me. You're such a liar, I don't even know who I'm speaking to."

"Do you tell the full truth to everyone you meet? For instance, were you honest with me about your friend, the drunkard?"

"Now, wait a minute. He's not a drunkard. He's clever, kind, and beautiful. He'd had a few shots too many, but don't act like you people don't enjoy the blood of Christ."

"The point is, he's not just your friend, is he?"

Her silence spoke volumes.

"You see? You, too, are a liar."

She gasped with outrage. "No. No. We're not the same. You're a criminal mastermind. You're the Talented Mr. Ripley, okay? I'm exactly who I say I am. I've never broken the law. I barely break rules. I don't cut off the tags on my pillowcases! I'm honest. You led me on. You made me feel like we connected in a special, rare way."

"Allora, I must stop you there," he said calmly. "I didn't lead you on. I didn't make you hire a detective. I didn't make you track me down or figure out who I was. With all due respect, you led yourself on."

This stung.

Gobsmacked, she took the phone from her ear and stared at it. He was right. And she was an idiot. She'd gotten swept up in the adventure, in the fantasy of this whirlwind, international romance, and she'd lost hold of good, common sense. Instead of being satisfied with some fun, titillating, in-flight chemistry with an attractive stranger, she tried to turn it into something epic. Something real. But you couldn't force "real." In fact, when "real" happened, sometimes it felt so natural and obvious that it snuck up on you unawares. Sometimes it showed up in the form of an old acquaintance.

From a million miles away, she heard Teo repeating, "Sasha? Sasha?" through the phone. Without thinking, she clicked off. And then blocked him. She sat on the bench staring at the phone until seconds turned into minutes. She had led herself on. It was true. Now she had to forgive herself for the crime of being a lonely person in an indifferent world—and seeking salvation in a stranger.

Chapter 26

DEAN W. SEELY

"Good morning, everyone! I'm Sasha Cruz, your casting director today. So excited to welcome such inspiring talent today. I've chosen each one of you personally and can confidently say that you're the cream of the crop. No matter what happens after this audition, please remember—I believe in you. Now, I only have five slots to fill. And there are thirty of you. But again, I love discovering talent. So, even if you're not right today, you might be right next time. Or I may know a casting director who has the perfect project for you. Ha! I'm kidding, why would I share talent with a competitor?"

A modest wave of laughter rolled through the crowd. Sasha was addressing the hopefuls in the back of the audition room, who were grouped on folding chairs. Everyone had a bookable look. Everyone had experience. And everyone was nervous. The casting was being held at Tribeca's Splashlight Studios, in an industrial chic, whitewashed, sun-dappled space with thirteen-foot ceilings. A few members of Seraphina's executive class were perched at a conference table to the far right, quietly observing the proceedings. But it was Sasha's show. She looked the part, too—decked out in a mini vest dress, chrome stiletto sandals, and a sleek bun. She was in business demon mode.

Sasha Cruz was *on*. And she was doing something she'd never done before. Giving a pre-casting pep talk.

"I had a thought on the train this morning. I wanted to give you some inspiration. You do this all the time. Far be it for me to tell you how to do your job. But I know that, sometimes, inspiration fails you. I know that the business can dull your shine. Make you second-guess your talent. It might even make you forget what drew you to acting in the first place. I want you to remember who you are. The good things, but especially the negative stuff. The scary things. The part of your personality that gives you pause, or may be a bit too 'real,' too 'authentic' for this world. Use those elements. Because that's what's going to set you apart.

"Now I, myself, am not a vulnerable person." She'd begun to pace slowly, hands clasped at her butt. "I don't confide in people. Instead, I sit alone with my thoughts, letting them consume me. For example, I experienced a traumatic incident about four years ago. It sent me into hiding. I felt like a victim, and I was too scared to face the world. But my perspective's changed! I wasn't a victim. I was scrappy, resourceful, and brave. Without getting into too many details, my bravery involved light parkour."

"Period," someone whispered from the audience.

"Recently, when I found myself in yet another tricky situation, I channeled that strength to empower myself. To stand tall and get on with life. And honestly? I think I turned a corner. I feel free for the first time in, well... maybe the first time, ever. Do I still have general anxiety disorder? Sure. But I have it. It doesn't have me.

"In your audition today, I urge you to use your shame, your secrets, your hidden histories. Use them to be a fully embodied performer. We aren't one thing. There's no either/or way of looking at yourself. We're all sexy and gullible and brave and scared and yearning. People are prismatic. So today, don't think of yourself as a type. I'm not looking for a type. I'm looking for complex human beings. Give me everything. Your performance will be the better for it."

A flaming redhead wearing excellent jeans raised her hand. "I'm sorry, this is an audition for a lipstick campaign, right? My agent said there'd be no reading, just vibing on video."

"Yes!" Sasha cleared her throat, realizing she may have gone overboard. Time to wrap it up. "No, you're correct. This is the Seraphina commercial casting. You're in the right place."

With that, she wrapped up her little welcome speech and headed over to her desk. The click-clack of her heels on the polished cement floor sounded uncomfortably loud against the stunned silence of the actors. Palms sweating from mild embarrassment, she sat behind the small desk positioned on a blank, whitewashed set. The videographer had set up his equipment just a few feet away. She smiled at him. Gave a thumbs-up to the Seraphina team over at the table. Arranged her portfolio printouts. And then she pulled out her lucky pencil from her bag. It was chewed up, four years old, and sharpened down to a nub at this point. Of all her talismans, it was the most important.

Just holding it made her heart hurt.

When it came to the almost-untenable levels of yearn she felt for Wes, she was a coward. She couldn't count the number of times she had picked up her phone, pulled up his contact info, and then swiped out of it. She wasn't even sure what scared her so much. Rejection? What if he laughed at her? Told her that, in chasing windmills (waterfalls?), she'd missed her chance with him. What if feelings had an expiration date, and each day they didn't speak, she floated further from his mind? What if Imani had gotten her claws in him?

She'd never know. Because Wes didn't call her, either. And each night that passed without speaking to him was excruciating. Because she was too conscious of his absence. Everything reminded her of him. On a Hot Girl Walk, she passed someone barbecuing at the edge of Prospect Park, and she thought, *Wes could do it better.* A random person posted their Wordle score on social media, and she thought, *Wes could do it better.* The Rose tried and failed to give her a thrill, and she thought, *Wes could do it better.*

Wes made everything better.

But life rolled on. Her heart didn't stop, and neither did work. While Sasha was chatting with Destiny at her dining table, she got a late call from the creative director at Seraphina—she finally had a date for her live audition. It was Friday at 11:00 a.m., one week after the Two Tunics gala.

"Time to work, folks," she announced into small handheld mic. "First up on set, Reem-Marie Badir."

Reem-Marie, the kid sister of a B-actress she'd cast on a series about slutty social workers, hustled over and gave it her all. Unfortunately, she didn't have big sis's charisma. Pasting on her pleasant, neutral casting face, Sasha called the next actor—and hoped she'd find the right talent, fast. It was eleven o'clock, and Seraphina had booked the space till three. She was nursing too much heartbreak to keep up this level of enthusiasm that long.

But, two hours later, she'd only gotten through eleven auditions. Energy was lagging, and each minute was dragging.

Why is this so hard? she thought. *Oh, that's right. Because I prepped them like they were reading for some Oscar-bait role. I encouraged them to Method act out their most intimate moments for a lips casting!*

One actor pantomimed the worst kiss he'd ever had by French-kissing his palm. Another stood in front of Sasha's desk and, with her fingers, yanked her lips in several directions to indicate her shame about being a gossip. Another slicked on black lipstick and delivered an off-the-cuff poem about how being a middle school goth informed her political views. The auditions were messy, overemotional, and off the mark.

Wait. Were they off the mark or brilliant? She gasped. Her posture went ramrod straight. Sasha wasn't a screenwriter. (And writers notoriously loathed input from nonwriters.) But she could influence, and there was something to the idea of lipstick—and lips!—as a metaphor for inner consciousness, memory, and identity. She grabbed her pencil. For good measure, she kissed it. And then, she began scribbling notes on the back of a printout. She had to act fast, as she had nineteen actors awaiting their turn.

As she was writing, Sasha felt a tap on her shoulder. She looked up with a start. It was April MacGruder, her fellow Spelman alum and Seraphina HR contact.

"April, hi! I didn't see you on the call sheet for today."

Sasha stood up and gave April a friendly, but professional, hug. A part of her felt antsy seeing her old college acquaintance in person. They'd only spoken on the phone since the email debacle.

"Great seeing you, Sasha." As per usual, April's tone was clipped and corporate. "You're right, I'm not on the call sheet. And apologies for the interruption. I just popped over to drop something off for you."

"For me? What is it?"

Pulling a file folder out of her bag, April addressed Sasha in hushed tones. "I know you harbored some complicated feelings after sending that email."

"Which email?"

April looked at her blankly.

"I'm joking. I'm trying to see the humor in it, as part of my healing."

"Ahh. Funny!" The HR representative didn't laugh. "Well, you'll remember that your company email was disabled after the incident. To give you some peace. But now that the project's coming to a close, I thought you'd want to see these." She opened the folder, flipping through several email printouts. "Your flight story launched a worldwide search. Dozens of Seraphina employees began looking for your fellow passenger. No one found him, I hate to say. But they all found their own loves. Isn't that wonderful? Look at all the good that came from you meeting Seat F."

Eyes wide, Sasha took the papers from April. Her mortifying foible inspired strangers to find romance? She was gobsmacked by this information.

"This is... I... I'm amazed. I don't know what to say."

"Say nothing and get back to work!" April smiled; she got weird around too much emotion. "I just wanted to hand these to you in person. But I should get going. Have a great casting, Sasha."

And then she was gone. With a thud, Sasha sat back down in her seat. There wasn't enough time to read through the emails now, but one caught her eye. It was from Maxi Morgan, the Fiorello Airport manicurist.

> ...I made a small mistake. I remember telling you that you'll experience a chance meeting that'll set off a chain of events that'll end in happily ever after... But I'm now realizing that the "chain of events that'll end in happily ever after" is referring to *other* people. You're going to meet a man, and somehow, that meeting will bring love to strangers. Many, many strangers. I don't know how I messed that up!

Her jaw dropped. Understanding slowly dawned on her. It was just another drop in the bucket of reasons the entire Seat F debacle was an utter misfire. At the time, it was fun to believe Maxi's prediction. It gave Sasha an (admittedly shaky) excuse to embrace such an unlikely love story. Turns out, Maxi's prediction was never about Sasha's love story—it was about everyone else's. Which was lovely. In such bizarre, fractured times, the world needed a romance epidemic. But Sasha hoped Maxi was working on upgrading her palmistry skills. Because, damn. That was the Cadillac of errors.

The videographer, a guy named Abe wearing muttonchops and circa-2009 hipster overalls, cleared his throat. She looked up and he asked, "Is everything okay?" She nodded quickly and called the next actor. But now she was distracted. All she wanted to do was call Wes. She wanted to tell him about the emails. She wanted to read them with him. God, she just wanted him. Why hadn't he called her? Why didn't she have the nerve to call him?

The rest of the auditions flew by. By 2:55 p.m., Sasha was 99 percent sure she'd found the right talent for the commercial. The Seraphina execs were nibbling on leftovers from the lunch spread and packing up to go. Just then, a studio manager rushed over to her, explaining that she had one person left to see. A latecomer, a name she didn't recognize. Dean W. Seely. This was odd, as she had handpicked all the actors, herself. Had she forgotten to add this person to the call sheet?

"Sounds like we have one more," announced Sasha, on the mic. "Dean W. Seely, you're last but not least. Come on down."

Tapping the pencil against her cheek, she quickly rifled through her papers, searching for this person's info. Hearing Dean walking onto set, she looked up. And then emitted a gasp heard round the world.

"Hi," said Wes, looking equal parts thrilled and nervous. And then, unnecessarily, he added. "It's me."

"Omigod. Omigod. Am I hallucinating?"

Her heart was thundering. Her soul was shaking. Her core was quivering. It was Wes, looking so unnecessarily rugged and casually sexy in boots, denim, and a navy knit tee. His eyes were twinkling under the professional lights. She'd never seen such an exquisite man.

What the hell was he doing here? She hadn't realized she'd asked the question out loud, until he answered.

"You've been trying to get me to audition since forever. So, here I am. Also, you're bad at anagrams."

She gasped again, frozen in her seat. "Dean W. Seely is..."

"Wesley Dane." He shot her a small, lip-biting smile. "It's good, right?"

"It's good," she said, her eyes welling up. "It's damned good. Get over here."

He walked up to her desk, hands in his jeans pockets. His face was a bashful, exhilarated, dimply vision of perfection. She wanted to kiss every inch of it.

"Why are you here, for real?" she whispered this so the videographer and execs couldn't hear. "Because I know you're not auditioning."

"You're right," admitted Wes. And then, he dropped the friendly pretense—and looked at her with a soul-stirring, heart-stopping earnestness so intense she could barely hold his gaze. Her pulse raged under her skin.

"I'm not here to audition," he repeated, his voice hitching a little. "I'm here because I love you."

The world seemed to sharpen around Sasha, then. No shadows, no vagueness, nothing dull. The room went incandescent.

"I've loved you since you showed up in my office, bossing me around in wrecked pajamas. I love your thoughts, your strength, your bottom lip, your laugh, the wildness of your brain. I crave you so badly, it's like...I see now why I've never felt truly at home in my life. Because I needed you. And I wanted to tell you, before. But your attention was...elsewhere, and I didn't want to get hurt. But in the end, I don't care. I don't care that you didn't choose me. I don't care that you loved him, first. I'm fucking yours, Sasha. I—" Wes stopped, looking down at the table. He zeroed in on the pencil.

"That's...the one from that night?"

Sasha nodded, eyes blazing and welling up. "I told you I kept it."

Wes looked at her with wonder, blinking in silence. His mouth opened, as if he was going to respond, but he shut it.

"Wes, I never said I loved him."

"You did." He sounded emotionally wrecked now, like he was barely keeping his cool. "I heard it through your earpiece at the gala. You said you were in love with him, but the odds were against you."

A tear rolled out of Sasha's eye, but she let out a laugh. "Did you hear the rest of it? I was talking about us, dummy! I said I was in love with you!" Her chest was rising and falling rapidly. "I am in love with you."

"You are? Me?" A slow smile brightened his face. He reached across the table, wiping her tear with his thumb. "You're in love with me."

"Yes, you, Dean W. Seely."

A slow smile of relief melted the intensity in his face. "Thank fucking God. Get over here."

And then, she flew out of her chair and into his arms. They stood there forever, in full view of the heart-eyed Seraphina execs and the frustrated videographer, sealed together in an impassioned, airtight embrace. At some point, Wes pulled back a little. Gazing at her with wide-open worship, he slipped one hand in her hair and cupped her jaw with the other.

His face was one kiss away from hers.

"You realize I'm at work, right?" she murmured. "It's rude to ambush me here."

"Oh, so *now* you care," he said with an amused chuckle. And then, he kissed her. As she lost herself in the soft, sensual drag of his mouth against hers, she had a thought.

In a way, Maxi also predicted Wes. Her chance meeting with Seat F hadn't just brought romance to the world. It worked for Sasha, too.

ACKNOWLEDGMENTS

Endless thanks to my friend Rasmus Greve, whose anecdote about a colleague's email snafu prompted this entire adventure. Tusind tak!

Massive thanks to "Wild" Bill Stanton, who taught me the ways of private investigating (and lives up to his nickname)—and to Phil "The Grill" Johnson for generously sharing his food truck experiences. And I couldn't have written Sasha without interviewing Leah Daniels-Butler and Jill Anthony-Thomas, who were so candid about their lives as casting directors.

So grateful for the all-hats brilliance of my literary agent/forever friend, Cherise Fisher—and for the encouraging spirit and positivity of my Grand Central Publishing editor, Karen Kosztolnyik. Huge thanks to Kat Burdon, my Quercus editor, for absolutely getting it (and me). I owe my stunning cover to mind-readers Albert Tang and Stina Persson. And I'm forever indebted to Cordelia Calvert, Tiffany Porcelli, and their fabulous teams, for their dedication and creativity.

Shout-out to my parents, Andi and Aldred, for their razor-sharp pop culture tastes. When I was growing up, they exposed me and my sisters to phenomenal movies, books, and shows—filling up our brains with a creative alphabet we use every day. An extraordinary gift.

Relatedly, I'd like to thank *Moonlighting*, seasons 1–3.

Thank you to the readers, independent booksellers, book influencers, book clubs, and libraries for being so supportive of my work, for so long. It's such an honor to be a part of the bookish community with you. Go romance!

And to my little family—Francesco (my half-Gallipolino husband), Carolina (my Afro-Dominican daughter), and Aksel (my darling toddler who has yet to inspire a character but JUST YOU WAIT)—you're my world. Love you forever.

ABOUT THE AUTHOR

Tia Williams is the bestselling author of *The Accidental Diva*, *It Chicks*, and *The Perfect Find*—now a Netflix film starring Gabrielle Union. Her novel *Seven Days in June* was an instant *New York Times* bestseller and a Reese's Book Club pick. Her NAACP Image Award–nominated bestseller, *A Love Song for Ricki Wilde*, was named one of the year's best romances by the *New York Times* and Amazon. Her YA rom-com, *Audre & Bash Are Just Friends*, was an instant *New York Times* bestseller and GMA Book Club pick. Tia lives with her family in Brooklyn.